SHADOWPLAY

SHADOWPLAY

Karen Campbell

WINDSOR
PARAGON

First published 2010
by Hodder & Stoughton
This Large Print edition published 2011
by AudioGO Ltd
by arrangement with
Hodder & Stoughton Ltd

Hardcover   ISBN: 978 1 445 85561 5
Softcover   ISBN: 978 1 445 85562 2

British Library Cataloguing in Publication Data available

Printed and bound in Great Britain by
MPG Books Group Limited

Third book in, and another huge thanks to the usual suspects: the ever-helpful Garry—arise Detective Inspector Deans; my editor Suzie Dooré, who chisels, chides and chivvies with good grace and humour; the lovely Leni for inventive PR; Jack, Francine, Bob, Penny Isaac and everyone else at Hodder; my sterling agent Lisa Moylett, ably assisted by Juliet Van Oss.

For technical expertise, much appreciation to Chief Inspector Kenny Graham and his staff at Giffnock Police Office for my re-orientation exercise; my good pal Alan Forbes and William Connolly of Strathclyde Fire & Rescue for guidance on chemicals; my brother-in-law Dr Ian Campbell for keeping me right with medical stuff; most helpful writer Amit Varma for a crash course in Indian dialects; Maureen Wheeler and Omar Kettlewell for some Spanish insights; Suzie again, for her prowess in Spanish, and my writer-buddy Helen Fitzgerald for sound advice.

Indeed, a special thanks goes to each of my friends and family for their support and encouragement; not least Mum and Dad for all their marketing efforts—national and international! And, last, but always first, my love and thanks to my husband Dougie and my girls Eidann and Ciorstan.

To Ciorstan, who is all the colours of the rainbow,
and more

PROLOGUE

On a hill swept by oak, a single soft glow shines from a darker bulk. Grey on grey, faint smear of bruising in a sky that undulates, lifting lines of shape from shadow. Close to, the bulk becomes a building, an old mansion house so far weathered and worn that nature's creeping grasp is a blessing of disguise. Hefts of ivy and moss might be all that stitch the crumbling lumps together. That and the piles of scaffolding, propping wall unto wall.

The security guard presses his face against the window, trying to see out. Dawn soon, and all is quiet. It is always quiet here, it is fine. And he can pray when he wants to. A cousin found him the job; it means he can study in peace too, by the light of a 40-watt anglepoise which plugs straight into a tangle of wires on the floor. The men are coming soon to raggle the walls, gouge channels then smooth plaster over the live cables that will dance and spark life through this skeleton of stone. A renaissance of luxury flats.

It was a museum once, a nature display, where the spoors and splays of long-dead animals lay alongside a desiccated wasp byke and trays of thin-pressed leaves and butterflies. He has seen pictures of the glass cases and the tea room, with its potted palms and silver service. This room was the park ranger's— the sign is still screwed to the woodwormed door. Before that, it was a country house, built by a sugar baron with the proceeds of his trade. Cutting cane in the West Indies, shipping sweet and sour along the River Clyde.

The guard had learned about it as he wandered the city's rain-slick streets, took shelter in its libraries and museums, which were free and splendid. Glasgow had been the Empire's Second City, a proud centre of trade and wealth and industry. Even now it revelled in its sturdy antiquities, offering history trails past refurbished warehouses, issuing glossy leaflets proclaiming the city's most famous sons, who slept under marble mausoleums in the Necropolis. But Glasgow didn't like to boast about the murk beneath the money; of souls being sold with bracelets on their ankles. Some of them passed through, some were kept, as pets. Maybe another black man like him had once stood here. Stood at this window and prayed he was back at home.

He'd seen a painting, in a museum in town. Done for the Glassford family, tobacco merchants who gave their name to one of the city's busiest streets. Serene mother, stern father, all the primped and becurled children in their vivid, lush silks and satins. And a darker smudge in the background, where their black page had been painted out.

Once his studies are over. He will work hard, become rich, and return home to his boy.

Then he can pay back what he owes, and the debt will be squared.

But for now, he must live in this quietness. He has been told to expect a delivery, and has cleared the basement as instructed. They never told him when, or what, and he has never asked.

Watch the wall, my darling, while the Gentlemen go by.

Kipling was a wise man.

He turns off the lamp as the sky yawns and stretches. It will be fine.

x

CHAPTER ONE

The Chief Constable patted her shoulder. A manly pat, a comradely one.

'My staff officer will see you out.'

Anna Cameron saluted, then turned towards the door. Felt her back foot spin too far, her supporting leg get confused. She managed to correct her gait, watching her flat black shoes find their place beneath flat black ankles, devoid of any shape now they were at right angles to the floor. Viewed from above, her legs were not her strongest attribute. *You're all up and down, you*, her grandpa would say. *Not a pick on you*. But even the most curvaceous of women would be hard pushed to find this uniform flattering. The sycophancy, however, was.

'Congratulations, ma'am.'

The inspector, the wee gingery inspector who'd briefed her as an equal but ten minutes previously, extended an orange-tufted hand once they were outside.

It felt so good. *Ma'am*. Not marm, as in school-teaching spinster, but *M-AH-m*, as in Ah.

Aaaahhh.

Bloody AAAHHHH.

That magic extra pip glinted at Anna, winking from a triumphant shoulder. 'Cheers. That me then?'

'You'll not stay for the tea and biscuits? I've heard tell they've got ginger nuts this month.'

'Is that right? Well, if it's ginger nuts you're offering me . . .'

1

No, Anna. Don't. You're a chief inspector now.

'Aye. That and a nice hob-nob with the Chief. Never too early to get your face on the radar, you know.'

Oh, her face was well on the radar already. Though for all the wrong reasons. How Anna Cameron had managed to achieve another promotion was something that troubled her almost as much as her colleagues. *Gender Agenda,* Colin Keenan had sneered, even though Anna had been an inspector nearly a year longer than him. However, Colin had not yet been the subject of two discipline enquiries, some dodgy rumours and a just-filed-away grievance alleging clandestine lesbian favouritism. Try saying that ten times quickly.

Paradoxically, that was the one that seemed to have finally tipped the scales in Anna's favour. Some disgruntled cop trying to find a reason for why he'd been overlooked for a shot in plainers. Apparently, he'd been keeping a record. And the record clearly stated that Inspector Cameron had, over a period of seven months, put Constable Arlene Winetrobe on plain-clothes duties during five of those seven months, while he, Stuart Wright, had been allowed just one brief week of sporting his M&S jeans and Clarks sneakers. And, furthermore, everyone *knew* that Constable Winetrobe was living with a member of the Scottish Women's rugby team, and was a particularly attractive young lady, and Inspector Cameron was . . . well, no one was quite sure, but she didn't have a man, ergo . . .

Ergo . . . Constable Stuart Wright was shite. At his job, at his communication skills, and, crucially,

2

at his powers of deduction. And Arlene was an excellent thief-catcher, who would sail daily from the office like a rosy apple picker, returning with another good crop of windblown, maggoty neds. But the cut and dried clarity of it all hadn't stopped Professional Standards from sitting Anna down for a 'chat'. One of those oblique ones, with lots of nods and trailing sentences that hung, and smelled, like apologetic smoke.

Of course, it's none of our business how you . . .

As you know, we actively encourage diversity . . .

However, this is an allegation of . . .

Very sensitive issue . . .

Anna's response had been more trenchant. 'Look, the guy's an arse, and he's crap at his job. Would *you* put someone on plain-clothes duty after they'd trailed into the office with two bags of frozen food from Iceland, and told the divisional commander they'd been doing their mum's shopping for her, because "things were a wee bit quiet"? In Easterhouse? When we're in the middle of a bloody drugs war?'

Like I said, we appreciate that this is a sensitive issue . . . Shall we say we've discussed matters, and leave it at that?

And now this. A quick Divisional Panel, an even quicker Force Panel, and promotion to chief inspector. At last, at last, at bloody last. Before she was forty, too. By just over a year, but then who was counting? Not Anna. Not every day, twisting time over her shoulder, looking down the barrel of where she'd been. Who she'd been. Forty. *Forty.* Futile, faded forty. A woman who'd never worn make-up, who'd relied on sharp brains and even sharper cheekbones, now looking at age-

3

replenishing moisturisers and wondering if they really worked. A woman who, in molten horror, had just found her first grey pubic hair. She'd tried to pluck it out, but the wiry wee bugger was rooted deep.

The speed of her surprising, jolting ascent to promotion, after years of swinging stalled in mid-air, unnerved her. 'Well done, lass. Glad to see the back of you,' her divisional commander had chortled, offering his congratulations when the news came through. And she'd laughed back, while her thoughts chased her belly down in a lurching pirouette. What if she'd been subsumed by the Peter Principle? What if that's exactly what they were doing—promoting her beyond her capabilities, in order to bump her out of the division, with minimum hassle and maximum protection?

She remembered standing on the beach as a child, feeling the sand guzzling from beneath her feet as the sea sucked in and out. All tumult, confusing movement and her, stock-still, just trying to keep her balance. Her daddy's hand coming down to help her. Anna's confidence in her abilities, in her right to reach up and demand, had been ground out of her as surely as it was from those poor defeated shadows you saw at the Women's Refuge. Receding youth and relentless mundanity had rubbed back her fine, sharp corners, blurring them flat and weary.

She'd come to Easterhouse Police Station as a shining star, with only a slightly tarnished tail. Well, everyone was allowed one misdemeanour, one learning experience. Hers had been the Wajerski case. And Jamie Worth. Discipline

4

Hearing number one. But she'd recovered from that, excelled at the training school, and been promoted to inspector. She'd heard sufficient appreciative noises from Personnel to suggest that her stint as an operational inspector would be a brief one. *Six months on the street, then we'll look at some lateral development, eh?*

This force still did things the old-fashioned way. If you looked on websites of police forces down south, places like Greater Manchester and the Met, their entire senior management team were about her age. Bright young things with power and vigour, beaming beneath their braid in cyberspace. Strathclyde, however, liked you to take the scenic route—a wee shot of this, a sojourn in that. Slow and steady up the ladder, paying all your dues as you went.

Anna had nodded, and smiled and taken her medicine. And had been a competent—if frustrated—shift inspector. She could do the job standing on her head. The sergeants did all the work in any case; Anna was just there to take the shit for her shift. But then, there had been her unexplained appearance at a crime scene in HMP Garthlock. Her unauthorised use of a United Nations identification card. And, once more, Jamie Worth. Discipline Hearing number two.

And then there was nothing.

Nothing but a dull ache of something closing over, a lump you'd never press; would pretend you couldn't feel. But still, she had her job, if not her career, and still she turned up for duty, day in day out, week on week, month into month. Three years, in total, of sprawling Easterhouse, until she knew every lane and gushet and alleyway and ned and local worthy and piece of political manoeuvring and threadbare patch of grass and miserable railing and brave, thwarted effort to paint a wall or form a youth club better than she knew herself.

'Come on Anna, time to get the lippy on. That's us off for our photies!' Alex Patterson, slick, dark-haired, skirt-chasing Alex from the Flexi Unit, kissed her cheek. 'Well done you, by the way. About bloody time, eh?'

'Well done you, too.'

Alex picked imaginary lint from the silver thread of his sergeant's stripes. 'I know.' Leaned closer in. 'Fucking mental, in't it? *Me*—a gaffer!'

'No more mental than me, pal.'

'Away. You were always destined for greater things. After you, ma'am.' He gave a courtly bow, and they followed the others across the road to the Identification Bureau, where they formed an orderly queue to get their picture taken.

'Which paper will we send this to?' asked the girl.

'Ach, don't bother.'

'No, we need to send it somewhere. What's your local?'

'The Bay Horse Inn.'

'Sorry?'

'Em, I think it's the *Southside Sentinel*.'

The girl scribbled something down on a form.

'Any biographical information to give? You know, Chief Inspector Cameron lives with her husband and two children in Shawlands, that kind of thing.'

'Nope.'

'Well, what am I going to put?'

6

'Chief Inspector Anna Cameron has been promoted back to G Division. Scene of her earliest triumphs, and not a retrograde step at all.'

The girl sniffed. 'I'll just make something up, shall I?'

'Fine. Can I go now?'

'Do you not want a copy of the photo to take away?'

'No thanks.'

'They make lovely gifts.'

For the cat? But she took one anyway. She could post it out to her mum, with a note attached. It would save the usual awkward phone call that neither of them looked forward to and from which, she suspected, each came away feeling worse.

Outside the brushed steel and glass doors of Headquarters, Anna paused. Let cold sunlight slip across her face as traffic rumbled and Glasgow bustled on, taxis touting, office girls with thin blouses and folded arms hurrying in their brittle heels to queue at sandwich shops. An *Evening Times* salesman stood on the corner of Pitt and West George, strangulating pitch and vowels as he yodelled titbits from the early edition.

'Coming for a drink, *ma'am*?' Alex grinned at her from the midst of a crowd of cops in half uniform, civvie jackets thrown over police trousers and shirts.

'No . . . I'm hardly dressed for it.'

'Och, button up your coat and no one will know. It's a wee lock-in anyway.'

'At lunchtime?'

'Chief Inspector Cameron, did you learn nothing when you worked in A Division?' He winked at her. That Alex wink which told you all is

7

well with life when you've got black hair, white teeth and a groin-grabbing strut to charm man and beast alike. 'C'mon, woman. My pint'll be going flat.'

It was the 'woman' bit that did it. Against her better judgement, against everything her head was telling her, some visceral surge came open and up. They were buddies, her and Alex, part of a team going way back. And it was good to have a comrade, someone who knew exactly who she was, and how she was feeling right now. Here in this moment, where a benevolent universe had beamed its goodness direct on her, expanding her ego and bubbling her brains.

As she went to answer him, an old lady in a wheelchair tried to wedge herself through the slight gap between Anna, Alex and the road.

'Ho, come on yous. Gie an old bird a break, eh? This thing's mair skew-whiff than a shopping trolley.'

'Sorry,' said Alex. They stepped aside to let her pass.

'Do you need a wee hand?' asked Anna.

'Do I buggery.'

Alex's eyes widened; suppressed, shared laughter making a bridge from him to Anna.

She waited until the wheelchair had squeaked by. *'Charming.'*

'Well? Are you pubbing it, ma'am, or what?'

'Aye, alright, then . . . Just the one though. I'm working tonight. I'll catch you up in a minute.'

'Right you are. We'll be in the back bar at D'Arcy's. And you're buying, what with your vastly inflated wages and all.'

'Can I remind you, Sergeant, you'll probably be

earning more than me, all the overtime you'll be racking up. Us chief inspectors just do it for love of the job.'

She watched the jostle of back-slapping arms and puffed chests spill left towards Sauchiehall Street; the Alley of the Willows that had paved over its trees, grown crops of shops and pubs instead. A much better prospect for a drink. There was little to keep you in Pitt Street, save the red-brick heft of Headquarters and a discount tourist hotel. The very first time Anna had come to Headquarters was as a child, for a Christmas party, just before her dad had died. These doors had seemed huge and heavy then, the black-glazed tiles inside like glossy liquorice. As they were led downstairs to the Assembly Hall, she'd pressed her hands against one of the tiles, watching her fingerprint form and fade. All these other policemen and their children, her dad the tallest of them all, holding her hand and getting her a bottle of fizzy juice with a straw.

On you go, Annie-kins. Away and have fun.

Kids standing awkwardly in the middle of the room, bursting balloons and playing tig, the parents in a circle round the edges. Mostly clusters of men in ill-fitting jackets, some joking, calling her dad nicknames she didn't know. The lady helpers all seemed to be typists and office staff.

Her dad had walked through these doors on his last day on earth. Been up to collect some urgent thing, parked the panda on the double yellows and bounded in. He was always big and springy, her dad. Like Tigger. What was the *thing*? They never told them what the thing was—a production, some incident tape, a gun? A box of shirts for his sergeant? But the *thing* never got to its destination either.

She refocused her eyes. The old lady had stopped by the kerb, just a little further along. She seemed to be struggling to get up from the wheelchair, but every time she put her weight on her arms, the chair would slip, and she'd collapse back into the plastic seat.

'Excuse me. Sorry,' said Anna, going over, 'I think you need to put on your brakes first.'

'Put on my brakes? I'm like a bloody tortoise as it is, hen. If I gang any slower I'll stop.'

'No, to stop it skidding like that, I mean. But are you sure you should be standing up anyway?'

The woman's pupils punched out across cloudy irises, like a cat before it jumps. 'Listen hen. Ma hair's a mess, I've had this dress on three days now, and ma daughter-in-law's trussed me in a big nappy to take me out. I can walk fine—just no fast enough for *her*. I've no very much dignity left, but what I have, I'd like to keep.'

'Of course. I . . . I'm sorry.'

The old lady leaned a bit closer. 'But if you could just gie me a wee punty up, I'd be awfy grateful.'

'Sure thing.' Anna slipped one arm beneath her elbow. Slowly, with equal effort on both sides, they got her on to her feet.

'So, where is it you're off to?' said Anna.

'I want to go to Watt Brothers and get a new frock, but that bitch of a daughter-in-law willny take me. Ah, oh, that's better.' Her eyelids fluttered in utter bliss. 'Oh, there's nae support in they seats—ma back was bloody louping.'

Anna stood with the woman a moment as she let

her back stretch straight. She smelled powdery, like a baby. The top of her head, her wild, black-grey hair, came up to Anna's shoulder. Unnaturally black, with remnants of perm; you could see where the dye stopped and broad, truthful white emerged. Whiskers on her chin, too. She must have sensed Anna looking, for she scratched her fingertips on the transparent bristles. Frowning, she looked at her fingers, then her elbow, then at Anna's face.

'Who are you?' The black sharpness of her gaze had vanished. Eyes completely vacant, one drifting slightly to the left.

'I was just helping you. You said you wanted to stand up?'

She blinked, and it was like another person, the first person, had returned. 'Och, that's fine hen. That's just lovely. Right.' The woman began the process of folding herself away, 'Back down we go. Ah . . . that's it. Now, if you could maybe gie me a wee hurl across the road . . .'

She broke off as a blonde in a velour leisure suit and white trench coat flapped towards them, thin jowls and ponytail bouncing.

'Mum! Mum! Where the hell have you been? Whit in the name of the wee man did you think you were doing?'

'I was *trying* to go shopping.'

'Now what have I told you, ya stupit besom?' The younger woman seized the back of the chair. 'You'll no be getting out again, that's for sure. Come on now, or I'll be getting another bloody parking ticket . . . Christ, I don't know. I try to do a nice thing, but see you? You're nothing but a . . .'

Her voice fragmented off the high walls of the

11

city buildings, then disintegrated as she bustled away. In her chair, the old lady shifted round. A mournful face looked back at Anna, features and hope receding.

A sudden, skipping guilt-trip. Was that how Anna's mother looked, every time their phone conversations ended? Or when another summer rolled by with no visits and no excuse? Anna had no idea. Had no idea how her mother was looking at all, in fact, not since the Christmas letter and the snaps of her-and-Teddy's-cruise, when her mother had seemed scrawny, almost, in her halter-necked dress.

Ach, why not send her the stupid photo? And, if that prompted another invite, then maybe this time she'd go. Maybe.

Some man clipped her leg with his briefcase. A tut as he manoeuvred round where she stood, still watching the judder of shrinking shoulders from tears or Parkinson's or merely uneven pavement; watching the flow of a hard, busy city, and a woman being swept away. The man brushed past Anna up the steps into Headquarters, pulling hard through the glass and steel doors, which whumped all the air and left a hissing vacuum.

That drink was calling.

*   *   *

Nearly half past ten when Anna made it back to E Division. She'd had to take a taxi straight from the hotel. Her car was still at Pitt Street, and she was probably over the limit in any case. Pulling on her crumpled uniform; leaving Alex sleeping on his back.

Oh God forgive her. Alex.

She closed her eyes and was back in the daytime dark. The half-shut curtains of a half-decent hotel room, cloth curving round a crescent of window light where the two panels of fabric joined. Faint, unfamiliar furniture; a trouser press, that little casket where they kept the tea bags, all soft-sketched; but she could see enough. Flat belly facing her, sinewed muscle rippling like tongues. Him up high, almost vertical, the dimples dark at his groin, pulsing as his hips moved, slowly at first, rotating, screwing tight, and tighter, fully in, and still gyrating as she folded her legs across his back, pulling him deeper, further, faster.

'Oh God, oh God. Anna, I've wanted this from the moment I saw you. Anna. You're so beautiful.'

Her lapping it up, sucking on his fingers as he moved inside her, letting damp hands trace her face, which gravity stretches young and taut again. Nothing more than indulging in extra cream on top, an extravagant party-popper, and Anna, what is wrong with you? What are you so scared of that you would prostitute yourself for a couple of pints? She remembers sitting in the pub, Alex's arm draped loose across her back, his hard, blunt fingers stroking the flesh beneath her hair. Casual, proprietorial, insistent, until she was loose inside. Couldn't wait to get there. Her credit card, her treat. Her need.

She sees her body sprawled wide and wanton. Nothing more than a cheap, pished shag. She flies above herself, ashamed, yet still she watches them. One dark, one fair, curved in a heart shape, but the heart is empty. Then he stirs and tugs her head down.

13

'Suck me, Anna . . .'

If it was nothing, then why is she still there; growing lighter and clearer? She witnesses herself take Alex's prick in her mouth, her tongue running over.

'Oh, Anna,' he whimpers. 'Oh, you dirty wee cow.'

Then she bites on his thigh, on the soft inner flesh, until he yelps like a dog.

'Something to remember me by,' she says later, when the bruising has come up, and he is climbing on to her again, gone crazy with the need to be inside. And she lets it happen, riding high on the moment and his ten-years-younger prick.

Her last glimpse: him, lying there, asleep. One arm flung high above his head. Just a boy, with his smooth, wide brow and solid-orb biceps. A beautiful boy, who should go home to his wife, or his girlfriend; they all had one. Anna felt grubby, her head hurt. She was never doing this again. In the morning, when she got home, she'd flush all her contraceptives away. No pills, no shagging—a simple equation even Anna could master.

She had the taxi stop a few streets away from the office, got out and walked the last wee bit in the fresh air. Or as fresh as it could be in Easterhouse. Sometimes, the yeast of the distant brewery crept as far as here; other times faint fruit and fish from the markets at Blochairn. Tonight, the air was redolent only with greasy chips and dogs' dirt, and the lorry-loads of intermittent noise and monoxide that swept down from the motorway; sounds and scents augmented by the lack of intact streetlamps along Bogbain Road. But it was worth the walk to see the sharp spring sky. Deep blue and clean, the

14

same matt-dark of her favourite Christmas bauble, which was midnight velvet ribbon over eggshell, studded with pin-tip golden stars. Her dad had made it, before she was born. It was he who had shown her how to weigh your egg, testing to see if the shell was sound. Then a tiny tap either end with the special bodkin he kept in the tin, and out, out damned spot, on to a saucer, yellow ooze on white. The shells that broke, they'd make into mosaics. Amazing that it was still intact, that bauble. She stored it boxed and cotton-wrapped every year. It was older, even, than her.

Easterhouse Police Station lit her way, a recumbent lighthouse in the dark. No banners or balloons for her there—well, that wasn't true. There were plenty of balloons there, mostly with superior airs and shiny red faces. Anna slipped through the door, past the big mosaic of a knife being binned. Kids at a nearby primary had made it, children not yet in their teens who lived daily with gangs and ghettos. *Don't be Afraid—Trade Your Blade*, the little tiles demanded, with a childish courage and certainty she wished she could preserve. But experience had taught her differently. In a few years' time, many of these kids would be forced to choose fight or flight, would spend their days working round an intricate series of demarcation lines, spray-trails of who ruled where. They would take wide detours, change buses, go on foot. Avoid football matches, reject jobs, refuse dates, all to avoid encroaching into enemy territory. And some would tool up. For protection at first, then for kudos. Then for fun.

Anna went into her office. Her shift were due to start the night shift, and this would be her last time

15

mustering them. They were a good bunch in the main, keen and productive, and she would miss them. Arlene, with her ribald jokes and eerie ability to see around corners; young Emma, who was a nurse before she joined; Stuart, whose name she glided over quickly because he never quite fitted; Big Al and Spike, who were like Laurel and Hardy; and Grandpaw Broon—Peter Brown, who had silver sideburns, the quiet, practised dedication of a military man, and slightly more service than Anna. Then there were her sergeants—shit-hot Sarah and world-weary Fred, who began each day by opening his Scope record on the computer, and relating exactly how many days were left until he could retire.

It was an alchemy, this coming together of disparate minds and moralities. Shaping them into a single, smooth entity that had an ethos and a drive, recognising their differences and pushing them to places in which they would thrive. 'Ahem.' A cough outside her door. 'That's the troops ready for muster, ma'am.'

'Okay, Fred, I'll be right through. Sorry I was late in—I got held up . . .'

She hoped he'd prepared the e-brief already, checking through the day's crime reports, confirming vulnerable premises, areas requiring extra attention, bail checks to be carried out. Anna normally came in early to oversee this process. She gave her hair a quick brush, sprayed some Gold Spot in her mouth. Another sparkle from her shoulder. It was okay, it was. She wanted to stroke that sweet silver bump. Next stop, a crown, and then she truly would be back on track.

Enough, Anna, enough. One step at a time. But

already, it was shifting. Like a sleepy animal stretching awake, a forgotten ember that had smouldered unseen, ambition stirred. She was allowed to feel the sun on her face again. Entitled. She glanced at her watch; her clock and all her gear were already packed away. There was still time. She sat back down, pressed the contacts list on her mobile. Scrolled down until she found it.

It was answered after seven rings; her limit was always ten.

'Hello, Mum? It's Anna.'

'Anna? What's wrong?'

'Nothing. Nothing's wrong. I just wanted to—'

'Then what are you doing calling at this hour? Teddy's *sleeping*.'

'I'm sorry . . . I just wanted to let you know—'

'What? Are you ill?'

'*No*. I just wanted to tell you something.'

'Tell me what?' A sharp catch of breath. 'Oh God!'

Anna was convinced she could hear her mother gulping.

'Oh, Anna. You're not *pregnant*, are you?'

That chiding lilt, borne not of empathy, but despair. No matter how hard Anna tried, she would always be a failure to her mother. She was her father's daughter, you see.

'Bloody hell, Mum. Quantum leap or what?'

'Well, I just—'

'No, no, it's nothing like that. Anyway, after all this time, I thought it'd make your day if I was.'

'Oh darling.' The hard edges of her mum's voice dropped away. 'Of course it would.'

'Well, I can assure you I'm *not*. I'm phoning to say I was up at Pitt Street today—'

'Are you in trouble again?' Immediately, the shrivel in her mother's voice returned. 'Honestly, what *is* it with you, Anna? Why do you always have to make life so difficult?'

A warning clench at the back of her eyes; that redness again.

'Fuck knows, Mother. I have no idea where I got that particular skill from.'

'Don't you *dare* swear at me—'

'Look, I won't keep you. Just wanted to let you know I got promoted today. I had this weird notion you might be interested, but hey ho, we mustn't disturb Teddy, must we?'

'Promoted?'

'Aye. And don't sound so bloody surprised.'

'I . . . I'm, well, no, that's lovely, dear, well done. But—it *is* rather unexpected, isn't it? I mean, with your track record and all . . .'

'Jesus Christ, Mother. Is it impossible for you to be pleased for me at all?'

'Oh, I *am* dear, I am.'

But Anna was talking over her, blotting out the clangs of anticlimax in her mother's words. 'Aye, so you bloody are. Just don't bother sending flowers, alright? In fact, don't bother phoning me back either, because I won't be in. Sorry I bothered you—and *Teddy* of course. *Adi*-fucking-*os*.'

She laid her forehead against the surface of her desk, anchored by the weight of skull on neck, the pulse in her temple. She must still be drunk. Never had Anna used that amount of foul language before; not in her mother's presence. It did not feel cathartic, the way swearing normally did.

Two palms flat on the nice, cool wood, two knees unlocking. She stood, took off her tunic,

18

smoothed down her shirt. Her hand trembled as she straightened her cravat. No time to change the ridiculous skirt for her usual trousers. Well, her legs would be hidden behind the desk in any case. Her mobile stared at her, unblinking, and she shoved it in the drawer.

'Ma'am,' said Fred. Impatient. 'You ready?'

The muster hall was dark and airless, small high windows screened with dislocated blinds. Her shift sat in their usual places, Spike fiddling with his hair, Big Al stuffing the remains of a packet of Maltesers into his mouth. Anna whispered to Fred, 'Where's Sergeant Black?'

'Be in in a second, ma'am. She just got held up. Oh, and Stuart Wright's phoned in sick.'

'Is that right? Surprise, surprise.'

'Hmm.' Fred smoothed the pages of his blotter. He was going bald on top; she'd never noticed that before.

'Right folks,' said Anna. 'Will we just get started then? Sergeant Graham, over to you.'

Fred led them through the muster, reading off the computer in front of him as the same words lit up the projector screen behind, allocating cars and duties and CRs for investigation, a rundown of the top ten offenders (in no particular order of merit), advising them of a special lookout for a vehicle involved in a robbery, reiterating memos about domestic violence indices, and the importance of wearing your hat in patrol cars, then asking them to check the list of forthcoming officer safety training courses to make sure they were up to date.

Anna sat quietly, looking at the faces in front of her. She'd never do this again, never have her own shift to nurture and groom. Chief inspectors were station managers, a further step removed from the bustle, blood and bluster of real-life policing. 'And that's your lot,' finished Fred.

Anna waited for him to say something, maybe offer her some congratulations, but none was forthcoming. Was that it? Were they all just going to wander off without even saying cheerio? Well, she wasn't. Couldn't. Anna held up her hand.

'Em, before you go guys, I'd just like to say a few words. I'll be around for the rest of the shift, obviously, so I'm sure I'll get the chance to speak to you all before I go, but, I just wanted to say, well, thank you, I guess. I know we've had our differences at times, but,' she smiled, 'you've been an excellent shift. We've had some hairy moments—remember the siege at the post office, Peter? And we've certainly had some triumphs too. Emma, there is a little girl who, but for you having got down on your hunkers to deliver her in the close, might now be walking round called Tracey-Chantelle McGurk instead of Emma.'

'Aye, but her big sister's still called Shangri-La,' Big Al called out.

'True. But every one of you has played your part in making my role as your inspector easier, by your commitment to your job and to this community. You've grafted exceptionally hard for me, and I'm very proud to have worked with you all.' She stopped abruptly. 'So . . . well, that's it really.'

Her shift gave a few curt nods, Emma a little dimpled grin. All sitting lightly on their chairs, poised forward and alert. They looked as if they were waiting for something. Then she realised what it was. That same itchy starting-block frisson Anna used to feel. Looking for a signal to go out

20

and get on with it.

'Okay, yous lot,' said Fred. 'Away and fight crime.'

As one, in silence, they stood. Then a roar of cheers and clapping woke up the mustery dust, and Sarah, who had been there all the time, came in with a cake. *Good Luck Gaffer* iced in blue.

CHAPTER TWO

Giffnock Police Office had changed little in the years since Anna had seen it last. A bit of a face-lift, some redesign of the foyer, but essentially it was still an old grey sandstone house, joined on to the District Court at one end, where the buildings curved on to the main road, and with a terrace of neat houses running in an L-shape from the other side. Parking, as ever, was dire; but now she would get her own space in the yard. This had been her first posting after she joined the police, nearly twenty years ago now. The wee green park with the flowers and the bench where Mad Maggie used to sit watching traffic had gone, turned to weeds and litter, but the handy newsagent's and the Orchard Park Hotel remained. All you needed, really—rolls and the paper and a drink at the end of the day. Anna's ground-floor office was bright and functional, and its door gleamed *Chief Inspector* on beautiful brass.

All you needed, really. It would have been nice if her friend Elaine still worked in the division, but she'd moved to the council; too long gone to give Anna any useful pointers about her new work colleagues. There was a senior management team meeting scheduled for nine a.m., so she'd meet her makers then anyway. Her colleagues and competitors: the subdivisional officer she would deputise for, who would guide her hand and write her appraisals; the divisional commander, holding both reins and purse strings for the whole division, who could condemn her to another lifetime in an empty shit-strewn nest, or could fold warm wings across her shoulder and help her fly. No pressure, then. Anna knew little about the commander, Marion Hamilton, other than she seemed to get a bad press. But then, she was a woman with rank, so that was hardly surprising. While men became dynamic leaders, their female counterparts assumed the mantle of narky bitches. Anna was looking forward to working for a woman. It would be a change in the dynamic, having a bit of female solidarity. Yes, it would be good. And, from what she knew of the deputy commander, Superintendent Donald Sangster had a reputation as being very fair. So, decent bosses and a return to her old stamping ground, where she knew her way about both the office and the streets. Plus, thighs still chafing from an unexpectedly fine—and final—illicit shag. Couldn't have asked for more, really. Only. This was the same division in which the Brisbane shooting had taken place, the same division she'd helped to hold up to the light and be scrutinised and shamed. But that was two years ago. Wishart had retired, that bitch Nikki Armstrong had resigned, and Coltrane had been dismissed. Nothing *criminal* you understand, just inexperience . . . confusion . . . uncorroborated allegations. But they'd all gone, at least they'd gone. Safe enough to raise her head above the parapet now.

Anna took a little photo of Alice from her purse, leaned it against her computer. Tomorrow, she'd bring in a frame. A brown one, to match Alice's fur. That cat was getting fat, mind. Next, her penholder. *A Present from Rothesay*. Not strictly hers, but it had kept her company on her desk at Easterhouse for so long that, on impulse, she'd stuffed it into her bag just before she left. And her clock. Her beautiful, unique clock that nobody ever got. Carefully, she unwrapped it from crumpled paper. The clock was mounted on wooden feet, and set inside an ostrich egg that she'd blown and painted herself; soft golds and pinks, with traceries of gentle blue. But fragile as osteoporosis. Virtually impossible to inset the timepiece without breaking the shell. She'd had several abortive attempts, triumphing on her fourth go. A friend of a friend who worked at an exotic animal farm did her a line in eggs. Offered her some llama wool too, but she declined. Enough bad taste in the egg.

'Anna?' A smiling man knocked at her open door. 'Sorry I wasn't here to meet you when you arrived—it's been bloody chaos here this morning. Anyway, welcome on board. I'm Johnny O'Hare, your SDO.'

She stood up, extended her hand. 'Good to meet you, sir.'

His accent was Irish, his handshake warm. 'Please, call me Johnny. We're all very informal here. Well, most of us. Though I'd maybe better check—do you prefer to be called Miss Cameron or—'

Anna laughed. 'Anna will do fine, sir . . . Johnny. There's no need be all polite on my account, you know.

'Anna it is, then. So you're not one to mind your Ps and Qs, eh?'

'Well, I can give as good as I get, put it that way. Mind, I've heard Mr Sangster is very old school; no swearing allowed, that kind of thing. Don't worry, I'll try not to shock him.'

'Too late, I'm afraid. Old boy heard you were coming here and keeled over with a heart attack.'

'Oh, very funny.'

'No, seriously. Took him into the GRI last night.'

'Shit. Is he alright?'

'Well, he's stable, but he's already had a bypass a couple of years ago. I don't see him being back actually. He was due to retire at the end of the year anyway.'

'So, is that you getting bumped up until they decide who'll take over?'

'Me? No chance. Apparently I can't be trusted with the division for more than a day—'

'Johnny! We've to go through now.' The panicked face of a man Anna knew vaguely came into view, half striding, half running through her door. 'We're not even having the tea and scones this morning, just . . . oh, hi there.' He paused when he saw her. 'You must be Anna. I'm Tony McGraw, your other half at Govan. Look, we'd better get in there. She's been through me already, just because I parked my car where she usually puts hers.'

'She?' said Anna. 'Are you talking about Mrs Hamilton?'

24

'JC, you mean?'

'I'm sorry?'

'Well, her full title is JCMM—Just Call Me Ma'am, but we like to abridge it. Plus she thinks she bloody *is* Jesu—'

'Have you met Mrs Hamilton before, Anna?' asked Johnny.

'Not yet.'

'Well, come on through and I'll introduce you.'

'Is she here? I thought we'd be going over to Govan for the meeting.'

'No, no, she likes to rotate where they are,' said Johnny. 'Keep us on our toes.'

Tony shook his head. 'Aye, check we're doing the dusting right, that kind of thing. It's like when my bloody mother-in-law comes . . .'

They made their way through to a larger office along the corridor. But the room was empty.

'Shit, where's she gone now?' said Tony. 'We should get her tagged.'

'Maybe she's in my office,' said Johnny. 'That's where everyone else is.'

Anna's colleagues, her team. The Divisional Senior Management Team. Again, that sigh of silver, drawing Anna's eyes down and across to gloat at the epaulette on her shoulder. Which was suddenly jostled by a shorter, shinier shoulder.

'Ho! Can we move it elsewhere, people? This isny a bloody bus stop.'

'Morning Mrs Hamilton,' said Johnny. 'Just showing the new girl round. Ma'am, this is An—'

Although small and splay-footed, the chief superintendent exuded bristling energy, self-important bosom quivering inside her crisp white shirt. Her cropped grey hair was too severe for her

25

rounded face and body—made her head seem like an afterthought. She shoved on a pair of thick black specs. 'I'm well aware of who this is, Superintendent. Though you'd be hard-pressed to believe this was the finest Strathclyde had to offer.' Her eyes raked claws across Anna's face. '*Chief* Inspector, eh?'

'Yes, ma'am. Thank you.'

An involuntary response. It was just Anna's mouth was hinging open, and the words seemed to float of their own accord.

'I wisny offering my congratulations. Right—do I have to round up anyone else, or is that us all here now? We're in your office, John. And send up some biscuits. I've no had my breakfast.'

'Yes, ma'am.'

The meeting was a brief one. Mrs Hamilton gave them an update on Mr Sangster's condition—*plugged in to the mains, with a drip full of pure alcohol, knowing him*—then berated them for failing to meet their local objectives for that month.

'Juvenile crime down. Down, that's what we promised. And then we get a frigging drunken rave at Rouken Glen Park. Cars vandalised, sheds burned down—and some wee shite knocked a swan from the frigging pond. And do we have any apprehensions? Any witnesses? Any names in the frame?'

'No—but we did get the swan back, ma'am.'

'The swan, Chief Inspector McGraw, was found locked inside a council recycling lorry, wearing a baseball cap. Hardly an investigative triumph. I want you to get on to your community cops, get them going into the schools, the youth clubs, and

26

find out who the hell organised the thing in the first place.'

'Yes, ma'am.'

'You know, it could have been a lot worse,' said Johnny. 'If we hadn't recovered the swan, I mean.'

'That's right,' said Tony. 'Swans mate for life you know. We'd've had to get swan counsellors in, the cygnet social workers—'

'Enough! Is this some kind of comedy act to impress the little lady here? Superintendent Greene, if we can have your overview of progress in the minority ethnic reassurance campaign in Pollokshields, please.'

Anna listened to the super's report, fingernails tight against her palms. This woman wasn't even giving her a chance. She could understand if she'd pissed her off in some way, but all Anna had done was turn up, take off her coat and say hello. Hamilton was an enigma. Anyone Anna had enquired of before her arrival at G Division had either proclaimed Hamilton to be 'brand new' or a 'total boot'. One girl even told her that the 'Mrs' was a misnomer, that Hamilton had no husband, but lived with her ancient mother, who had also been a policewoman sometime in nineteen canteen. That would have been when women staffed an entirely separate department in Turnbull Street, and worked points and shoplifters and missing kids and female escorts. When a woman patrolling on night shift would have been an abomination, and it was deemed unseemly for gels to continue working if they became (whisper it) *married ladies*. Only Mrs/Miss Hamilton senior had not been married, so the shocking story went. She had been required to resign, pregnant and in

27

purdah, and little Marion had been the result.

'Right.'

Mrs Hamilton was clearly winding things up, even though Greene was in mid-sentence.

'I think we've got the gist. We have been consistently advising a softly-softly approach. The council, on the other hand, are wanting to raise ASBOs against these teams of Asian youths. Well, *certain* councillors, shall we say.'

Greene sighed. 'I've explained we'd be as well lighting a blue touchpaper, ma'am, but they're not listening. Councillor Heraghty is demanding we supply clear evidence, so the council can go to the Sheriff Court. You know, give them more intelligence, names. Information-sharing protocols and all that.'

'Well, this is my division, and you are *my* police officers, so the council can go take a fuck to themselves—don't minute that, Irene. You report to me, not Councillor Heraghty, Steven, is that clear? In fact, a timely reminder to you all—you listen carefully, nod politely, then filter all requests back through me. *I* drive this division's strategies—and I expect you to follow where I lead. Bottom line is—you're either on my bus, or you're under the wheels.'

Anna laughed. A flash of red drove through her thoughts, a bespectacled driver scowling through the window. That's who Marion Hamilton reminded Anna of: Postman Pat, but with steel-grey hair.

'You think I'm joking, Miss Cameron?'

'Well, I was assuming a degree of irony, ma'am.'

'You can assume all you like. But, see, when I want you to laugh, I'll tell you. Giggling and

28

simpering might impress our male colleagues here, but it will cut no ice with me. Understand?'

'Yes, ma'am.'

'*Alright*,' murmured Tony. 'Bitch fest.'

*   *   *

One week under her belt, and Anna was still afloat, kicking knackered legs through seas of absence management, appraisals, applications, grievances, meetings with her inspectors, trying (and failing) to get round all the shifts both here and at the outlying offices, endless, endless checking of databases and updates and correspondence, dealing with a parade of local worthies, an inter-schools netball competition and a stubbornly blocked toilet that just refused to flush. Yes, maintenance of the leaky old building was also, it would appear, part of Anna's duties. In one week, Anna had become a politician, counsellor, administrator and janitor. The only time she would get to be a cop was when she donned her body armour and went on call. Even then, the other chief inspectors said they used the quiet times to catch up on admin.

Anna kept blinking, lubricating her eyes. It had been a long day, past nine o'clock, and the community council meeting in Busby was just concluding.

'One last question from the floor,' said the chair, 'and then I'll draw this meeting to a close.'

As well as Anna, there were some officials present from the council. The chap from Education had been getting a roasting; the police had escaped reasonably lightly. Maybe they were being gentle because it was her first time. She began to consider the prospect of dinner.

A woman got to her feet, her chair strident on institutional vinyl. 'We've heard a lot about gangs and bullying tonight. I'd like to ask Chief Inspector Cameron her own thoughts on bullying.'

'Well . . .'

Bye bye chicken bhuna.

'First, I'd agree with Mr Blair here, that bullying is everyone's problem, not just the schools'.'

'No, you misunderstand me, Miss Cameron. What I mean is bullying within the police force.' Her face was tight, angry. Laden with agenda. On a gentle simmer for the last two hours no doubt, waiting, just waiting, for this moment, when her boiling point had come.

'Sorry?'

The woman fanned a brown envelope, the paper slapping against her cheek. People around her shifted back, edging their chairs from agitated air. 'That's his sick-line here, by the way. That make you happy?'

'I'm sorry. *Who* are you?'

'I'm Stuart Wright's wife. You remember Stuart, don't you?'

'Yes, I . . .'

She was shaking, the woman. Rippling with rage in Saturn-rings that seemed to encompass Anna. 'Do you have any idea what a good man my husband is? The kind of person he is, his character?'

'Look . . .' The chair stood up. 'Whatever this is about, madam, I don't think this is an appropriate forum . . . I . . . Do you even live here?'

'Mrs Wright, I have no desire to get into a

30

confrontation with you.'

Anna tried to affect a smile, but the audience were muttering to one another, gleeful whispers that loudly declaimed: *Ooh. Now it's getting interesting.*

'Well, don't. Just bloody listen.'

A hollow, desperate crack in her voice.

'Chair,' said Anna. She had to move this woman out of here. 'Perhaps I might finish this conversation in private?'

'Certainly.' He flicked his hand, embarrassed.

Anna got up, walked towards Mrs Wright. A hundred necks craned to follow.

'Shall we?'

'Aye right. Too feart to talk to me in public are you?'

'Mrs Wright, if you want to talk to me at all, then we're doing this outside.'

They left the hall, went into a little cloakroom off the foyer. In amongst old coats and a badminton net, Anna sat down. The wooden frame she perched on wobbled, a shoe stand or umbrella rack, and she gripped it either side of her body.

'Okay, Mrs Wright. I don't really know what this is about, but go for it.'

Mrs Wright was roughly Anna's age. Plumper, greyer, with tired brown eyes that ignited every time she said her husband's name. 'Go for it? *Go for it?* How dare you? You need to understand what you've done. My Stuart is loving, brave and loyal. And he works so bloody hard. He might not be one of life's big shots, he maybe doesn't shout as loud as some of the other cops, but he's given Strathclyde everything. Got his tickets: nothing. Went and did an HNC: nothing. Applied for CID:

31

nothing. Plodded away, on this shift and that, doing his best, never a shining star. A plodder, yeah, not one of your sort at all—'

'Mrs Wright. I don't have a "sort". The fact is—'

'Let me finish.' Lower, slower, like a eulogy. She would say this whether Anna sat there or ran away. 'You ask the folk he works with: the kids' club he runs in the summer, his mum, who's got Alzheimer's—but he still visits her every bloody day. You ask him about his Crohn's Disease he got ten year ago, jumping in the Clyde to save a wee lassie. Swallowed God knows what, and his guts are twisted in pain every bloody day of his life.'

'He's never said . . .' Anna had the same church-hall taste in her mouth that she used to get at Brownies.

'Of course he hasn't. That's not Stuart's style. He just turns up to work, takes his pills and doesn't grumble. He doesn't want much any more. No, don't worry about that; any dreams he had of being a high-flyer have been well and truly kicked out of him. All he wanted was a bit of respect.'

She shook her hair away from her face, one agitated thumb working round and under the strap of her shoulder-bag. 'And you wouldn't even give him a poxy turn in plain clothes. Do you know the nights we talked about it, before he took out that grievance? Me urging him to do it, him going, no, no, it'll all work out. The job won't let me down. All I need is a chance, I don't want to make a fuss. But then he does, and look what happens—you get a promotion, and he gets shafted even more. Made into a bloody laughing stock.'

'Mrs Wright. I'm genuinely sorry if Stuart feels—'

Foot-in-mouth, brain mincing words. I'm genuinely sorry. *Is there any other type?* I'm truly sincere, I'm uniquely apologetic, *I am choosing my words to reflect not what I feel, but to protect my position as I erect a wall of platitudes against you.*

'You have destroyed him.' Metallic. Precise. 'Do you realise what you've done? My husband, the man I love, he's signed off sick, with stress. And I can't see him coming back. That's how his career with Strathclyde Police will end: washed up and wrung out, because he somehow pissed *you* off. And the thing is, he doesn't know yet what he did wrong.'

She took a small brolly from her bag. Was she going to hit her? 'So you enjoy your promotion, Anna Cameron—you *deserve* it.'

Mrs Wright shook her head, a fury-fizzing figure heading out into evening rain, leaving Anna in the cloakroom, her balance gone. It was as if she had caught her foot on a flight of stairs, stuttered as her belly fell, then steadied herself. In time, but not. From the main hall, she could hear a tide of chairs roll back. Her car was parked outside; if she went now, she would avoid all those curious looks. Her stomach had gone that gurgling way, when all it had consumed for hours was its own acid. Above all else, Anna needed to eat. She remembered seeing a chippy, perched on the concrete bend facing Sheddens roundabout—less than two minutes down the road. Into her car, not looking at any of the passers-by, who *of course* did not know she was a callous cow, but she felt the weight of their collective opprobrium anyway. She parked up outside the chip shop and went inside. She would grab some food, go home and lick her paws.

33

Therein lay the pleasures of living alone. And she would not think of Stuart Wright and his harpy wife, nursing their wrath at home.

A small blond charmer, with a grin bigger than he was, took her order.

'You sure you want just a single fish?'

'That's what I said. A single fish.'

'Well, how about I do you a special fish? Wee bit more pricey, but you get a much bigger piece of fish—and the batter's ace. Made it myself,' he beamed.

'Is that right?'

'Yeah, special ingredient that makes it really light.' The boy leaned forward. He must have been fourteen, fifteen. A local Clarkston lad perhaps, well spoken. 'Elio's got me on trial here. He says if the punters like my own-brand batter then he'll move me on to doing pizzas.'

'*Pizzas,* eh?'

'I know. So, what do you say? Special fish—and I'll throw in a pickled egg. How's that?'

This wee lad could sell coals to Newcastle. Give him a few years and he'd probably be running his own chain of businesses. 'Okay, you win. Special fish it is, but hold the pickled egg. Please.*'*

'Nae bother.' A quick rummage in the fryer, then a suspiciously luminous piece of fish was flicked on to a polystyrene tray. Two crisp turns of white paper, and he handed her the parcel.

'By the way—what *is* your special ingredient?'

The boy looked over his shoulder, at the two girls chopping and rolling behind the pizza counter.

'Irn-Bru,' he whispered. 'But don't let on you know.'

Known as Scotland's other national drink, Irn-Bru was a sticky orange carbonated soda, reputedly made from iron girders, yet tasting suspiciously of bubblegum.

Outside, the packet's heat damp on her hands, Anna noticed a gang of youths on the other side of the roundabout. Eight of them, walking with the united swagger of wide boys sniffing out sport. Several held cans and bottles of cheap blue alcohol and cider. Local byelaws made it illegal to drink in public, and they all looked underage in any case. In her early years, Anna would have rushed across, demanded that they hand over their bevvy, tried to take down all their names. Only she would never have got to that point, one against eight, her off duty, no radio, no phone. Ach, the CCTV cameras would follow these boys. If they had the resources, a cop would be dispatched. If not, pragmatism would prevail, and these low-level neds would carry on transmitting their low-level crime waves, shattering their bottles and scribbling their tags and menshies in some desperate need to advertise who they were. Anna knew how people worked, what signals they emitted. At least, she thought she did. She thought she had everyone sussed. The keys were in her hand, ready to unlock the car when a shout went up.

'You're fucking ripped, ya Paki cunt!'

In a breath, the casual tenor of the group had smashed, its shards refracting shrieks and speed. The air charged and hungry as a body leapt, struck glass on wall, and they were running, all running, a pack of howls. White trackies, red eyes in a single, focused surge, and she could see another figure, further down the road, freeze and flee in seamless terror, round the corner, out of sight, pursued by the gaining mob.

Instantly, she dropped her food, tried to dodge the looping cars. Feet unsteady on the roundabout's pointed paviors, placed to deter pedestrians from crossing there. No bloody car would give her quarter as she hovered, and drew back, then burst across to hoots and shouting. By the time she'd made it to the other side, got to the street the gang had run into, there was no one there. She waited, panting. Hands on knees. Listening. The street was straight, long; they should still be in it. Yellow slabs of streetlight shone bars through city dark. Where would you run, if you were running for your life?

Looking up, along. Looking right and left.

Luxury flats, neat and pebbledashed, with wooden palings beneath the windows. Quiet blinds drawn, a grey metal railing at the side, running between two blocks and up, up. Marking the line of a high, tree-fringed concrete stairway linking this street to a higher, parallel one.

You would run to the hills.

Again, Anna listened. Nothing but traffic, and the sound and smell of trees, the gentle smirr of rain. Sharp, woody resin, a fresh-snapped branch, squint like gallows where it had been broken back in the rush. Cautiously, she climbed the stairs. They were inky and narrow, room for two abreast at most. If the gang came running back down, they would crash straight into her. And if they were still at the top, it would be an easy thing to take her in such a confined space. One brief circle, above and below, and Anna would be trapped.

A thin square landing, where she stopped again;

stood still to listen to the sweeping sounds of evening: the crack of a car door, a bleep of alarm being set, the grinding of a wheelie bin being rolled out down below. But no battle-cries, no shouting. As if the gang, and their quarry, had melted. Two more steps and she could see another lozenge of sickly light, shining from the top of the stairway. It must be the next road; the whole passageway was clear. She'd climb up anyway, have a quick look in that street too. The concrete here was broader as the incline eased off. Too busy, making her way and looking up at the light, to see the crumple at her feet until she stood on it, soft and warm.

A body, a boy, tight-curled round his belly.

She gagged at the telling sourness. On her knees, trying to ease him open, still breathing, breathing blood. His wild eyes falling back, quivering, her taking his hands away from his abdomen and seeing the signs. One single stab-wound like an open eye, blinking out life. Quickly, trying to staunch the blood, wrenching off her jacket, tearing the lining to make a pad. 'What's your name?' She was shouting at him, not caring if the gang heard. 'Can you tell me your name?'

Neck jerking as he tried to speak, but only tears came, mingling in his mouth. Something white, he was choking on froth.

'Ssh, ssh. It's alright, pet. Don't worry. I've got you.'

She could leave him, run for help. But it would be too late; he was going to die, whatever she did. He was just a teenager; and the last thing he would ever know was this concrete step. His body spasmed, vicious, his arm shot up.

'I've got you.' Scattered beside his hair, two

37

ragged triangles of bread, the filling spilled and soaking blood. Anna shifted her body so that she was lying alongside him, supporting his head and shoulders on her chest. Coughing, choking. She hooked a finger under his tongue, trying to loosen the phlegm, but it was bread, a chunk of bread and meat caught in the gap behind his wisdom teeth, the space where you would feed medicine to dogs. Even then, with his airways clear, he couldn't breathe. His lungs were filling. Flailing now, his body drowning him. Face on to her, the terror building.

'I know. I know.'

She held the boy in her arms as saliva bubbled blood and his eyes faded, fast and dark.

* * *

'Here.' Johnny placed a mug of tea in front of Anna.

'Cheers. Any biscuits?'

Her fish supper lay in Clarkston, scattered on the pavement, and she was starving. Even after seeing that poor boy die, her legs still damp with blood, Anna needed food, something solid to press down on liquefied guts. She pulled her fingers through the mesh of the crocheted cardigan they'd found her. It was itchy, as were the jeans. Her gear had been seized for forensic examination; not to prove it was blood, real blood that coated her clothes, but to discount her mess and fibres from the others they would hopefully find.

'Want some of my chips, ma'am?' said the DS sitting beside them. Stumpy, pale digits, smothered in tomato ketchup.

'No, you're alright.'

He read Anna's statement back to her.

'So, no sign of anyone by the body, no sign of any weapon?'

'No. All I can speak to is seeing the chase, giving pursuit, and then discovering the boy on the stairs. I can't even say I could ID any of them again, beyond what they were wearing.'

'Disny matter that much anyway, ma'am. Nae offence. I mean, we've got them running down Clarkston Road on CCTV—you can confirm at least that the clothing on this footage matches the description of the guys you saw, and that one of them shouted: 'You Paki cunt.'

'That's correct. But I couldn't say who.' She took one of his chips after all. Cold and fat and comforting, the tang of sweet tomato and the blandness of floury chip. 'Have we got a name yet? For the boy?'

The DS nodded. 'Sabir Aziz. Would have been nineteen next month.'

'Local?'

'No really. From Shawlands. We havny established what he was doing up in Clarkston, particularly on his own.'

A DC knocked at the open door. 'Hey, boss. Uniform have hoovered a load of neds by the viaduct in Overlee Park.' He grinned. 'One is currently topless. Gordon Figgis—ever heard of him?'

'Don't think so.'

'Claims he was about to dive into the river, but the cops reckon he's lobbed his clothing down into the water there. They could see something white caught on a rock. Might be a poly bag or

39

something, but they're going down for a look.'

'Excellent.' The DS jumped up. 'Gotta go. Cheers, missus. We wouldny have got them this quick if you'd not been there. Give yourself a gold star.'

'Ta. Can I just get the rest of your chips instead?'

'Sure.' The DS went outside, then almost immediately popped his head back into the office. 'If we parade them once we've interviewed them, say tomorrow maybe, d'you think you'd pick any of them out?'

She stuffed three chips in at once. 'Doubt it, but I'll do my best.'

Silently, resolutely, Anna munched her way though soggy chips, sucking off the ketchup, then chewing each chip down. Johnny watching her, annoying her.

'Well, that was a quick night's work, Ms Cameron. Community Council *and* you solve a murder. Well done.'

'I hardly solved it. I fucking let it happen.'

'And how do you reckon that?'

'Well, if I'd been a bit quicker. If I'd had my phone on me . . . I couldn't even protect the locus properly, afterwards.'

She picked at the crispy batter crumbs remaining in the poke. 'I had to leave him and go thump on the nearest front door till someone called the police.'

'Anna, kids like these mill about every night, in every part of Scotland. Gangs fighting over territories, girls, what race or religion or school you're part of. If they'd not got him tonight, they'd have got him some other time. Or got some other

40

kid instead.'

'Maybe so. But they got this kid, tonight. And you didn't watch him die.'

'Yeah, well, we do what we can do, and that's it. And you did a good job, don't forget that.' He stood up. 'Shall I escort you home?'

'Nah. I'm a big girl now. Think I can sort myself.'

Johnny clicked his briefcase shut, picked up his jacket. Taking his time, zip, cough, fumble in the pockets. Anna sensed there was something more to come, some wise adage from the Bumper Book of Polis Proverbs.

'Look, I know you've had a shit day . . . but do you want to grab a quick drink?'

On another day, Johnny's attentions would have been very welcome. Given her a wee frisson, even. But not tonight.

'No, cheers. That's a nice thought, but I'm really knackered. Maybe another time, yeah?'

'Sure, no worries. Night then.'

'Night.'

Anna came out of the office to a lacquered wet sky, rain sheening the concrete in deep, long drifts. Headlights broke the black, sweeping into the yard. She got into her car, saw they were bringing a load of kids in. Lowering them out of the van now, a cop each side to steady the boys as they came down, since their cuffed hands couldn't help them if they fell. It looked like the same pumped-up warriors of before, same pale nylon joggers and gel-smooth heads, only now they were silent and twitching. Staring at their feet.

Anna drove on, wipers swishing the seconds past. She still felt hungry and she still felt sick.

41

CHAPTER THREE

The notes lay in piles of twenty. One heap of £50s, smooth, flat green, the top one with a picture of the Falkirk Wheel on the front. Three piles of £20s, and the same of £10s and £5s. £2,300, just lying there. Enough to pay off Anna's credit card bill—and buy a decent dress for Elaine's wedding. Not quite designer, but something subtle from Whistles or Hobbs.

'So. Can anyone spot the difference?' The Fraud Squad DCI sat back, hands over his comfortable gut. Typical CID; hair too long, and he seemed to be experimenting with sideburns. 'Apart from the obvious: i.e. some are Bank of England and some are Bank of Scotland.'

Dense silence in the room. It was Mrs Hamilton's own office they were in, all institutional green and fawn, nary a spider plant nor snap of a grandwean to cheer the place up. Just a pinboard sporting an array of coloured rosettes, and a calendar featuring the 'Ferret of the Month'. Seriously. It would seem that each month boasted a ferret in a different pose. 'Action Ferret' (it was pointing with its nose and paw) was this month's special, but little titled inserts round the main picture revealed the delights to come: 'Sniffing Ferret'; 'Sleekest Ferret'; 'Ferret at Rest'. She could swear that a faint animal odour emanated from the wicker basket below the window, too. When she looked more closely at the rosettes, she could make out that they were from the National Ferret Association. Most said 'Best in Show'.

Nobody wanted to speak or point, in case they got it wrong. Anna picked up one of the fivers, a Bank of England one. The paper felt crisp, as it should, not glossy or waxy like some of the dodgy ones she'd seen. Proper notes were printed on a thin cotton weave. She held it up to the light. The metal foil, which appeared as silver dots and dashes when lying flat, became one continuous strip. Again, all present and correct. The Queen's head watermark was faintly visible, as were both Britannia and the value of the note in the hologram on the front, flickering in and out as she moved it. The two other chief inspectors began to copy what Anna was doing. Johnny O'Hare had lain out a couple of notes too, and was comparing them, running the top of his pen along the serial numbers. Mrs Hamilton's breasts spilled from under folded arms, the eyes behind her glasses radiating prior, superior knowledge. Anna put the note back on the table, rubbed her thumb across the design.

'Am I right in thinking that real notes are still printed on intaglio presses?' she asked the DCI.

'Ten points to the lady,' he nodded. 'You're absolutely right.'

'So, should the ink not feel more . . . raised?'

'Right again.'

'Okay. Well, I think this is a fake.'

'And see this one?' Johnny held up one of his twenties. 'I think they've hot-foiled this on top of the note: the strip doesn't weave right through the way it should.'

'Mrs Hamilton, your troops are good.'

She pursed her lips. 'Aye. Took their time, but.'

'But that's understandable; these notes are top

43

of the range. Actually, they're all counterfeit, every one. I've brought along a selection to show you how they've evolved. Some of the earlier ones, like yours, Superintendent, have had a thin foil laid on top, rather than through the paper. With yours, Anna, they've conquered the foil issue, but are still using commercial presses, hence the flat quality of their work. But, with some of the newer ones circulating, the printing's textured, and even the holograms appear authentic.' He raised his eyebrows. 'For those of you who don't know, kinegrams and holograms are produced by embossing microprofiles with thermoplastic films.'

'Och, we knew that,' said Tony McGraw.

'Shut it, Tony,' said Mrs Hamilton, 'unless you've something constructive to say. Carry on, Mike.'

Anna suspected the DCI had been practising in front of the mirror. His demeanour was that of a kid about to recite his times-tables, lips slightly mobile as his eyelids flickered, before globs of words splashed out and engulfed them. 'Well, a hologram is applied using the interference of light from different sources in a specific pattern, and kinegrams are produced with achromatic and polarisation effects, resulting in a 3D image when lit from different angles.'

The DCI paused to observe a table full of gormless faces. Ah, see, thought Anna, you pitched it too high.

'Basically, when you tilt the note, the image changes.'

They all nodded in agreement.

'Now most forgers never go into that much detail. But this one has. His later versions are practically a work of art.'

'And do you think these are all coming from the same source?' asked Anna.

'I do indeed. And, without going into too many details—because, if I tell you, I may have to shoot you—we think that source is somewhere in dear auld Glesca toon.'

'So, Mike, what is it you'd like us to do?' said Mrs Hamilton.

'I'd like you to brief your cops, obviously. But without letting them know we think the forger is from hereabouts. Just make them aware there's a quantity of well-crafted dodgy notes circulating, and advise them of what to look for. I'll leave a couple of samples, and I've prepared a wee check sheet which you could maybe circulate.'

'And do you want us to warn local shopkeepers?'

'No. Not for now. I'm worried we might alert this team to the fact we're closing in. For the moment, I'm just looking for as much information gathering as possible. These notes are so sharp now that I think the only way we'll find the source is via intelligence and observations. But there's bound to be some of the earlier prototypes still in circulation. So, if any of your cops receives a report of counterfeit cash being tendered, please pass all details of where, when, how much and, most importantly, any IDs of *who* passed the notes, to me at the Fraud Squad. If possible, seize CCTV recordings which might cover the periods any transactions were made, and we'll collate that too.'

He swept the notes like playing cards. Together, shuffle, sort. Smooth, straight, thickened paper in satisfying handfuls. Was he ever tempted? Surrounded by all that money, and him on fifty grand a year. Wads and wads of customised notes that even the experts could barely discern from the real thing. Enough money to buy . . . anything. To crush and rustle them through your fists, smell the wealth they offered up. Money bought you respect, security. The ability to demand what you deserved, to tell your boss to stuff it up her arse, walk free, free into the glorious day and be . . .

Be what? Be anything she liked.

Anna would like to make things, she decided. Craft structures with her hands, sculptures perhaps, and not give a stuff who liked them. She would fill her garden with wirework horses, leaping cats and twisted men, then move out into the street, her neighbours' gardens. She would work secretly, in the darkness, spilling silver wire through night air, a burrowing mole here, by the drain that cut through the gutter, and there, in the park, a louche droop of human; dryad; tree? A copper-headed Narcissus mirrored in the littered duck pond? Who knew, who would ever know, just Anna and her lightning hands, pleating soft, thin metal until her fingers bled, like the girl who spun gold in fairy tales.

People asked that sometimes. Are you ever tempted? You know, to help yourself? To remove some stolen goods maybe, to sort out a nice wee stash of drugs, to take that tenner in the petty cash? Anna could only speak for herself, but the honest answer was no. And it would be no, always, even if it were only whispered inside her head, and not said out loud for effect, or because it was the right thing *to* say. Knowing she was better than that, than the 'them' she locked up and looked down on. Some days that pure, clean gut-down knowledge was the only aspect of this job that she still felt sure about.

'Well, we appreciate you giving us the heads-up, Mike.' Mrs Hamilton rose from her chair; a signal she was done and dusted with him. As she shook the DCI's hand, the door clattered open and a burly, grey-haired man careered in.

'So sorry I'm late, ma'am. We've that murder on—'

'Ah. DCI Cruikshanks. How nice of you to join us. Big queue in the baker's, was there?'

'Thomas!' Without thinking, Anna cried out. Thomas Cruikshanks, her old DI from A Division. Grown fatter and older and even more scruffy, if that were feasible.

'Anna Cameron,' he laughed. 'How you doing, my old mucker? And well done you—you're some kid, so you are.'

'Oh, I'm so sorry.' Mrs Hamilton assumed an overly polite, Kelvinesque drawl. 'Friends Reunited, is it? Would you two like us to leave?'

'Och, I've no seen this wee lassie in years, ma'am.' He winked. 'And I have to say, she's a distinct asset to the division. I take it you know it was Anna who kicked off the murder investigation last night?'

'Hmm.'

'And we've got a name in the frame already, by the way. So,' he turned direct to Anna, 'how you been?' His grin was the warmest Anna had seen since she'd arrived at the division. No shark-smiles there.

Mrs Hamilton banged her folder on the desk. 'Ho, Cruikshanks. Take it outside. If you canny be bothered to get here in time, then I'm no wasting

47

time with you.'

'Eh, sorry, ma'am. Sorry. I'm interrupting here.'

'First correct thing you've said today. Michael was done here anyway, so maybe you'd like to take him back down to CID and he can give you a wee remedial lesson on what you've missed? Seeing as it would be quite nice if my CID had a basic knowledge of this month's divisional policing issues.'

'Aye, talking of which, ma'am, I've a bid to put in for extra bodies on the seventeenth.' Cruikshanks held out a typewritten report.

'Put it with the others and we'll draw straws.'

'But ma'am, this is really important—'

'And so's my time, Cruikshanks.'

This Tasking and Co-ordinating meeting was held every fortnight. Policing priorities for the next two weeks were worked out, and resources allocated accordingly. But of course, everyone's priorities were urgent, and so a bidding system had evolved, where each senior officer had to prepare a report stating what their specific problems were, what they proposed as a solution, what resources this would need, and how this fitted in with ongoing divisional objectives. And how those ongoing divisional objectives fitted in with Force objectives. And how those Force objectives fitted in with the Joint Police Board's objectives, who, ultimately, dished out the dosh. Mrs Hamilton picked up the sheaf of papers in front of her, flicked through them.

'Right, let's see. A Farm Watch initiative to combat the mysterious case of the missing combine harvesters in Eaglesham—haud me back—versus . . . school gate parking . . . piss off . . . versus . . .

extra attention to licensed premises . . . versus a series of indecent exposures in Linn Park. Hmm. Okay, we'll start with this one. Johnny, over to you.'

Tom Cruikshanks remained by the door, as did the Fraud Squad DCI. One of the DCI's hands was creeping through the gap between door and lintel, while the rest of him hung in an embarrassed apostrophe, neither in nor out, here nor there, yet car-crash gazing all the while. In which camp would he place his feet, Anna wondered? She sensed the intake of Johnny's breath which would preface his report, dunted him with her elbow. As he looked up, she tipped her pen towards Cruikshanks. A tiny tilt, but enough to make him notice Cruikshanks' expression.

'Excuse me, ma'am?' Cruikshanks' mouth was rigid, pale in a red-splotched face.

'You still here, Thomas?'

'I'd prefer to submit my bid in person. Particularly if that's the reports just being heard the now.'

'Aye well, tough. You've got to get yourself up to speed on our counterfeiting problem, and Mike here disny have all day to—'

'Ma'am,' interrupted the Fraud Squad DCI, 'I've a few other visits to make nearby, but I'm happy to come back.' He turned to Cruikshanks. 'In an hour, say, Tom, and we can discuss how you'd like the liaison between us to work. We'll be adhering to NIM obviously.'

'Obviously,' smiled Cruikshanks. 'That's the National Intelligence Model, ma'am.'

'I know fine well what it is, Thomas. D'you think I button up the back? Right, on you go, Mike. You,

49

Thomas,' Mrs Hamilton pushed out a chair with the tip of her toecap, 'sit your arse down and we'll get rattled through these. Okay Johnny; gie's your flasher sob story.'

On the other side of Anna, Tony whispered, 'She's getting worse.'

Anna listened as her boss began his shopping list. Then it was the turn of Govan, then Cathcart, then Gorbals. Eventually Cruikshanks got his moment in the sun; an impassioned bid for plainers to help combat a spate of car-jackings on Cathkin Braes. Anna would be expected to have her own list of initiatives next time. As quickly as they all spoke, Mrs Hamilton fired back questions, then expletives, then more questions. It felt like being back at school, struggling to keep up, not sure when to enter the fray, and fervently resisting eye contact with the teacher, lest she begin to pick on you. Finally, it was the turn of Pollok to put out their begging bowl. Of all the subdivisions in the South, this was the one with fewest saving graces, cobbled round a massive dose of poverty, a vacuum of decent jobs—albeit with a vast new shopping centre plonked dead in the middle, an acute injection of drug abuse, and a splendid collection of burned-out cars lodged in every local stream. Pollok reminded Anna of what she thought she'd left behind at E Division. Hopelessness.

'So, in conclusion ma'am, this mobile crack den has been reported at three schools in the area— one of them a primary. The kids all seem to know what day it's due where, but we don't have a scooby. All we know is it's disguised as a chip van, and there's bloody hundreds of *them*. As I said, my bid would be to utilise the services of the

Divisional Flexi Unit for a period of five days, to work on a rotational basis, taking observations on clusters of secondaries and feeder primaries—'

'I'll give you them for three. But no overtime. Fucking CID are scooping my budget again.'

'Done.'

'Right. If that's us, I need to prepare for another meeting.'

'Eh, ma'am,' said Johnny. 'About last night's murder?'

'What about it? We've jailed the wee shites. Hip hip hooray. Are yous wanting a chocolate Noddy?'

'What I was really looking for, ma'am, was a steer on how we should play this. With the community, I mean.'

Johnny was right. It was too soon to point fingers or cast aspersions, but whether Aziz's death had been purely racist or born from territorial dispute, the problem of gang violence had now erupted into murder. Until this point, it was only acne-aggravated anguish they had been dealing with: the Busby Cumbie, the Clarkston Young Team, Young Stampy Derry; some were new gangs, some had reappropriated names with the baggage of past violence. But all they'd been displaying were the actions of truculent kids. And the police's role—which they couldn't get away with now—had been markedly low-key. A few extra men going round the drinking dens, some anti-vandalism talks in schools, when what was really needed was some parents with the balls to deal with their loutish kids.

Oh, no. Not my boy.
Who you calling antisocial?
My kid's a good kid.

51

It's the school's fault, the polis's fault.

Everyone's fault but theirs. But what did it culminate in? Did kids like Gordon Figgis murder kids like Sabir Aziz because they were *bored*? Feral children, gone to seed. It was endemic; one of the reasons Anna's own mother had left Scotland. Sick of the persistent, petty drizzle of shattered glass and disaffected youth which clinked and punched and piddled through her town. Which cowed with foul language and fouler music on the buses, and made shadows of decent folk skirting trouble-seekers in their city's streets. Children who tooled up with chibs, articulating arguments with knives. So Caroline had headed for sangria and sun, to a place where youth and age could coexist and family was all. Except the family you left at home, of course. But still, Caroline had 'the girls' for bridge and golf, the hirsute Teddy for everything else. And neither did it rain in Spain.

'The *community*?' repeated Mrs Hamilton. 'Well, Superintendent O'Hare, I don't think it's very difficult, do you? Least sign of trouble, whether they're black, white, orange or green, and we clamp down hard—no matter what "the community" thinks. Clear? Right,' she hit the desk, 'back to work, the lot of yous. Oh, Anna,' she added. 'Could you stay behind a minute?'

'Ma'am.'

As they trooped out, Cruikshanks squeezed Anna's elbow. 'Good to see you, doll. I was fair chuffed when I heard you were coming here.'

'You were?'

'Aye. C'mon down to CID and we'll have a wee chat when JC's done with you.'

Anna needed to get back to Giffnock. She

52

hadn't even gone through her correspondence yet, or her emails. Or checked the Vulnerable Persons' Database, which she was meant to do first thing. But there were two complaints against the police to deal with, and then this councillor had phoned. The same one that had phoned her yesterday, and the day before that, bleating on and on about dangerous Dobermans in the park. They'd gone for his poodle, twice now, didn't she know? And what, exactly, was Anna going to do about it? She'd arranged for him to come in and see her. It would also be a good opportunity to brief him about the murder last night, keep him sweet.

Five minutes of chat would offer a respite though.

'Well, I've . . . Yes, that would be nice, Tom.'

'Good stuff. I'll away and put the kettle on. And whatever you do,' Cruikshanks whispered, 'don't let her see the whites of your eyes.'

Mrs Hamilton waited until the room had emptied.

'So,' she frowned. 'Settling in?'

'Yes, ma'am.'

Anna tilted her hip slightly, settling her posture. This had to be a precursor to something big. A well done for her efforts last night, maybe a performance review note in her file. Then perhaps an apology, or an explanation at least, of why Hamilton had not given her a fair reception. A girly chat about the hair-width tightrope linking femininity and power, a hidden warmth of mentorship creeping from behind those steely specs—but never, ever, expressed in front of the boys.

Fair enough.

'Good, good. Right, I've a wee job for you.' Mrs Hamilton seemed to be rummaging for something under her desk. 'I've to go to the swearing-in ceremony next week up at Jackton. Another load of tender new sprogs for us to let loose on the public.'

And . . . what? Did she want Anna to accompany her, get a feel for the ceremony, the sort of duties she'd be expected to carry out when she became a divisional commander? Maybe Mrs Hamilton was one of these women who was tougher on other females than she was on men, but only because she didn't like to show favouritism. Yet, underneath those forbidding bosoms beat a heart of—

'Aye.' Her right shoulder was tilted low, her right hand hidden. Was she sorting her tights or something? 'So . . .' rising back to upright, holding something bulky in her hand, 'I'll need my shoes bulled.'

Like they were a prize, Mrs Hamilton handed Anna a pair of black court shoes. Still warm inside from where her feet had been, their moist heat rising through Anna's hand to her face, her head.

'And you're asking me, because . . . ?'

'You worked in Training for a while, didn't you?'

'Yes, but—'

'Well, you'll know how to get a good shine on them. Just the toecaps, mind—and use water. I don't want you gobbing on them. And I'll need them back as soon as. I've only got the one other pair, and they pinch like buggery.'

There was a smear on the window behind where Mrs Hamilton sat. Almost a handprint, enough mottled puckering of pressured cells to dot-dot-dash a thumb at least, and the pad of rounded palm-flesh. Did Mrs Hamilton stand there, watch the comings and goings in the yards below? Was she spying on her domain, or contemplating that big, final hurl?

Thank you very much go fuck yourself was jumbling all in the one breath, one person, one thought, and still this desperate desire to be approved of by the person whose hand had just proffered this stinking pair of shoes, which could have been dog-shit or two fingers in a V. Was this a battle or the war or just mundane, to laugh at later? Anna didn't know, just knew she could close her eyes and take the medicine for an illness she did not have. Or state her case with insolent eloquence, walk out proud and punctured, or . . . or . . .

Or be not Anna, but someone new.

'Certainly ma'am.' She secured the shoes under her arm. 'We'll have them so shiny you'll be able to see your face in them.'

Hamilton blinked, a lazy frog meets fly blink, and nothing more was said.

Down in CID, Cruikshanks had two mugs and a plate of Chelsea buns waiting.

'Survive whatever it was?'

Anna dropped the shoes on to his desk.

'Oh, aye. As long as I bull her bloody shoes.'

'Jeez. Has the wumman no heard of Odor-Eaters? Put them away.'

'What the hell am I supposed to do with them?'

He swiped the shoes on to the floor, where they lay pouting like sulky mouths. 'First rule of management, doll. Pass it down the chain of command. Bun?'

'Too right she is.' Anna helped herself to the

biggest, curliest daud of pastry she could see, using the hand that had not held those smug black shoes. 'And she was a total boot to you and all. How do you all put up with her?'

'She's got worse since Sangster's been away. He used to keep her in check, as much as he dared. I tell you, she wouldny have spoke to me like that if old Donny-boy had been there. Fellow fisherman, you see. But now she's going sky-high loony.' Cruikshanks spoke through clouds of crumbly bun. 'Tell you, any minute now, you'll see her on her broomstick, flying off up to the moon.'

'I wish. So, tell me about my murderer?'

'The boy with nae top? Well, it *was* his sweatshirt in the water, and it did have blood on it. Found a blade down there too. Once we confirm it's wee Aziz's blood, we'll have Figgis greeting by lunchtime—you wait and see.' Cruikshanks gave a weary sigh. 'Aye, they're no so tough once you get them on their lonesome.'

'Was there history between him and Aziz?'

'Only a few hundred years.'

'Pardon?'

'What I mean is, nothing personal that I've established so far. Sabir Aziz was Asian, Gordon Figgis is white. Figgis runs with the YSD, Aziz with Ubu Roi.'

'What the hell is Ubu Roi?'

'Team of wee scrotes fae Pollokshields. I don't think your Aziz was an angel by any means.'

Anna digested this information, reconciled it with the scared child dying on her lap. 'So he was in a gang too? So what? He didn't deserve that.'

'No. No, he didny.'

'Did he have any family?'

56

'Only child, far as I can establish. Neighbours say the father died last year, and the maw's in India. God knows where—we've asked the consulate to check.' Cruikshanks swallowed the last of his cake. 'I mean, you'd think he'd belong to *someone.*'

They both waited a while, letting the silence settle.

'How long've you been here anyway?'

'Near two years now,' said Cruikshanks. 'I replaced a lassie called Armstrong. Heard of her?'

Anna stopped chewing. 'You taking the piss?'

'Course I am doll!' A little belch. ' 'Scuse I.'

'So, does everyone hate me in CID then?'

'Ach, away. You done them all a favour. I don't think many folk liked Nik-ki-ki with a "k" much at all. No from what I've heard.'

'Didn't look like that to me. She aye had a wee band of willing young DCs round her.'

'No, I think you'll find Nikki Armstrong was one of those women who use charm and sex appeal to climb up the first few rungs of the ladder, then oppressive conduct and sexual harassment when it all goes south.' He popped the last of his pastry in his mouth. 'Nae offence, like.'

Anna stared at him, at his busy, chomping jaws, until he finally started laughing.

'Oh, you soor-faced cow. I'm only joking!'

She knew he was. That's why she liked him—not that she'd ever say, mind. An electronic riff beeped from Cruikshanks' desk.

'There's your raspberry going, hen.'

'It's not a raspberry, you diddy, it's a BlackBerry. Or something like it, anyway.'

Anna picked up the digital unit he was

prodding. They'd all but replaced the traditional notebooks, which would bulge with elastic bands and bits of pencils and blank forms for sudden deaths and missing persons and aides-memoires about what to do in the event of a bomb call or if you came across a terrorist in the local bus station. It could be your best friend in a crisis; the very act of withdrawing it was a signal that things were about to change. It was your bible in court. And it would keep all your secrets, particularly the ones you inadvertently rewrote. But these digital units were something else; storing facts, photos, forms and fixed penalties, you could key in all your reports on site, and just download at the end of your shift. If only you could do that with your head. Anna looked at the digits on the side.

'Is that yours too then, that Airwave thingy? Because I canny find mine.' He waved crossly at her personal radio, which lay beside the digital unit.

'Yup. See, I wrote my ISSI number on it.' She showed him the strip of white label, complete with her personal ID.

'This job's too full of numbers. What happened to people? I canny mind my own date of birth some days, let alone all this crap.'

'But ISSIs are great. You can talk direct to any cop on duty, anywhere in the UK.'

'Aye, and they can talk to you right back. Boom, boom, boom. I preferred it when you sent out telexes and waited for someone to pick it out the machine. You've nae time to think any more.'

'Ah, but neither have the bad guys.'

'Ach, piss off, Pollyanna, and get on with your work. I'm away to set myself in aspic.'

Anna checked the message on her digital screen: a reminder from Mrs Hamilton about her shoes. And telling Anna she'd also have to prepare a presentation for . . . EWomF?

'Tom, what's Ee Womb Eff? Is she swearing at me now by BlackBerry?'

'Let me see.' He looked at the screen. 'Och, that's Eastwood Women's Forum. Businesswomen, lovely yummy-mummies and that. I mind her freaking that the Chief had passed it on to her.'

'And now she's passed it on to me.'

'I love you, Mini-me,' Cruikshanks squeaked.

'What?'

'That's what she's grooming you for: a mini-Mrs Hamilton. You're gonny be her stunt double.'

'Fuck off.'

'My God—she's creating a monster!'

First person Anna saw when she arrived back at Giffnock was Claire Rodgers, the Three Group inspector. Not intentional, certainly not planned, but Claire would do. She always looked so perky that woman, even though she was just back from maternity leave. Perky and pert and perfect. And very pleasant too, which annoyed Anna greatly. She would have preferred a tangible reason to find her irritating.

'Claire. Can I have a word?'

'Sure. But Councillor Heraghty's here for you.'

'Shit. Already? Look, I hate to ask, but could you get someone to . . .' Anna pointed to the poly bag, not quite sure how to say it.

Claire looked inside. 'Bull Mrs Hamilton's shoes? Yup, no bother. I'll get one of the probationers to do it.'

It felt like passing the torch. 'I'm really sorry to

59

ask you, Claire. I know it's ridiculous. And she needs them back up the road as soon as you can.'

'It's fine, honestly. At least it's not her order from Damart needing collected.'

'You *are* joking?'

'No, no. She likes to get her thermal underwear in the Easter sales. To keep her warm at the football.'

'Of course.'

Anna left the shoes with Claire, went along the corridor to her office. A pale, faded man was sitting on the plastic chair outside. He rose at her approach, hand outstretched in welcome.

'Chief Inspector?'

'Councillor Heraghty. Pleasure to meet you. Please, come in.'

His fingertips were ochre, as were his teeth. Clean shaven, but with a trace of white stubble lurking like dandruff on his chin, his wattle-neck held steady by a stiff, light green shirt and matching tie. There was a coffee table and a couple of easy chairs by the window. Heraghty settled himself down in one, unbuttoning his tweed jacket, stretching out his legs. Anna took the other chair.

'Coffee?'

'No, no, you're alright.' He smiled again, his eyes journeying round the room. 'It's good to meet you at last. Unexpected pleasure this, getting to see the chief inspector.'

'Really? Well, I hope we'll be seeing a lot more of each other. I think it's vital that we have a strong working relationship—'

'Sweet music, Ms Cameron. I couldn't agree more.'

Anna pushed her hair behind her ears. 'Now, about these dogs...'

'Och, c'mon. I rather think circumstances have overtaken us, don't you? Can we be frank here?'

'Of course.'

Up front and obvious, a simple and efficient philosophy. Anna had watched too many gaffers contort themselves, concealing and obfuscating nuggets of information, dispersing only the least incriminating or most innocuous fragments on a 'need to know' basis. But folk like councillors did need to know, and would glean the details from other, more convoluted sources if the police didn't get in there first. Filter out what you don't want told, then feed them every lump and twist of gristle that remains. Stuff them full of it, ladle out abundant helpings and they'll go home thinking you're their new best friend.

'I imagine you'd rather talk about last night's murder. I've actually prepared a short briefing note for you, Councillor.'

'Really? My goodness, that *is* remarkable.' Thin, pink tongue moistening his lips. He glanced at the memo. 'Mmhm, yes. Pretty much what I'd heard already. Oh, all very factual, thank you. But, sadly, it's not often I get the ear of the local cop shop, so let's use this meeting to both our advantage, eh?'

'Can you be more specific, Councillor?'

'Well, I mean, the aftermath. Things are going to hot up big style now, aren't they? Tension, retribution, interracial violence.' He almost sounded excited at the prospect. 'My constituents need to know what you're going to be doing to reassure them.'

Without warning or pre-emptive knock, Anna's

61

door swung open. In marched Johnny O'Hare, hair sticking to his brow as if he'd been running.

'Anna. Councillor Heraghty. How are things?'

He assumed a referee stance, arms folded, legs wide, his body carefully positioned in the no-man's-land between them. Solid legs he had; she'd noticed that before.

'Eh, fine.'

Why was he frowning at her?

'Mr O'Hare,' said Heraghty, 'long time no speak. I was just saying to your charming colleague here, how nice it is to find a senior officer who actually wants to converse with me.'

'Councillor, we're always happy to speak to you.'

'Is that right? Just a shame I've to do all the running though, isn't it? That's four times now I've had to ask for an update on recent crime stats. You know, it would be nice if, once in a while, someone actually got a bit proactive. Gave me the rundown on what was going on in my area, rather than me have to read about it in the local paper.'

'Well, I'm sure we can sort that out, sir,' said Anna, eager to smooth some salve on the heat beginning to spark. Clearly, there was some background she wasn't aware of. But Heraghty was *her* guest, she could deal with this. 'In my last posting, in Easterhouse, I had an excellent system for keeping our councillors up to date. On a monthly basis, I'd get my community cops to—'

'D'you hear that, Mr O'Hare? See, it *can* be done.'

'Councillor, it *is* being done. According to proper protocols. But I can't have you coming in here and harassing my staff.'

Anna opened her mouth, then shut it. In one

swift movement, she'd been shoved out of a game she didn't know was being played, let alone what the rules were, or whose side she was on. She could be watching this through a window, present but detached, for neither of the men was giving any cognizance to her presence now, just strutting and posturing, each clucking a little louder.

'Harassing your staff? Ms Cameron invited me here. She's like a breath of fresh air. Honest to God, I've never encountered such a secret squirrel set-up in my life before.' Heraghty's volume increased as he stood up. 'Your Mrs Hamilton would rather eat her own ferrets than give me the time of day. I've left several messages for her now about this murder, and she's no even lifted the phone.'

'Sir, Mrs Hamilton has been in meetings all day, and is now en route to Aberdeen for an ACPOS seminar.'

'Well, it would be nice to have known that.'

'Sure, it's not incumbent on Mrs Hamilton to provide you with details of her weekly diary.'

'Look, Superintendent, as a local member, as vice convenor of Community Safety, not to mention as a member of the Joint Police Board, I have every right—'

'I'll have to ask you to stop raising your voice, sir.'

'Don't you speak to me as if I was a piece of shit, laddie. That woman has one rule for some—'

'Right, that's enough.' Johnny dropped to a don't-mess-with-me baritone. 'I'm going to terminate this meeting forthwith, and I'm going to have to ask you to leave.'

Heraghty hesitated.

'Immediately, Councillor.'

All the broken veins on Heraghty's cheeks had united in one glorious, scarlet pulse. The councillor was scrutinising her. Anna could see herself reflected in his eyes—oh, not literally, but you could see the sense of it, the slowly hardening perception of who she was, apparent in the crook of his fingers, the rigidity that prefaced his defeat.

'Ms Cameron.'

'Councillor.'

He nodded at her, then Johnny. 'You haven't heard the last of this, Mr O'Hare.'

Johnny held the door open. 'Likewise, Mr Heraghty.'

Heraghty left the room. Air churning, Anna paddling in its wake.

'Fucksake.' Johnny dropped into the chair vacated by the councillor, shut his eyes.

'Do you mind telling me what was going on there?'

'Anna, that man is like a stick of dynamite. I don't know what you were thinking of, inviting him in.' He wiped the heel of his hand across his mouth. 'Bet you're glad I was here to rescue you.'

'I wasn't aware I needed rescuing.'

'Is that so? Sure, you've a lot to learn, kid.'

It would appear she had. 'So tell me.'

'Not now Anna, eh? Just be warned. Give the man a very wide berth.'

'I don't see why.'

'Because it won't go well with Mrs H if you don't.'

Nothing Anna did went well with Mrs H in any case. And Heraghty did have a valid point. 'Well, what *are* we going to do regarding community

64

relations? There's bound to be some repercussions after Aziz's murder.'

'Aye, if folk like him start winding people up, there will be.'

'What do you mean?'

'Anna, you heard the commander. We take our orders from her, not Heraghty.'

'I don't think he was giving us "orders". The man was merely entering into some dialogue with us.'

'Leave it Anna, okay? I'll take it up with Mrs Hamilton, I promise.'

Johnny was not for talking further. Just upped and departed as quick as he'd come, leaving Anna to wonder where else she should fear to tread. She was not in the mood to play Machiavellian politics.

CHAPTER FOUR

It is late when they come. This time, the Mirror Man is with them.

The guard has seen him only once before, from a distance. It was in the place where they had given him his uniform . . . but, oh, the sense of him, even through two open doors and a glass-partitioned wall . . . it was the thick, close creep of death, the godless watching of shaded eyes long after the guard had left the room. They had ushered him into an outer office the moment the Man appeared. A creak of leather, an incision of white in the space where a smile might sit was all the guard registered, before they took him out, through a corridor of interconnecting doors. From down the boxed tunnel of office after office, the guard had pretended not to look, seeing only obliquely as the Man struck a young boy, a teenager. Fist across screaming face, the boy falling to the floor. Then the Man had turned, his eyes behind dark glass, and the guard had felt his soul wither.

'Who is that?' he had whispered, as they were pressing a mess of jumper and torch and dark jacket on him.

'That is none of your business,' said one.

'That is the Mirror Man,' said another.

And now, the Mirror Man is here, in this dark and lonely place; the guard's lamp silhouetting his profile, rising jagged on unplastered wall. The Man removes his glasses, an infinity of forty-watt bulb-pricks refracting from glossy lenses. On the table where he lays them is a carton of Chinese food, and in one clean swipe he knocks it to the floor, spraying rice and waxy egg.

He folds his arms, and his eyes stretch wild. They are tiger-gold and brown, the colours flit like birds inside a cage. 'Who brought you this?' His voice a dull chisel; it is the first thing he has said.

'I . . . I got it. From the—'

'No one comes here and you do not leave. You do not leave and you do not speak. Understand?'

The guard nods once. His neck remains bent as he watches the wall, watches ruby sauce drip and puddle on the floor.

*   *   *

Anna sat upright, confused, aware of a presence. A stuttering consciousness that there was someone in her room, and that the sky outside the window held a liquid shimmer; rain, or dawn; some shift in

66

light. Alice stared back at her, throat-purr revving as she kneaded paws on Anna's pillow.

'Hey. It's you,' Anna whispered. 'What time is it?'

And then the phone rang, like it had been waiting for her. Six a.m.

'Hi boss, sorry to disturb you. Alan Harkness here, night-shift inspector.'

'Morning Alan.' Her fingers, pushing her eyelids back. 'What's up? You on about that murder?'

'No. Bit of a busy night all round, ma'am. We've two juveys absconded from the children's home at Eaglesham, *and* an old dear gone AWOL from The Meadows up in Mearns. Myself and Claire from the early shift are just looking for a steer on how we should prioritise things, ma'am.'

'Bring me up to speed on what you've done so far. The juveys first. Are they habitual runaways?'

She was dressing as she spoke, fumbling for socks and clarity as her brain uncreased.

'The male is, ma'am. But he's off with a female this time. Fourteen years old, first time in care.'

'And how old's the boy?'

'Sixteen. Wee toerag—known to be violent too. We've searched the home, questioned the other kids. They seem to have taken a load of clothes and around eighty pounds in cash.'

'Sounds like they don't plan to hang around then. And the old woman?'

'That just came in. It's a nursing home; the care staff went in and her bed was empty. Actually, there were two beds empty—her and her roommate's, but they found that one under the bed.'

'Alan, are you winding me up?'

'No, straight up.'

'So does she not know where her buddy is, then?'

'Canny talk, apparently. Anyway, I've sent a couple of cops up there, to search the home itself. So far nothing—although they do report that the back door was lying open.'

'Brilliant. So she's gone for a walk in the dark?'

'Looks like it. I've put in a request for Support Unit assistance when they come on, but I need to know if you want the helicopter to come out too, and also, where you'd want it and the Unit guys deployed. And if you want the night shift kept on to help with searching.'

Anna thought a moment. The kids were more likely to make for a friend's house, or go straight to a bus or train station, whereas an old lady in her nightclothes, wandering round in wild April winds . . . but what if the young girl hadn't gone of her own accord? She was vulnerable too—only fourteen, and with a known offender. If Anna kept the night shift on, would that scoop their overtime budget? Johnny had talked about monthly allocations and emergency reserves and fiscal autonomy and authorisation, in amidst an avalanche of other information, but the specifics had been vague.

'Have you spoken to the SDO?'

'Eh, no ma'am. It kind of works in a reverse pecking order . . .'

'Fair enough.'

The buck stopped with Anna. Until she decided that she couldn't cope, and had to call in the big guns. Which would be never. No way would she give Marion Hamilton one sliver of suggestion of any weakness or indecision.

Anna moved round her bedroom, seeking shoes, shooing Alice out the way. 'I'm heading in now anyway, Alan. Retain half the night shift—'

'We've only got three on, ma'am. One of the lads up at the old folks' home is a day-shift boy who'd just come in early.'

'Ah. Okay, retain all your night shift at present, but don't deploy them. How many have you got on the early shift?'

'Two single crewed cars, ma'am—including the lad at The Meadows. And one of the early shift's got court at ten.'

It was farcical. If the public realised how light a sprinkling of polis night-dust there was, there'd be an outcry. And yet, instead of employing more cops, the politicians kept playing with the figures, promising the equivalent of a thousand more police, and translating that figure into faceless cameras and a new batch of community wardens, those ersatz police. Overexcited and overexposed, they did their best, were well-meaning people in the main. But, the fundamental issue was, they weren't cops, and, in her view, that just made things worse. You go to hospital, you want a doctor, with a degree and clinical experience. You go to school, you want a teacher to educate your kids, not a classroom assistant. As soon as 'aides' and 'auxiliaries' and 'support staff' get brought in, the demarcation lines bleed and everything becomes everyone's job—and no one's responsibility. Now, if *she* was Chief Constable . . .

'Ma'am?'

'There's a lot of open ground around the nursing home, isn't there?'

'Aye, scrubland, couple of burns, then a new housing estate.'

'Right. Request the helicopter to scour round there in the meantime, and, if both incidents are still ongoing when the Support Unit come on, ask them to report to me at Giffnock. Use your early shift crews to respond to normal calls, and get one of the night shift to stay up at the children's home, in case the kids come back there. Get another night-shift cop to contact SPT; check out their CCTVs for Giffnock, Clarkston and Whitecraigs railway stations, and find out what time the buses start running from Eaglesham. Has anyone been in touch with the old girl's family?'

'Believe the care home staff are doing that now.'

Think, Anna, think. This was her first chance to shine. Or to screw it all up and see her credibility dissolve. She tapped some Whiskas into a bowl for Alice, who sniffed at it once then walked away.

'Okay, Alan. You sound like you've got everything covered. I'll be in in ten minutes or so— and I'm on my mobile if there's any developments.'

Pale charcoal dark outside, a smoky-pink kindling in the east. The quiet smell of earth and damp waking with the birdsong. Anna shivered; no coffee inside to warm her up. She didn't want to waste time waiting for the kettle to boil. In the films, she'd have had some handsome partner, sorting out her wholesome packed lunch as she saved the world on her cell phone. And she'd be five years younger, with Manolo Blahniks and much nicer clothes. Off to investigate a gory, glamorous murder with the help of Morgan Freeman.

There was a bakery in Kilmarnock Road, the

70

main road leading from Shawlands to Giffnock. She could maybe pick up a coffee there. And a roll and sausage. With potato scone. And sauce.

Before she'd even turned on to Kilmarnock Road, her mobile went.

'Ma'am, we've got the juveys.'

'Excellent. Where?'

'Clarkston train station, like you said. They'd walked it all the way from Eaglesham.'

'Both okay?'

'Fine. They were huddled up together on a bench, sharing a bottle of Irn-Bru.'

'Aw.'

'Turns out he's the girl's boyfriend. Has been for ages. We think she may have purposely engineered getting into Muirbrae so they could be together. I've a cop taking statements just now.'

'Okay. Good work, Alan. Just stand the night shift down then.' She checked her watch. Six twenty a.m. Yay—no overtime incurred. 'I'll go straight up to the nursing home, see what's happening there. Any word from the Support Unit?'

'Not yet, ma'am.'

'Well, just keep them on standby until I've been up there myself. Hopefully we'll not need to start beating bushes and trawling culverts yet. And give my regards to the happy couple.'

She felt relieved. Yet a nip of sadness too, that the kids had been caught. All that planning, creeping through the dawn, their thudding hearts as they began to think they'd made it. Teenaged feet given speed and spirit by that blundering, driven love which would have you break through walls and see brighter things than you ever thought possible—like the sharp, high shock of a butterfly,

71

each colour too perfect to believe. And worse, knowing you will never feel that shock again, no matter how many butterflies you net and gas and pin on boards. Marvelling at azure even as it fades to grey. Anna missed that feeling.

Alan was saying something else. 'Ma'am? D'you want to come in and speak to them yourself?'

'Nah. No need now. I'll leave that for you to deal.' Anna yawned. This was what happened when you were too keen to be involved and indispensable. See if she'd just sat and had that coffee, she could probably have been climbing back into bed now.

'The old lady's still outstanding, yeah? She's not turned up in the loo or anything?'

'No, definitely not.'

'Well, I'll carry on up to The Meadows then.'

She drove straight towards Newton Mearns, where the nursing home was. This was all different now—fewer trees, more developments. The Meadows had been an old farmhouse, back when the Mearns was just wide swathes of moorland, sheep and stubby trees. Now, Newton Mearns was an ever-burgeoning, upmarket housing estate, eating more greens than the hungriest herbivore. Still, she thought this was the right road . . . ah, there it was. The craw-stepped gables of The Meadows shone indignant, indigenous stone against the clamour of red brick and neo-Georgian mock-mansions chewing up the hill on which they all stood. What would have been the kitchen garden was now hard standing for cars, and a purpose-built two-storey wing was tacked on to the original farmhouse. Anna parked the car, walked to the front entrance.

THE MEADOWS—Caring For Your Fragile Loved Ones.

Made it sound like a china repair shop. She pushed the supposedly secure front door and found it open. Inside, the hall was well lit and empty, a vase of flowers drooping on to a melamine desk. Blue chairs, yellow cushions, pink nylon carpet. Woolworths prints, puppies and a *Hay Wain*. An unappetising air-soup of cabbage, boiled stockings, urine and synthetic fresheners. A generator hummed in some back room, and she could hear footsteps overhead.

'Hello?' she called upwards.

'Who is it?' A pair of plump white legs at the top of the stairs.

'Chief Inspector Cameron, Giffnock Police.'

The legs descended, bringing a navy blue dress, hot face and white cap.

'Oh, what a palaver. We're still searching upstairs. They've never done this before, you know. Mad as a brush, the pair of them, but normally very good.' The woman patted at her uniform, which was covered in white dust. 'Och, look at me. I've even been up in the loft. Sorry, I'm Jill Gray. Matron here.'

Anna looked behind the reception desk. No CCTV screen, no intercom. 'What's the lady's name? The one that's still missing?'

'Cassie. Cassandra Maguire. One of my girls went in about five thirty, and saw the beds were empty. We had a good look round, but no sign.'

'But not under the bed, I take it?'

'No.' The matron kept scrubbing at a speck on

her uniform.

'And the lady you recovered?'

'Manju?'

'Have you spoken to her?'

Jill Gray shook her head. 'Manju doesn't really speak much. Never has.'

'Have either of them done this before?'

'Not really. They play at dressing up, stuff like that, but Manju can't get about much and, to be honest, Cassie's not as sharp as she used to be, either. She can't have gone far.'

'Your security seems pretty lax. I understand the back door was lying open, and I noticed the front door was unlocked when I came in. Is that normal?'

'What? No, no, we normally keep that locked at night . . . both of them, I mean. There's just been so much coming and going . . . but we *do* lock everything up at night, honestly.'

Anna tapped the hook by the door. A bunch of keys hung there. 'With these?'

'Yes, but—well, we need to keep the keys close in case of fire.'

'Has Cassie's family been informed?'

'We tried, but I keep getting an answer machine.'

'We can send a cop out.'

The matron spoke sharply. 'I'd rather not, until we absolutely have to.'

'They'll need to know, even if we do find her. My guys still searching?'

'Yes. Both up the stairs.'

'What about down here?'

'All been checked.'

'Everywhere? Basements, storerooms, cupboards? Inside the washing machines? You'd be surprised where we find folk.'

The matron rubbed reddened hands along the sides of her nose. She looked as though she was praying. 'There's a wee warren of rooms through the old scullery—I don't know if anyone's gone through them yet.'

'Fine, I'll take a look there. You got a torch?'

'Under the desk, I think.'

Anna set off through the kitchen. The walls were thick here, obviously part of the old farmhouse. The aroma of just-turned food was overwhelming, despite the draught coming from the door on the far side. You could see the orange of the sunrise coming through the glass. Anna checked the door. Unlocked, as the cops had said. It opened on to the back yard, and the hill and houses and hundreds of acres beyond. She shut it again. She didn't want to think about all that wide expanse, not yet. Instead, she carried on down the hallway, to the very back of the property. Linoleum gave way to slate tiles as she stepped down a few centimetres into another era. Did she imagine a smell of cattle, in where the ploughs and hay would have been stored? There was definitely a harsh burr, breathing in and out as she opened doors. It was bowel-dark, just one weak bulb hanging from the corridor's ceiling, most of the storerooms with no lights inside. She did her best, delving her torch beam far into corners, disrupting boxes, deckchairs and decades of grime, as that tight, hard twist of panic began to lace up her back. Searches induced fear. Always. Fear of what was missing, fear of what you might find. Fear of what you might miss, what you'd have to explain. And that primitive terror of plunging yourself into dark recesses; of not coming back out intact.

Only one door left, hidden under a gloomy slope which must be the underside of the staircase. Anna eased open the latch. Fousty black nothingness, then the hall light behind her, beckoning wild shadows of serpents and spears. Anna cracked on her torch, saw vacuum nozzles and brooms askew on nails. Smelled excrement. A sewer trail, growing stronger as she entered the press. There, behind the packing cases, a soft-heaped comma of Winceyette, some lurid strips of green satin. Beside the satin lay a slipper; burgundy velvet with the heel squashed flat.

'Cassie?'

On her knees, she shuffled under the stair treads, between the cases.

'Cassie?'

Her hand went out, expecting to touch a hand or face. Sweet, vile stink. The ground moist and yielding as her fingers sank into human faeces.

'Shit!' She snapped her arm back. Nothing but a pile of shite. Literally.

Anna radioed the office—with her clean hand. 'Get the stations at The Meadows to come to the rear scullery behind the kitchens. I'm in the cupboard under the stairs. And tell them to bring the matron.'

She crawled back out, to where the air was fresher. From here, only moments to reach the kitchen and the back door. Anna retraced her steps, shining her torch across the floor, trying to augment the light. Was the woman wearing slippers? Bare feet? Was she wearing anything, or did she wander outside in just her old, bare body? The cops and a nurse came running, Jill Gray toiling behind on stubby legs.

'Have you found her?'

Anna gestured to the open cupboard.

'Look under the stairs. And don't touch anything.'

'Oh God. Is it bad?' The matron stuck her head inside. 'I can't quite see—'

Anna shifted her torch. 'There. See between the packing cases. Is this what Cassie was wearing when you put her to bed?'

'Oh, dear God. Yes. I think so.'

'Okay. Matron, I want you to go up to her room and check through all her clothing. See if she's taken anything else.'

'You don't think she's gone outside, do you? With nothing on?'

'You tell me where else she can be. Right,' Anna turned to the cops. 'One of you get on to Inspector Harkness. I want the Support Unit out here now to do a ground search, and a dog van if there's one available. Matron, who's your boss? Who runs this place?'

'Um—Mr Macklin. He's a consul—'

'Well, I suggest you call him out too.'

'What about Cassie's family?'

'Don't worry. We'll send someone round to do that.'

'Can we not just wait—'

'No, we bloody cannot just wait, Ms Gray. They should have been notified immediately. I need to know everything about Cassandra. Her state of mind for one. Is she able to look after herself? How far can she walk unaided? What medications does she take?'

Jill Gray's thumb and forefinger, twisting her

77

lips. 'Of course.' She sniffed, touched her nose with the back of her hand. 'Padma, could you go and get Cassie's medical history file, please?'

The nurse nodded, but still she lingered by the cupboard door. As if continual vigil would force Cassie to rematerialise.

'Did Cassie ever intimate that she was suicidal?'

'No. Definitely not.'

'Ma'am.' The younger of the two cops broke off from his radio conversation. 'Inspector Harkness says: do you still want the helicopter?'

'Tell him yes. In the meantime, I want you two to—carefully—go out the kitchen door and walk round the full perimeter of the nursing home. Spread out slowly, check every bush and tree stump. If she *is* naked, I don't know when hypothermia would set in, but I don't reckon it would take very long.

'Ms Gray, let's head up to Cassie's room, check out her clothes, yes? And . . . Padma, is it? I could be doing with that medical history now.'

'Excuse me. Ma'am?' It was the younger cop again, a tall, fair-haired lad. 'Yes . . . Sorry—what's your name again?'

'Fraser, ma'am. Fraser Harris.' The cop coughed.

'Well? What is it?'

'I just think it's really important that someone speaks to Cassie's roommate. I mean, she's the only obvious witness to whatever's happened. I tried when we arrived, but the . . . well, I was kind of discouraged, put it that way.'

The matron held up her hand. 'Constable, I simply said that Manju was confused and dehydrated.'

'No, you actually pushed me out of the room. I heard you shouting at her.'

'I did no such thing.'

'Matron, we distinctly heard you saying, "You and your bloody nonsense. What have I told you about getting out of bed?" Then I'm pretty sure you called her an "old witch". Isn't that right, Laurence?'

The older cop yawned. 'Aye, something like that.'

'Ms Gray,' said Anna. 'I think I'd like to see Manju now.'

Anna and the matron followed the nurse along the corridor. No one spoke, just the rush of nylon tunics and the squeak of Anna's boots. She hadn't taken her Airwave set home last night, had never expected to be called out, and she missed its reassuring chatter.

'You said before that Cassie was "mad as a brush". What did you mean by that?'

'Look, she's got dementia. But she's a happy wee soul, honestly.'

'And Manju?'

The matron was panting again. 'Manju is Manju. She can be . . . difficult.'

'But you're positive Cassie's never done anything like this before?'

'No.'

The nurse slowed, looked over her shoulder. 'What about the flying, Matron?'

'Flying?'

'Och, it's just daft. The two of them sometimes pretend they're birds. They put on Manju's saris and fly about the room, you know? Arms flapping, with the saris for wings.' Jill Gray shook her head.

79

'Always the same time of the month too. You know how women living together start to have their periods at the same time? Well, I think it carries on into old age. In here, they all have their mad turns together. Moon tide, we call it. All they need is a big yellow moon, and they're away.'

Time and tide; it was all a nonsense. Just two old dears who were batty and bored. But some of that fabric in the cupboard had been satin.

'Was that a sari, in the cupboard with her nightie? Were Cassie and Manju playing that game last night?'

'I have no idea.'

Padma half opened her mouth. 'No, but she was the other day, Matron. Mind when—'

'Padma, the notes?'

The nurse shrugged, then branched off at the first-floor landing.

'We'll need details of Cassie's next of kin too,' said Anna. 'Oh, and do you happen to have a photo of her?'

'A photo?'

'Yes. For the media.'

'Oh God.' Jill Gray covered her eyes. But was it at the enormity of the situation, or just the thought of bad publicity? Anna checked her watch. It was now seven fifty a.m. Cassandra Maguire had been missing for two and a half hours.

'This is it, in here.'

Cassie's room was on the second floor of the newer wing. Nicer than downstairs, the carpet was soft rose, walls beige. Cassie's empty bed was high and narrow, the metal guards slid down. On the other side of the bedside table, Cassie's roommate slept on in her own cot. Nothing more than a crumple beneath bedclothes, some fronds of dark hair. Behind her, orange flowered curtains were drawn over the window, a thin rag of daylight pointing through. An unwelcome memory came into Anna's mind, of dim shapes moving in a hotel room. She tugged the curtains wide.

'I take it that's Manju?'

'Yeah. I told you, you'll get nothing out of her. Conked out like a light, soon as we got her back into bed. This is Cassie's wardrobe. Shall we just work our way through it?'

Manju looked peaceful enough. There was a porcelain sink attached to the wall. First things first. 'Is it okay if I wash my hands?'

Anna didn't want to appear unsympathetic, but she still had a fistful of crap clinging to her fingers. The soap was liquid, emerald, and she could feel it drying out her hands even as she rinsed, the dense pine smell masking everything else.

'Hey, look! Her sheepskin boots are missing!' Jill Gray was shouting, louder than she needed to. She shook an empty hanger. 'And her coat. In fact

. . . yes, I'm sure there was a blue dress here earlier too. Blue or green anyway—a kind of swirly pattern.'

'Okay good. At least we know she's not starkers with one bare foot.' It came out flippant, but Anna was relieved. She had found a small, calm barrier, like applying a plaster to a stinging cut. It was a blank on which she could project some pictures. Cassie had taken clothing. Cassie had soiled herself. Ashamed, she had taken clean clothing, and she had hidden herself away. But why had Manju hidden too?

81

'Can we wake up Manju now? I really do need to talk to her.'

'Em . . .' The silvery noise of rustling coat hangers faded. 'Probably not for an hour or two, to be honest. I actually gave her a wee sedative earlier, just to calm her down.'

Brilliant.

'Did she need one? Was she distressed?'

The matron tutted. 'She tried to hit me, okay? And she might have tried getting out of bed again. She could've hurt herself. We were all tied up looking for Cassie. I mean, we can't be watching them twenty-four hours a day.'

'Is that right? Here's me thinking that's exactly what your job is.'

Jill Gray sighed. 'You try working here. Anyway, you'll not get anything out of Manju, whether it's morning, noon or night. Look, you wanted me to go and phone Mr Macklin?'

Anna felt herself being moved towards the door, a gentle ushering of air propelled by a heavy blue dress.

'Yes. And get me a photo, please, and the contacts for Cassie's family. I'll need to speak to Mr Macklin as soon as he comes in. How long do you think it'll take him?'

'I really don't have any idea. He's not due in today—he'll have to make arrangements—'

'Arrangements? I mean, we don't want to inconvenience him or anything.'

'It's not like that.'

'Look. There are a million and one things I need to be doing right now, if we're going find Cassie safe and well. Just get him to call me, okay? I'll leave my number.'

The matron was half out the door. 'Okay. Write it down for me—I'll be back in a minute. I'll just get you the Maguires' address.'

'And a photo!' Anna called out.

'If we've got one. Which I doubt.'

Anna rested against Manju's bed. Her right hand sought her hip pocket, to take out one of her cards. As her hand went back, she sensed spiders scuttle, a sudden bracelet of bones that sprang round her wrist. She tried to pull away, but the grip was insistent, strong. From the blankets, Manju stared, deep brown furrows above black brows, skin like flaking mud. Her shoulders were wrapped in a vibrant sari. When she spoke, the old woman's head swayed like a snake.

'He will be coming back, yes.'

In her eyes, a burn of calm insanity.

Then she smiled, revealing a flat white tablet concealed beneath her tongue. 'You came back.'

Anna pulled her hand free.

'What do you mean? Dr Macklin? Is he coming back? Or do you mean *she*? Do you mean Cassie, Manju?'

She untangled the vibrant cloth, which Manju had wound round each wrist and was gripping in her fists. The old woman began to wheeze, a gathering of fricative air, pushed out in a song. 'They . . . will carry you off, my child-oh . . . They . . .'

Her neck fell back, limp.

'What do you mean?' said Anna. 'Tell me what you mean.'

But Manju had closed her eyes once more, her features set in sleep.

CHAPTER FIVE

Of course, Manju was mad. No one could have reverted to sleep as rapidly as that, yet nothing Anna did would stir her. In truth, Anna hadn't tried overly hard; she had extracted herself from the room. Well, there was so much to do; she had to organise an early shift sergeant to attend and co-ordinate operations, liaise with the Support Unit when they arrived. Then there was the elusive search for a photo—the one Jill Gray dredged up was a group shot, and was useless, Cassie's face imperceptible from a clutch of other grey ladies; there were the Maguires' details to obtain, the cop to be dispatched to inform the family and bring them up to the home. Anna was a leader now, not a doer. So she had left The Meadows and returned to Giffnock; her presence at the home would add no further value. All that she could have done for the moment had been set in motion, and she did not want those wild eyes to attach themselves to her again.

Anna was certain she knew Manju from somewhere. She could not shake that feeling; it clutched on to her like the old woman's fist. Her first reaction was that it was only the madness she recognised, but it was more than that. Anna finished her coffee. It would come back to her, if she didn't think too hard. Anyway, she was going to go back and interview Manju herself.

She felt foolish now, bathed in the sensible yellow light of her office. In need of some small victory. Like falling from a horse, the best thing to do was get straight back on.

'Ma'am?'

Claire Rodgers stood in Anna's doorway, hands crossed neatly, feet in ballet first position. Well, not quite, but that was the effect she gave.

'Claire, sorry. Can it wait? I'm just heading back up to The Meadows. I take it there's been no further updates?'

'No updates, no. Half the Support Unit are still searching, the other half are helping our guys do door-to-door in the surrounding area, but so far we've no witnesses, no leads.'

'Shit.'

She scrubbed her fingers through her fringe. Every hour that slipped away took them further downhill. Anna's ostrich clock showed ten thirty. Five hours gone, yet not one single soul had laid eyes on Cassie. Mrs Hamilton was still in Aberdeen, and was not to be disturbed. Johnny was in a meeting at Headquarters, would not be back until the afternoon. They had agreed if there was no trace by then, they would put in a bid to get Cassie on the evening news. Failing that, tomorrow's papers.

'Oh, there is one thing,' said Claire. 'The family have finally arrived.'

'Only now?'

'Weren't at home. Cops knocked up the neighbours, went to the son's work, and eventually traced them to a hotel in Edinburgh. Anyway, they're there now—and greeting all over the shop apparently.'

'Deep joy. Och well, I can speak to them while I'm up there. And I've still not heard from that bloody doctor.'

85

'I think he's already given a statement to Ross.'

'Yeah, but I asked him to speak to *me*. Right, I'm off.' Anna stood up. 'And I'll see if the family have found a better photo too—that one the matron gave us is shite.'

'Eh, ma'am. You're remembering you've got that meeting?'

'Meeting?'

'I left the details on your desk.' Gliding forward, one arm out in third position. 'See, there.'

It was another of these multi-agency things to tackle youth disorder. Number one on the agenda was: 'Diversionary Tactics'. Get some nice ping-pong tournaments set up, that'll sort them all out. Anna may have moved to the other side of the city, but the work was depressingly similar. However, here, as Tom Cruikshanks had pointed out, you got the added twist of gangs drawn on ethnic, as well as tribal, lines. Second- and third-generation Asian youths, intent on throwing off the shackles of respect and hard work for which their parents were renowned, and replacing them with souped-up cars and drug-running. Proper Glaswegian assimilation, even down to the glottal-stopped swagger. And Anna didn't have the answers. Would anyone else? She ran through the sederunt for the meeting. Plenty of cooncil wallahs, a local minister, someone called Roz Dick from Young Action Now! and a Raju Nayar, listed as 'local businessman and community leader'.

Anna wanted to find Cassandra Maguire, not spend hours round a table of philanthropic faces. She was not prepared for this meeting, had no recollection of being told about it. Sabir Aziz's murder would feature, implicitly or not, in everything they discussed, and Anna would have to walk the line between calming fears and justifying the actions of the police. Only thing was, no one had told her what those actions were to be. Yes, they had a boy in custody, but no suggestion of what came next. Already, the division had featured prominently in the news: *Racist slaying in suburbs.* Yeah, it had been absolutely no problem to generate media interest for that. And that was before any more trouble kicked off. Tom had done his best to provide gravitas and reassurance; looked almost presentable, actually, once he'd been extracted from his fishing anorak and put in a decent suit. But what if retribution was planned; what if the streets erupted this weekend? What if, what if, what if?

Resources were an issue for a start, both in terms of money and manpower. Surely Marion Hamilton should be developing an anti-violence strategy, or fronting a local media campaign, instead of stuffing her face at a conference buffet in Aberdeen?

'I've typed up a brief report for you, ma'am.' Was Claire still here? 'Outlining the Saturday Saturation initiative.'

'The what?'

'Oh, nothing major.' She flounced her hand as if she was brushing off a fly. 'Just a wee idea of mine, to swamp the place with all available stations on a Saturday night. A kind of zero-tolerance approach, you know, after that poor kid's murder. Word is it's going to get worse. We got a couple of cops up from Aitkenhead Road, a few from Govan, and the Support Unit agreed to swing by when they could. Should be helpful for your meeting. I . . . I thought

87

Mr O'Hare would have told you?'

'He probably did.'

Anna took the neatly labelled report. Bound in a nice red folder too. What was Johnny playing at? He hadn't told her anything about this. Did he want her to make a tit of herself at the meeting?

'Thanks. I'll read before I go. Wherever it is I'm going again . . .'

'Council Offices. At Eastwood Park? I could go if you like. If you're too busy, I mean.'

'No, you're alright. Anyway, you've got a shift to run, Claire.'

'Och, that lot run themselves—they're very good, you know.'

Anna reached over to log off her computer. 'I'll keep that in mind when I'm awarding Brownie points.'

Her tone as crisp as cracknel. It was meant to be a joke; she tried to ghost a smile across her lips, like it had always been there and Claire just hadn't noticed it before. But it was too late. Claire merely nodded, and left the room.

*　　　*　　　*

The Meadows seemed worse in daylight. At night, the dark drew covers over the cracks. By day, all those drowsy shapes were seated to attention, on parade in high-backed, wipe-clean chairs. Legs splayed, mouths agape. Liquid eyes, liquid diet, knotted fingers over patchwork quilts.

'Just go through to Matron's office,' said the receptionist. 'There's plenty polis there already.'

The smell was worse by day, too. Salted air, oozing with lard-drenched cooking, only half masked by plug-in air fresheners. But still, still, over it all, that awful acknowledgement of too-damp pads, of fading control of bodily functions. As Anna moved through the Day Room, the occasional hopeful eye would lift, a tiny tensing of cardiganed shoulders, like a dog wondering if it should wag. Then the gaze would slip, would fall as Anna carried on, and drift back to the behind-the-scenes-of-a-hospital show, which someone had left on too loud. Rows of once-weres of every hue, but who knew now, who cared? Old soldiers, housewives, professors, postmen. Had any of them thought they would end their days here? Never let that be me, thought Anna. Let me die fast and private, somewhere that doesn't stink of rot. Because who would visit me then?

A woman in green overalls stood by a trolley. She was breaking open a capsule, powdering the contents into a bowl of thick green soup. Other bowls lay full and congealing on the table beside her. Her eyes ran down the list that lay beside the phials of medication, ticking off another name.

'I'm looking for the matron's office?' Anna wasn't sure they'd been in there earlier.

'Through the swing doors at the end, and it's the office facing you.' Raised voices told her she was heading the right way. The door was open, and she could see a man in a white coat, slouched next to one of her cops—that tall boy, Fraser, from before. Well, that was an affectation, right off. White coat—*woo-oo, I'm a doctor. Get me*. Even hospital doctors hardly wore white coats any more. It was like those men who left their hard hats in the rear parcel shelf of their cars—white, of course, not common, brash yellow. White was *candidus* in

Latin; she remembered that from school.

Anna's sergeant was seated at a desk, on the phone; he raised a hand in greeting. Jill Gray was there too, trying to pacify a weeping man, and a small, bird-like blonde who was shouting at the assembled group.

The matron was patting one arm of the long leather coat the woman wore. 'Ssh, now. Don't upset yourself.'

The woman's face was taut, exhausted, thick eyeliner and red lips too harsh for her little-girl frame.

'Ma'am.' Fraser acknowledged Anna's entrance. 'This is Mrs Maguire's son Ronnie.'

A tear-bloated face stared from a cradle of fingers.

'And her daughter-in-law, Sheena.'

'Hi. I'm Chief Inspector Cameron—'

'Oh, that you brought in the big guns now, is it?' said the woman. 'Shame you couldny get your arses into gear last night, when Cassie went missing, isn't it?'

'Mrs Maguire, I was out here at six a.m., soon as we heard your mother-in-law had gone.'

'And what have yous all been doing since then?' Sheena Maguire pulled her arm away from the matron. 'Fuck all, far as I can see. This is a bloody farce. We don't fork out the ridiculous amounts this lot charge each month just so old biddies can wander off into the sunset. We expect twenty-four hour supervision, nurses on standby . . .' She punctuated each statement by striking the edge of Matron's desk, the gold pendants at her cleavage jangling.

The doctor spoke. He looked about forty, stark-

90

blue eyes, black hair; the fringe too loose about his forehead. Same Celtic colouring as Johnny, but without the pecs. Louche, the planes of his shoulders rising as he unfolded his arms, eased his body from the supportive wall. He lacked . . . crispness. Even his voice was low and slow. 'I totally agree, Mrs Maguire. And I promise you that the staff here provide an excellent standard of care. You know that, surely?'

'No any more I don't.'

A clasp of hand on chin. Earnest, appraising? Never trust a man who covered his mouth when he spoke; any cod-psychologist could tell you that.

'Look, we've got to have a balance between caring for the complex needs of our residents and allowing them some freedom. I thought that was the reason you chose The Meadows in the first place? Would you rather we sealed them into their bedrooms at night?'

'No!' Ronnie sat up straight. 'I don't want my mammy getting locked up!'

'No, but it would be an idea if you at least secured them somewhere inside the *building*,' said Anna. 'Or d'you think it's okay for your residents to go on night rambles too? Some septuagenarian Duke of Edinburgh Award scheme you're running maybe?'

He had a long face, the doctor. Fine and elegant, if you liked that kind of thing, his hand brushing hair from his eyes.

C'mon coat-boy. Bat it back.

He offered merely a weary smile. Anna was disappointed. It was a poor effort, weak against the whiteness of his coat. The doctors in hospital, that time they had kept her in, they all had the same

91

beatific, flat *cleanness* about them. Like insipid milk.

'Mrs Maguire,' she said, 'I know this is a side-issue at the moment, but I *have* asked my officers to carry out a security review of the premises. You can rest assured that—'

'Chief Inspector,' said the doctor, keeping the same even tone. 'We're already fully approved and regularly inspected by the local authority. We have our Fire Safety certificates, our Health and Safety certificates—'

'I'm sure you do. But, nonetheless, I have some serious concerns regarding how your premises are secured. When I arrived last night, the front door was unlocked and unmanned, as was the back door.'

'See what I mean?' said Mrs Maguire. 'This place is a bloody joke!'

'Oh, for fucksake.' Ronnie's lips began to tremble once more. 'I *telt* you we should never have put her in here.'

'Chief Inspector, I think that's a very unfair observation.'

'Dr Macklin . . . I take it you *are* Dr Macklin? Did you get the message to contact me?'

He rested his hands together.

Here is the church and here is the steeple. His mouth was fluted, an upward curve. Did he think this was *funny*?

'I did.'

'And were you planning to?'

'I was just about to. Desperate as I was, of course, to speak to you, you'll understand I had a lot of other issues to deal with as well. Not least the welfare of all of my residents and staff. We're a

92

family here—we're all very fond of Cassie you know; this is very upsetting for everyone.' He drew slightly away from her. 'And it's *Mr* Macklin, Robert Macklin. Not doctor.'

'Is that relevant? You run this place, right?'

Anna was scribbling in her notebook; it was quicker than trying to type on the tiny keys of her digital unit. Unnerved folk whatever way you did it, making them think they were being committed to memory, to some mysterious database. And she wanted to unsettle that slight smile.

Trust me, I'm a doctor.

Well, I'll be the judge of that, Mr *Macklin.*

'I'm a consultant geriatrician, based at the Mansionhouse Unit. However, I'm also the major shareholder in this establishment, and I'm on call to provide medical advice and assistance as required.'

'Major shareholder? So The Meadows is an investment to you, is it?'

'It's a business interest as well as a professional one, if that's what you mean.'

At last. A reaction, a slight twist of metal in his tone. Then: 'You're supposed to be finding Cassie; why are you so interested in me?'

He had a point. Why was she goading this man? *Because I don't like the cut of your jib, pal.* Need there be a concrete reason? It was a perk of the job that Anna still enjoyed, this random umbrage that you could take, and contort and play with.

'I'm asking the questions, Dr Macklin.'

'Excuse me,' Sheena Maguire interrupted. 'See when yous are done with your verbal sparring, any chance of telling us what the fuck you're doing to get my mother-in-law back?'

'Of course.' Anna put her notebook away. 'I'm so sorry. Mr and Mrs Maguire, I promise you that we're doing everything we can to find Cassandra. We've got the helicopter out right now, and police chapping every door. I know my officers have already taken statements from you, and we'll be visiting every single place you've suggested your mum might make her way to. We're also making plans to generate a media appeal, but hopefully it'll not come to that. And I'm in the process of appointing you a family liaison officer. They'll be with you throughout, keep you updated on everything that we do. But,' she sat firmly on the edge of an over-stuffed armchair, her spine facing Macklin, 'what I'd like to do right now is have a wee chat with you both. I want to get a feel for what Cassie's really like.'

'She's a saint, that's whit she is,' wept Ronnie. He seemed to be channelling Elvis, with matt tar hair which drooped in a ludicrous quiff. 'My mammy is the salt of the earth, raised me on her own since I was a boy. And whit do I do? Stick her in here like a dug in a fucking kennel.'

'Ronnie, gie it a bloody rest,' his wife muttered. 'She is *not* a saint. She's a thrawn old besom. And this is just the sort of thing she'd do to prove a point.'

'How so?' asked Anna.

Sheena opened up the palm of her hand, scrutinised it. Her vision shifted to the edge of some distant place, then tumbled back. 'Cause she disny think she should be in here. Thinks she's missus independence, and that she should still be in her own house.'

'Well, it was her house, Sheena. We shouldny

94

have—'

'Aye Ronnie, the same house she half torched when she left the bloody gas on. Chief Inspector—the woman is a menace. She's been a menace since the day and hour we got married, and she just keeps getting worse.'

Filigrees of thread veins round Sheena's nostrils; thin lines where her lipstick had started to bleed. Her cheeks were uniform beige, but her foundation was slipping where she had sweated. Coming here, post-haste from their trip to Edinburgh, Sheena had found time to make up her face.

Anna leaned closer to study her clamped expression. There was a familiarity to its shape, its set of resignation.

'Excuse me—but have we met before?'

Sheena slipped a piece of chewing gum into her mouth. 'Not that I know of. How?'

'No reason. I just thought I'd seen you before, that's all.'

'No me, doll. I'd have remembered.' Sheena picked at a polished nail. 'I tell you. That old besom is doing this just to spite us.'

'For God's sake,' cried Ronnie. 'She's eighty-two years old.'

Matron clapped her hands together as if she'd thought of a jolly good wheeze. 'Would anyone like another cup of tea?'

'What I'd like to do is to speak to Manju again,' said Anna. 'And on the way, Dr Macklin, you can give me Cassie's medical background.'

'Again? I've already put it in my statement.'

'Again, and again, and as many times as I deem it necessary for you to tell me, Doctor. Do you have a problem with that?'

He lowered his eyelids, the *I'm-bored-already* blink that Alice sometimes did. 'Not at all. If you'd like to come this way, I can show you exactly how our security arrangements operate too.'

'Ho, Fraser.'

'Ma'am?'

'You can come and all.'

At the door, Anna stared again at Sheena, who blinked back at her as she lowered herself on to the sofa beside her husband. Crossed her legs, tapped burgundy-tipped fingers.

'I definitely don't know you from somewhere?'

'I'm just a hard-faced Glasgow blonde, hen.' The gum slid in Sheena's mouth. 'There's plenty of us around, eh?'

The doctor led Anna and Fraser outside. 'I'm sure she didn't mean anything . . . Sheena's upset, Chief Inspector.'

Cheeky bastard. Mirroring the hard pip of sentiment that she was rolling over in her own mind.

'I never thought she did.'

'Get tae hell away from me!'

In the hall, an old man was struggling to get up. He had been placed alone, in a green plastic chair, a *Daily Record* strewn at his feet. He was screaming, throwing punches at the air. Then he saw them, grew still.

'Oh, oh. C'mere, nurse,' he beckoned. 'C'mere.'

Anna drew as close as she could, frightened he'd start punching again.

'I'm terribly sorry, hen,' the man whispered. 'But I think I've shat myself.'

An arm passed between Anna and the man. 'It's

alright Frank, I've got you.'

It was the woman in the green overalls. 'C'mon luvvie, that's you.'

They got him off to the bathroom, the nurses and the care assistants soothing his tears and remonstrations. These poor women had to do this every day, truss up old legs, wipe wrinkled arses; and know one day it might be them.

'Lock all the doors!' he was yelling. 'Lock us all up!'

It was probably best that his lights had gone out again. That must be the only way to cope here, thought Anna, by living somewhere else. Those moments of absolute clarity must be the most terrifying of all.

'Sorry about that.'

The doctor tried to disarm her with another smile. Did he want a face-off? *His* face off, because she'd do it, she bloody would. He *farmed* these people, he made his living from the cultivation of bedsores and sodden chairs and he whirred on wheels of calmness through them all. Through all this.

There is a buzzing building inside her. She thinks it has been there all day: it is tiredness. It is the tiredness of stolen sleep and it is becoming a roar, a call to action. Summoning her to shake this man, to overturn his equilibrium like a jug of complacent cream, to scream at him *You have a patient that has disappeared!* and strike the supercilious bastard, and make him cry. It is the thing she has been waiting for, from the moment she awoke in that unsettled air. Something is coming, something must . . . break. And then the roar drops, and in the space it leaves, the doctor is staring at her, and she feels him reach out to hold her wrists, but her wrists are at her side, as are his, and she has imagined it.

Fraser, too, is staring at her. She needs a drink.

'So. What's wrong with Cassie exactly?' Her throat is parched. 'I mean, why was she in here?'

The doctor frowns, then licks his lips. 'Oh, just the usual combination: dementia, diabetes-induced reduction in vision, increasing frailty . . .'

'Quite a list. And yet you don't seem that bothered that she's disappeared.'

He is fiddling with his chin, the scores between his eyebrows deeper.

'And how do you make that out? How can you possibly know what I'm feeling?'

'You just seem very . . . business-like about it all.'

'As do you, Chief Inspector. Professional hazard, maybe?'

The noise abates, her heart rate slows. She swallows.

'You were going to tell me all about your second-to-none security arrangements, Mr Macklin.'

They had reached the front desk, which was empty.

'Well, as you can see, we have a door entry system.' Macklin indicated a yellow wall phone behind the desk. 'This desk is usually staffed during the day, if resources allow, and if not, the buzzer goes through to Matron's room—and the nurses' staff room up on the first floor. Same thing at night time.'

'So does that mean that someone could be buzzed in without anyone actually seeing them?

98

Say, for example, if I said I had a delivery, could someone just let me in remotely without checking who I was?'

'Well, I suppose in theory . . . Are you suggesting that someone came *in here* last night? At five in the morning?'

She ignored him. 'So, if I *did* get buzzed in, then I could just wander about and take my pick of the doped-up residents' property.' She stretched over to lift up a paper bag, emblazoned with *Lloydspharmacy,* and sealed with a prescription strip. 'And any excess medication lying about. Fraser, I hope you're noting all this down.'

'I'll take that, thank you. It was delivered just as the Maguires arrived.'

'And left here for anyone to help themselves to.' She read the label. 'Benzodiazepines. More sedatives, I see. You like your sedatives, don't you?'

'They also help with anxiety—which many of our residents suffer from. May I?'

She lets him take the package, and their fingers do not touch.

'So, that's the front. Now what about the back door?'

'Locked at night. Usually open during the day. For deliveries and so on. I mean, there's always someone in the kitchen.'

'But even when it's locked, you leave the keys hanging up.'

'Not any more.' He strummed a dissonant rhythm on the bag. 'We've already moved the keys since you visited us earlier. Matron advised me of what you'd said. We've also got a fire alarm, a burglar alarm and a panic alarm—and a security

99

firm that responds to our alarm system if it's activated.'

Fraser interrupted. 'Could I just confirm the name of the security company, sir?'

'It's All Star Security. They're very good. They take a drive past once a night too—'

'Is that to round up your escapees?' said Anna.

'No, we actually introduced it because we'd been having trouble with local kids congregating outside—drinking and stuff. And your office was . . . let's just say, a little *unresponsive* about attending.' Macklin eased the knot in his tie. It was narrow, spinning concentric circles in purple and blue. The kind of pattern that would give you a headache if you stared at it for too long.

'Chief Inspector, have I done something to offend you? Personally, I mean?'

'Not at all.'

'So are you always this aggressive in your approach?'

She clocked Fraser, trying to hide a grin.

'Mr Macklin, believe me when I say that this is me being far from aggressive.'

'Well, maybe we could start again then?'

'There's nothing *to* start. Why don't you show me where you keep the keys for the front and back doors?'

'Through here.'

He took them into a small office behind the reception desk. 'Inside this cabinet. And from now on, we'll keep this office door locked at night. But the night sister will have a key.'

'And this alarm system you mention. It wasn't activated last night?

'No.'

100

'Was it set?'

'I . . . No. I don't believe so.'

'Okay. So we've got the nurses snuggled up watching telly, Cassie wandering downstairs to take a night-time dump in the cupboard, helping herself to the back door key and strolling out. With no alarm going off to let anyone know.'

Anna leaned against a filing cabinet. 'Fraser, you get on to the security firm, find out what time they drove by last night. Mr Macklin, in your opinion, could Cassie really have made it all the way downstairs by herself?'

The doctor held the paper bag, crumpling the top down. A thin, loose wedding band glinted against the white of coat and bag.

'Meaning?'

'Could she have been put there deliberately? Maybe as some kind of punishment?'

'That's an outrageous suggestion.'

'Look, I have to investigate every possibility. And let's face it, your employees arny exactly Florence Nightingales. Since I've been here, I've seen little form of stimulation or interaction between staff and residents at all. In fact, other than the impromptu toilet duties there, the only activity I've seen is that slightly grubby cook force-feeding people drugs by hiding them in the soup. I also noticed your matron was very keen to sedate Manju after her ordeal, rather than take the time to listen to what she was saying.'

'Which was that she was a bird of paradise, I believe?' Macklin shook his head, face glum as a churchyard angel. Minus the moss. His skin was remarkably pale in fact, almost translucent beneath the eyes. 'Chief Inspector, you clearly have no idea the amount of time and care my staff devote to our residents. We have t'ai chi, a mobile hairdresser, reminiscence sessions—'

'Now, calm down, Mr Macklin . . .'

'I'm perfectly calm, *Miss* Cameron.'

Oh, he'd gone for the jugular now, clocking her spinster-fingers and putting her in her place. She noticed Fraser had wandered off, back through to reception. He was either the soul of discretion, or he was looking for something. If she'd stuck in and done a PhD, Anna could have been a doctor too, had a nice sterile title conferring androgyny and respect. Still, chief inspector did the job just as well. It was a beautiful, hard hammer to open doors and claw out answers.

'Good. I'm glad you're calm. Now, what's the update on Manju?'

'Manju's doing fine. She was a little dehydrated, a little feverish, but we've upped her fluids and brought her temperature down.'

'Is *she* active? Could she have helped Cassie to get to the scullery?'

'Manju? Not a chance. She used to go walkabout in her time, but she's virtually bedridden now. Has the odd spurt of energy, when Cassie gets them dressing up and so on, but there's no way she could make it down the stairs.'

'She made it out of bed though. Under it, in fact.'

'I know. It's very strange. I can only assume they were playing hide and seek or something. I've given Manju a thorough examination and she's absolutely—excuse me a minute . . .'

A nurse was standing at the office door, Fraser behind her. 'Sorry, Mr Macklin—that's your

102

daughter here. She's outside . . . I didny know if . . .'

'Look, do you mind if Nancy here takes you up to see Manju?' he asked Anna. 'Only I'd hate my daughter to think I was being huckled by the police.'

'I don't huckle, Mr Macklin. I've got plenty of officers to do that for me. But yes, I've got no more questions for now. Thank you for your time.'

'My pleasure, Chief Inspector. I take it we'll be liaising through this young man here?'

'Yup. Fraser or his sergeant. But I'll be visiting frequently, don't worry. Every hour on the hour, until we find Cassie.' She smiled, a narrow glint of teeth; the kind you'd offer only to be polite, at a social gathering say, when someone had told you an inappropriate joke. 'One of us has to give a shit.'

She saw him flinch.

'Sorry. We professionals don't swear, do we?'

You go ahead and paint your lovely t'ai chi pictures, Mr Macklin. Anyone can put on a prearranged show, like the mad round of refurbishment that had gone on at Easterhouse, just before the Chief Constable paid a visit. Beat-up old cars moved out, yards hosed down and cells scrubbed. Hand-picked young cops marched in to proffer sycophantic questions. Hardly a snapshot of the truth. No, you had to sneak up on reality, seize it unawares. Still, this place was clean enough, she supposed. The rooms were nicely decorated, the residents looked well fed. And old folk go wandering all the time.

She could see Macklin through the little office window, opening out his arms to an auburn-haired

103

girl of ten or eleven. A glad, wide smile as he kissed the cheek of the woman standing with her.

'Tell me,' Anna asked the nurse beside her, 'is it a mix of NHS and private patients you've got?'

'Oh no. It's all private, I think. Once you start with the NHS ones you get stuck with them. Canny shift them on, know? Private patients are easier to manage.'

Anna watched Macklin put his arms round wife and child, and walk them towards the entrance. A devoted, handsome family, cushioned by old money. The oldest you could get.

'You were wanting to see Manju again?'

'Please.'

'Ma'am.' Fraser was at her side. 'Can I have a quick word first?'

'Excuse us a wee minute, would you?' said Anna to the nurse. She waited until the woman left the room. 'What's up?'

Fraser dropped his voice. 'I was thinking. I wonder if someone *did* come in here, right enough, maybe frightened the old dears enough to make them want to hide. Then Cassie got confused, wandered outside. Easy done, especially if they'd left the back door open.'

'But who?'

'Well, there's a wee team doing the rounds at the moment. Mostly hospitals and GPs' surgeries. Housebreaking when they have to, just walking in off the street when they can, stealing drugs, equipment, scripts. Rifling patients' lockers too, up at Stobhill. They've not been particularly active in this division yet, but it's been rife over in the North.'

Anna took a closer look at the young cop beside

104

her. He couldn't have been more than twenty-two, twenty-three. 'How do you know all this? I've not heard anything about it.'

'I keep my ear to the ground. And know my neds, ma'am. I stopped two boys not far from here the other day. I didn't recognise them as Mearns boys, and they just had that . . . look, you know? So I chinned them. Anyway, one of them was carrying a couple of prescription pads. So, I was just thinking . . . maybe they're starting to move their operation into the south side.'

'I'm impressed. And you'll be firing all this in to Divisional Intelligence?'

' 'Course.' He grinned at her, and his freckled face flashed handsome. 'I'm a regular contributor.'

She returned his smile, a little envious of his youthful enthusiasm. 'Well, there's no real sign of a break-in, nothing missing. Doesn't mean I disregard your theory, though. Stick the details of the two neds down and we'll add it to the pot.'

'Fair enough. I just thought you should know, what with the lack of security in this place anyway.' Fraser raised a sandy eyebrow. 'I mean, you might want to drop it into your next conversation with Mr Macklin . . .'

'Indeed I might, Constable Harris. Right, you better go see what your sergeant needs you to do next.'

He grinned again. 'Please God it's not more under-the-bed searches. There's only so many old slippers and screwed-up tissues I can take.'

Nancy, the nurse, was waiting for Anna outside. They began walking up the stairs. 'How's Manju doing?'

'Ach, alright. Her and Cassie were awfy close,

but. Disny say a lot, does our Manju, but she's heart-sore, I know that much.'

'What else can you tell me about Manju?'

'Nothing really. Been with us six or seven years. No relatives that I know of, no visitors. Here we are. Manju,' she whispered, 'Manju hen. I've a wee visitor for you.'

The curtains were closed, lending the room a greenish, underwater tinge. Anna went over to the bed.

'Hi Manju. It's me, Anna. Remember? From this morning? I just wanted to talk to you about Cassie again.'

The nurse flicked the light switch on the wall. Manju groaned at the brightness, eyes rolling backwards, head trembling. Everything became sharp and rapid movement; her fingers flicking air, blue-veined legs jittering as her whole body flailed in tiny flea-jumps, and yet she hardly seemed to be breathing. She let out a feeble whimper, then slapped Anna hard across the cheek.

'Oh, hen. Oh, I'm so sorry.' The nurse rushed over. 'Here, away out the road while I try and calm her down. She just needs a wee drop medicine and she'll be right as rain, won't you pet?'

Anna stood in the corner of the room as the nurse fussed and patted at Manju, adjusting her pillows, smoothing her hair. Eventually, the old woman lay on her side, asleep and rasping. The nurse came over to Anna.

'Look, I think you'd maybe better leave it for now. She's just no herself, poor lamb. She went like this the other day too, when Cassie was telling all they stories. I think she gets herself feart, then it's like her system canny cope. She just shuts

106

down, you know?'

'Of course.'

Anna's cheek was stinging still; she imagined deep crescents where the woman's nails had caught her. Manju had hooked the slap, her hand crabbed, like little barbs on jellyfish. The nurse switched off the light.

'C'mon away downstairs hen, and I'll put some iodine on that.'

'You said Cassie was telling stories. What kind of stories?'

'Och, I couldny shut her up. The pair of them were hyper. Cassie bawling: "I'm no as green as I'm cabbage looking, you know!"'

The nurse laughed, sucking her teeth. 'And I says: "I bet you're not." "No," she goes. "I telt them I couldny go anywhere without changing my pad. They werny having it but then"—oh here, this is awful hen, excuse my language, but Cassie says she asked them if one of them wanted to change it for her, cause it was a right shitey one! And her and Manju both start hee-hawing like donkeys. Then Cassie says something like: "So then they let me go to the toilet—and that's when I gied them the slip!"'

'Gave who the slip?'

'Well, that's what I says. "Who did you give the slip to, Cassie?" And she goes: "They big black men. The ones that came into my room." Then she starts singing at me, something about Saracens carrying you off.'

Immediately, Anna recognised the line. 'Was it "carry you off my child-oh"?'

'That's it! "The charge of the mighty Saracen will carry you off, my child-oh . . ." How, d'you know it?'

'No, but Manju does. She was singing it this morning.'

'Ach, well I don't know what the pair of them were on. But they were happy, know? I like it when they're happy. Och hen . . .' The nurse seized Anna's hand, burst into tears. Great packets of salt water, coming from nowhere, as brief and unexpected as Manju's slap. 'I hope you find poor Cassie soon.'

'Me too.'

Once upon a time, Alice had gone missing. First one night had elapsed, then two. By the third night Anna was distraught, not with the bare reality of the matter, that the cat was not there, but with the creeping absence of facts. Huge empty burdens into which she poured nightmares of laboratories and experiments, of cages and live-skinning, claws scraping to get out, get in.

The missing person was an everyman. That's what happened; they became every lost soul who had slipped out of your reach. And yet she was Cassie, streaking round her bedroom. Anna could see her, if she shut her eyes; a thrawn old bird wearing nothing but yellowed pants and a brilliant coloured cloak of brocade-trimmed satin, which flew behind her as she ran. Arms outstretched, ancient dugs slapping flat on feather-ribs.

'I'm a bird of paradise!' she yells, flapping hard as the nurses take an elbow each. Then a horrified gape, a face suddenly sentient. Anna knew that face; knew that particular flip of knowledge from oblivion.

It made her want to break into a run too.

CHAPTER SIX

Claire was still in the office when Anna returned to Giffnock. Still super-keen. Anna had twenty-five minutes before this youth disorder meeting began. *With a sandwich lunch.* And it was now six and a half hours since Cassandra Maguire had got up, selected a change of clothing, and vanished into the wide, cubic landscape of the Mearns.

Anna's clock squatted on her desk. Whether she was there or not, it imperceptibly nudged its two black hands round and round and back to the start, each dour hour dropping from the circumference. She could feel them, smug discs piling up, dragging at her ankles.

'Ma'am,' said Claire. 'The Divisional Intelligence manager's here to see you.'

'Is he? Did we have a meeting?'

'No, he said he'd tried to catch you when you were up at Divisional Tasking. I've put him in your office.'

But I've got no time, I've got no time.

'Claire, sorry, but I'm up to my oxters in missing old ladies. I need to get on to Corporate Communications, see if we can make *Reporting Scotland*.'

'I got the impression it was quite urgent. Also, the roof in the Engine Room has fallen in.'

'What?'

'Aye. That leak finally did it.'

Anna wished she could go off sick. Two days with a pillow over her head and Alice at her feet would just be perfect. The Engine Room was where they collated all the crimes and incidents in the subdivision. Staffed by one cop and a civvie, it was in the oldest part of the building. The bay window had been leaking for the past six months at least, a fat brown stain seeping spider-legs across polystyrene ceiling tiles, perpetual thick drips like a snotty nose greening the wall. Anna had reported it to Property Services, as had her predecessor, and been told to patch it up with some tape and a black bin-bag meantime. As had her predecessor.

'Is anybody hurt?

'No. Luckily, George was over at Blochairn, at the CCTV cameras, and Ness was on her piece break. It's not the whole roof, mind, just the bit above the bay, and then half the plaster off the rest of the ceiling. Made a hell of a mess though.'

'Shit. We'll need to find somewhere else to accommodate them.'

The Engine Room was crucial to the smooth running of the subdivision. Without them to plot courses and plan operations, Giffnock would be rudderless, and the whole stinking station might fall down.

'Claire, give me five minutes to think about where we can put them. We'll maybe need to get the community cops to share with CID.'

Claire snorted.

'Aye, I know. Well it's either that or the typists. And it's only temporary. Though we've got that plainers operation next week . . . they'll need a room too.' She sighed. 'Right, let me think this through.'

Anna escaped into her office before anyone else could waylay her. Except, of course, the Divisional Intelligence manager, who was already lying in wait. He stood as she entered, making her jump.

'Hi there, ma'am.'

'Oh, Jim. It's yourself. Grab a pew, please.' She made her way round to the other side of her desk, sat down. 'And what can I do for you?'

That can't wait, that is.

Jim pulled his navy cardigan tighter round his shoulders. 'I've a wee bit of a sensitive issue I need to discuss with you, ma'am.'

Her heart swooped low. This wasn't going to be a quick in and out, then. 'Right. Fire away.'

'It's about Constable Harris.'

'Harris?'

'He's not long joined us from the Support Unit? Tall, fair-haired laddie—nicknamed the Hoover?'

'Oh, Fraser? I know him. Was just talking to him actually. Why do they call him Hoover?'

A pitying glance. 'Because he hoovers up neds?'

'Ah, see, that's why you're in Divisional Intelligence and I'm not, Jim. Look, if you're here to tell me what a great job he's doing, I really appreciate it, and I *will* pass your thanks on—but I'm kind of up to my arse in alligators at the moment.'

'Pardon?' Jim's cardigan was threadbare, he wore it wrapped tight as his pursed-up face.

'I'm busy?'

'No, I'm afraid it's not about that. Well, it is I suppose, indirectly, but not *exactly*—'

'Jim. *Please.* Just tell me what it is, so we can sort it out, yeah?'

He tugged his chair a little closer to the desk. 'I've received information that Constable Harris is being targeted.'

Anna tried to keep the impatience from her

voice. 'For what? By whom?'

'Dissatisfied customers, shall we say.'

'Jim, I know you're kind of in the secret service, but will you stop talking in riddles?'

'Neds, ma'am. Disgruntled neds. Ever since he's arrived in this division, Harris has been like a one-man whirlwind, stopping cars, searching gangs, turning houses, checking pubs. Don't get me wrong—it's brilliant, and he's been feeding us some really useful intelligence, but I think he's been stirring up a hornet's nest for himself too.'

'Yeah. Exactly like you said: disgruntling the neds. I mean, come on. Who's feeding you this stuff anyway?'

'Ma'am, this is graded intelligence. You know I can't give you any details regarding the source. All I can tell you is that it's credible. Extremely credible.'

'So what *are* they saying?'

'The opening phrase was . . .' He considered his notes. 'One of your cops, Fraser Harris, is "being watched". Informant then went on to say that a black or navy hatchback has been seen following Fraser Harris home from work on several occasions. They were very specific about giving his name, and could say exactly what car Fraser drives and where he lives.' He put his notes down. 'I've had a look at CCTV covering Giffnock yard, gone back through the last month or so, and they're right. Twice, I could make out a blackish car come out of the lane at the side of the office, and head off in the same direction Fraser was driving.'

'Have you got a registration number?'

Jim shook his head. 'Couldn't make it out at all. The picture quality was rubbish.'

112

Physician heal thyself. Why would the closed-circuit television system for a police office be an exemplar of clear, sharp focus and precision engineering?

'And does your source know who might own the vehicle?'

'We're working on that too. All I know at present is that Harris has upset several people, and that a couple of "major players" are getting angry.'

'Major players? Have I just moved to Sicily?'

An earnest frown. 'Believe me, we've some heavy-duty neds operating—and living—very close to home, ma'am.'

'I don't doubt it. But taking observations on a cop? To what ends?'

'My belief is it's just to put the frighteners on him. For the moment.'

'And have you told Harris this? Is he even aware he's being warned off?'

'Not yet, ma'am. It's really up to you to decide how we play this from here. But what I would say is that it's imperative we interview Fraser as soon as possible.'

He was right. Intelligence could gather information, CID could investigate if needs be, but as deputy SDO she had responsibility for all personnel and welfare issues.

'Okay,' she said, 'I'll speak to him, find out if any direct threats have been made to him or his family, anything that he's not telling us about. Then I'll need to do a risk assessment, look at who he's dealt with recently, who he's jailed. Check the route he travels to work, who his dependents are, that kind of thing.'

'Obviously, we'll keep you updated as to any

more intelligence we receive.'

'Sure. And you've really no idea *who* at the moment?'

' 'Fraid not. Fraser Harris is pretty unspecific about who he jails—and the tout was even less specific. But, if you're happy that we move on this, we can start being more proactive about gathering intelligence too.'

'Absolutely.'

As soon as Jim left, Anna started jotting notes. First thing was to establish who was behind this, haul them in for questioning. She might have to get some extra attention to Fraser's house too: CCTV, or cops taking observations. Enough padding to make him feel he was wrapped up safe. If they couldn't protect one of their own, what chance had they of protecting anyone else?

If you let it, each new imperative could flood the ones before. Fifteen minutes before her meeting with the council. Media first, then admin, then she'd read over Claire's report. Anna stuck the phone under her chin, dialled the tie-line for Corporate Communications and tapped into her email file. Only twenty more had arrived since she left for The Meadows. Clearly, things were slowing up. Her fingers begged leave to delete them all. How anyone was meant to work productively when they were being attacked by emails every second—then berated for denying all knowledge of something important they'd been sent in among a batch of spam . . . would somebody answer their bloody phone? Of course, it was lunchtime. They'd all be out entertaining journos on expenses.

'Hello, Katy?'

'No, it's Eleanor.'

114

'Eleanor, you'll do. This is Chief Inspector Cameron at Giffnock. We have a missing OAP, and I need to try and get a media broadcast on her. What are the chances of it making something like *Reporting Scotland*?'

'Hmm . . . doubt it. What's the angle?'

'There *is* no angle.'

'Well, how long has she been gone?'

'Since five a.m. this morning.'

The girl drew in her breath. ' 'S'no really that long, is it?'

'Well, see, the idea is, we don't wait until the woman's actually deid. I thought it might be fun to see if we could generate some interest while we still had a chance of finding her alive.'

There was a pause. 'You were up here the other week, weren't you? You're the one that didn't want your photo from the promotion parade.'

'Oh, for the love of God. That's not exactly relevant, is it? Look, you want an angle? How's this? It's possible the woman may be naked. And she's from Newton Mearns. A rich, naked old burd—would that do?'

'May . . . be. Do we think it's sexual then? Sex sells, you know. Why don't you email me a wee briefing note and we'll see what we can do?'

'Yeah, great. Cheers. Let's do lunch to discuss it, shall we? And just pray it disny get any colder out while you're deciding.'

Anna hung up. Opened a few emails, looked up the number for Property Services, and started cobbling a press statement. Oh to be like many-handed Vishnu; embodiment of mercy and goodness, the preserver and protector of creation, the one who never sleeps—and, crucially, who

115

would be able do all these many tasks she was attempting without dropping the damn phone.

'Ma'am.'

Claire again, her cheeks more pink, less twinkly.

'Sorry Claire. Unless it's a wee man with a ladder and a bag of ceiling tiles, it'll have to wait. Can you find out if Mr O'Hare's back yet? We need to make a decision about where we go next with Cassandra Maguire. Oh, and while you're here, can you shout Fraser Harris on the radio. Tell him to come in and see me, please? ASAP.'

'Ma'am, sorry. The bar were trying to ring through, but your line was engaged. It was someone called Teddy on the phone for you. Said he couldn't wait.'

'Teddy?'

'Yes. From Spain I think? He was phoning about your mum. Ma'am, I'm really sorry. Would you like a cup of tea?'

Anna put the receiver back on the cradle. 'No,' she said quietly, 'I'd like you to tell me exactly what he said.'

*   *   *

Hot slap of feet on tarmac, a warm evening folding like custard around languid mutters Anna didn't understand. It was the same day as the one she had woken up in, but here she was, in a different place. A hand outstretched to return her passport.

'*Gracias.*'

Dark men with shades and tight-tucked khaki shirts waving people through, jolly holiday-makers all new-clothed and eager being led to the right coach by tanned and sturdy lassies in sky-blue

116

skirts, their heels catching on uneven tiles. Anna pushed through it all, looking for a taxi, or Teddy's anxious face in the crowd, or her mum saying 'Don't be silly darling, I'm fine, I'm fine.' Then they'd peck the air and chat about inconsequentialities, and have dinner in 'this little place'. She could smell garlic from the cafeteria, see families greeting families, lovers hugging lovers. Anna had only been here, twice was it?, in ten years, and both times her mother had picked her up. She went the other way from the tourists, found the taxi rank.

'*Hospital Arrixaca*.' Showed the driver the name of the hospital, in case she hadn't said it right. Even with all that saliva flowing.

'*Vale. Cincuenta euros*.'

Fifty euros? Was *cincuenta* fifty? 'Okay.'

On the plane, she'd read, eaten, done crosswords; filling slabs of slack time. Her body was mostly still, while her mind flew from Cassie to Caroline, Caroline to Cassie; she was abandoning one old soul to run to another. Nothing she could do to make the plane fly faster or the seas recede or land stretch out to hasten their passage over hundreds and thousands of miles she couldn't change. So if her mind only dealt with the words on the page or the food that she chewed, it could make ballast to press on this twitching, cold-pouring dread that had crept with her into the taxi. Flat dry landscapes scudded by, studded with dusty green scrub and white buildings. This last bit was the longest, the point where she could almost run there.

It would be dark at home, pitch dark. It would not be warm, like here.

'*¿Usted tiene frío?*'

'Pardon?'

The driver turned his head and tried in accented English. 'You . . . cold? I turn air con down?'

'No, no. I'm fine.'

She folded hands beneath her thighs, still hunched, but not so obvious.

The hospital was a large teaching hospital, spread out like a small town, but the reception staff were kind. One spoke enough English to show her where to go.

Cuidados Intensivos. Room 42.

Sick-burning starbursts in her stomach. Now that she was here, outside, she wanted to leave. Why confront a stark reality that she could not change? What was the point if you couldn't *do* something? At work, she had control. Not here though. Never here, in the places where her mother was. But she went inside, because she'd come all this way, and it was what people expected.

Anna had expected to see Teddy's head bent over her mother's pillow, but she was lying alone, her hair spread loose, cheekbones high. She looked *young*. Like when Anna was wee and her mum wore her hair long, with a scarf tied in a hairband, sweeping it off her brow. There was a squint photo, somewhere, of Anna and her dad and her mother, laughing on a boat in St Andrews. The wind was strong, and Anna's mum had held her on her knee, shrieking as her dad rocked the boat, pretending that he'd dropped the oars. He set up the camera on a pile of their coats, clicked the timer, and clambered over the wooden seat to collapse beside them. Made it just in time, before the shutter closed. Her mum had worn an orange

118

scarf that day, with prints of horses and gypsies dancing. Anna remembered the flap of it on her cheek, tickling her nose with Coty L'Aimant.

She put her bag down, walked closer to the bed. The floor was slippery with just-mopped dampness, everything bleach-fresh round this unfresh form. Her mother smelled *bruised* somehow, like fruit.

'Hi Mum.'

You should talk to people in comas.

'It's Anna.'

She sat beside the bed, hands resting on the starchy cover. She should not feel this guilty scurrying in her gut; was it really for Cassie? No, there were others who would be looking out for Cassie. Right now, Anna's mother had only her. Was it alright to touch her, disturb her peaceful sleep, for surely, if Anna kissed her, she would wake? Such clear, smooth skin, stretched on such fine bones. Only the music of the beep, beep, beep and the dancing, jagged, lit-up lines to give it away. On the other side from Anna, a viscous cord of saline dripped from a plastic bag, lapping into her mother's bandaged arm. A clear tube had been inserted into each nostril, beaded with the condensation of her mother's breath. That was good, a good sign that she was breathing on her own. Anna leaned in closer. One tube looked a little dirty at the top. Carefully, she dipped the end of a tissue into a glass of water, dabbed at the fleck. Stubborn, stubborn spot. Then she realised it was a glob of dried blood, still attached to something inside her mother's nose, and that actually, Caroline's face was very lined close up, and there was blood in her hair, too.

119

'Oh, Mum.' She took her mother's hand, held it to her lips, then leaned over to kiss her hot-cold forehead.

She had no memory at all of the last time she'd kissed her mother, properly, with love instead of duty. It scared her. All those stiff niceties which had seeped in over the years, filling the vacuums of unanswered questions and closed-up doors, sluicing over the rawness of slights and sharp words. When had teenaged angst turned to adult disdain and the gulf grown so deep? Had it always just been Anna who imagined the worst, who misread signals, felt rejection when it wasn't meant? Packing it down, all that undiscussed resentment, until it became too big and amorphous to be defined. But her mother had been the adult, for a long part of it at least. Anna hadn't imagined a cold, brittle house where friends were not welcome; a mother who turned from tears to turn up the telly, who cut up photos and banned the mention of Anna's father's name. Who read Anna's prizewinning essays and noticed only missing punctuation.

Or were Anna's memories tempered with yet more guilt? At ten, at parents' night, caught between a shocked mother and confused teacher. *I'm so sorry, Mrs Cameron. Anna told me you were very ill*. Her sixteen-year-old self, screaming at her mother that she was a frigid old cow, and *what would you ever know about love anyway*? Evenings just walking past the light of the living room, going straight up to her room, leaving home as soon as she left school. Being busy, always busy.

'You're going to be alright, Mum.'

Anna's fingers hung over her mother's hair,

pressing lightly on the springy cuticles, dried from years in the sun. Her own hair would end up this grey-salted blonde, would feel like bristles on a broom. She could sing; old ladies liked singing. The nurses said it calmed them down. A thickness in her throat as words rose, a lilting tune that seemed to match the stroking of hair on pillows and deep-breathed sleep.

Slumber gently, goodnight.
Stars give thee their li-ight

'Carnation and rose, watch over thy repose.' Humming at first, she sang the last line out loud, stopped as the echo of her voice caught and shattered. All the wrong way round.

Her mother knew lots of songs, old Highland airs and English folk songs, and lieder about earl kings and Loreleis. Anna should have asked her to write them down. She would, later, when Caroline woke up. It could be therapy. If Anna had remembered the right words, she could have sung them to her, triggered something. Gently, she tried to unstick the hair from the dried scalp-blood, but it was too matted and she wasn't sure if she should wet it, didn't know if it would hurt, if it was internal blood that had oozed from her ear, or splattered blood from the fall. And where had Teddy been? How long had Caroline lain there, where was bloody Teddy now?

Her mother's nightdress felt clammy. There were no more in the locker. Anna should fetch some clean stuff from the flat. She would, she'd go in a while, once she'd seen the doctor. But there was no rush.

121

'Alright, Mum. I think I can remember "The Skye Boat Song".' She took off her jacket, scraped her chair as close as she could to the bed. Tried to ignore the staleness breezing through Caroline's breath. 'You just join in when you're ready.'

*   *   *

The little complex in which her mother lived was smart and white, low bungalows ranged round a pool, then steps to the terrace and the bar. Beyond the bar, a golf course, its sprinklers wheezing like a sibilant brook. Some of the houses had deckchairs outside, some geraniums. Some had gnomes. Caroline's had two wrought-iron chairs, and a blue and white wooden plaque above the door. Anna recognised it as one she'd picked up years ago in Fort William, sentimental with cider and the triumph of just finishing the West Highland Way.

Our Hielan' Hame.

'One day, one day, I'll have one of these for real,' she'd laughed, picking up the plaque amid groans of derision from the girls she'd been walking with.

'It's so tacky, Anna,' her friend Elaine had said. 'Here, d'you not want a wee tartan coo to go with it?'

But those had been her dad's exact words. He had promised. Driving back to Glasgow after a week on the Isle of Skye, listening from her makeshift bed in the back seat to her dad promising they'd go back; that one day he'd buy them their *ain Hielan' hame*. A nice wee crofter's cottage, not a conversion in Shawlands. Elaine was right; it was tacky. She'd felt stupid when she got

122

home, put the plaque up in her loo. Her mother had asked if she could take it, last time she was over. As far as she could remember, Anna had simply shrugged. Two years ago, that would have been, when Caroline and Teddy came for a friend's sixtieth birthday, and an awkward dinner *à trois* at Anna's.

All night, she had dozed and wriggled in the chair by her mother's bed. Her limbs were stiff, there was a ping at the base of her spine as she stepped on to her mother's patio. Her mobile rang. Claire Rodgers.

'Hi, ma'am. Sorry to bother you. How are things?'

A ratchet of unasked-for sympathy. 'Not too good.' Anna could feel her throat tighten, her voice squeeze thin. 'My mum's still in a coma, and no one can tell me much about her prognosis.'

'That's terrible. Have you seen the doctor yet?'

'Yeah, but all they say is to give it time, you know?'

'Look, I'm really sorry about this, ma'am, but I've had Mrs Hamilton on, asking what's happening. She's been going on about unauthorised absence—says you should have informed her before you went. You were meant to be on call this weekend? And she wants to know about some presentation to Eastwood Women's Forum. What will I tell her?'

'I . . . I need to sort some things out here. I don't know how long my mum'll be staying at the hospital, or where they'll . . .'

She didn't even know if her mother had medical insurance. Teddy would know—probably had the forms stashed in his suitcase.

'It'll be another couple of days at least. I need to make sure my mum's settled, pay for anything extra that needs to be done.'

'What about flying her home? Do you want me to make enquiries from this end?'

Home? Spain was Caroline's home, where her friends were, her life was. As Scotland was for Anna. Bringing Caroline 'home' wasn't something that had even crossed her mind. Was that what you were meant to do? Uproot the invalid, drag them halfway across the world to a place they thought they'd escaped from; dump them in another clean white bed with crappier food and wet grey views from the window?

'No. I'll just need to wait and see what the doctors say. But thanks. Claire—is there any word on Cassandra Maguire yet? Please tell me you've found her.'

Anna hadn't slept properly in over thirty hours. Sitting, just sitting by her mother's bed. She'd only come away to get her some clean nighties. Pulses skittering up her bones, her teeth; a head full of pounding . . . there was something else she had to do.

'Sorry, no. We've got nothing. It's like . . . I dunno, like she's been spirited away.'

'Right, go through the entire file again. I want you to revisit everything that's been done already, I want you to check that the security firm has been contacted . . . there were two housebreakers seen nearby—verify that they've been interviewed too; and you'll need to insist on that media appeal. In fact, get Mr O'Hare to phone me—'

'Ma'am, it's all in hand. I promise. We will find her. Trust me.'

'The first few days are crucial.'

As if Claire didn't know that. But she handled it well, remained pleasant as she rerouted Anna's efforts to steer by remote control.

'Look, this thing about the women's forum. Hamilton's doing her dinger. I think the Chief Constable's wife is a member, that's the problem.'

'That figures.'

'Well, will I say you'll reschedule it when you get back?'

Yes, that's right, jolly, clap-on-the-back Claire. Number one priority on my list, so it is. Pipping my dying, incontinent, inconvenient mother to the post, soaring above the pile of work that is building in my absence, the unanswered emails, the unallocated reports. Sweeping away my lonely cat, my glowing failure of a love life, a disgruntled councillor, a dead Asian youth and the unobliging old woman who simply refuses to come home quietly. All, all subsumed by Mrs Hitler Hamilton and her ugly, gleaming shoes.

'You can tell Mrs Hamilton to go and—'

'Anna, Anna. Walls have ears. I'm at the office now,' Claire continued brightly, in that way you do when you're putting on a show, or spea-king cleeer-ly fo-or the be-ne-fit of the tape. Aye, maybe Hamilton did monitor the airwaves. So what? She deserved all she got, then. People who listened at doorways never heard good of themselves.

'Could I do it, maybe?' said Claire. 'What is it?'

'That's brave; volunteering for something before you know what it is.' Anna kneaded the back of her neck. 'Canny mind exactly. Some crap about being "A Woman in a Man's World".'

'Ach. A doddle. Don't you worry about Mrs Hamilton—I don't mind braving the Witches of Eastwood. You take as long as you need, and I'll sort things out here.'

'Hopefully it won't . . .' Anna stopped herself. The girl was only trying to help. Few folk did that any more. Felt almost . . . it felt kind. A kind of weakness in allowing it, but . . . Anyway. There it was, the gesture smiling up at her. 'Yeah. Okay, Claire, thanks.'

'Really?'

'Yeah, why not? You're just as qualified as me. Probably more so. I mean, I don't have to do all that child-juggling stuff as well.'

An inflection of genuine surprise. 'Well . . . thanks. I think.'

'Mind and bake some cakes to take along, just to show all that nasty police work hasn't de-feminised you.'

'Well, I am a cordon bleu chef. Not to mention a demon with the Hoover.'

Yes, you probably are, thought Anna.

A thud amidst the pounding.

Hoover.

Jesus. *Hoover.* She'd run out the office so fast, she'd completely forgotten.

'Claire . . . I've just realised something. Something *bad.*' Quivers in her nose, she could feel it building, in with the tiredness and the splitting head. As if that would be much use to the poor guy.

'It's Fraser Harris. *Fuck.* I've left him totally exposed.'

She pulled air through her teeth, let it settle. Then gabbled out what the intelligence manager

126

had said, and what she should have done.

'I did make some notes, and I'll draft a risk assessment, I promise. I'll fax it to you, tonight.'

'Don't worry. Honestly, it's fine. I can deal with that at this end—'

'*No.*' She almost shouted it. 'It's my responsibility, Claire, it's me that's let him down. But can you get the super to speak to Fraser—you sit in too, of course? Just say to Mr O'Hare that—'

'We'll handle it, trust me.'

'And don't delay, please. Fraser should have been warned yesterday, as soon as I was told.'

'I promise. I'll go and speak to Mr O'Hare right now.'

Soothing, calm; the sort of there-there tone she must use with her children.

'Claire, promise that you'll keep me in the loop. About Fraser *and* Cassie Maguire. I mean it. Make sure they're doing everything they can. Interview the family again. The daughter-in-law—'

'Don't worry. Done, done and done. You just focus on your mum, yeah?'

'I will.'

My mum. Anna rarely called her that, not to her face. Never called her it since she was wee, in fact, not until she had uttered it in the hospital. To that blank, ageless face that could no longer nag or chide. *Oh Anna. What a state you are.* It was unforgivable, leaving that young cop unprotected, in the dark. No matter how sympathetic Johnny might be, Mrs H wouldn't see it that way. Just one more coal to stoke the fire.

And still no bloody Cassie. She felt so tired. But it would be no different if Anna were there, she told herself; the searchers would be no less

127

professional, the interviews would still be as thorough. Claire and Johnny had worked together before Anna arrived, and would continue to do so in her absence. She, Anna Cameron, was not the missing link in the convoluted chain that sought to anchor Cassandra Maguire.

She put her phone back into her bag, let herself in with the key the complex warden had given her. Anna had asked the warden where Teddy was, but the woman had just shrugged. The hospital hadn't known either.

'Señor Steed brought your mother in, and stayed while we made her comfortable. I talked with him after, to tell him it was a cerebral haemorrhage.'

'That must have been when he phoned me. Has he been back?' she'd asked the doctor.

'I do not know. Now, your mother is very ill, you understand that?'

'Yes.'

'All we can do is keep her stable, keep her blood thin with medication, and wait.'

'Will she wake up?'

'I hope so.'

Caroline's house smelled fousty. It was dark inside, curtains drawn. Teddy had phoned Anna's work mid-morning, so she was guessing it had happened at night.

It. *It.*

The stroke.

A smooth hand passing on your brow, a feather's caress, an affirmation of midnight. From the looks of things, Teddy had not been back since then. Anna pulled open the cheery yellow curtains in the kitchen. Blades of light flashed across the aluminium sink, ricocheting from walls and tiles,

128

across the floor darkly smudged with dried-up blood. Another smear on the wall—at a sliding height. Anna crouched to look at the marks. Had the bastard not even thought to clean this up? It was like he'd fled the scene, or couldn't face coming back. Perhaps he'd panicked. Men were like that; weak men like Teddy. She stood, turned on the tap. Her mum would keep cloths . . . there, in the little drawer beside the stove. Not the one beneath the sink. Ha. She was right. What a thing to feel triumphant about.

She let the tap run hot, moved into the living room. Everything was neat and ordered, flowers on the polished table, macramé plant holders strung in the window. The two fireside chairs from home, covered now in duck-egg checks. Just a rug knocked squint between here and the bedroom door. She pushed it straight with her foot, switched on the bedroom light. The double bed was in disarray, pink sheets all rumpled and . . . rank. That same bitterness of the old folks' home at The Meadows; of soiled old people left to unravel. Caroline must have lost control as it was happening, staggered into the kitchen, and fallen against the wall. Her brain cells popping, flooding through memories, motor skills and speech, all leaking on to her ceramic tiled floor.

'Oh for God's sake.' A man's voice, in the kitchen.

'Who's there?'

Anna ran through, saw Teddy scrabbling at the tap, hot water pouring from the sink, bouncing down the cupboard below.

'Teddy.'

'Oh, Anna. Didn't think you'd get here so soon.'

He was grey beneath the tan, face-folds accentuated by his unshaven jowls, his generous moustache. A dirty big bloodhound in an open-necked shirt.

'Where have you been?' she asked.

'At the hospital.'

'Bollocks. I've just come from there.'

'Anna, your mother doesn't like you swearing, you know that.'

'Fuck off. *You're* not my dad. Where were you?'

'I had forms to fill in, stuff to—'

'How come you left the place like this?'

'I meant to . . .' He wrung out the cloth.

'I was with her all night, Teddy. Where the hell were you?'

'I was . . . staying with a friend. I couldn't . . . I didn't want to come back here.' The cloth hung in his hands, dripping limp down his Farah slacks.

'Give it to me.' She took the damp rag from him, started scrubbing at the floor, crouched in a squat to keep her knees clean. The edges of the stain were wiping away, but where the blood was thickest, it wouldn't shift. She had to scour with her fingernails through the mesh of the fabric.

'So. Are you going to tell me what happened?'

'I told you on the phone.'

'You told me my mum had had a stroke. But when, how did it happen? Had she been feeling ill? What?'

Teddy moved round her and into the living room.

'Where you going?'

He didn't answer.

'Don't you worry. I'll just clean up my own mum's blood, will I?'

130

Still it wouldn't shift. The cloth wasn't very absorbent, clear drops of liquid shaking on the surface as she moved the fabric up and down. It looked like a piece of old T-shirt clipped neatly with pinking shears. *Waste not, want not.* One of her mum's favourite Presbyterian pieties, designed to make you wash out your jam jars and save your paper bags and eat up your mince in a three-day cycle. Tuesdays, that was the day it always began. Mince and potatoes, all gristle and flecks of white fat, swimming in a film of yeasty grease. *Marmite.* No one else used Marmite to flavour their gravy. And the pale orange cubes of boiled-soft turnip, dissolving as your fork hit home. All hail Vesta curry days, with their Caroline-proof sachets that required only ten minutes on the boil. But she tried, God love her. Making cakes with packet mix, putting the egg in with the icing sugar by mistake. Both of them gamely munching the resultant crisp biscuits. And making mosaics with the smashed-up shells.

Still this wouldn't shift. On Anna rubbed and rubbed, her palms growing damp with dilute mother-blood. Under the quick, under the skin. Is that what it meant to be a mother? To scrape and mop and make and bake and not feel sick or want to run away? Anna, bound by circumstance and blood; braver than Teddy because it was all she could do.

From the bedroom came sounds of creaking, slamming. She straightened up, gave up. They'd need to get bleach or something for this last bit. She let the cloth steep in the basin and went in search of Teddy. He was chucking T-shirts and socks into a suitcase, all frenzied like he was going

131

to be late. Anna touched his arm. 'Hey, I don't think she'll need all this, Teddy. Just some clean nighties, maybe a bed jacket for when she's sitting up.'

He opened the wardrobe, brought out ties and jackets.

'What are you doing?'

'I'm packing.'

'Aye, but it looks like your stuff.'

'It is.'

'Why?'

'Because I'm leaving.'

'You mean you're going to stay at the hospital?'

'No. I'm going to stay with a friend.'

She slammed the lid of his case. 'What the fuck is going on? You can't leave my mother lying in a hospital bed.'

'You're here now. You can deal with it.'

'It? *It?* "It" is the woman you've been living with for fifteen years. Who are you running off to, *Teddy*?'

Teddy was always a little scared of Anna. Wary at first, but confident he'd win her round. Then just wary, then, finally, afraid. She'd threatened him one night, when he and her mother still lived in Scotland. They were both a little pished, her mother gone to bed. He'd put his arm round her in the kitchen, a fatherly gesture, she was sure, but she'd hit his hand away, told him she wasn't part of the package.

'You don't look, and you don't touch. Clear?'

'Anna, please, I just want to be your friend.'

'Look, you're no my pal, you're just shagging my mother. And if you touch me again I'll break your arm. Oh, and while we're on the subject, if you

132

ever hurt my mum, I'll do much worse.'

Then she'd raised her glass, so he'd know it was all friendly like. 'So. Are we on the same page, *Tedster*?'

No more pretending after that. He knew she hated him, and she didn't give a toss what he thought. But he loved her mother, or needed her or something, and so they had to tolerate each other when Caroline was around.

'Ho. I'm talking to you,' she said.

Calmly, Teddy opened up the suitcase again, Anna's hand sliding from the lid.

'Anna. You, of all people, should be pleased.'

In went another pile of jumpers; Pringle pastels slipping like sliced ice cream.

'Finally, finally, I've taken the hint. I'm moving out of your mother's life.' He stretched over to press the clothes down, then looked around the room. Half a wardrobe hanging empty. Two open drawers, bereft of any socks.

'But why?'

Up too close against her now, breathing in her face. His fat paunch pressing on her belly in the airless, stinking room.

'I've had enough.'

She wouldn't back away.

'What kind of a man walks out on his partner when she's ill? When she might be dying?'

'We're all dying.' He snapped the case shut, picked it up. 'All of us, every day.'

'Why are you leaving her? Tell me what happened to my mum, you big shit.'

Teddy stood for a moment in the doorway. 'She had you. All downhill from there, wouldn't you say?'

133

Anna should have stopped him. Got details of where he was going, a phone number at least for when her mum woke up. But she let him walk away, heard the door pull to, his clicking shoes as he crossed the patio, the shrump of the dragging case. Then nothing at all but her breath and insects chirping and the hissing insistence of water sprays.

She sat on the bed, let her head come to rest on her knees as she watched an ant process beneath the bed, its black-lacquered body following a line of grout. The tiles on the bedroom floor were chequered. Cream and blue, like the lino in their old house. She remembered their kitchen, blue tiles, white Belfast sink. The chopping boards and the rolling pin and the smash-crunch of wood on shell. It *had* been her mum that had made mosaics with her. Not her dad.

*   *   *

The Mirror Man is waiting in the basement.

The shock is absolute. The guard is carrying a bowl of food, a beaker of water, and the liquid spills in wide flourishes. He heard no door open, saw no one come inside.

The Man is squatting by the bed the guard has tried to fashion; bits of cloth, her wrap, some packaging he'd found strewn upstairs. Fresh newspapers, which he changes daily like you would for a cat. She is asleep. Or she is paralysed with fear, or dead. The Man's hand rests on her collarbone, on the open, untied flap of her cotton nightgown.

He smiles, but does not move his head as he speaks. 'Stop up my breasts. It's an excellent sentiment. Lady Macbeth—you know it?'

134

The guard shakes his head, says nothing. He does not know what he is meant to say, all he knows is that the Man must be removed from here.

The Man stands. 'Do you know that some warriors collect women's nipples? They wear them like trophies.'

He unbuttons his shirt. Takes his own black nipple, squeezes it between his fingernails. 'Don't you wish you were numb to pain?' He comes closer so the guard can see his own, twinned reflection looking back at him. One in each glimmering lens.

'You are a piece of shit,' the Mirror Man roars, battering the bowl from the guard's shaking hands. It strikes the wall, explodes in rice and shards of cheap, powdery china. 'I collect shit, I own it. My life is built on shit, shit like you.'

Flecks of saliva hit the guard's cheeks, spatter warm and salty into his mouth.

'Waiting downstream for the flotsam and the jetsam—I dirty my hands with your shit—and this is what you do. Who told you to feed her?'

'No one,' the guard stutters.

'Fucking no one.' When the blow comes, it is almost a relief. He feels the rupture of his nose, a dense, dull compression and then pure liquid fire, sending starbursts to his eyes, his teeth. Briefly, he cannot see.

'You are no one. And so is she. Now, give her this, then fuck off out my sight.'

The guard feels a small, hard object pushed into his hand. He blinks, forces open his eyes. Is aware of the Man at her body again, this time at her feet. Pulling something sticky from his own elbow. A tape, a bandage?

'Do you have a pen?' the Man asks. Deep and

135

slow and calm once more.

The guard looks down at his hand, at the object thrust on him. It has the long curved thinness of a pen. But it is not. It is a plastic syringe, filled with colourless liquid.

CHAPTER SEVEN

Day two—or was it three? It was Saturday morning, in any case, and Anna's mother was still 'comfortable'. Once or twice, she thought Caroline had moaned, or moved, but the doctors could see no change. Some golf club ladies came to visit, bringing flowers that spilled gold pollen on white linen, and were removed by the nurses.

Anna remained in the chair by Caroline's bed, leaving occasionally to find food or check her messages, feeling each hour become shakier and more surreal. And still no word on Cassie Maguire. Well, hundreds of words—she phoned frequently for updates—but none of any consequence. She spent some of her time writing out the risk assessment for Fraser. It had to be treated seriously; prepare for the worst-case scenario, then work back from there. She listed all the dangers inherent in allowing him to keep working, then, in bullet points, charted all the ways they could help keep him safe. That was Anna's role, making lists; Divisional Intelligence or CID would carry out a similar procedure for assessing potential suspects. She persuaded the lady at the hospital reception to fax the report for her too, and then stopped as she was in the act of handing the scribbles across.

Where was her brain? An open fax in a foreign country, listing every possible way one of her cops might be harmed? On top of an overseas call made on an unprotected mobile? However unlikely, however fanciful her imagination, one thing two decades in the polis taught you was: *you never know.*

Anna pulled her jacket tighter round her shoulders. The air conditioning came on at six, clicked by a central control, a daily drying of her throat.

'You need to get some rest, pet.' It was one of the 'golf girls'. 'Won't do your mum any good if you get ill too, will it?'

Even her hair felt thirsty. 'I know, but I can't leave her.'

'Course you can. Off you go back to Caroline's flat and get a nap, and we'll sit with her, won't we, Peg?'

'What about Teddy?' asked Peg. 'Has he been helping out?'

Anna's mother had always been intensely private. If these women knew nothing, then that was how it would remain. The other lady took Anna's arm.

'Come on, dear. I'll walk you over to the lift. Have an hour at least, eh? Some fresh air, a nice coffee?'

The corridor was cool and sterile. Metal doors, lemon walls. Modern art in blue and green showing calming seas and flowers. You could be in a nice apartment block, if it wasn't for the clinical smell.

'He's buggered off again, hasn't he?' said the woman.

'Again?'

'Look, it's none of my business, dear, but I think you should know: that Teddy's a bad lot.'

'You think?'

She patted Anna's elbow. 'I'm Joan, by the way. Known your mum for years, I have. And *him* too. Never liked him.'

Anna pressed the arrow by the lift.

'He left her last year too, you know. Came back when his money ran out.'

'Did he?'

'I know, I know. I must sound like a terrible old gossip, but I promise you, I'm not. All I'm saying is, if he *has* gone, then good riddance to him. But don't you worry, dear, we'll all rally round. Take it in turns to sit with her till she gets back on her feet.'

'If.'

Joan smiled. 'There's no cheering you up, is there? Let's cross that bridge when we come to it. It's early days yet. Plenty of folk older than her recover from strokes, you know.'

'After being unconscious all this time?'

'Nature's way of healing, love. And it's only been since Thursday, eh?' She let go of Anna's arm. 'Anyway, no matter how long she's in here, we'll all take our turn. She's a lovely woman, is your mum. Do anything for anyone, she would. And you can't stay here forever, Anna. Not when you've such an important job back home.'

Anna looked at her, surprised.

'Chief inspector now, isn't it?'

'How d'you know that?'

'Because we all got summoned to the celebration, love. Cocktails on the terrace and everything, all in your honour.'

'Oh.'

Joan's rings shifted round wrinkled fingers as she touched Anna's hand again. 'Your mum's terribly proud of you, you know. Talks about you all the time.'

The lift tinged open, a cold, clean vial into which to pour herself. Anna stepped inside.

'Joan?'

'Yes dear?'

'Teddy wouldn't *hurt* my mum, would he?'

Joan frowned. 'Oh, no, dear. They told you it was a stroke, didn't they? I mean, she's had high blood pressure for years, you know.'

'Has she?'

'Yes. That last time she was over in Scotland . . . she'd been getting tests done. Some new drug trial. Did she not—'

'Oh. Yes. So she did. I forgot. Thanks . . . Joan.' Anna let the doors slide shut, pressed the bottom button. It would either take her to the foyer and the *churros* counter, or to the basement where they kept the boilers and the bodies. Coffee or corpses? Let the god of lifts decide. A sugar rush would be good, but formaldehyde always gave her that wee buzz too. A slight sickness in the sweetness. Her mum had been ill for years. Years of downing pills and potions which she shared with Teddy, not her, and yet her mum talked about her all the time. All the time, you know. That was a West of Scotland thing, that grim acceptance of your offspring to their faces, while lavishing praise on them behind their backs.

The lift opened up at the foyer, before she was ready, with the tears still wet on her face. Still, it was a hospital, and folk were used to these things.

Who did she know here in any case? That was it, she thought as she walked towards candy smells and warm roast beans.

Cerrado.

'You're closed?'

'*Sí.*' The waitress shrugged as she straightened the sign, locked the door. Then she pointed out through the main foyer doors.

Directly across from the hospital's entrance, Anna could see a café, tucked in a courtyard on the other side of the road. It had a plastic sign for San Miguel above the door. That would do. She darted between the traffic, the hot sun like fire on her back after the cool of the hospital.

'*¿Qué quiere tomar?*' asked the man behind the counter. It wasn't just *churros* this place had, there were croissants too, and little olive things and fresh coffee and rows of bottles. Civilised, thoughtful, lovely Spanish. Anna pointed to a bottle marked Torres Gran Reserva. She'd had it before. Tasted of toothache. 'Brandy, *por favor*. And one of them.' The *churro* was full-fat grease, deliciously tepid folding round her teeth. She chewed and balanced and found a table near the window.

Outside, long fronded trees bowed and birds pecked on pebbled ground. A couple of little girls played in the courtyard, two women watching them from the shade. One woman was in a wheelchair. The other scooped ice cream from a little tub, carefully waiting and placing the confection in the other's drooping mouth. What was she: carer, daughter, skivvy? Sticks and stones and names stamped on you, covering you over with the labels folk like to see, to save them from making their own minds up. Too many times, Anna had been

140

stamped. Difficult, arrogant, aloof. Cop, spinster, misfit. Frigid, promiscuous, bitch. Bolshy, selfish, wrong. Wrong, wrong, wrong.

No one knew her here at all. If she wanted, she could cry and rail and beat her breast; nobody would care. The brandy swirled dark gold, each lap on glass a sticking lick. A stamp. What was Anna stamped with?

Outside, the ice cream dribbled down the woman's chin, her daughter reaching to catch it, upending the entire tub on the paving stones. At once, the birds flurried and fought, cawing for the spillage.

Anna had thought Ronnie Maguire was comical, this grown man bawling like a baby. Not any more. Her brandy crackled comfort, plumping out the *churro* dough in her mouth. More tears came: tight, sore ones that offered no relief.

Brandy splashed on her hand, it jerking as she saw the daughter outside suddenly scoop the carton from the ground. She was screeching, was thrusting it into her mother's terrified face and, as she did, Anna could see *Cassie* cowering, could see that skinny harridan dragging her away. Not a daughter, but a daughter-in-law.

She fumbled for her mobile, switched it on. Frustrated as the tendrilled bar surged out, ebbed back, searching for a signal. She had no idea which shift was on, but she still had Claire Rodger's mobile number in her memory card. Two rings and it was answered. 'No, Sophie. Put it down! Colin? Where the hell are you? I'm due out now.'

'Claire? No, it's Anna Cameron. Listen, has any consideration been given to treating it as a criminal investigation?'

'What?'

'Cassandra Maguire. Are we still treating it as a missing persons enquiry?'

'Any reason why we shouldn't?'

'I don't know exactly. It's the daughter-in-law. She's too angry—she's not upset. I just . . . I just don't trust her, okay?'

There was the suggestion of suppressed laughter. 'And that's it? Ma'am, I *really* think you're overreac—'

'I'm over *what*?'

Over land and sea? Oh, Anna could fire ice darts from halfway across the world, you cheeky bitch.

'Nothing.'

Let's just both pretend it was a bad line.

She could hear Claire's sharp, clipped breathing. 'Okay, sure. Well, why don't I get someone to interview her again? I'm going back up later anyway. That doctor, the one that runs it—he's been really helpful you know.'

'Macklin? I bet he has. Scared his wee cash cow is going to get shut down.'

'It's not like that at all. He's been out searching himself, he's helped us with interviewing the residents . . .'

Was the girl for real? 'Claire, I'm not convinced he's not involved in some way too.'

'Oh. Okay. What about the old lady's roommate? You think we should bring her in for questioning too?'

'I don't know. Maybe. She was going on about black men being in her room.'

'Ma'am. Have you managed to get any sleep at all?'

'Don't speak to me like that. I'm not an imbecile, I'm your boss.'

'Yeah, and I don't start work until two o'clock this afternoon.'

Oh.

It felt like a wall collapsing; that fury that had been holding her up, suddenly knocked away.

'Claire, I'm sorry.' She got the dusty words out, before they choked her. 'I know I've called you up at home, and . . . look, I'm sorry, okay? I'm just tired, that's all. I feel totally useless stuck here. I can't help Cassie, and I can't even help my mum.'

'You *are* helping her, of course you are. Is there any change?'

'Nope.'

'So, she's stable. That's alright, eh? Don't give up hope. What you need to do is forget about work, Anna, okay? I promise I will interview Sheena Maguire myself—'

'Try and get the measure of her, you know? See if there's a history of her bullying Cassie, if the staff have ever seen anything untoward.'

'I will. Will you please relax and trust me?'

Claire's singsong lilt was smoothing down the edges. Anna's neck felt looser, her shoulders more at ease with their joints. But there was one more thing. She filled her lungs with coffee-scented air. 'And what about Fraser?'

'Sorted.'

Thank you, thank you, thank you.

'We've had a chat and—'

'Anything more from Divisional Intelligence?'

'Not yet.'

'I couldn't send the risk report. I wrote it, but then I thought it wouldn't be safe.'

143

'Don't worry. Mr O'Hare and I have done one. Fraser's cool. Totally unfazed by the whole thing.'

'Well, just tell him to be careful. Tell him I'll speak to him as soon as I get back.'

'Will do. And, here, d'you want some good news? Your ned's full committal was yesterday. You know, Gordon Figgis, for the Aziz killing? He's virtually put his hands up to it already, is what I've heard. Amazing! Imagine him going down without a fight, eh?'

Anna could no longer get excited about anything much. Her reserves had drained; the world gone thin and flat. 'Maybe he thinks there's some kudos in being a bona fide killer.'

'Well, it'll stop it dragging on for Aziz's family. And it's bound to help things settle down here. Place was mental last . . . anyway, I better go. I think that's Colin at the door. Oh! Will I make it chocolate or jam?'

'Pardon?'

'The cake for the Eastwood Forum? What flavour do you think they'd like?'

'Goodbye, Claire.' Anna hoped she could hear the smile in her voice. 'Have a nice shift.'

'*Adios.*'

The brandy was working its magic, massaging her back, filling the flatness up with gold; Spanish sun baking through tinted glass. The children in the courtyard were squabbling, squeezed in beside each other on a single chair. Anna wondered why they didn't pick a bench each, these two little girls in emerald dresses. Then she realised they were twins. That was the sort of thing twins did, wasn't it? Curl up together like they were inside the womb. Their mother was still shouting, wild hands

144

gesticulating at the woman in the wheelchair, who sat unblinking and absorbed it all. A mournful face, looking back at Anna.

'*Señorita.*'

Another glass of brandy appeared beside the first. Anna glanced up, the barman smiled.

'Oh no, I didn't order—'

'*Por favor.* For you.' He nodded, walked back to his counter. Kept his head down at the sink so she couldn't say no, or maybe so she knew no conversation was expected. She sipped this one slower. Wondered what she should do next. She'd asked about medical insurance, been told her mother was covered for 'acute care' only. No one could quite give a definition of what this meant, or how long it lasted, but clearly it was finite. Anna would have to consider other options, other places, if Caroline did not improve. The barman was staring at her. He draped his dishtowel over the taps, began to move again round the zinc counter. She downed the dregs of brandy, and returned to her mother's room.

In the filtered sunlight, she watched Caroline sleep, thought of Cassandra Maguire. Was she sleeping too? Was she safe against the cold, did she have her coat and her sheepskin boots, really? Or had they simply been removed, to push assumptions down another path?

Trust nae cunt.

Every cop should have that tattooed across their knuckles.

Hello, I'm Sheena, and I just murdered my mother-in-law. It probably *was* a lurid notion, born of breakfast brandy and the appalling magazines her mother's friends had brought to keep her

145

company.

My smack-head stepson tried to kill me.

Struck blind, but I can still see the love in his eyes.

Cassie was a diabetic, Macklin had said. It was seventy-two hours since she had disappeared. How long could she go without insulin?

Saliva oozed from Caroline's puzzled mouth. Anna reached to catch it, realised she had no tissue. Let it fall across her fingers anyway, warm mucus from her mother's mouth. She wiped round Caroline's mouth with her fingers, thought she felt the puckering of her lips follow. A sigh; a full, shuddering rattle of old air expelled. Was this it, the last of her lungs clearing memories? Then she moaned, mouth curling, smacking her swollen tongue, neck falling slightly, to the left where Anna sat and when she opened her eyes, when her mother opened her always-blue eyes, Anna's were the first thing she saw.

CHAPTER EIGHT

It felt so cold, being back in Glasgow. Fresh, sparse air, clean blue sky. A breeze biting at the newborn leaves, which quivered and clung in hopeful green. All the shops had Easter eggs in, big glossy dark ones and gold-foiled ovals; nut clusters and chocolate bunnies. Anna bought herself a dark Lindt fondant-filled 'bombe', then another, slightly bigger one, to give to Claire at work. Well, she could give it to her kids or something. It was just a token, that was all. Claire hadn't needed to fire tranquillising darts at Hamilton—or indeed book

Anna's flight back home. Anna had phoned Claire again yesterday, to tell her, of course, about her mum—but also to check if Claire had spoken to Sheena Maguire.

'Sorry, ma'am, no. Neither of the Maguires were up at The Meadows when I went, and we've been flat out. I'll get someone to their house today, I promise. Look,' she had neatly segued, 'how about I try and book you a flight from here?'

Meekly, Anna had agreed. Trying to organise anything from the hospital had been a nightmare. No Internet access, her phone running out of credit, her apologetic Spanish-sounding snorts and hisses not actually compensating for the fact that she could not speak, far less understand, more than two words of the language. Her mum was sitting up now, able to slur a few syllables and suck milky, chalky stuff from a beaker. But the staff had been making noises about moving her on, that this bed was for *casos urgentes, urgentes, entiende?* Anna was knackered, brain-blasted, panicking about the practicalities, and the language and the costs. Like a child, she'd wanted to flee for home, she'd had enough of sweet-tasting milk and too-dry, artificial air.

I know, sí. I understand. Okay? There was nothing else for it. She'd have to bring her mum back with her. Not a decision to be taken lightly, for either of them, but with Teddy gone, what else could she do? Her mum was still a UK citizen, there had to be provision for getting her into an NHS hospital, at least until she got back on to her feet. It would mean Anna could return to work, then pop in and visit Caroline on the way home. Or something. She hadn't quite worked all that out yet. But it was a decision, the first she'd made in days, and was therefore something solid on which she could predicate further decisive actions. The English-speaking lady at reception was nowhere to be found, so Anna attempted explaining—via the art of mime and a kindly tour rep she'd dragged from a neighbouring ward—that she would make immediate arrangements to bring her mother home. Thinking they'd be glad. Instead, immediate, angry chaos prevailed. Lots of head shaking all round, fingers waggled repeatedly. Eventually, she grasped she was being told that her mother could not fly, not for three months at least, following a stroke.

But Anna had to come home. She wasn't bailing out on her mum, who was getting better all the time and had friends to come and sit and spoon-feed. In Glasgow, Anna could look at her options, get advice from those who knew. Knew what exactly? How to find, and pay for, the best stroke care in Spain, or how to transport her mum back to Glasgow, and, once there, where the hell to put her? Not with Anna, no, no way, neither of them, both of them would hate that. To take her mum to the toilet, touch secret skin she'd not been intimate with for decades, build handrails on the bath? God, no. No, horrid, thoughtless daughter thinking thoughts that weren't allowed. What was the alternative, then? Anna had folded her mum's clean nightie, smoothed the ribbon-tie flat.

One of those places, those ugly, fetid places like The Meadows, where they'd sedate her and pad her and stick her in a vinyl chair.

There were bound to be better places than that—she could draw up a shortlist, go and inspect them. Once she was home. Yes, Anna must go home. There was Alice, whom the neighbour had been feeding, and—she could feel her shoulders tighten—there was work. Even the golf club ladies agreed she had pressing issues to contend with.

They had no idea.

It was now six thirty on Monday morning. The average heart beats seventy-two times per minute, and Cassandra Maguire had been gone for over one hundred hours. Four hundred thousand beats of time, opening and closing. If Anna kept visualising that, focusing on the beat like artificial respiration, then she could visualise Cassie alive.

'Morning ma'am,' said the bar officer. 'Good to see you back.'

She smiled at him. 'Thanks, Joe. Much happening?'

'Same old same old. Five minutes, and you'll think you've never been away.'

Oh, but she had. The fresh-draughting current that entered her office with Anna cut through sleepy air, which had been quite happily minding its own business, morosely pushing dust across the coffee rings and silent clock. She opened the brass plate at the back of the mount, began to wind the little mechanism inside. Switched on the computer, typed in her magic numbers to unlock the screen. Black, black, all thick bold black screaming hundreds of unopened emails. She closed it up again, wished she could throw away the key. Another password, another heart-sink. Twelve new entries to be updated on the VPD. In what, four days in total since she'd last sat at her desk? Fair enough, there'd been no time to arrange proper cover, but could Johnny not have done the VPD at least? Her role was to deputise for him, but surely it worked both ways.

Anna spread her hands across her cheeks and eyes, watching the world through little Vs. They'd have set up an incident room for Cassie now: a vulnerable OAP who had slipped from the face of the earth. They always used the long, thin room by the gents. Five minutes and she'd go up and see what was what. Not yet seven a.m. She'd come in deliberately early, suspecting the worst and hoping for a little window of quiet in which to read, reply, prioritise or bin before the new day's assault began.

First thing after Cassie would be to have a word with Fraser Harris. She checked the rosters, saw he was backshift the next day. Okay then, first thing tomorrow afternoon, she'd speak to him. And, in a couple of hours, she could call her mum's old doctor. The same one that had given Anna her rubella jag, nursed her through suspected meningitis, told her she was pregnant. Nice old man, Dr Struthers. He'd know what to do. He'd find her mum a good place to recuperate. Get her some speech therapy, physio. And then, then, the time would be right to ask her mother the question that plucked this constant, irritant string. Once Caroline was rested, once the swelling had subsided and the bruising faded to blush, Anna would ask her what it meant, this spasming of her head; the desperate, regular nodding which had begun when her mother woke. And she'd ask her mother why her only waking words had been *Teh-ee, Tegh-ee*, uttered mournfully slow. Once she could say more, Anna would ask her.

'Ma'am?' Joe was holding a sheet of paper. 'You

150

got a sec? Only, I meant to say. We've some news about your old woman.'

'Cassandra Maguire?'

Anna's response was hesitant. 'News' could be a limp, curved body found in a ditch, if it meant a form signed off and resources released.

'Aye. Last night actually, but the request to put this out only came in the now. So it'll no have been marked off the VPD yet.'

He slid a flimsy global message across her desk:

To All Forces.
Missing Person Cancellation: Cassandra Maguire

'Look. Traced, safe and well.'

Like the swift rush of blood that came with resurfacing, Anna realised she'd been holding her breath. 'Oh, Joe, that's brilliant news. Where was she?'

He laughed. 'Only got herself on a train down south, and presented herself at her sister-in-law's door. Bloody Liverpool.'

'You are joking!'

'I know. Sergeant Duncan's just phoned me to put this out on STORM the now. Apparently she was sick of being "treated like an eejit", I think her exact words were.'

'But how did she get out the nursing home?'

'Booked a taxi, if you please, on her mobile phone. Then let herself out the back door. What a wumman, eh?'

A swift vision of the doughty old dame, scurrying from her room like she was in *The Great Escape*, dodging nurses and searchlights, with a coat draped over her nightie.

151

'Oh. Oh, Joe—that's fantastic. I'm *so* chuffed. Is someone going down to bring her back?'

'No, I think she's staying in Liverpool. Word is her daughter-in-law wants nothing more to do with her. And vice versa I believe.'

Ga'un yersel Cassie.

A beautiful feeling of looseness was gathering at the base of Anna's skull. Some generous, benevolent puppet master was untangling the strings. She took her left wrist in her right hand, raised both above her head. Stretching until she felt the T-shirt pop from her belt. 'Joe, I tell you. That has fair made my day.'

Joe scratched his elbow. He seemed embarrassed, then she realised. Not only was she grinning like a loon, but her belly button was on show.

'So,' drawing her arms down smartly, 'keep me updated, eh? I want to see the whole file once it's completed, yeah?'

'Nae bother, ma'am. Eh . . . I'll leave you to it.'

Anna looked at the Easter egg she'd bought for Claire. Claire, who was off for four days' skiing, all healthy and bobble-hatted with her gleaming, pine-fresh kids. A fine big egg it was. Too big really. Anna cupped the fat round golden head of it, feeling hexagonal dips like phrenology. Flexed and raised and formed a fist. Punched slowly, triumphantly, the chocolate folding in a concertina beneath crumpled, tearing foil. *Here's to you, Cassandra Maguire. Wha's like you?* She bit a piece of chocolate, crisp-bitter on her tongue, then fixed her mind on other work, starting to shuffle through the pile of reports and memos and applications and letters that leered at her from on high. There was so much *stuff,* it made her head ache. But it would not ache today. Not while she had this perfect, silken taste of molten chocolate and victory. It did not happen often, and should be savoured when it did.

'Here, ma'am? I brought you the missing persons file. Most of it seems to be filled in already—I think they were just waiting for confirmation this morning.'

'Okay, great. Just leave it there, Joe.' Her fingers were sticky. 'Want some chocolate?'

'No, you're alright.'

She just wanted to check it all in black and white, then she would update the VPD. Flicking through all the four-page forms until she came to the one marked: *Cassandra Maguire.* Turned to page two, saw the global Joe had freshly stapled and attached:

To All Forces.
Missing Person Cancellation: Cassandra Maguire

Beautiful, fat black confirmation. The latter entries on the form were a hopscotch of handwritten scrawls and photocopied faxes between Strathclyde and Merseyside. The last one from down south came at nine o'clock last night. *Identity confirmed. Statement from Mrs Maguire to follow.* Anna looked for the statement, but there was nothing else. Yet Johnny appeared to have signed it off, last night, long before this cancellation was circulated. So what had they been waiting for? There were no medical reports, no further contact with the nursing home either. Was Cassie actually compos mentis? Did she *know* that

153

she wanted to stay in Liverpool? Ten minutes, that's all it took to finish things off properly, but everyone was always too busy, skating on thinnest ice, scrape-tipped fingernails hanging and whoosh, we got away with it, it was fine, fine, until the next time. And each time, every time they skimmed and skimped, even if they did get away with it, something else was lost.

Anna clicked on her electronic diary. She was down for Subdivisional Tasking at nine, and a meeting with Community Policing at eleven. She could squeeze a quick visit to The Meadows in between. It would simply be a courtesy call, no criticism of Johnny's professionalism implicit at all.

The Tasking meeting dragged on and on, Johnny keen to offload as much crap on to her as he could. But she couldn't stay pissed off with him; he did it with such broguish aplomb. Although he'd still not explained why he'd omitted to tell her about Claire's Saturday Saturation extravaganza—or given her the full story regarding Heraghty.

'Sure, only if you think you can manage that too, Anna,' he smiled, at some final, detailed request. 'I know you've a lot on at the moment, particularly with your mum and all. But we're just glad to see you back. Place hasn't been the same without you.'

Was that a wink? A twinkle at the very least. The sinew on his forearm undulating as he gathered up his papers. Johnny was in operational gear that morning, some recce visit he was doing later at Hampden football ground. Few senior officers suited the crude black nylon T-shirt sculpting over their middle-aged, status-filled bellies. But Johnny was surely of the Black Irish, long-boned and lean. He asked her to wait behind

154

as the rest of them were leaving.

'So. How are things? Really?'

'Good, thanks. My mum's out her coma now, they're giving her therapy. It's going to be fine.'

'Good stuff, good stuff.'

Sometimes, in the temptation to stay happy and whole, Anna chose not to dip behind the scenes, seeing or hearing only that which was sufficient to maintain a façade; of being popular, being right, in control; whatever. But then it would start to gnaw, this need to *know* and seek the truth, even if it might hurt. Deep breath, and out with it.

'Johnny. I need to ask you about a couple of things.'

'Fire away.'

'First off: what's the script with Cassandra Maguire? Why did nobody tell me she'd been found?'

'Because it was late last night and you were flying back from Spain?'

'You could've left a message.'

'And why, Anna, would I do that? I knew you were back in today, I knew you were fretting about your mum. And, quite frankly, I knew I could handle it—all on my own, as well.'

'I didn't mean it like that, it's just that . . . well, I'd like to have known, that's all.'

'Well, now you do.' She saw him check his watch. She was *meant* to see him check his watch.

'And what about Councillor Heraghty? I'm still not clear on what went wrong there. I thought it was my job to liaise with my councillors.'

He nodded, thoughtful. 'Well, I'm glad you mentioned that Anna, because we do need to have a wee word there. Actually, Mrs H has requested

155

the pleasure of your company regarding same.'

'Why?'

'Like I said before, she's been having a lot of trouble with that man, Anna. He's a shit-stirrer, bad-mouthing this division every opportunity he gets. Personally, I thought his behaviour was bang out of order.'

'I didn't think he was that bad—'

'Anyhoo, why don't you give Mrs H a ring? She just wants a chat, check everything's good with you.'

That didn't sound like Mrs Hamilton.

Johnny opened his desk drawer. 'Here, I know you're just back and that, and I don't know how you're placed, but . . . um—do you like curry at all?'

Curry? She was a cop. It was what they ate for breakfast.

'I do. Why?'

'Well, I've been given two tickets for the opening of some new curry house up in Mearns.' He handed her an envelope. 'Gala buffet, local celebs—d'you fancy it?'

The invitation read: *Coriander. A new experience in fine Asian dining.*

'You realise that'll mean wee dinky portions on big white plates, don't you?'

'Ach well,' said Johnny, 'we can go for chips after. If you fancy it, that is? It's this Friday.'

'Sure. Why not?' She passed the envelope back to him, her self-esteem unfurling a few notches. Perhaps she had misjudged him, misjudged it all. Perhaps she was entering a new five-year cycle of boom instead of bust? Then she thought of her mum and her poor withered hands, and felt a little

156

sick.

'Hey, I thought it might cheer you up.'

'No, it will, it does. Sorry. I've just got a lot on my mind. And, that was the other thing I wanted to ask you about. This Saturday Saturation gig?'

'Yes?'

'It's just, well, I thought that was the sort of initiative we'd work on together. And you hadn't mentioned anything about it before.'

'You mean before your mammy took ill?'

'Yeah. It would have been really helpful to have had sight of the proposal, for that meeting I was scheduled to go to.'

Johnny leaned back in his chair, T-shirt moving with the muscles underneath. 'I never mentioned it because Mrs H hadn't agreed we were doing it yet.'

'But Claire Rodgers presented it to me as a fait accompli.'

'Well, Claire Rodgers had got a bit ahead of herself then. Of course I would have discussed it with you, Anna. You're my number two, aren't you? But, I'll tell you, that girl can be way off the mark sometimes. Speaking of which: Fraser Harris?'

Heat flushed Anna's cheekbones. She could feel the skin tauten, waving little red flags of complicity and blame. 'Johnny. I'm really sorry about that—'

'Ach, away. Sure, you've got nothing to be sorry for, Anna. If Claire Rodgers had got her arse in gear a bit quicker, then the poor boy might not be nursing a sore face at all.'

'I'm sorry?'

'Fraser. D'you not know the full story? He went to remonstrate with some boy racers outside his house, and got a black eye for his troubles. Of

157

course, *then* it turns out they weren't boy racers at all, but part of an ongoing attempt to intimidate him. But no bugger had told me that, had they? I only sussed it out when bloody Claire Rodgers came to see me, all snot and apologies that she hadn't passed your message on sooner.'

Anna stared at Johnny's mouth, with all that jumble pouring out of it, like bubble words in a comic.

'Anna, don't look like that. It's not your fault. I totally understand you had to rush and get to the hospital. Fraser's grand. He's been back at work already—he's coming in to see you tomorrow, yeah? And Claire's learned her lesson, so it's all cool.' Johnny stood up. 'You know, we should only have to say things once to sergeants and inspectors; it's not our job to be their mammies. Oh . . .' He sucked in his bottom lip. 'Sure, I'm sorry. That was crass. Look, I'll need to shoot. Anyway, the report on Fraser's all there on your desk.' He patted her shoulder as he passed. 'You take it easy. You're looking right pale.'

Claire wasn't back until next week, but this couldn't wait. Anna still had her mobile number. She started dialling it before she'd even got back to her office, power-walking past people saying 'Hi, ma'am' and 'How are things?' Tough shit if Claire was careering downhill on a bobsleigh. She'd have her phone on anyway, of course she would—she was one of those women who were perpetually primed and ready to go. Just add boiling water . . .

'Claire? Anna Cameron here.' Shutting her office door, rummaging through her in-tray, to find the damn report.

'Oh, hi, ma'am. Is that you back?'

158

'Yes.'

'Get your plane ticket alright? I had a right bother getting—'

'Claire. What's this crap about you not getting the message regarding Fraser to Mr O'Hare? After everything I told you, you—' Anna had found the report, was reading it as she ranted. Was reading it again, trying to make sense of the dates. Looking at her calendar, and back at the page. Time was slipping uncontrollably at the moment, was lapping itself in horrible, relentless waves, but she knew she was not mad. The report said Fraser was assaulted on Thursday, the night Anna had flown to Spain. But it was the Friday morning that she'd spoken to Claire.

'Claire. What's going on?'

Anna could hear the giggles of kids in the background, the clatter of cutlery. Claire not speaking.

'*Claire*. Why does Mr O'Hare think you forgot to pass on my message?'

'Because I told him you gave me it the day your mum took ill. The Thursday, not the Friday.'

'And why the hell would you say that?'

She sniffed, gave a little sneeze. 'Oops, sorry. Got a bit of croissant stuck there.'

'Claire?'

A sigh. 'Just before I went to see Mr O'Hare, after we spoke, I mean, I saw Fraser had signed off sick. I did a bit of digging and found out there'd been an incident at his house already.'

'But why didn't you tell me that when I phoned again? And why did you not just tell O'Hare the truth?'

'I got the feeling . . . look, have you spoken to

159

Mrs H yet?'

'No. Why?'

'It doesn't matter. I just thought you had enough to be dealing with, that's all.'

Anna paused for a moment, absorbing Claire's statement. Soaking in under her skin, round the back of her yellowed guts.

'You mean—you felt sorry for me?'

'Anna, I really admire you. I think you're a great boss. You don't take any crap, but you don't talk it either. It was a spur-of-the-moment thing—I knew Hamilton would crucify you, but she seems to *like* me at the moment, for some weird reason . . . so . . . well, I blubbed some rubbish about one of my kids being sick, and how sorry I was, took the bollocking, and that was it really.'

'Claire. I don't know what to say . . .'

'You don't have to say anything. It was my decision, you didn't ask me to do it, and if you say anything now, then we'll both be in the shit. At the end of the day, Fraser's fine, we've got an action plan in place—plus he thinks he could maybe ID one of the neds responsible—if we ever track them down.'

'But, even so . . . Claire, I've been a horrible cow to you.'

'Yeah, but you're a horrible cow to everyone, Anna. That's what I like about you. There's no side to you—not like Hamilton. One day you're in her "groovy gang", next she's bad-mouthing you to your shift. I hate women like that—they're just bitches, and the job's getting full of them. It seems to me the more women we get up the ranks, the more bullies we're getting too. And you're not a bully, Anna. You're tough, but you're fair.'

Whipping air round her face, like someone had thumped her, hard.

'Shit. All I can say is . . . thanks.'

'Och, thanks, shmanks. At the end of the day, I was acting in my own self-interest. I'd like to keep you as my boss. I mean, I've got to have *some* decent role models to learn from, if I'm going to be Chief Constable in ten years. Hey, got to go. The minibus leaves in five, and there's a black run with my name on it looming.'

Anna put the phone down, placed the report about Fraser directly in front of her. Tried to focus on the words on the page, not those zooming inside her head. Effectively, she was guilty of dereliction of duty, yet Claire had taken the blame. Would Anna have done that? Or would she have put the boot in so firmly that Claire would now be counting traffic cones in Gourock? For all Anna had been intrigued by the notion of a female divisional commander, she had never cleaved to a sense of 'sisterhood' in the job. You got where you got on your own merit.

Anna reread the first paragraph. Fraser had come out of his house about nine in the evening, to put the bins out. Had noticed a black Nissan Primera parked across his driveway. He'd asked the occupants to move, knowing that his wife would be coming home from her mother's. In his statement, he said he'd been perfectly reasonable, explaining politely that she'd need access to the drive. Both male occupants had then jumped from the car, the driver actually slamming his door into Fraser's groin and stomach as he'd exited the vehicle. While Fraser was winded, his assailants had struck him several times about the head and body, before the men returned to the car and made off north towards the main road. As he hit him, the male who Fraser believed to be the passenger had said: 'Take a fucking telling, pig.'

'At no time,' Fraser stated in the report, 'did I identify myself as a police officer.'

It was not Fraser who had called the police, but a neighbour who came across him lying on the pavement. By the sound of it, they must have knocked him unconscious. The males were described as late teens, one sallow-skinned, possibly Mediterranean, one—the passenger—white, with peroxide blond hair. Both spoke with pronounced Glaswegian accents. The darker male was approximately five foot six or seven inches, while his companion was well over six feet. An odd couple, yet none of the neighbours, not even the man who found him, had seen a thing. *Following a hospital check-up*, the notes said, *it was noted that Constable Harris had sustained a broken tooth, facial abrasions and bruising to his abdomen.*

She closed the folder, raging. At herself, as much as these shitty neds who'd given one of her cops a doing in his own front drive. She tried to get on with the rest of her work, but kept returning to pictures of Fraser lying on the deck, and then of Claire, being martyred on her ski poles. Criss-cross in the snow, St Andrew in salopettes.

That Claire *liked* her, was loyal to her, astonished Anna. That she felt secure enough to say so made Anna numb. All through her service, Anna had squared up, dressed down, kept things tight. She might bluster and shag her way through the job, but it was never done in a specifically *female* way. Not intentionally. There were always

162

potential prejudices lurking, of course there were, but it was up to you how you dealt with them. You could either back away at the merest hint of discrimination, or charge straight through—and run the risk of bursting your nose as you crashed against a brick wall.

If you did charge, though, and it worked, you were vindicated. *Tough.* And it felt so good. But then you'd do it again, and again, until you were in danger of becoming more macho than the men you tried to match. Anna had seen it happen, knew she had atrophied that little bit too. Stopping up the milk of human kindness, so scared you might be perceived as weak that you would overcompensate, grow more antagonistic, more quick to confront than the worst of the men you worked with. Margaret Thatcher syndrome. No, it was Mrs Hamilton syndrome. Something that probably originated as a defence mechanism for Marion Hamilton had turned into a ruthless drive for power at all costs. And an inability to show any hint of being female at all.

Claire, on the other hand, had it sussed. She seemed to have found a third way, neither overaggressive, nor meek and ineffectual. Like Jenny Heath, or young Arlene Winetrobe, even. The uniform might be one size fits all, but the women Anna had worked with were just as diverse as the men. Some with nurturing qualities, some who worked instinctively, methodically. Some were cerebral, while others could knock down an angry man at ten paces. And some, like Hamilton, were out-of-their-depth bullies, trying to prove a point their younger colleagues had already made.

Claire admired Anna. So Anna had to be doing

something right. Cheered by this new dynamic, she decided she *would* visit Macklin at The Meadows, actually call in in person. Because Anna was tough, but fair. With an extra serving of compassion. And she'd buy another Easter egg on the way.

'Joe,' she called to the bar officer as she was leaving, 'I'm just nipping out. If anyone's looking for me, I'll be back by eleven, okay?'

'Right ma'am.' He smiled. 'Secret mission, is it?'

'Eh, no?'

What kind of a smile was that? A pseudo-knowing one? Is that what they thought of her in here, that she was aye rushing off to get her hole or something?

'Joe, this is a business call. Were you implying something else?'

'Jeez, no ma'am. No, not at all. I was just . . . it was just banter . . . I—'

'Aye, well you'll be bantering your arse straight into a free transfer to Arran if you keep that up, pal.'

She let the back door slam shut. Took a full, sore breath, and thought about crouching on her hunkers with her head buried in her armpit. Of course poor Joe had been joking. That face of mortification was all for her, not him.

You've let down your bar officer, you've let down your station—but most of all, you've let down yourself. Insert 'school', 'family', 'cat', 'mother' at the appropriate juncture, and there you had it— the story of Anna's life.

She drove slowly up to the Mearns, trying to remember the yoga breathing Elaine had taught her. You'd to pick a soothing mantra, but all Anna could come up with was 'bollocks'. Still, repeated

164

slow and sure on the out-breath, it engendered a curious calm, which lasted all the way to The Meadows. The face regarding her in the driver's mirror was only slightly mottled. She collected herself, pushing her hair from her brow. Automatically thinking of Macklin, and his similar habit.

Gusts of wind fretted as she crossed the empty car park. The door, this time, was locked. They should have made it into a stable door, in keeping with the rustic theme. Keep the bottom locked and the top open for visitors to shout into. None of the oldies could have vaulted that. She buzzed the intercom. 'Anna Cameron for Mr Macklin.'

Macklin was waiting in the hallway, his face slightly flushed, and she realised he was pleased to see her. The thought reared, confusing her.

'Chief Inspector. You got my message then?'

It was a bitter day, the heating on full blast, fermenting unpleasant air. The kiss of almost-death.

'What message?'

'I left a message, asking you to speak to me. Urgently. Is that not why you're here?'

'No. But I take it it's about Mrs Maguire? I came to finalise a few issues about her anyway.'

'You did?' His voice lifted. 'Like what?'

Was that a wee tweak of panic there?

'Why don't you tell me what you wanted to see me about first?'

Deeper splashes of colour in his cheeks. 'I . . . look, I want you to know, I'm not trying to make a complaint or anything.'

You're not making a complaint! Bloody right you're not. You'll be lucky to come out of this whole

165

thing without losing your licence. Or permit, or whatever it is you need to run a nursing home.

'Do go on.'

Cruikshanks was right. She'd slipped to icy-polite, just like Mrs Hamilton.

'The thing is . . . I'm not sure you've got the right person.'

'Pardon?'

'The lady, the one your guys recovered down south. Well, I'm pretty sure it's not Cassie.'

Anna didn't close her eyes. She didn't let the small, brief 'ohforgodsake' whimper from behind her bitten lips; didn't even scowl, as far as she was aware.

Because Anna was tough, but fair.

People did it, she'd seen this before. They blocked out the possibility that the bad stuff could pass. And it was usually cases like this, where there was no violence, just a void. It was the not-knowing, it went far deeper than simple death. Just you and the empty space, and your head fighting the mind-whirling that would wake you, fighting the visceral twist of your fears, and you, not able to stop it. With all *that* gnawing, some folk could only hold themselves numb.

So when the truth came, you couldn't accept that either.

Anna sat on the edge of the hall table. 'Mr Macklin, I promise you—we've found her. It's fine.'

'It's not, it's really not. Look, I went up last night, to see the Maguires. I wanted to . . . apologise, I suppose.'

'*Wow.* Bearding Sheena in her den—that was brave.'

166

Macklin half smiled. 'I took her up some flowers. Freesias.'

Anna's favourites. All the live, light colours of the rainbow. They didn't overpower like lilies, or sit petulant like carnations. As she was thinking it, Macklin's face seemed softer, his jaw less tense. For twenty years, Anna had seen the calluses and carbuncles that crept round police officers; bright, decent folk who started out with kindness in their hearts. Perhaps it was true of doctors too.

'That was nice. Did it calm her down?'

'Actually they were both very quiet. Quite nervy, in fact. But the point is—'

Anna stood up again. This could go on all night. 'Look, I maybe shouldn't say this, but we haven't interviewed Cassie yet. If I were you, I wouldn't be admitting to anything yet. Let's just wait until—'

'*No.* I really don't care about all that liability nonsense.' He was coming towards her, palms up. Automatically, Anna repositioned herself, so she was facing him, square. Ready for . . . what, exactly?

'The point is, when I was at the Maguires', I saw a fax. It must have come from the English police. It was a photo of an old woman. And, I promise you—that woman was *not* Cassie.'

Macklin was standing over her; she could feel the warmth of his breath, his words unravelling in fluid air. Words that made no sense.

'You have to believe me.' Mouth up close, enunciating every syllable. 'The woman you think you've recovered is *not* Cassandra Maguire.'

CHAPTER NINE

The office was Baltic. Johnny was a fresh-air freak, had all the windows in his office wide, blinds rustling like long grass behind Anna's head. The wind had been bullying clouds and brollies all day; it was something to be shut outside, not invited in like a colleague. Side-on to the gasps and whistles of the corner window, Johnny's hair rose and sighed as he spoke.

'Sure, woman, do you not have any proper work to do?'

'But the doctor says it isn't her,' Anna argued.

'And the *daughter* says it is.'

'Daughter-in-law.'

'Whatever.' Johnny ran his pen down the last page of the report. 'Look; not only did the cops ID her, but the family did too. Says here the son spoke to her on the phone, so did his wife. Both happy she's safe and well, no further action required. See, quite clear: *N*,' each letter highlighted with a rap of his biro, '*F, A*. So,' he shut the file, 'if the family is happy, if the investigating officers are happy, if the fecking missing person herself is happy, then why, oh why, oh why, do we need to take another look?'

Anna pulled the file back across the desk towards her, opened it again. 'Yes, but, like I said, her doctor isn't.'

'This the same doctor you were convinced was running an unsanitary granny farm last week?'

'He's alright actually. And he's adamant we've got the wrong woman.'

'We haven't "got" anyone, Anna. This isn't an

arrest, no one's done anything wrong.'

'You know what I mean.'

'So who the hell is the old biddy in Liverpool then?'

'*I* don't know, do I?'

Johnny eased back in his chair, hands behind his neck. 'Tell me again why Dr Evil is so convinced?'

'Well, he said it was just a feeling at first.'

'A *feeling*. Sure, that's very scientific for a medical man. Then did a wee magic voice, a wise old gnome perhaps—'

'Would you let me finish?'

'Ah, you're a hard woman, Anna Cameron. Go on, shout at me again.'

She ignored him. 'Look, initially the daughter-in-law was going crazy at The Meadows staff, while the son was a waste of space. Greeting all over the shop and blaming the wife for putting his "old mammy" in there in the first place. Nearly had a stand-up fight, the pair of them, I saw it myself. Anyway, all that day, and right through the next, they were frantic, Macklin says. Never left the nursing home, panicked phoning to everyone they knew, much gnashing of teeth—you get the picture.'

' 'Tis a lovely one that you paint.'

'Thank you. I *am* very artistic you know. You should see my eggs.'

Did his shapely jaw not drop?

'I beg your pardon?'

'Doesn't matter. Anyway, end of day two, after there was still no trace, Macklin finally got the family to go home for a rest. He said he expected them to come back, all guns blazing. But only Sheena arrived, around mid-morning, and she was

169

very subdued. Saying she was sure the old woman would turn up soon, and that they didn't want to waste everyone's time.'

'Delayed shock,' nodded Johnny.

'Maybe. But I checked our missing person entries for Saturday, and Ronnie did the same thing here. See.' She slid the book over to him again. 'Arrived at the front desk, asked to speak to the officer in charge—'

'That would have been me.'

'Well, duh. But did he speak to you?'

Johnny screwed up his eyes. 'To be honest, I can't remember. Nah, I don't think so. I was flitting in and out a fair bit, covering the on-call, plus I was trying to arrange a media appeal—'

'Which got cancelled.'

'Sure. Because they found her the next day.'

'Yesterday.'

'Aye, yesterday. And . . . here we are again.' He folded his arms. 'Just gone round in a nice big circle.'

The clock behind him was stuck on ten past six. Every time he looked at it, Johnny could congratulate himself. He was either in early, or working late, a fine, satisfying way to spend each of his days. Anna had had to cancel her eleven o'clock meeting after Macklin's revelation, and she still had to catch up with Divisional Intelligence too. They were one hour ahead in Spain; her mum would be having lunch. She'd need to phone the ward soon; one of the golf or bridge club ladies should be in for visiting, could maybe give her an update. It would be too difficult to get much from the nursing staff beyond, *Your mother is the same. When can you make arrangements . . . ?'*

170

Anna would also ask if anyone had heard from Teddy. There was no point in trying to keep his absence secret any longer; they'd all have seen it for themselves by now.

'Anna?'

'Oh, sorry. Anyway, yeah . . . look. If you read what the FSO said here,' she carried on, 'the lassie that dealt with Ronnie Maguire, she states he was insisting he wanted no press coverage. And this is the Saturday mind, a full day before Cassie allegedly phones and goes: "Coo-ee. I'm here!" Does that not strike you as a bit odd?'

'Not really. And is that it? The basis of your doctor's hunch?'

'No, of course not. It's what we in the trade call circumstantial evidence. Maybe you don't have that in the Emerald Isle . . .' Anna registered the glimmer at the edge of his mouth. 'When was it you transferred here again?'

'When you were still a wee sprog in nappies, lady.'

A sharp trill of an insistent phone. *Ding, ding. Seconds out.* ' 'Scuse me a minute.' Johnny reached for the receiver. 'Yes? Oh, hi, boss. Yes, yep, no bother. Here she is.' He passed Anna the phone, one palm covering the mouthpiece. 'It's JC. For you.'

'Hello ma'am.'

'Did Superintendent O'Hare tell you I wanted to see you?'

I'm very well, thank you. And how are you? Oh, my mum? Yes, she's still clinging to life. Very kind of you to ask.

'Yes, ma'am. I was just about to—'

'Phone me? Well, I saved you the bother. And

171

I've no got much time, so let's cut to the chase. Councillor Heraghty?'

'Yes?'

'Don't "yes" me. What the fuck did you think you were doing, inviting him in? Were you not at the meeting at which I stated, clearly, stated, that he was persona non grata—'

'In fairness, ma'am, I didn't realise I wasn't permitted to talk to him.'

Johnny's eyes were cartoon-wide, head shaking vigorously. Anna turned her chair slightly away from him.

'Well you do now. In future, you reroute any communications from him via me. Clear?'

'Crystal.'

The instruction was, not the motive. But there was no point in asking why. Like the rampage of the crowd, you couldn't reason, couldn't quell it.

A sniff. Hamilton was probably inhaling essence of Easter Ferret. 'Tell me this. Did Heraghty smell of alcohol?'

'What?'

'Had the man been drinking?'

'No. No, he was perfectly—'

'Was his face red?'

'Well, yes, but he was upset.'

'Hmm—irate, erratic, possibly inebriated—'

'Ma'am, that's not how he appeared to me.'

'Aye, but then you're not the most observant girlie on the block now, are you? Couldny even find a team of murderers when they were waving at you across the street.'

'Now, that's not fair—'

Johnny tugged on her chair so she would look at him. He was leaning over the desk, index finger

172

sawing across his throat. Anna's teeth pressed on her tongue. She was going to start laughing.

'And what about this Fraser Harris debacle?'

An instant dissipation, the bubble of mirth exploding. Leaving an expectant space, as sweat cools and runs. *Inside* her.

'Bad enough you buggering off and leaving us in the lurch all weekend. I don't care what kind of an emergency it was. To arrange no cover, leave no instructions . . . It was your job to pass that information on, *not* Inspector Rodgers'. I have to say, Chief Inspector, I'm no very impressed with your performance to date. Not impressed at all.'

The moment gone. One second it was there, the perfect gap in which to slot the truth, then life had rumbled on. Hamilton talking too fast, Anna's conscience waking too slow.

'Anyway. You're still on call until Thursday, right?'

'Um . . . I just assumed that you'd done a swap . . .'

'That *I* had done a swap? Suffering God. Do you think I'm your bloody nursemaid or something?'

'I didn't mean you personally, ma'am. I meant . . . well, whoever's filling in for me, I could fill in for them when it's their turn.'

'You could, could you? Well, that's very good of you. But now that you're back, you can bloody well finish this turn too. Understand?'

'Yes ma'am.'

'Right. Well, just so you're aware, there'll be a sergeant and four from the Support Unit coming out to do a backshift all this coming week, starting tomorrow. We're going to extend that saturation thing. Been a bloody good initiative—we want to keep the momentum going.'

'Right you are, ma'am.'

Extend it? But Johnny had said they hadn't decided if they were doing it yet. Hadn't he? Hamilton kept talking at her, Anna struggling to keep up. Keep playing the game, the shitty game.

'Aye. I want any trouble hammered down, instantly. So I expect you to make yourself visible too. I want you to do the backshifts yourself. Tomorrow, Wednesday and Thursday. Treat it like you would the weekend on call—attend the musters, get out and about—oh, and you can check the prisoners every night as well. Do you have a problem with that?'

Not unless I had a life outside the job, ma'am, no. This wouldn't be you hammering down on me, *by any chance?*

'No problem. I'll do a patrol of the back lanes myself, shall I?'

'No, there's no need to do that. Just make your presence known on the main streets, particularly where the neds have been gathering. You know, the chippies, the play parks, the off-sales. Focus particularly on Clarkston, Mearns and the Broom shops.'

All the leafy suburbs.

'What about Pollok? Or Barrhead?' said Anna. 'It was pretty wild there the last few weeks. The Barrhead Bowery's been strutting their stuff.'

'Yes, but our two elected members on the Joint Police Board don't bloody live there, do they?' Hamilton coughed into the phone. 'Right, I need to go. Oh, and tell Claire Rodgers that her proposal for that Eastwood thing is excellent.'

'Will do, ma'am.'

'Doesn't quite balance the scales, mind. You can

174

tell her that too, from me.'

Say it, say it, say it, she willed herself once more. But Claire had been right—what good would confession do now: Anna full of belated virtue, and Claire doubly condemned? She'd make it up to her. Give her a cracking appraisal. Anna waited until Hamilton had hung up, then continued speaking into the receiver. 'Pleasure as always.'

'You bollix,' laughed Johnny. 'I know she cut you off.'

'Old hypocrite, so she is. All that Gloriana crap about "I bow to no one", and now I've to do a stint of backshifts and polish the front yards of our local cooncillors too. Heraghty's as well—even though I'm not actually allowed to speak to him.'

'Yeah. I heard she'd been getting her arse felt.' He shuddered. 'What a thought. Aye, but you realise old Heraghty's house wouldn't be getting any extra attention if it wasn't in Newton Mearns too, don't you?'

'Is that because Councillor Nayar lives there as well? What's he like? I haven't met him yet.'

'Mrs Hamilton likes him. That's all you need to know, little girl. Anyway. Back to your dastardly plot.'

'So, right. Where was I? Yeah, when he heard last night that Cassie had been found, Robert Macklin went up to see the Maguires. Took some flowers and that.'

'To avoid being sued.'

'Possibly. But still nice that he went, eh? He could've just sent the flowers.'

And it *was* nice. He could have bade the Mad Maguires farewell from the safety of his phone, posted a curt, clipped letter of contrition with the

175

final bill. Instead, he had trekked to their house himself, stopping to choose flowers on the way.

'So he's a hero now. I get it,' said Johnny.

'The thing is, Macklin was expecting the Maguires to be all jumping for joy, but they were both very quiet. "Edgy" was how he described it. But, but—*this* is the but.'

'Glory be to God and his blessed mother. At last.'

'On the hall table, as he was leaving, Macklin saw a fax. It must've been a copy of the one from Merseyside. You know, the photo the cop took as confirmation?'

'This one?' Johnny took out a flimsy mug-shot of an old dear with dyed black curls.

'Aye. Well. Macklin says it's not her.'

'Ach away. You've seen the other photo, the one we circulated already. You tell me that's not the same woman.'

Anna turned the fax round to face her. Smudged and varying greys of bags and jowls, a Crimplene collar. *Is this it, then?* said the uplift of the woman's fraying mouth. A mournful face, looking back at Anna . . .

It was, and it was not.

Deep-set, skin-draped eyes, their brows tipped slightly in a quizzical acceptance of whatever she saw before her. A birthday cake perhaps, or her newest grandchild, because that's when the cameras came out; for something pretty or a day of import. Not simply to record a spent face.

It was an old lady, and they all looked the same.

'I don't know.' Anna pushed the fax away. 'But, the point is, Macklin swears it's not her. Says Cassie has a cataract on her left eye. And this

176

woman hasn't.'

'How the feck can he tell from that picture?'

'Diagnostic skills? He said her eyes looked a bit funny in real life.'

'Funny? Sure, you can't get more specific than that.'

'Well, according to her *doctor*, Cassie's left eyelid droops a bit too, and this lady's doesn't: that's what he noticed first. That she was staring straight at the camera, both eyes focused straight.'

'And did your man say anything to the family?'

'Nope.'

'For why?'

'Because,' Anna shifted her elbows forward on to Johnny's desk, 'he thinks they might have bumped her off. Okay. That's me done.'

'Aye, you will be too, for wasting my precious time.'

'Och Johnny, c'mon. What would be the harm in me speaking to Cassie's family . . . ?'

'Absolutely not. On what grounds? As far as everyone in creation—apart from you and your man there—is concerned, the old woman is alive and well, living happily in a shell suit in Scouseland.'

'Well, can I at least speak to the cop in Merseyside who took the statement off her? It still hasn't arrived here.'

'If you like.'

'And could we maybe send someone down there?'

'Feck off woman. I'll pay for a phone call, then that's your whack.'

'Oh, you're too kind, *sir.*'

Tingly, sparring air. A thick pause in the midst

177

of it all, a waiting for someone to decide. But he had bestowed one gift on her already; that she could rummage a little further, with his blessing. Was that because he also had concerns about Cassie Maguire, or because Anna had charmed him? Because of the simple fact of her elbows, pressed on his desk? This dinner, on Friday; Anna was not sure what it meant. Should she keep dancing, duck low and fire off another wee joke? Or wait for him to lure her in, then—

'So, how's your mum doing really?'

In the words of Johnny: Feck.

'Ach, alright. She's sitting up, mumbling a bit, that kind of thing. According to her doctors though, she is no longer *urgente*. Thing is, I can't move her back from Spain for three months, but the hospital she's in won't keep her. And I don't really know where to begin with finding out what benefits she's due, or if the NHS will look after her here, or pay for her over there or what. I need some geriatric guru to come to my rescue.' Anna half raised her coffee mug, set it down. 'I mean an expert in old folk—not an expert who's very old.'

'Why not ask your doctor friend then? Keep him from creating new conspiracy theories.'

'Hmm.'

She clicked her pen against her mug. Of course she'd thought about Macklin. But asking him for help would entail a tilt in their professional equilibrium, leave Anna in debt. And, after this morning, she felt uncomfortable already. Something imperceptible had shifted. She was no longer sneering at him. And he was no longer someone Anna thought she had sussed. She took a mouthful of coffee. Och, it would be so good just

178

to take folk at face value. For once, just to switch off that natural default of suspicion and go with the happy flow. That was it, that was their common ground, she and Robert Macklin: conspiracy theories.

'Anna.'

'What?'

'Do *you* think they've harmed her?'

'Who?'

'Your Mrs Maguire. Do *you* think the family are telling porkies?'

Did she now? Did she really, in the soft grey Glasgow light of the real world?

'Hard to say.'

'But Anna. *Matricide?* Really?'

It was a ridiculous word; made you think of a giant mattress, all old with the springs poking out, hoisted aloft, then squished hard and fast on some unsuspecting mother. Arms and legs starfished beneath striped ticking.

'Ach, no. Of course I don't. Ronnie's a big woose, but still . . . That daughter-in-law—she's a torn-faced cow. You didn't meet her, did you?'

'No.'

'Well, I did. Even so, I'd probably disregard the good doctor too, but for the fact that . . . I just got this suspicion, you know? The same kind of niggles, I suppose. When I was in Spain. I kept thinking about *my* mum, and how you just freeze. The anger and the panic comes afterwards, but at first, you . . . well, the thing is, when I saw Sheena Maguire, she wasn't upset at all, just furious—and very keen to apportion blame.'

'Methinks she doth protest too much?'

'I dunno. But Macklin *is* pretty convinced that

that woman there isn't Cassie. And I couldn't settle if I didn't . . . I just want to put it to bed, you know?'

'I do indeed. And I salute you.' He swung his chair round.

'So?' Anna stood. 'Permission granted to tuck it up?'

'What?'

'Tuck it up in bed, I mean. You know, like we were saying . . .'

Johnny had already begun checking his emails. 'Sorry, what?'

'Nothing.' She left to go to her own office.

Even the walls were frowning at her. *Anna, get a grip.* It was like her pheromones were off-kilter. Or was it the peri-menopause? She'd read about that, when your fluctuating, gloom-stalking hormones tricked you with a kind of preview of the real thing; just enough hot-flushed angst and antics to make you dread the next ten years. But *did* she, would she? Should she find Johnny attractive at all? What was worse: shagging your boss or shagging a passing sergeant? Or not shagging anyone at all?

She couldn't believe Hamilton was making her do a run of backshifts.

Anna turned her Airwave set in her hand. Airwave was your personal radio and a mobile phone combined. Very nifty. She had preset channels for all the Scottish forces, but not for down south. Probably the best thing to do was email Merseyside, and get the Liverpool cop to phone her. She reread the fax. PC Auden was his name, and there was an email for both his Force HQ and his Divisional Office, St Helen's. Protocol probably dictated she should go via Force HQ, but

180

protocol meant another layer of bureaucracy and time. So she emailed St Helen's direct, asking that the cop get in touch with her, ASAP. Not quite a blue-light emergency.

Despite her goading of Johnny, Anna didn't really know what she thought. She had been utterly relieved when she'd seen that global message, had no desire to create more clouds where the dust had settled. And she truly doubted that Ronnie Maguire could have been so abjectly, man-like-a-headless-chicken distraught at Cassandra's disappearance if he'd harmed her himself. What would his motive have been anyway? Not that you always got one. He was clearly a well-off man in his own right; inheriting Cassie's collection of cardigans and Mint Imperials was hardly likely to augment his coffers much. And he genuinely seemed to dote on his mother. But Sheena? Ah, Sheena. *We don't like Sheena.* All she exuded was bile.

All this speculation was immaterial, anyway, until Cassie was properly identified. Anna fired off her email to Merseyside, tagging it high priority, then set to compose a tasking report. She wanted it to be good. Sharp, focused, eloquent, and bound to be disregarded by Mrs H. The last of Claire's chocolate egg—which she hadn't replaced—lay crumbled in bite-sized chunks. She scooped them up into her mouth. With perfect timing, her digital unit rang.

'Hmmw?'

'Hello there. PC Auden looking for . . . Annie?'

'An*na*. Shorry, got my mouth full here.'

'*Aye aye.*'

She gulped. 'Cheers for getting back so fast.'

181

'No probs. What can I do you for?'

'I wanted to talk to you about a missing person enquiry you dealt with for us. Cassandra Maguire?'

'The old girl? Yeah, what about her? Scarpered again?'

'I'm looking for the statement you took from her—still not arrived, I'm afraid.'

'Ah, well, you see, that would be because I've not got it yet.'

'Pardon?'

'Nah, well, the old love was a bit shaken up after all that travelling, so we agreed I'd come back today. But it seems she's gone off on her holidays now.'

'How do you mean?'

'Well, that's what her sister-in-law told me.'

'Was it not her sister she was staying with?'

'Whatever.'

'Where did she say Cassie had gone?'

'Dunno.'

'Did you ask?'

'Now look, love, I dunno how it is with you Jocks, but down here, we don't have time to—'

'Ho. I don't know how it is with you *Scousers*, but here in Scotland, we address chief inspectors as ma'am, not love.'

There was a brief silence. A sorry swallow, that fair warmed the cockles of her heart.

'Em. I didn't realise. It just said to phone Anna, ma'am. I'm ever so—'

'Useless? Right. I want you to go back there, find out exactly where Cassie is and when she'll be back. Don't let on there's anything amiss; just say you need to get the paperwork finished or something.'

182

'But *is* there anything amiss, ma'am?'

'Nah, I'm just bored up here. Thought I'd noise you up, PC Auden.'

'Noise me up . . ?'

'Yes, I do think there might be "something amiss" actually. In fact, I'm not even convinced we've found the right woman at all, but I'll not know that until we've spoken to her. So, chop chop, PC Auden. There's a good laddie.'

'This isn't a wind-up, is it?' The boy had slipped to sounding barely out of his teens.

'Can you hear me laughing?'

'No, ma'am.'

'Well, there's your answer then. And find out exactly when Cassie's back, will you? I think I might pop down and have a wee blether with her myself. Come and kick your arse in person too, eh Auden?'

'Eh . . . right ma'am. I'll get straight on it.'

'Cheery now.'

Och, these ISSI numbers were fab: no faffing about going through sergeants and inspectors. Straight to hassling cops direct. Anna: Queen of All the Polis. Maybe she could phone wee Rutger in the UN too, and direct operations in Darfur, or wherever they were this month. She rolled the smooth black plastic of the Airwave set in her hand. Her two years would just about be up, if she had got that UN job. Two years as a chief inspector, coming home to possibly a super's job. Two years during which she would have been out of the country and far away from.

From.

No. No matter what had happened, with Jamie, and David, and that dark, serrated pain that caught

183

like hangnails, Anna regretted nothing. Without her, Jamie Worth would be a prisoner, and he wasn't, not any more. His conviction had been overturned, his freedom reinstated, his wife, his kids: Anna had given him all that. She had given him back his life.

She let the Airwave drop on to the desk, wrapped her arms around her shoulders. She wanted to be held. Not as a groping prelude to sex, but the kind of all-encompassing hug you could sink into, breathe deep into someone's hair. A hug that held you upright, even after it was done; that you could come back to again and again and again.

The ostrich clock beside her gave a tentative ping. When she'd chosen all the gubbins to go inside, the man in the clock shop—a burnished, ticking time warp of knotted-wood panels—had tried to sell her a brass-and-bells confection that chimed 'London's Burning' on the quarter-hour. Too rude, too maddening. A single, hourly ting was ample—and polite. Two p.m. If she phoned the ward now, she might yet catch one of her mum's daily visitors. They ate their lunch late there.

There were no call bars on a chief inspector's phone, not even for international calls. Although, when JC caught sight of the next bill there soon would be. Click, burr, *y hola España*. Just as easy as calling Edinburgh. Only not quite. At first she got someone who spoke no English, then someone who spoke in fragments.

'*Mi madre*. Caroline Steed?'

'*Sí, sí.*'

'She is well?'

'*Sí, está bien.*'

'Is there anyone with her?'

184

'*¿Qué?*'

'Can I speak to her friend please? *Amigo*? With
. . . em . . . *con* Caroline?'

'*Ah, sí, su amiga, vale.*'

A clatter and an empty echo. Shuffle, shuffle,
quavery Brit.

'Yes?'

'Hello. Who's that?'

'Who is this, please?'

'It's Anna. Caroline's daughter.'

'Oh, Anna dear. It's Joan. How are you, dear?
Are you bearing up?'

'Oh, I'm fine, fine. How's Mum?'

'Just the same, dear. They had her at some
therapist this morning. Gave her a ball to squeeze.
Big red thing, like a tennis ball. She's got it with
her now. Poor love's a bit tired though.'

'Can she say any words yet?'

'Not really. You get to know what she means
after a while, but it's all a bit . . . well, she gets
herself flustered, you know?'

'Any walking?'

'No, dear. No.'

Joan waited while they both digested this.

'What about Teddy? He reared his ugly head at
all?'

'Swine's not been near her, love. Just as well, I
say. Or I'd swing for him myself.'

'Do you know where he actually is, Joan?'

She sniffed. 'Well, I have my suspicions, but it's
not for me to say.'

'Please. I need to know . . . stuff.' Anna
improvised rapidly. Vaguely. 'If they had any more
health insurance . . .'

'Oh, well, it's hardly a secret here anyway.' A

185

wheezed reluctance. 'You'll have to find out sometime. He's staying with Myra Todd.'

'Who?'

'Rich divorcee with a face like the Blackpool tram tracks.'

It was nothing less than she'd expected. But the confirmation felt like a door slamming.

'Is this a new development, or was he seeing her before?'

'Before?'

'Before my mum took ill.'

'Darling, that's probably *why* your mum took ill. Poor love was at her wits' end. Terrible it was. Absolutely terrible.'

'What was terrible?'

Cold, lithe fingers at the nub of her neck, seep, seep, seep along her shoulder blades like wings.

'All that fighting. Shouting and swearing, night after night. Him driving off, her sobbing in the street. I even ended up taking her in one night myself. Shaking, she was. But then he'd come back, and it would all be quiet for a day or two. That last night though . . .'

Anna had thought, she had sensed, and had compressed it like compost. The noxious product of her midden-raking mind. Trusting all the low opinions about her, yet not trusting her own. But that first, base instinct was always the purest. It was not the devil talking.

It was Anna being right.

'Go on.' Though she didn't want to hear this.

'I really didn't want to burden you with all this. Your poor mum would be mortified if she thought I was telling you.'

'Please.'

Joan took one hard gasp, then launched her slings and arrows. 'At first it was the usual; shouting, then crying. Slamming doors; you know, you forget in hot countries that everyone has their windows open. And these places are built right flimsy. Anyway, I could hear this awful banging and thumping. Your mum was yelling *No Teddy. Please don't*—all sorts like that. I couldn't hear him say anything, just all these clatters like the house was falling down. Then I heard her screaming. Awful it was, same words again and again.'

'What was she saying?'

'*Please don't leave me.* That's what she kept screaming, four, five times, then it all went quiet.'

Anna closed her eyes. 'And what did you do?'

'Well, I went round of course—I'm not scared of him. But he'd already left.'

'What time was that?'

'Oh, I'm not sure. Ten, ten thirty perhaps? Made her a cup of tea, straightened the place up a bit. You know, I tried to get her to come back to mine, but she wanted to wait. In case the bastard came home.' Joan's voice dropped. 'Oh, I wish I'd just made her come back with me now, I really do.'

'Joan. Do you think Teddy hit her? Was that what you heard?' Her own voice came back at her, a sharp echo down the line.

'No! I honestly don't think so. Caroline was upset, yes, but she didn't have a mark on her . . . There's absolutely no way I would have left her on her own if I'd've thought that. No, Teddy threw some stuff about maybe, but he never hurt your mum.' A dry, distant laugh. 'Not physically, I mean. But I've no doubt that fight must have led to her . . . oh, Anna dear. I'm so, so sorry I didn't do

187

more.'

Anna's Airwave phone began to ring. Fingers slippy as she picked it up. A number she'd only recently keyed. Auden again. *Shit.* Good. *Shit.*

'Look Joan, I need to go. Will you give my mum ...'

What? Flowers, a kiss? An injunction against Teddy? A pot of yoghurt?

'Will you just say to her I phoned? But don't tell her what we've been talking about. I don't want her getting upset. Okay? Bye.'

She snatched the still-shrilling phone up to her ear. 'Hello?'

'Chief Inspector. Just about to give you up for dead. PC Auden here. Look, I popped round like you asked, but the place was all locked up. Seems the sister's gone too now. Curtains drawn, mail on the mat. Asked the lady next door where they were, but she didn't know.'

'Shit.'

Think Anna, think. Expand your vocabulary at least. But her brain was sliding small and withered in her skull, all her energies still conversing with Spain. Stinking fat old bastard whom she'd always hated. Great blocks of anger thrumming, smashing flat and pure like bone on unforgiving tile.

'I know,' said Auden, somewhere in the distance. Talking about someone else's mum. She tried to fix on his words, ignore the bright, sharp taste in her mouth.

'Sorry?'

'Dead duck, so it is. What about your end, ma'am? Anyone you can talk to there?'

Anna would have to speak to the family immediately. If everything they'd said was the truth, then the Maguires would know exactly where Cassie was. And if it wasn't, then the urgency of Anna's visit would be even greater.

'Look, I don't know if this is any help or not,' said Auden, 'but, the night we found old Cassie here, we took her down the station so's we could take her picture. For the ID, you know. We'd have done it in the house, save the old soul the trouble, but the telly was knocking on for an antique, so I didn't reckon they'd have decent cameras. Well, I remember she'd put on her coat and headscarf— was a bit parky out. Only, she forgot to take her scarf home with her. Left it lying here. I've been meaning to take it back . . .'

'You've still got it?'

'Yeah, it's in my locker.'

'Not exactly pristine storage conditions.'

'I know, I know, but I wasn't thinking of it as a production, not then. Might have some bits of fluff from the back of me locker on it, but it's bound to have some of her hairs too, eh ma'am?'

'Uh huh?'

'I mean, I know it won't be scientific, or evidence or that, but if you can match the old lady greys on it with anything you might have of hers up there—'

'We'll know if it's the same person or not. Clever boy.'

'So, shall I bag it and send it up?'

'Yes please.'

She gave him Giffnock's address as she was rifling through the missing persons file. There was a phone number, somewhere, for the Maguires. If she could get them to come into Giffnock, it would save her a journey and a couple of hours out the

189

office, especially since her entire week's schedule had just been flushed away by Mrs H. And there was always a quality of gentle menace inherent in attending a police office. It sharpened the senses, even if you had done nothing wrong. Barely registering the boy's goodbye, Anna dialled the Maguires' number. It was answered almost immediately.

'Yes?'

'Mrs Maguire, this is Chief Inspector Cameron here—'

'Look, she's back, alright? Can you people no leave us alane?'

'Mrs Maguire, I'm as delighted as you that your mother-in-law has been found; however, there's still some paperwork we need to complete. How are you and your husband placed to come in—'

'Aye, aye. Alright. We'll come doon the night, okay?'

'About five thirty say?'

'Whatever. I've got to go. Gonny no phone me again?'

Nice talking to you too, Mrs Maguire. At least they'd agreed to come to the office; that had to be a good sign. Oh Jesus. She could not get the thought of her mother, terrified and alone, out of her head. The receiver was still in her hand. Anna hung up, blew her nose. Dabbed at her mouth, the hanky blushing at the embarrassment of it all. She'd wondered why she'd been tasting blood, realised it was coming from her lip.

*　　　*　　　*

The guard must give her an injection every day. That

190

is what the Mirror Man said, before he left. The guard lives in an ecstasy of fear that he will return. That the Man will see he is still sharing his food, that he sits with her at night, this Scheherazade who tells him tales, and asks for nothing in return. For how can he administer drugs and water, then walk away?

Far better if he did not have to see her at all, if he could pretend she was not there. But she is, and so is he.

Evil is not a presence, it is an absence. It is a blank and terrible vortex that consumes. He no longer thinks about studying, rarely leaves the room. If he tells someone she is here, the Man will kill him. Of that he is sure. He has lost the ability to think with coherence. God knows he cannot speak; what words would he say to her? She will think that he is mute, or has no English, and that is fine. But he can sit beside her. He can listen.

'Did I tell you about ma dream, Ronnie? I was going up the stair in ma house.'

Her speech, each day, is weaker. Yet conversely, each day, it is more full of words. They tumble and pour in confusion, and he must sieve them sometimes into sense. He sees her shuffling her tethered legs in a parody of walking, and he cannot bear it.

'Aye, no thon big swanky place of yours, son, but ma wee terrace in Brigton. Mind it? Mind thon side window that was too high to clean. It was aye streaky when the sun shone in. Well, I could see it, I was nearly at the top, know?'

Her voice dips. Very faint. 'Aye, that bit where the dapples hit the carpet, where you used to sit when you were wee. Do you remember that Ronnie? You telt me you were catching the sun's fingers.'

191

She has her eyes shut, he does not need to respond.

'Well, I seen ma pal Manju on the windowsill. All cooried up, like she was on a perch, with thon beautiful blue robe of hers, and you were there, and Sheena. Waiting at the top. Aye, Sheena, the bitch. She gies you this fast smile, son, then next thing I know she's shoving me oot, far oot like I'm heaving into space.' She laughs. 'I tried to kick her, you know. But I couldny reach.'

Her feet are tied tight, ankle chafing ankle. There is a noise upstairs.

CHAPTER TEN

The Maguires, despite their promises, failed to appear. By the time Anna had realised, it was almost seven o'clock, and a tight dullness had permeated the spaces behind her eyes and nose, its pressure building. The weight of a hand clamped over her skull, determined to squeeze out the last drop of life. She would go tomorrow, doorstop them when they least expected it, armed with more evidence of hairs and headscarves; she had no idea how long these things took to analyse. Tom Cruikshanks would know: he knew everything.

She must have put the fear of God into PC Auden right enough, because the headscarf arrived next day. But it turned out to be an unnecessary acquisition.

Tuesday night, gone six p.m. Anna, back at the nursing home. She'd gone to see if the staff could scrape up some of Cassie's hairs. Realised it was a mad idea even as she was asking Robert Macklin.

She'd been ushered into his office, surprised, actually, that he was still there. She would have come earlier, but she'd not had a moment to breathe since starting at two. Not even to speak to young Fraser. Mrs Hamilton's idea of on call meant donning your breast-crushing body armour, being het for every problem, query and complaint that merited a senior officer's attention, buzzing about from call to call—so you were 'high profile' and 'visible', but, in reality, simply getting in your cops' way. Best of all, you had the privilege of checking an entire division's worth of smelly, stir-crazed prisoners.

At least it was only a weeknight; Anna could whiz round them pretty quick. Weekends were altogether different. A weekend lie-in did not have the same sleepy resonance in police stations that it had in the outside world. Rather, for those who had the misfortune to be arrested on a Friday, and who were of no fixed abode, or were likely to reoffend, or were serious baddies, or were possessed of an unfortunate face or attitude, it meant they would be kept within the police station until court on Monday. And it was just your Donald Duck if you were stupid enough to get arrested on a bank holiday weekend, because then you'd be in the jail till Tuesday. Which was a beautiful slice of summary justice, but did mean that the cells got packed with the great unwashed.

Still, whatever night of the week it was, the prisoners were as thrilled to see Anna as Anna was them. Being on call was also code for *no social life for you, doll.*

Robert Macklin was turning into yet one more dissatisfied customer.

193

'Hairs? What on earth for? I thought you believed me. Do you think I'm lying, that I make up weird fantasies because my day job's so dull?'

It was hot in Macklin's office; so hot she'd taken off her fleece. Macklin's face was blood-coloured, him standing in the middle of the room, arms tight at his side. Why had she not just phoned? His adrenalin was stretching him taller than she recalled, broader too, his chest without its white coat filling more of the space around him.

'Now look, sir . . .' Her hand up, restraining. Foot forward, body open; it was how you punctured tension. Displaying yourself. Unthreatening. When, in reality, your other hand was hovered over your stick or your spray or, in Anna's case, was itching to give him the finger.

'I know this is all very distressing—'

'Are you for real?' The solid length of him advancing. That flapping fringe, made you want to cut it, or touch it . . . he was grabbing her elbows, holding her. They were, suddenly, lip-high perfect, and she did not want to move.

A tremble and hum, fury as she pushed him back.

'What the *fuck* do you think you are doing? Don't you dare put your hands on me.'

'I'm sorry, I'm sorry. But please, can you not do something? Just go and question the family, anything? Good God, Cassandra is a vulnerable old woman, she's an insulin-dependent diabetic, and you're fannying about—'

Anna burst out laughing, couldn't help it, at the incongruity of his playground swearie-words and his six-foot, coiled-spring stance. At the insanity of wanting to press hard up against him.

194

This was madness. This would not do. Was she *in heat*?

'What? Did I say something funny?' A belligerent, doubtful face.

'No, not at all. You are absolutely right. It is ridiculous.'

She recognised that anger. That was all it was. Macklin twisting with the same frustration Anna felt, every time she thought about Teddy. Even if she hunted Teddy down and lynched him herself, it wouldn't change how her mum was. But it might make *her* feel better.

That was all it was.

It was forgivable.

She would call him sir again and it would all be fine.

'I'd actually asked the Maguires to come in last night . . .'

Swallowing, swallowing, but the feeling was not receding. Oh *God.*

'. . . but they failed to appear. Look, I'm doing a backshift, I need to muster some extra men we've got coming on. But then I'll go up to see the Maguires myself. In person. I promise.'

'That would be superb.'

Macklin took off his glasses, stuffed them in the breast pocket of his shirt. He looked tired. There were red pinch-marks where his glasses had rested. He was a married man.

'I'm really, truly sorry I shook you.'

'You should be really, truly grateful I'm not arresting you right now.'

He looked up. 'Could you?'

Her laugh was curdled, dry.

'No, I mean, really.'

A long, slow silence. Anna's skin, rising in scales. 'Can we get back to Cassie please?'

He bridged his hands, smoothed them down and away from his nose. 'I know you think I'm being daft, and I probably am . . .'

'So you don't really think her family's done her in?'

'Och, I was getting desperate for someone to take me seriously. I suppose I got carried away, I don't know. What I am absolutely positive of is that the woman in the fax isn't her. And,' he looked straight at her, 'I was hoping you would listen to me. Maybe pull some strings?'

Anna could do nothing for her own mum just now. Couldn't force Teddy to return to her bedside, couldn't feed her or make her walk. Imagine if she could, though; imagine if she could tug on thin air and watch her mum move again. Or slice frayed ropes and watch Cassie drop from wherever she'd been concealed. Maybe somewhere, in a balanced universe, if Anna could do that, the energy released would surge into Caroline's limbs.

'Well, I am listening to you, okay? And it sounds like a reasonable suspicion to me. I promise you, we'll take it seriously. Sir.' Added as a full stop, as a line drawn definite and firm.

'Please, it's Robert, not "sir". Rob, actually.'

She held out her hand. 'Anna.'

His palm was smooth and dry. Artist's fingers. She needed to leave. On with the heavy-duty fleece. They had plastic-coated lettering on the back, these fleeces. *Police* in reflective bands. As if the chequered bowler hat and stick-swinging utility belt wasn't confirmation enough. Still, it gave the neds somewhere to aim their spit.

'One more thing.' Her voice sounded tight, or tired. It sounded strange. 'Can you check for me exactly when it was that Sheena Maguire told you to scale things down? You know, on the Saturday? I want to see if it's the same time Ronnie turned up at Giffnock Police Office.'

'I'll get Matron to look it up. We keep a log of every visitor, now . . .' He took his glasses back out of his breast pocket, put them in their case. The man was a fidget, fired with nervous energy for all his professionalism, like cling-film with liquid moving underneath; and always that quiet, muted smile.

'Matron. I mean, her name's Jill. It's daft, isn't it, the way you carry on at work? As if your job title sums it up when all it does is put up a great big barrier—'

'Oh, Mr Macklin,' a nurse came hurrying in. 'Quick. Agnes has taken another wee turn.'

'Excuse me,' said Macklin, following the nurse out, Anna after him, halting when she saw a huddle of residents, a stockinged foot protruding from a twist of Crimplene on the hall floor. Macklin crouching down, one arm gentle beneath the old lady's head.

'It's alright Agnes, alright. I've got you. That's right, you just take it easy.'

All the while he soothed and murmured, he was taking her pulse, easing her sideways into the recovery position, running fine fingers over her to check the strength of porous bones. Surrounded by bunioned feet in carpet slippers and a trellis of canes and walking frames.

'Padma, can you go and get me Agnes's tablets

197

please?' he asked the nurse. 'She was due a dose at bedtime, but I think we can take them now, eh Agnes?'

The old lady coughed, and he squeezed her hand. 'And ask someone else to come and give you a hand to get everyone back to the Day Room, please? Arthur, Mr Bell'—Macklin waved to two of the residents, one stiff-backed and buttoned in a collar and tie, the other smaller, stocky, in a lemon waistcoat and tweeds—'would you mind escorting some of the ladies back through, so we can give Agnes more air?'

'Certainly, Doctor Mac.' The smaller one began to shoo his fellow residents like they were straying sheep. 'C'mon Golden Girls—last yin through gets the pishy seat.'

'Arthur MacGregor, you're a mucky bugger.'

'What's that he said? Are we having something to eat?'

As the spectators shuffled off, Anna stooped down beside doctor and patient.

'Can I do anything?'

'No, it's okay.' He smiled. 'Thanks. Unfortunately Agnes has her wee turns quite a bit, don't you, missus?'

'Aye,' whispered Agnes. She seemed much more comfortable, reaching out to pat Macklin's hand. 'You're a good lad, son.'

'Ach, I keep telling you to stop falling for me, Agnes, but will you listen?'

She chuckled, closed her eyes.

'She'll just sleep for a bit now,' he said to Anna. 'That's the usual pattern—ah Padma, cheers.'

The nurse had returned with Agnes's medication, but Macklin waved it away.

'Let's get the trolley chair and get her off to bed. She can take them later, it won't matter. Just make sure she has them by ten, okay?'

Another nurse arrived with a sit-up stretcher, and they began to hoist Agnes on to it, one on each side. Macklin held her head, while Anna put her arms under the old lady's back.

'Woah, health and safety, Anna,' said Macklin. 'Just leave it to the professionals.'

She stood back, let them get on with it. Though what did he think happened out on the street? If an old dear collapsed and Anna was walking past, she'd hardly leave her lying until the appropriate winching gear came along. And a few days ago, she'd probably have said as much to Macklin. But either he, or she, was mellowing, because she couldn't help thinking how *kind* he looked as he was dabbing and fussing at this fragment in the Crimplene dress. Still talking softly, even though Agnes was pegged out in her chair. One final pull at the hem, so it covered the bumps of stockinged knees. 'That's you, my love.'

He straightened up, brushing carpet threads from his trousers. 'I'll pop in and see you in a wee while.'

The nurses wheeled Agnes away down the hall, Padma's hand on the old lady's shoulder.

First impressions. Anna always set such store by them. Bish, bosh, sorted. Good guy, bad guy. Just like dealing with your in-tray. If you spent all day deliberating each action or equivocating on all the subtleties of what lay between the lines, you'd achieve nothing. She'd always believed that was the essence of that 'cop's instinct'—not some sixth sense at all, just prosaic and practical, oven-ready

199

leadership skills. Make a decision, move on. Yet the older Anna got, the less wise, it would seem, she became. The less sure of anything at all.

'You know, I wish they were like that in my mum's place.'

She hadn't meant to speak aloud. Next she'd be hearing voices.

'Whereabouts is your mum then?'

'Och, nowhere you would know, don't worry. She's in Spain—she's just had a stroke, and they're desperate to get rid of her. But I can't let her fly for three months, and—'

He was looking at Anna the same way he'd looked at Agnes. Creased brow and concerned head-tilt.

'Sorry. I wasn't trying to get a freebie consultation there.'

'No, I—'

'Look, I'll need to head if I'm going to make that muster. Maybe you could just email me the exact time Sheena got here? You've still got my card?'

'Sure, no problem.' He hesitated. 'I mean, if you need to, I mean, if you'd like to talk about your mum—'

'No, no. If you can just send me the details . . .'

'Oh.' He took his specs out again, gave them a little polish with the end of his tie. 'Okay. Well, thanks. You can let me know how you get on.'

'Will do.'

'*Please* don't miss them and hit the wall.'

'The Maguires?'

'Yup. I reckon without her insulin, Cassie's got one more day at most.'

Macklin walked her to the door. Every second

200

stride, Anna could see a clump of spidery-blond fibres bouncing at the corner of her vision, as his arm swung in time with his step.

'Fluff.' She nodded at his elbow.

'Pardon?'

'You've still some fluff on you.'

'That'll be my dog. Her hairs get everywhere. Still,' flicking the hair on to the floor, 'the residents love it when I bring her in.'

'You bring your dog to work?'

'Yeah. Perk of being the boss. Plus it's therapeutic. All that stroking and licking.'

He was opening the door, maybe she hadn't heard him right. Then he laughed. 'Great for morale.'

'Goodnight Mr Macklin.'

'Goodnight, Chief Inspector Cameron.' Up close, he smelled of linen, not death.

Good guy, bad guy?

*   *   *

Fraser Harris was waiting for Anna as she returned to Giffnock. She didn't want to see him, felt like one more tiny push would bring her down.

'Fraser! How are you?'

Please say 'I'm fine'.

'Good, ma'am, I'm good. Inspector Rodgers told me to come and see you today, when I got the chance. Is now a good time?'

Forty minutes before the muster—she had time. And he deserved that small courtesy at least.

'Sure, come on in.'

Fraser was six one, six two, and he wore his stature power-packed, hinting that he could uncoil much, much further, if he wanted to. Probably nondescript in civvies, but the uniform gave him a presence. Solidly confident. Black for concealment, black that didn't show the stains. It made no sense. Doctors wore white, yet they must get as dirty as cops. How were colours ascribed qualities? Red for anger, green for calm. Black for authority. Not that it always worked; a colour could only convey so much. Forced as a probationer to wear a male cop's raincoat because the female ones were too short for her, Anna's very first appraisal had stated that 'Constable Cameron would do well to smarten up her appearance, as it would appear that the uniform wore her.'

She slung her fleece on the back of her chair. 'Sit down, Fraser.'

'Thanks.'

'I just wanted to catch up with you—find out how you're doing. And I think we need to set up a meeting with you, me and the DIO, just so we can—'

'Ach, there's no need ma'am, honest. It was just a couple of neds, trying to wind me up.'

'Even so, Fraser, it's my job to look after you guys—in *and* out of work. You're no use to me lying in a hospital bed.'

'I can look after myself. And I'm not having some wee scrote tell me who I can and can't jail.' Arms and legs folded, and that was the end of that discussion.

'But do you know who they were referring to? When they told you to back off?'

'I've been through all this with the DIO already, ma'am, given him a list of everyone I've dealt with

202

since I came to this division.'

'And? Anyone jump out?'

'Ma'am—the list is pages long. We're talking . . .' He started counting off on his fingers, '. . . four or five housebreakers, a load of breaches and assaults, those kids with the prescriptions, couple of fraudulent credit cards, bit of dodgy money I traced back to the petrol station on Fenwick Road—'

'Notes? Does DCI Cruikshanks know about that?'

Fraser nodded, then took another breath, 'Shoplifters—from the same petrol station . . . cars, cars . . .' He rolled his eyes. 'Actually, I don't know how many cars I've turned—found a couple of machetes in one, drug seizures, some other weird chemical stuff I've sent off for analysis—oh, now that one did go a bit loopy. It was this irate motorist I did for obstruction and an out-of-date tax disc. Of course, I always give their motors a wee once-over too, and I found this unlabelled tub, about the size of an Elastoplast box, with some gritty, grey powder in it. Guy claimed it was for athlete's foot, and that I was harassing him. So I seized his wallet for good measure too!'

'You did what?'

'Well, all that dodgy money flying around. He had a roll of fifties, and the paper felt a bit thin.'

A fixed, thin grin played only round Fraser's mouth.

'What was the guy's name?'

'Em . . . Avalon. Dougie Avalon—but everyone calls him Frankie.'

'So you know him? You've had dealings with this Avalon chap before?'

Pupils dilating, a brief delay in his response. 'Few times. He owns the Tammy Lin pub in Tradeston. You know, that famed reset joint and knocking shop.'

Arms folded once more, quitting while he was ahead.

She wrote *Tammy Lin* beside Avalon's name. Wondered what Fraser's previous involvement with Frankie-boy was. Couldn't get the Roxy Music song out her head now either. Or the curve of pale skin, the lazy black hair.

'Anybody else of note?'

'No really.'

'What about before you came here?'

He puffed out his cheeks. 'Oh, now you're asking.'

Anna got the feeling he was quite enjoying this. Not her concern for his welfare, but this proud cataloguing of his achievements, stacking them high like tins in a supermarket.

'I broke up a dog-fighting ring in Greenock—that was quite big; it stretched nationwide—down to England too.'

'Names?'

'Havny a scooby, ma'am—I'd need to check.'

He was right. It was some list. Anna clicked her pen. 'That all you can think of, then?'

'No.' He sounded slightly aggrieved. 'Eh . . . I had a run-in with a nightclub owner a while back. Jazz Chaddha. Big-time ned.'

'I've not heard of him before,' said Anna. 'Is he local?'

'Govan. Big fuck-off mansion near Ibrox. Drives a Merc with the reggie Jazz 1. Keeps a low profile in terms of the hands-on stuff, mind. Calls himself

204

a "businessman" now.'

'So what's Chaddha's history?'

'He was a total skull when he was younger—key player in one of the biggest gangs in Pollokshields. The Support Unit were frequent visitors to their wee soirées. Bastard's given me a sore face more than once, that's for sure.' He blushed. 'Sorry ma'am.'

'But he's not active now?'

'Would appear not. Apparently he's been rehabilitated. He says he's a property dealer, mostly pubs and clubs. Anyway, I stopped his car a month ago, when I was with the Unit. Wasn't him driving, unfortunately, just one of his minions, but I turned the vehicle, just in case. Once a ned, always a ned, I reckon. The boy had been coming back from the printers, I think—there were boxes of business cards in the boot.' Fraser felt around in his pocket. 'Here.' He passed a card to Anna.

Lap It Up dance club. With the tasteful adjunct: Asian Babes a speciality.

'Don't think there's a law against that, I'm afraid. Much as I'd like there to be.'

'No, but there is against having 200 grams of superskunk in the glove compartment. Of course, I spoke to Chaddha about it, but he denied all knowledge. Said the car must have been taken without his permission. Sacked the lad on the spot, right in front of me. So all I could do was charge the boy with taking and driving away, and possession with intent to supply.'

Anna frowned. 'Why did you stop the car in the first place?'

'Eh—went through a red traffic light?'

'Is that right?'

205

'Of course it is, ma'am.'

His stare was too steady, like a challenge. Or a smoke-screen gauze.

'Fraser, I know you love job creation, but you need to be careful just now. Just curb your enthusiasm for a while, yeah?' She scribbled down Chaddha's name as she was speaking.

'Without fear or favour, ma'am. That's how it goes. Talking of which—you want the rest of my list? Dealt with three or four domestic disputes, a fraudulent credit card—oh—and there was a Chinese restaurant I reported to the Environmental Health.' He shook his head, smirked. 'The DIO suggested we consider Triad connections.'

'Don't laugh. There was a Triad murder in town about twenty years ago—in a Chinese restaurant.'

'Even so, ma'am, it's hardly likely is it?'

Anna eased forward, clasped hands on her desk. 'You seem very unruffled by all this, Fraser.'

'Well, it's just part of the job, isn't it? If you start to get scared about what might happen, you'd never walk out the office, would you?'

'But what about your family? Doesn't it bother you that these people know where you live?'

She was supposed to be reassuring him here, not making him feel worse, but it was vital he understood this wasn't some game. Whoever these people were, whomever they were representing, they had the audacity to track a cop to his house, then beat him in a public street.

'Ma'am. Please don't bring my family into this.'

'But they already are. What have you got—one kid?'

He sighed. 'Two. A wee girl, and we've not long

206

had a baby boy. My wife's still on maternity leave.'

'Well, we have to protect them too. At least until we know who's doing this. Have you been offered CCTV for your house?'

'That'll just freak Maria out, ma'am. I told you, I don't want her getting scared. It's me that's got the problem, not her. She wasn't even in that night; she was visiting her mum. And . . .' the muscle in his jaw twitched, '. . . and I didn't exactly tell her what they said.'

'Why?'

'Because *I* can handle this. She doesn't need to know.'

'And what if they come back, Fraser? What if they come back when you're not there?'

'Look, I didn't tell her because I feel bloody stupid, alright?' Fraser shoved his chair back, getting up. As his body unfurled, there was an almighty crash. All so quick, a bang, a burst, Anna's window caving in, crystal-clinking glass chunks in her face, her hair. The thud of something solid on her desk, it hit her clock sideways, skidding on to the floor. Where was Fraser, where was Fraser?

'Ma'am! Ma'am? Are you alright?'

Anna shook the glass from her eyes, saw newsprint round a brick. Was on her feet, running to the window. Heard a car, several cars, the usual traffic puttering by. On her radio, shouting. 'Get me stations to assist. Stations to assist outside Giffnock Police Office. I repeat, Braidholm at Fenwick Road. Stop any youths on foot, cars in the vicinity. Someone just put a brick through the chief inspector's window.'

Everyone came running: the bar officer, the

207

community sergeant who'd been in doing paperwork, cops having their piece in the refreshment room. One guy in shorts who'd been in the gym, a nearby patrol car, all scouring the streets, searching for . . . whoever. But whoever it was, was gone.

*   *   *

'But was it kids?' asked the community sergeant later. 'Or a car?'

'I don't know, Mark,' snapped Anna. 'By the time we looked out the window, there was nobody there. Get the Engine Room to check through the camera footage—'

'Ma'am. We don't have a camera at the front.'

'What?'

'Just the back yard and the side bit. I guess no one ever thought they'd need one at the front.'

She drew a hand across her hair, felt tiny bites of glass there. 'Well that's just bloody brilliant.'

Search over, the cops had returned to whatever they'd been doing before, leaving just Anna, Fraser and the community sergeant. The three of them stood, peering through the shattered pane as if they would find some hidden clue. There was a paved area directly under Anna's window, which ran the length of the old building, just wide enough for a single row of cars to park. Beyond that, only a couple of metres away, was a low wall separating the police office from the street. Anyone could have stood there, lobbed hard, and run.

The missile had streaked straight past Fraser's head. 'Near took my ear off. I mean, I actually felt it, you know, the draught as it passed.' He went to pick the brick from Anna's desk, but she stopped him.

'Ho—don't touch that. We might be able to get prints.'

'From a brick?'

'From the newspaper round it.' She walked over, knelt to retrieve her clock. One side was completely crushed, crumbs of painted eggshell glistening amongst glass. All those hours of tongue-poking carefulness. Her breath was pushing fast in her lungs; dancing with her heart . . . she thought, at first, it had been an explosion.

'Right, Mark—I want you to get a Scenes of Crime officer down here immediately, to see if they can salvage anything.' She stood up. 'And, once they've been, get someone in here with a dustpan and brush please, and get this mess cleared off the floor.'

'Wee bastards,' said the sergeant. 'I mean, when they start vandalising the bloody cop shop . . .'

Anna bent nearer to the brick. The newspaper had partially unwound itself, enough that you could make out the headline.

'No,' she said, slowly. 'I don't think this was kids.' She nudged the newspaper wider with a pen. 'Fraser, I think this was meant for you.'

OFF-DUTY COP BEATEN UP AT HOME

'Jesus wept.' Fraser snatched at the paper.

'Put it down!' shouted Anna. 'Just leave it, like that. Look, you can still read it.'

She put her hands on the young cop's shoulders, turned him to face her. 'Now, calm down. We've both had a bit of a fright. Just calm down and let's

209

see what it says.'

'It's just the local weekly,' said the sergeant. 'You know, the freebie one.'

Fraser didn't look, just sank into Anna's chair. 'Aye, that gets put through every door in the fucking district.'

'What's the date on it?'

'Today's. It must be just out.'

'But how the hell did they get hold of the story?' said Fraser. 'Christ, this is the last thing I need.'

'Neighbours maybe?' said the sergeant. 'I mean, they all got interviewed, didn't they?'

'Yes, but they weren't given a blow-by-blow account of the entire incident either.' Anna read the article aloud.

Fears are growing that a campaign of intimidation is being mounted against local police officers after youths attacked a twenty-three-year-old constable in his own garden. It's believed the assailants had been following the young officer for several weeks, before pouncing on him as he exited his house in Ormonde Crescent. While police have no definite leads at present, it is well known that feuding gangs have been causing mayhem in the area, resulting, last week, in the tragic death of nineteen-year-old Sabir Aziz. One resident, who didn't wish to be named, said: 'This area is being overrun with gangs of boys—and young lassies too, drinking and fighting. I know the man that got beaten up—he doesn't take any nonsense off them, and they don't like that. But it's come to something if even the police aren't safe in their own houses.'

Following hospital treatment, the injured police officer has now returned to work. Strathclyde Police are refusing to comment on whether there have been similar attacks on other police officers.

'For fucksake.' All in a low-pitched groan; Anna could barely make out what Fraser was saying. 'Who wrote that shite?'

'Some woman called Lucy Manning,' said the sergeant. 'Never heard of her. Must be new.'

'Okay,' said Anna. 'I want to meet this Miss Manning asap. Find out where she got her information from and what the bloody hell she thinks she's doing. Corporate Communications were specifically asked to keep this out of the press. I mean—virtually giving your *address*? And Fraser; stop pissing me about now. You will do exactly as you are told with regard to security, do you understand?'

'Yes ma'am.'

'You will have CCTV installed at your home; you will be given an escort to and from work, and I will arrange for plainers to take regular observations on your house. I will also come out and speak to your wife—' she raised an eyebrow at his threatened interruption—'to *reassure* her, and explain to her exactly what we're doing. I will also provide her with a linked panic alarm, and arrange for her to be given additional security advice if required.' She paused. 'It's either that, or you hang up your cuffs and take a nice long holiday abroad. Seriously, your choice. No one will think any the less of you if you keep your head down until we get

211

this sorted out.'

'No way. *Ma'am.*'

'Thought you'd say that. Fort Knox it is then. I'll pass on this Avalon guy's details to Divisional Intelligence, see what goods they can produce, and then you and I will have a meeting with them and CID first thing Monday morning—agreed?'

'Agreed.'

'Okay, so. Look, do you want to go home just now? I can arrange for someone to follow you?'

He picked up his hat. 'I've still got three hours of my shift left, ma'am. And I'm working it.'

*   *   *

Two minutes to eight. Anna could just miss tonight's muster; the inspector could take care of that. However, work went on regardless—there was Fraser, zipping up his jacket and going back on the street. Nothing else Anna could do. Scenes of Crime were en route, as were Hurry Brothers to board up her window. She'd phone Johnny later, to check he was happy with what she was proposing to put in place for Fraser. And, forbye all that, the rest of the world would keep turning; cars would be screwed tonight, faces hurt. Some poor girl would have a lucky escape or a terrible ordeal, others would flash their tits at passing cars and laugh about it next day. The Maguires would still need to be interviewed; Anna's mum would suck and wheeze in parallel with old Agnes at the home. And Alice would prowl and stretch in an empty flat, aggrieved because she couldn't get out at the moon.

Anna was convinced that Mrs Hamilton would

212

put in an appearance at this muster, not least because it was Anna's first week on call. In fact, she could foresee Mrs H popping up at regular intervals in the coming week; a scowling face in the background of a group disorder; the dark shadow of a ferret, scampering up a lane.

So she went through, just as they were all taking their seats. The muster was a mix of Anna's own troops, two guys from Aitkenhead Road, and the sergeant and four from . . . *Jesus*. The sergeant was Alex.

Leaning back in his chair, legs wide, one arm draped along the seat back. Eyes like he owned her. 'Ma'am.'

'Sergeant.' She nodded, kept walking to the back of the room. No need for her to sit at the front, she hadn't planned to anyway. Far better to keep out the way and let the inspector get on with it. That was his job; she could chip in as required.

The inspector read out the detail, told them who would be working where, what areas required extra attention, and every time Alex moved, each languid scratch at the nape of his neck, each further stretch of his legs, she knew was directed at her. Had to be. The boy had so much . . . so much . . . had she really bitten him?

'Ma'am?'

They had all turned round to stare at her.

'Sorry?'

'Ma'am—do you have anything to add?'

To what? Can't you tell I wasn't listening?

'Um, no, no I think you've covered everything.' Her eyes careered around the room, anywhere, anywhere, except the middle chair in the front row. Flailing for a hint of the little speech she'd been

213

working on. 'Em . . . just remember to fill in your returns, act with integrity and . . . *yes, she had definitely bitten him . . . you wouldn't imagine something like that* . . . and, restraint and . . . keep yourselves safe. That's all.'

And now, she'd have to walk past them all. Or sit tight in her seat until they left. Unless Alex had the balls to actually come over to her . . . yes, of course he did.

'Hi *ma'am*.' Standing right over her, groin directly level with Anna's head. No matter how far down she slumped.

'Alex.'

'So, how are you?'

'Good. You?'

'No bad, thanks. Although I did have to go and get this rabies jag . . .'

Oh, piss off, sonny.

Pushing her gaze upwards, aware of the inspector shuffling his papers, again and again, and still not leaving the room. 'Sergeant, I expect all our overtime officers to be out on the street as of five minutes ago. That's if you want to get paid.'

The sulky lip of a hurt wee boy. Why did he think he was unfinished business?

'Anna,' he lowered his voice, 'I was hoping we could maybe have a chat . . . ?'

The inspector was coming over.

'Maybe later. If I've got time. Hi George. Good muster, well done. Do you want to show Sergeant . . . sorry. What's your name again?'

A tight-sprung shake of Alex's head. 'Cheerio, Anna. I know my own way out.'

The Saturation was in full swing, all available cops out on mobile and foot patrol, in all the places Hamilton wanted targeted. The area around Clarkston Toll, where Sabir Aziz had been killed, was particularly swamped—more cops than kids, in fact. So far, however, fears of retribution and running battles were largely unfounded. Yes, there'd been some trouble at the weekend, but getting an early arrest seemed to have contained most of the threatened surges of righteous indignation. It was quiet. Unusually quiet. Early yet, mind. Elsewhere in the division, at this time in the evening, you'd only get the pissed-out-their-faces schoolgirls, the boys tossing chip papers and mooning at passers-by. And some nutter chibbing rocks at police stations. It was later on that the real fighting would start, with the arrival of tanked-up neds who'd finished their stash of bevvy, and were truculent, fuelled and bored. So now was as good a time as any for Anna to visit the Maguires.

She should pass it on to CID, and she would, she would, if there was any substance to Robert Macklin's fears. She'd need to speak to Cruikshanks about Fraser anyway. But she didn't want to make herself look even more of a tube in the interim.

The Maguires lived in Newton Mearns, barely ten minutes from the nursing home they'd put Cassie in. Anna wondered why she was surprised. Should it not be a good thing to keep your loved ones so close? So near, and yet so far . . .

She drove into a gravel drive curved so wide and long that you couldn't see the house at first. It was nothing like she expected. An elegant grey and white villa, Art Deco influences and exquisite topiary flanking the front door. Neon blue night-lights gleamed from under the eaves, the sky

215

behind ribboned in a pink and gold backdrop. It was like a film set. Anna could count three, four, five windows stretching along the top floor, each one banded with thin metal strips. In amidst all this, they couldn't have found one single room for an elderly lady? Two rooms even; then they could have got a live-in carer too, and still never got their hands dirty themselves.

But this was hardly being objective. New, improved Anna no longer made snap decisions. She would assume nothing until she'd spoken to the Maguires. Assumptions and suppositions were two different things, though, and several possibilities were threading themselves through: that Robert Macklin was wrong; that Robert Macklin was deliberately causing trouble; that Cassie had set it all up to escape her tacky family. That her family had set it up to get rid of Cassie; thus, one or both of the Maguires were potential murderers. No, no and no again. None of these seemed plausible. Then again, when did that matter?

It was Sheena, Cassie's daughter-in-law, who answered the door, her scowl deepening as she saw the police uniform. Anna hadn't decided, until that moment, how she was going to play it.

'Good evening. I'm Chief Inspector Cameron. We met at The Meadows.'

Icy-polite, it would appear.

'Yes?'

'May I come in?'

'Why?'

'You were supposed to come and see me yesterday?'

The woman blanched slightly. 'And?'

216

'And, I'd like to come in. Is Mr Maguire at home?'

Ronnie Maguire was creeping down the polished hall. 'Who is it?' he hissed to his wife.

'Strathclyde Police, Mr Maguire—'

'Jes-*us*.' Ronnie scuttled to the door, looked wildly up and down the drive, as if demons were lurking. 'Get her inside, quick.'

He bundled Anna into the hallway, slammed the front door. Okay, this was weird. One who would rather poke out her own eyes than let Anna cross the threshold, the other virtually carrying her across it.

'Ronnie. Maybe the policewoman would like a drink?'

'What?'

'I said, away and get the wumman a drink. Let me deal with this, eh?'

'Actually, I've come to see you both. This the lounge here, is it?' Anna opened the white glazed door. 'Lovely. Very elegant.' Several leather Chesterfields were positioned round a Chinese claw-foot table. Jagged yuccas took the place of blinds at each of the three long window panes, a plush, russet pelmet the perfect colour match for the hearthside rug. Without being offered, Anna took a seat on the nearest squeaking couch, rested her elbow on the small table at the side.

'So,' she asked, smiling straight at Ronnie, 'how's your mum?'

Wet lips began to wobble. His hair was coiffed, not floppy like it had been at The Meadows. He wore an open-necked pale pink shirt, and as many gold chains as his wife, all quivering together.

'Aye, aye,' he nodded. 'She's grand.'

217

'Where is she again?'

The answer flew sharp from Sheena's tongue. 'At her sister's, down south.'

'No, I mean on holiday. Where is she on holiday?'

'She's no on holiday,' said Ronnie.

'So she's still with her sister? Definitely? Same house in Liverpool where she was found?'

A tiny whimper from Ronnie, then another nod.

Sheena folded her arms, positioned herself in front of Anna, her husband off to one side. You would think she was deliberately blocking Anna's view. 'Aye, that's right.'

Anna rested her hands on her rounded knees, the fabric rough. Tiny sparks danced in the lamp-glow, pinpricks of glass still caught in the weave of her trousers. She smoothed the flecks away, stood up.

'Only I had a police officer call round to see her, and the house was all closed up.'

She moved past Sheena to look directly on Ronnie's huddled form. You could almost see resolve dissolving. It was there in the slight loosening of his posture, like elastic stretched too far. It wouldn't snap, not now.

A deep suck of buoyant air, count one badwolf, two badwolf. Then PUSH IT OUT FULL BLAST.

'Does someone want to tell me what the *fuck* is going on here?'

She felt Sheena pull her forearm, trying to tug her away from Ronnie.

'Don't you speak to my man like that.'

'I'm no talking to you!' shouted Anna. 'So you sit on your arse and shut your face, you hear me?' She didn't push her, not one bit. Just stood over her long enough that Sheena succumbed to a comfy seat.

'Ho. You!' Anna pressed Ronnie's leg with the toecap of her Docs. 'I'll ask you one more time, and then I'm taking you down the road. Do you know where your mammy is now?'

'I don't know,' he wept. 'I don't. That's the God's honest truth—I don't know. They wouldny tell me.'

'Ronnie!' screeched his wife. 'You keep your stupit mouth closed.'

'Do you want the jail right now?' said Anna. 'Obstruction, perverting the course of justice? Impersonating a woman?'

'You cheeky bloody cow!'

'Sheena! Shut up. Shut the fuck up, will you?' Ronnie turned to Anna, tears flowing fast and hard.

'Ma mammy's been kidnapped. Kidnapped, you hear me?'

He held the cuff of Anna's fleece, a desperate grey stretch in his eyes.

'But yous canny do a thing. They telt me if we went to the polis then she'd be fucking killed.'

CHAPTER ELEVEN

Wednesday. This was CID's baby now. Anna still bore the scars of previous unwanted interventions. Indeed, Cruikshanks had posed, hands on hips, as she'd passed him her notes, all the times and details of her conversations with Mr Macklin and the Maguires, the phone calls with PC Auden.

219

Raising his voice for the benefit of the rest of the incident room: 'Now, is that everything, Chief Inspector? No secret witnesses you're keeping for yourself? A couple of your neighbours you've got tailing the suspects, perhaps?'

Anna leaned close into him. 'Up yours,' she whispered in his ear.

'Seriously, brilliant work, girl. You really should think about ditching that uniform. Let's hear it for Chief Inspector Cameron, lads.'

A half-hearted smattering of 'yays' and 'cheers, ma'am', but not one of them actually meant it. Why should they?

'Oh, for fucksake, guys,' said Anna. 'Just get on with finding the poor old soul, eh?'

How many of these detectives had worked under Nikki Armstrong? On top of her, even. That was Anna's first, churlish response; she had got their old boss the sack, and so they didn't like her. Before, it would have been her only response. But rank had stamped her somehow, bringing the security of stature, not in a self-aggrandising way. She'd noticed it creeping like a lengthening pool, ever since she got promoted. It must be how an actor felt when they got a good review, a poet when they won a prize, or a writer as their novel shot up the charts. You can know, and think, and trust that you are good, as you work away in secret. Yet you never quite make your mark. In your head, you tell yourself nobody understands you, that you don't care. But you do, you *do*, and you only know how much you do when the hurting stops. That head-raising glory when they stop hammering you down, and a wee, important man sticks a big gold star on your chest and goes: 'Okay, then. We finally agree.'

That stamp of approval was liberating, like just the right amount of drugs. Giving her the clarity and confidence to look beyond the knee-jerk. Hamilton didn't like Anna because Hamilton was a basket case. Anna couldn't change her commander's mindset, but she could live with it. And these cops might be pissed off with Anna, but it was not because she was an unlikeable boot. It was because she had done a good thing, and they had not. Two good things, if you counted Aziz. Stuff it, three, if you counted shafting Nikki Armstrong.

No one else here had thought the missing Cassandra was a crime; no one else had looked at the facts and said it wasn't right. Only Anna. And though the facts were as unaltered as they had ever been, that Cassie, who had been here, was no longer here, the abstraction contained by these facts had now shattered into crime. And that was down to Chief Inspector Cameron (and her trusty sidekick Dr Rob). And nobody likes a smart-arse.

Already, Cassie's abduction was being treated as a major incident. A HOLMES team was en route from Force Headquarters, as was the area detective superintendent. Three offices at Divisional HQ in Govan had been cleared so that an information firewall could be set up. This third room, where Anna was standing, was top of the tree, reserved for the Investigation Team. After today, it was unlikely Anna would be permitted inside. The chain began in Office One, used by the HOLMES operators, who would take every statement as it came in, index each one, then dictate them on to the system. A secure exit on one side of this office led in from the corridor, while another keypadded door on the facing wall would take you in to Office Two, the Intelligence Cell. This cell had been set up immediately, a dedicated unit to gather and protect every piece of intelligence and information relating to Cassandra Maguire. The Intelligence Cell was the hub of everything, feeding off the fodder and dross that came from the HOLMES operators in Office One, filtering each statement and scrap, washing it clean, smoothing it down or shaping it up, before passing an ordered menu on to the Investigation Team in Office Three. Again, a further secure door separated the Intelligence Cell from the Investigation Team, which in turn had its own secure exit into another corridor.

There was a whiteboard at the front of Office Three. However much Cruikshanks adhered to procedure, he eschewed a total reliance on modern gimmickry. 'I prefer to write it all up in big bubbles first—*then* we can see where we are.'

There were bubbles aplenty on his big glossy board; but none yet forming those satisfying links that reminded Anna of hydrocarbon chains from her Chemistry O Grade.

'You realise if you read this,' Cruikshanks continued, 'I'll have to kill you.'

'But I *gave* you most of this information already.'

'Two minutes, then you're oot. And I'll be pulling the blinds down too, so don't think you can sneak a peek tomorrow.'

Anna scanned the board.

Abduction
Cassandra Maguire née Sturgeon
DOB: 5/4/22
DATE & TIME—Between 2 a.m. and 5.30 a.m. on Thursday 17 March
i.e. 5 days cold as of notification: Tuesday 22/3

'Do you really think she's still alive?' asked Anna.

'I've got to, haven't I? Until we've evidence to the contrary. But I'm finding it hard to believe there's been no further contact in all that time—and that the Maguires would just sit tight and do nothing for nearly a week.'

'So, explain all that crap about "finding her" down south?'

Anna had stopped the interview, had called Tom from the Maguires' house as soon as the abduction had been confirmed. She had succumbed to proper procedure, and her nose was bothering her greatly.

'Apparently that was Cassie's cousin Elsie that they roped in. Soon as the warning came not to contact the police, Sheena was on the blower, promising a three-week cruise if Elsie pretended to be Cassie. Never told her it was an abduction, of course, just that there was some hassle about paying the home, and if they could pretend Cassie had run away, then The Meadows would waive the fee.'

'Quick thinking in a crisis.'

'I know. Crafty wee shites, eh?'

'They must've been really scared, though; I get the impression Ronnie dotes on his mammy. No so sure about Sheena, mind.'

'You really don't like that wumman, do you? Any road, they're both being interviewed separately the now.'

PLACE—from The Meadows N/H, Newton Mearns

An aerial photograph of the nursing home was pinned to the board, along with a sketch of the internal layout.

POTENTIAL SUSPECTS
Persons Inside N/H
Persons connected with/business associates of Maguires
Ronnie Maguire
Sheena Maguire
Other family members
Random housebreakers/Prescription fraudsters/panic

'Fraser Harris raised that about the stolen scripts before,' said Anna. She stopped, looked at Cruikshanks. 'You do know that, don't you?'

'*Yes*.' A slow-squeezed warning, which she pretended not to hear.

'And did he give you the details of who he pulled? For the prescriptions, I mean.'

'Aye. He's a smashing wee cop is Mr Harris. Mind . . .' Cruikshanks reached for an open packet of crisps. '. . . These anyone's?' he called. 'Naw? Ace. Aye, being a smashing wee cop is how you make enemies, though.'

'You heard about my brick?'

'I did indeed. Just as well you're as cool as a

224

cucumber, eh?' He coughed into his hand. 'I didny do it, miss. Honest.'

'You really are pathetic.'

'They got some prints off the newspaper, by the way.'

'That was quick.'

Where carbon powder would quickly reveal prints on objects like furniture and glass, the moistness of flesh soaked into porous surfaces, requiring more prolonged chemical treatment to reveal it.

'Aye, well. If you canny look after one of your own . . .'

'And?'

'No matches with anyone yet, but we'll keep working on it.'

'Well, Fraser has a list as long as your arm, but there are three possibles I would go for. First off, Jazz Chaddha.'

'Cheddar? Like the cheese?'

'Ch-ah-da. Some property dealer?'

'Ach, I know who you're on about,' said Cruikshanks. 'Buys and sells pubs and clubs?'

'And runs them too, it would appear.' She handed him the business card Fraser had given her.

'Asian babes for hire.' Cruikshanks grinned. 'Disny make you a bad person.'

'Okay, well what about Douglas Avalon—known as Frankie—'

'Oh, I know *him* alright.'

'Well, interestingly, he had a wad of potentially dodgy notes on him last time he and Fraser spoke.'

'Really?' said Cruikshanks. 'Now, that *is* interesting.'

225

'Third off, Fraser mentioned a dog-fighting ring, based in Greenock. Now, what do you know about dog fighting?'

'Anna, pet . . .'

Wide arms flung despairing at the chaos all around. 'I don't have a scooby. I'm kind of up to my neck here, know?'

'Yeah. Yeah, sorry. Look, I realise you're full on with this abduction. But I'd really appreciate a wee half-hour when you get a moment, just to go over where we are with Fraser—and what more we could be doing.'

'I'm never too busy to look out for a cop, hen. Tomorrow morning do?'

'Aye—no. Shit, I'm backshift again tomorrow. Can we make it around lunchtime?'

'It's all one to me, doll.'

'I'll get the DIO to sit in as well, will I? And Fraser's inspector? Claire Rodgers.'

'Aye, well named that lassie. *Rodger.*' He rolled the word with relish. 'Well, you would, wouldn't you? Crisp?'

Anna returned to the whiteboard.

MOTIVE:
* <u>Money 1</u> No ransom requested as yet. However, Maguires have income of circa £350,000 p.a. S runs cleaning business, R owns scrap-dealing company & various vehicle sales & hire dealerships in city. Reasonably high profile: Member of Rotary Club, sponsor of local boys' rugby team
* <u>Money 2</u> Do Maguires stand to benefit in any way from death/removal of mother?
* <u>Revenge/Leverage</u>—For   what?   Check

Maguires have no pre cons/outstanding complaints/warrants/issues. (Check with bank/Inland Revenue too)
* <u>Sadistic/Sexual</u>—Checks being run on all known sexual offenders/Register etc in fifty-mile radius. Check also with HM Bar-L, Saughton & Peterhead re. any recent likely releases
* <u>Punishment</u>—Of Cassie? Maguires? If so, likely to be carried out by staff within N/H? Check for any recent fights/issues/incidents. Background checks on all N/H staff—beginning with Robert Macklin

'Robert Macklin? Really? Why's *he* first on your list?'

She had woken last night, flat on her belly. Hand pressed under her navel, her face in a pillow that had been Macklin's mouth. And felt pathetic and wet and hungry all at once.

'He owns the place, and it's losing money hand over fist is what I've heard. Money is a terrible motivator, my child. See—very next thing on my shiny whiteboard. There is a logic to all this detective stuff, you know.'

* <u>Something against N/H, not Maguires at all</u>—Check all recent dealings relating to N/H, i.e. complaints to police, issues re. local authority licensing, press interest, money/tax/fraud, anything

<u>CONTACT MADE BY ABDUCTORS</u>
Initial statements from both Maguires correspond:

One phone call (records being checked re. where from)
Time: 4 a.m. approx
Date: Saturday 19 March
Male voice, Scottish accent, poss Glaswegian, but described as a little more 'lilting'. Words used (approx):
We have got her. Do not go to the police. Do not contact the papers. If you do, she will be killed. Await further instructions.
Call was then terminated by this male.

'Well, it canny be related to Macklin then,' said Anna. 'It *must* be about the Maguires. They knew it was Ronnie's mother, knew where to phone.'

'Aye, but how gaga is Cassie? I mean, is she sharp enough to know her own son's phone number?' Cruikshanks stuffed some more crisps in his mouth.

Anna thought for a moment. Could picture Cassie, near-naked in her room, proudly cackling how she'd 'gied them the slip'. 'Aye . . . I guess.'

'So she could have just told them, if they asked. All they say is "her", not "your mum" or anything like that. They could of just taken any old biddy; might not be any specific connection at all. See, that's you trying to contaminate my train of thought already. Away oot the road, and let me get on, will you?'

Anna finished reading the next segment. 'Ho— what's this?'

PUBLICITY
Hang fire at present—further risk to safety of abductee

V. urgent need to amass all available intelligence
CI Cameron to front if required.

'CI Cameron to front? Why me?'

'You're the deputy SDO, it happened in your area, and you've a lovely face for the cameras. Just come over a bit . . . sympathetic, for fucksake. Anyway, I've no decided yet—they're pretty clear about no going to the media.'

'Yeah, but soon as you start interviewing folk, it becomes public anyway.'

He sighed. 'I know. And we've no got that much time to play with, either. See?'

ADDITIONAL RISKS
Abductee is frail elderly. Requires medication for diabetes. Failure to provide likely to induce complications/hypo/coma, etc
ACTIONS UNDERWAY
Int Cell established
HOLMES Team
Additnl resources for intvws at N/H?
TO CONSIDER
RIPSA Surveillance (dep on Intel)
TO INTERVIEW:
Pcs Auden & Glass at Merseyside
Ronald Maguire (Want background checks)
Sheena Maguire (Want background checks)
Robert Macklin (Want background checks)
All medical, nursing & ancillary staff at N/H (want background checks)
All residents at N/H (background checks N/A at present)
Secondary intvws: All contractors/visitors

Anna tapped the board with her finger. 'Make sure you speak to the lady that shares a room with Cassie. Manju, her name is.'

Cruikshanks dropped a dainty curtsey. 'Please, miss. Will you let me know when I can wipe my arse too?'

'Look, they'll tell you she doesn't talk at all—but she does. I . . . I've heard her.'

'Oh, and what pearls did she give you?'

'Ach, just some rambles. She thought she knew me. But the point is, her and Cassie were friends.' She shrugged. 'They might have talked about something. Plus she was there when—'

When Cassie was singing her song about the Saracens . . .

'Hey!' Anna grabbed Cruikshanks's arm. 'Cassie said something about big black men just before she went missing—how she'd given them the slip. I just thought it was gibberish. But Manju was there too. If anyone had been in the room that time, Manju would have seen them.'

'Sir,' shouted one of the detectives. 'Can we just go over the timescales again?'

'Two ticks,' said Cruikshanks, walking Anna to the door. 'I promise you, I will interview your Manju lady myself.' He spoke quieter. 'Chill out, eh? I know things are a bit stressful at the moment.'

'No they're not.'

Tangled eyebrows rising. 'So how *is* your mammy then?'

'Okay. Let's not go there. I'm chilled, alright? I'll leave it with you.'

One hand on the curve of her back. 'That's the girl. JC'll make me bloody redundant if you steal all my glory. Okay, *our* glory. I take it you've been updated with the Aziz murder?'

'Good eh?'

'It is that. All done and dusted, virtually. Your man Figgis has been remanded, trial date's been set, but I reckon it will be a total formality. Word is he'll plead. I think he actually thought he'd get bail. It was quite funny seeing the shock on his face. I mean, culp hom's still serious shit.'

'What do you mean culpable homicide? I thought the charge was murder?'

Dense suction, like a punch going in. *Sell-out of the century. Come and get your plea bargains here, from our careworn, crammed-up justice system.* Wilfully depriving someone of life should mean murder, truth should be incorruptible and life should mean life. It rarely did. She shouldn't be surprised, not really.

'*We-ell*, it was, originally. Then it was kind of . . . fluid. When Figgis appeared on petition originally, he cited self-defence. Apparently he just picked up the knife to keep Aziz away.'

'Bullshit. It was a fucking ambush. I *saw* them chase Aziz. They just flew at him out of the blue.'

A sharp glance from the detective nearest the door. Clearly Anna and Tom's conversation was more interesting than the phone book through which he was leafing.

'Aye, but a wee while earlier Figgis and his mates say the boy Aziz had pulled a blade on them. So, when they saw him again, they felt obliged to make a citizen's arrest. For the good of the community, like.'

231

'Tom, are you taking the piss?' Fair enough, Anna was merely a witness, but it would be nice to be kept informed.

'You'd think, wouldn't you? Sadly that's the line Figgis's brief gave, corroborated by several of Figgis's pals, and the Crown bought it. So, the PF has recommended to Crown Counsel that we go for culpable homicide, and that's that.'

'Tom, I *saw* one of the neds smash a bottle and then they all ran hell for leather after him.'

'Aye, but could you ID which one done it?'

'No . . .'

'And were bits of bottle found at the locus?'

'No. Just the remains of a sandwich. In fact— what about that? He had a roast beef sandwich shoved in his mouth.'

'So? Maybe he was hungry.'

'And maybe someone stuffed it there. In self-fucking-defence.'

'Anna, Anna. Do you know for a fact that the boy wasn't in the process of munching a butty when the gang started chasing him? I mean, could you actually see from that far away?'

'No. You know I couldn't.'

'There you go then. Much as I'd like to cite that classic and ancient Scots Law sandwich objection, I canny. I'm afraid the final nail was when two of Aziz's own pals confirmed that the knife we found was actually Aziz's blade, and that he *had* pulled it on Figgis's gang a wee while before.'

'But Aziz was totally alone when I saw him. Where were his pals then?'

'Where indeed? But that's what it says in their statements.' Cruikshanks dropped his hand, rummaged in his trouser pocket. 'A-ha. Sweetie?'

he asked, offering a paper bag.

'No, you're alright.'

'Right. Well,' his cheeks puffing, 'ooh, soor plooms. Jeez, they're wersh.' They were in the corridor now. Cruikshanks stopped, lifted his hand.

'Oh—speak of the devil. The very man we were just talking about. What can we do you for?'

Fraser Harris was at the top of the stairs, coming towards them. Out of breath, his colour high.

'Are you alright?' said Anna. 'Has something happened?'

'No, no. I'm alright. But I just thought you should know. That All Star Security—the ones Mr Macklin said the nursing home used? Well, they're a shower of neds.'

Cruikshanks crunched his sweet. 'Yeah?'

'Yup. I've been doing some research. It's run by a guy called Callum MacLeod.'

'Callum MacLeod, eh?' said Cruikshanks. '*The* Callum MacLeod? Husband of the lovely Lori? Owner of two fat Rottweilers? Missing one finger and most of his brain?'

'The very same.'

'I don't think . . . oh, sorry.' Cruikshanks was using his pinkie nail to dig around in one of his molars. 'Bit stuck in a filling.' He swallowed. 'Aye, I don't think he's been up to anything since they post office robberies four year ago. And he was only jailed for three.'

'No, I know sir,' said Fraser. 'But when I saw his name registered as All Star's director, I thought it was worth flagging up. I mean, he's bound to have some of his buddies grafting for him. I'd love to know how he's made enough money in such a short

233

time too. I've checked them out, sir. All Star are pretty slick—they've got offices in Glasgow, Ayr, Stirling, all over the shop, offering private security, personal security, guard dogs—'

'*Rottweilers*,' nodded Cruikshanks.

'Aye—alarm fitting, maintenance and response, fast response patrol guards—you name it, they do it.'

'Hmm. I'm no totally surprised about All Star,' said Cruikshanks. 'Find me a Glasgow security firm who *disny* have links with the underworld. But, it's interesting. Very interesting. Thanks, Fraser. We'll look into it. And can I suggest, for the meantime, you keep your distance from Mr MacLeod. No more poking about, alright?'

'Sure, sir. Ma'am.'

They watched Fraser make his way back to the stairs.

'He's a good lad, him.'

'I know he is,' said Anna. 'That's why we need to look after him.'

'Right then, hen.' Cruikshanks patted her on the back. 'I'd better be getting back to where the action is; find your gadaboot granny.'

'Eh, just a minute. Gordon Figgis?'

Figgis was going to get away with murder. Nobody cared; Aziz was just another dead statistic.

Cruikshanks put his arm round her. 'Oh, Anna, Anna. Come on, lass. You and I both know that we canny fuck with the system. At the end of the day, it was a bit of ned-on-ned action, and I think the feeling is: we have a body in custody, that body is more than likely to plead when it goes to trial and, ultimately, we have no evidence to suggest the attack was premeditated.'

'Other than my statement.'

'Shit, I know, I know. But the boy's deid, another boy will get the jail, we get our backs slapped rather than our arses felt—plus we don't have a multicultural gang war on our hands. Will that no do for you, hen?'

'It's no really up to me, is it? You're the DCI. If you think justice has been served, all well and good.'

'Anna, come on doll. Don't be like that. There's mair important things to get your knickers in a twist about. You need to focus your energies on getting your mum well. Or getting her home at least, eh?'

She let her body go rigid. 'Right, yes. Sorry to have put you out.'

'Och stop that nonsense now, ya daft besom.'

'Look,' Anna pulled away from his paternal bonhomie, 'I need to go, Tom. Let you get on with this. But we'll still have that meeting tomorrow, yes? To discuss Fraser's case?'

'We will.'

'Right, well I'll see you then, then.'

Stuff the bloody lot of them. This office, these people, would survive whether she was here or not. They would find Cassandra Maguire; in fact, there was a sense of release in walking away. Anna had delivered the dilemma, gift-wrapped for CID. Justice, logic, ownership was all outwith her hands. Anna was going to book a flight to Spain.

The bright stream of daily updates from the ward had become muddied; now it was every couple of days, and the news was always no news. No change, no movement, no speech. Before she went, she'd do some research, check out a couple

235

of suitable nursing homes. English-speaking if possible, but it would only be temporary, until she could bring Caroline home. And, if she happened to get the address from Joan, well, she might just pay Teddy and Myra a visit too.

Out of the office, back to Giffnock, then on to the street. That was the best place for Anna. With her head up and her hands behind her back, she could be twenty again, sniffing up the dark, fresh air. There was an anticipation about the night, something visceral. On her own, she walked the streets, walked all the way to Clarkston and back, calling into the pubs, the Redhurst Hotel. *Oh nothing special. Just a licensed premises check, sir.* She loved that moment, when the music stopped and the cowboys sat, staring. Loved it even better if she got a cat-call or a jeer, because then the fun would really start. But there were no takers. As if the punters had already been warned.

Do *not* fuck with me.

Unlike last night, G Division was heaving. Twists and knots of kids everywhere, like an invite had gone out, but they couldn't find the party. Boys in hot hatches, not racing, but circling. Radio traffic reporting group disorders at Overlee Park, in Mansewood, up in Eaglesham. Come eleven, there were a load of prisoners for Anna to check. Hard to tell if the activities of the local youths had been more offensive than usual, or just, thanks to the Saturation, more observed. Were the police preventing crime or creating it? It was the same Support Unit officers out again, but she'd managed to avoid most of them. She had, however, checked who was lifting all the bodies. Maybe Alex was working off some frustration, but he hadn't stopped for breath. As soon as he got one ned processed, he was out to gather up some more. They were three to a cell in some cases, mostly youngsters. You knew it was a busy night when you stacked them three abreast. You'd only ever put one or three in a cell—two was the unlucky number of fist-fights and no corroboration. So, a cell either housed a single prisoner, where they could bang their own heads off the wall in boredom, contrition or indignation—and have no one to blame but themselves; or, if it was hectic, three in together, the third man providing the sandwich effect of a witness or referee. The bar staff were being run into the ground with calls for solicitors, extra blankets, the doctor or more bog roll.

Anna slid the observation hatch on one of the doors. Three in this one, all quite calm. She nodded to the turnkey to open the cell door.

'Everything alright?'

'Hullo there, doll!' waved one of the trio inside. 'You come tae give us a bed bath?'

She sighed, moved along to the next one. The truncated view through the hatch showed only cold gloss paint and the edge of a mattress.

'Can you open this one up?' she asked the turnkey. 'I can't see anyone inside.'

'Sure. It's just the one guy here, ma'am. He's been a total pain in the arse since they brought him in. Had the casualty surgeon out already, but there's nothing wrong with him.'

'Alright in there?'

A gust of sour body twined with alcohol.

'Naw. I want the fucking doctor.' Glowering at her, a bull-necked man with heavy, tanned arms

237

and receding hair. He thumped the wall with a tattooed fist.

'And why's that?'

'Cause I fucking do, ya boot.'

'Well, my understanding is that you've already seen him—and he's happy for you to remain in custody.'

'Aye, well I'm fucking not! You fucking thieving bastards.'

'No, I think you'll find that's you, pal.' Anna turned to her colleague. 'What's he on about?'

'Och, he's been screaming that some cop stole his wallet. But he didny have a wallet on him when he came in—just a wad of notes. And they're all counted and in his property bag.'

She lowered her voice. 'Well, you'd better get the outdoor inspector to come and take a report anyway. Probably is a lot of pish, but we need to cover ourselves.'

'Okay ma'am.'

'Ho! Gie me some fucking water, you!'

Anna kept smiling. That usually wound them up more. 'You've already been given tea.'

'Tastes like pish.'

'I see you didn't eat your dinner either.' Congealing square sausages like sliced brick on his plastic tray.

'A'm no eating that fucking muck. You can stick it up your arse,' he slurred. 'In fact—it probably came oot your fucking arse.'

'Lovely. Well it was nice talking to you.' Anna began to close the door.

'I want a drink of water.'

'Just lock it. Let's move on.'

As the door grated shut, his shouts grew louder.

'I said: I want a drink of fucking water. I want a drink of water!'

All along the cell passageway it drifted, a plaintive, angry cry, accompanied by a rhythmic kicking on the metal door.

'Alright in there?' she asked the next batch.

'What's that, miss? I canny hear you for that racket.'

The chant was being taken up by some of the other prisoners.

'I want a drink of water!'

'No, *I* want a drink of water.'

'Hey. If you're taking orders—can I get a latte?'

The cacophony spread and surged, until the whole corridor rang with thirsty cries.

'What's that one's name?' said Anna. 'The one making all the noise?'

'Eh . . . Avalon, ma'am. Dougie Avalon.'

'Avalon? Is that right? *That's* what he's going on about the wallet for. He'd money seized by one of our guys during a previous incident.'

'Is that right? I wouldny know. CID dragged him in, pished, at teatime. Breach, resist, the usual.' He shook his head. 'And they only went to bring him in on a voluntary as well.'

'Right, forget taking any complaint about missing wallets. Have CID questioned him yet?'

'No. Waiting till he's sobered up a bit, I think.'

Anna chewed at a sliver on the inside of her lip. It had a tangy taste, a bit like salted bacon. 'Alan, gonny get me a cup of water from the sink there?'

The turnkey filled a polystyrene cup.

'More. Right up to the brim, please.'

The turnkey would think her a generous sap. Anna took the beaker from him, indicated that he

239

should unlock the door. And chucked the water straight into the waiting prisoner's face.

'There's your drink of water, pal. Oh, careful now.'

The man yelled, lurched towards her, skidding on the wet floor. Slowly spiralling, coming to a halt against the wall. He wiped his eyes, blinking and winded.

'Better get that wiped up, Alan, where he spilled it. In case he slips or something.'

'Yes, ma'am.'

She crouched to whisper in the prisoner's ear. 'And you cool your jets, Frankie-boy, or you'll be here every night this week. We'll just keep pulling you in and kicking you out and pulling you in and kicking you out until you think you've lived here your whole fucking life long. And only *then* will the questioning start. Understand?'

'What questioning?' he whined. 'That's what *they* keep saying an all. For bloody what?'

'Och now Frankie, you just sit nice and quiet. Be a good boy and don't spoil the surprise, eh?'

'Ma name's no Frankie!'

She straightened up, returned to the passageway. 'Lock the door please, Alan.'

They finished the checks in relative silence. So, that was Dougie Avalon. Good. Maybe now they would get somewhere with the Fraser Harris issue, clamp it down before it escalated further. Avalon's swift (and—she was sure—entirely unprovoked) detention was another example of efficient, full-on law enforcement; you couldn't argue with that. All these arrests looked good on paper, sure. This merciless street-washing would mean happy councillors, and a few quiet nights as the ripples

240

spread out, the gangs congregating elsewhere until the tide of cops receded. But it couldn't be sustained: somewhere else would need the resources next week, next month; and then the returning trickle of wary neds would become a gallus flood.

Anna was truly knackered.

She thought about Cassie, out there in the cold. About her mum, equally lost, in a body that couldn't function. In a world that couldn't give a shit. Then she thought about a chicken madras, a warm cat and a comfy bed.

CHAPTER TWELVE

Johnny grinned at Anna from across the table, stretched long arms and yawned.

'Late night, boss?'

'Ah, but they're the best, sure, aren't they?'

Tomorrow, she would go and get her hair done. She'd have completed three backshifts on the trot by then; she was *owed* a morning off. *Sod it, take the whole day, Ms Cameron.* She would too. She could spend it all preparing for her big night out.

They were in the office lined with extra lockers that passed for a 'boardroom': her, Johnny, Claire and Cruikshanks. The meeting about Fraser was drawing to a close; Johnny had sanctioned all Anna's proposals, even the overtime for the plainers. The divisional intelligence manager had sent his apologies—citing the Maguire abduction, a spate of car crime and a heavy head cold—but had dispatched an underling bearing a useful two-

241

page report. Both he and Fraser were getting ready to leave.

'Just one other thing, Fraser,' said Johnny. 'See this newspaper report, where it says: *He doesn't take any nonsense off them, and they don't like that.* What are they referring to there?'

'Sorry sir, I'm not sure what you mean.'

'The bit where they speak to one of your neighbours. There.' Johnny fired a copy of the *Southside Sentinel* across the table. 'Sorry. I'd've thought you knew the whole article off by heart now.'

Fraser shook his head. 'I've no been able to bring myself to look at it, sir. I'm no exactly keeping a scrapbook about this.' He picked up the paper. The pages shivered fractionally as he held it. 'Who's that?' he said.

'Who?'

Claire Rodgers put her hand out to lower the *Sentinel* to her eye level. Fraser was pointing at a little inset beside his story.

'Oh, that's the boy that was murdered. Aziz.'

'Are you sure?' Fast and high, his voice almost accusatory. 'It's nothing like the photo they had in the *Herald*.'

Cruikshanks took the paper off him. 'Let's see. Nah, I think this is just a more recent one.'

'It is,' said Anna, without even looking. She knew Sabir's face well enough, knew each permutation of it that had appeared in the press.

'Aye, the Press Association got hold of an old school photie, I think; wired it to all the dailies—specs and a stripy tie. The picture of innocence.'

'Tom. The boy's dead.'

'Och, don't be such a—'

242

'Fraser,' Johnny repeated, 'what did your neighbour mean? Have you being coming over all vigilante on your days off?'

'No sir. No, I haven't. *Christ.* I haven't done anything wrong.'

'Alright there. Keep your hair on.'

It was a curious, old-fashioned turn of phrase. Sometimes, Johnny could be very twee.

Claire stood up, took the cop's arm. 'Ssh Fraser, it's alright. You're allowed to get upset.'

'I'm not upset.'

'Em . . . I'll just away, then.' The intelligence guy lisped quietly from the room, Fraser's eyes following him, shoulders slumped, fists balled. 'Is that us done, sir?'

'Sure.'

'You look after yourself, Fraser,' said Claire.

He ground past her and out of the room.

'So.' Johnny smacked his hands together. 'What are your thoughts, Tom?'

A subdued atmosphere, everyone contemplating, digesting. Cruikshanks, literally digesting, ploughing through a plate of rolls.

'Dogs,' he burped.

'Pardon?'

'Anna asked me to look into dogs. It's mostly tinks involved, but there's a couple of players fae Possil that lost their three best fighters in the raid Hoover Harris initiated. So we'll look at them next. You also mentioned this chappie Chaddha, but I've checked him out. He's no real convictions to speak of—bit of high jinks when he was a boy, but that's it.'

'Fraser seemed to think he was a big-time ned,' said Anna.

243

'Naw, I think Jazzie boy likes to give that impression, but he's pretty much a naebody. Plus, and I hate to say this, I really do . . . and I'm *no* a racist, but the guy's . . . well, the last thing we want to do at the moment is huckle folk fae the Asian community for no obvious reason. It's all settled doon after that Aziz boy, and I've nae desire to wind folk up. However, as regards Avalon,' he cleared his throat, 'I have to report as follows . . .'

He went on to read out a two-page report, the sum of which was that Avalon's prints did not match those on the brick; no black-coloured car appeared to be owned or stored by him, and he had sound alibis for both the evening when the brick was thrown and the night Fraser was attacked. Plus, he looked nothing like either of the boys Fraser had described. But the good news was that some of the notes Fraser had originally seized from him were, in fact, counterfeit. As the owner of a busy pub, Avalon could legitimately claim that 'money passed through his hands like water', but still, it was a tentative hook into something. Not sufficient to keep Avalon incarcerated, but at least he was on their list.

'Aye, we'll be keeping our eye on Avalon for a number of reasons.' Cruikshanks waved his roll and sausage like a flag. Spluttered. 'I'm sorry. *Avalon*. I laugh every time I hear it. I mean, what kind of a gay-boy name is that? Oh, sorry sir,' he added, glancing at Johnny. 'I mean,' he finished chewing, 'it is rather camp, is it not?'

Johnny turned a gracious head. He had a lovely, long neck, the kind of cropped-in hair that just sat perfect on the nape. 'And is that particularly relevant, Tom?'

244

'Well, no . . .'

'So,' Johnny moved to look at Claire. 'You're Fraser's inspector. How d'you think the boy's holding up?'

'I think he's got balls of steel.'

'Hmm, I'm not so sure,' said Anna. 'Personally, I think he's in denial. He's playing it down *too* much. Either that, or he knows more than he's saying.'

'How do you mean?' asked Claire.

'Well, like there's been some other incident or threat that he's not told us about. Or perhaps *he*'s instigated something he's not proud of—'

'Look, Fraser Harris hates neds, but there's *no* way he's bent.'

'Claire, I wasn't suggesting that,' said Anna. 'But he does have a low tolerance threshold.'

And there had been something in his demeanour when they last spoke—his reluctance to involve his family, or to discuss suspects and options—that belied his stoicism.

'I mean,' Anna glanced at each of her colleagues, 'let's be honest, we've all been there. Someone winds you up, you give them a wee smack. Dog their footsteps for the next few weeks. Stop their car every time you see them on the road, maybe turn up at their door in the middle of the night to ask some spurious "questions".' She waited for the shame-faced nods of recognition; felt virtual tumbleweed blow instead. 'No? Anybody? Shit, have I just divulged my modus operandi?'

'No, I know exactly what you mean,' said Cruikshanks. 'And, eh, I hate to say it, but there's one other thing naebody's mentioned: that it's got fuck all to do with the job at all.'

'Like a neighbour dispute?' said Claire.

'I was thinking mair like a pissed-off husband, one who disny like Fraser shagging his wife.'

'Och, come *on*.' Claire's cheeks were an attractive, preppy pink. 'That's not like Fraser at all.'

'But how do we *know*? These are all things we need to consider.' Cruikshanks picked up the intelligence report, then flopped it back down. 'Particularly in the absence of many other decent suggestions.'

Johnny clicked his fingers for the file. 'Let's just recap. Now, Fraser managed to get the first two letters of the motor: MD, then possibly a five and a two. Which narrows it down to vehicles registered in Manchester or Merseyside, in September 2002. Divisional Intelligence are saying there are several possibles for the originals, with the same combination of digits, but none relating to a black Nissan Primera. So, we're definitely looking at false plates.'

'But it'll still be useful to track down all the originals?' said Anna.

'Yep, DIO's currently getting that done. We've also got the descriptions of the two males—quite distinctive. Of course, there's always a possibility that these boys do work for Avalon—so Tom, perhaps you could get someone to do a bit of subtle poking around in the Tammy Lin . . . and its salubrious environs.'

'Will do, sir. I've also had Fraser go through pages of photographs, but no joy. Though what I'm thinking is we ask every cop in the division to look through the same pictures. You never know, we might get lucky; we could just circulate them at the

246

start of each shift.'

'Fraser won't like that,' said Claire. 'He doesn't want everyone knowing.'

'Tough shit for Fraser,' said Johnny. 'Everyone knows now anyway—special thanks going to our local rag. Anna, are you dealing with that?'

'Yup.' Her tone was grim. 'Miss Manning is coming in to see me this evening. And I'm going out to speak to Fraser's wife tomorrow, too.'

Bugger, so she was. No day at the hairdresser's for her then. Quick, slow, quick, quick slow. Like a sweeping tango, Anna's train of thought, her very sympathies themselves, spun in another direction. It happened every day, and it wasn't because there was too much on her mind; it had been like that for ages, was getting worse. To vacillate so fast, her concern for Fraser and his family becoming an irritation that they cast a shadow on her plans; was that normal?

'Good stuff,' said Johnny, apparently still talking to Anna. 'Claire, I want you to consider every case Fraser's done since he came here, any incidents, even visits to schools, whatever. Speak to each cop he's neighboured, find out if there's anything he's not telling us, okay? And then check with his previous division too.'

'Will do. Though he was in the Support Unit before, which widens the net a bit.'

'Sure, not for a smart girl like you. Checking every pissed-off ned in the whole of Strathclyde? A doddle. I expect your report by teatime. Speaking of which,' he checked his watch, 'Mrs H and I have a date, so if you good people will excuse me,' he rose, 'I think that's us for the moment.'

'Anna,' said Cruikshanks. 'Can I have a word?'

247

'Sure.' Anna went to sit beside him.

'You know that roommate of Mrs Maguire's?' said Cruikshanks.

'Yes. Manju? How did you get on with her?'

'We didn't, is the short answer. I tried, a DC tried, the doctor tried; even got one of the nurses to speak to her in Hindu.'

'Hindu isn't a language, it's a faith.'

'Well, even God didny help then, because she wouldny utter a word. So,' he chewed, 'I was wondering . . .'

'Mm?'

'Seen as Manju's already been having tête-à-têtes with you . . . could you have a go? See if you can pin down exactly when she saw Cassie last. Find out more about these big black men? Who they were; if they ever came back.'

'Oh Tom, I don't know.'

You came back.

Anna didn't want to come back. Manju, in her confusion, had patently mixed her up with someone else. Never play with Ouija boards: you don't know what doors you're opening. She'd already tried to speak to her again, and got thumped in the jaw for her trouble. Making some strange connection with a witness was rarely good; worse still was clicking with a suspect. And some did, they sought that click, they liked you. They thought you were their friend, because you smiled, had perfume and bobbed hair. Don't let them in, give nothing away. That was how you got hurt, how you got threatened like Fraser. He *must* have done something to trigger it.

'Anna? Will you? Please? We're running out of time with poor old Cassie. If I get no

248

breakthroughs today, then I'll have to go public.'

'And risk getting her killed?'

'Well, if I don't she's going to die anyway.' He batted his eyelids, dredged up a creepy wee-girl simper. 'Please?'

'Fine.'

Neither did she wish to visit Rob Macklin again. Not yet.

'And will you do it now?'

Cruikshanks got a DC to run her up to The Meadows. They'd been trying to keep a lid on things, but it was impossible to smudge the sharpness of prying eyes, to damp the ring of clipping heels, the essential muddle of an ongoing investigation. Unknown men in suits, not visiting their mothers, but slipping in the back. Clutches of pensioners taken in to see Matron, two by two for comfort and speed. All the staff agreeing to their fingerprints being taken, to racking their brains, but telling no one.

This can't go outside these walls.

Please understand how important this is.

If you care about finding Cassie as much as we do, then you won't mention this to a soul.

But someone did, of course they did. They always do.

Anna recognised the woman from the snap above her byline. It was unlikely two people would have the same scraggy red hair, parted in the middle and anchored in Pre-Raphaelite clumps round either ear. Lucy Manning, up close and personal, chatting to Rob Macklin. Little rounded teeth agleam as she nibbled on her pen. Anna pinched the DC's elbow. 'What is *she* doing here?'

'Who?'

'That woman. She's a journalist.'

'You're joking. How did she get in?'

'You tell me, Sherlock. And where the hell is Corporate Communications? They're not just there to feed these beasts—they're meant to corral them too. I want a press officer here, now.' She left the DC, headed straight for Rob and his pink-cheeked chum.

'Mr Macklin—Robert. Hi!'

'Anna,' he beamed. 'Tom said you were coming up. I don't know how—'

Anna arched past him to shake the journalist's hand. Tried to glower him into silence at the same time, but there was something lovely about his face. It shone on seeing her, a genuine pleasure that gleamed and broke around her. Then her antennae picked up on the journalist again.

'And you must be Miss Manning. Good to meet you, Lucy. Heard a lot about you. *Southside Sentinel*, is that right?'

Rob's grin slithered from his face. You could almost trace its progress down to the floor. 'I'm sorry? Miss Manning, you said you were with the press office.'

'No actually, I think I just said press.' Her accent was thickly English. Yorkshire, Lancashire? It held the unmasticated grit of puddings and ale, the spotted, murky stuff with peculiar names and bits floating in.

'And I think you were just leaving, is that right? I'm Anna Cameron, by the way.'

'Actually, I hadn't quite finished here.'

'Oh, I think you had.' Anna linked her arm through Lucy's. 'Let me walk you out. We can chat on the way. Saves us having our meeting later on.'

'Excuse me. Can you let me go please?'

'What? Certainly.' Anna already had her at the reception desk, could afford to loosen her grip. 'But this isn't the best place to talk. Why don't we use this office?'

She led Lucy into the office behind reception, pressed the door tight shut behind them.

'Are you telling me I can't move around freely here?'

'Are you telling me you identified yourself clearly on arrival, and stated the exact nature of your business?'

Lucy rolled pale eyes.

'Remember, this is a *private* establishment, full of vulnerable elderly people. Mr Macklin has a duty of care to all his residents, and he's well within his rights to ask any uninvited callers to leave. Or have them removed, if necessary.' Anna pulled out a chair for Lucy. 'Why don't you sit down, Miss Manning? Tell me, what exactly was it you came here to find out?'

'Well, I don't think it's any secret to you. We heard that there'd been a kidnapping.'

'No, sorry. No such thing.'

'Pardon? Sorry, can I just note this down?' Lucy flicked a spiral-bound notepad from her bag. 'You're denying that Cassie Maguire has been kidnapped?' She shook her head as she wrote. 'Incredible. Even though she's been missing for virtually a week now—you can ask any of the staff here, and they'll tell you. Yet there's been a total news blackout. Even now, you're still denying it.' She put her pen down, eyeballed Anna. 'How do you explain that? Is it because the police are trying to cover something up?'

251

'Not at all. No, what I'm saying is there's no such thing as kidnapping. You're in Scotland now, Miss Manning. It's called abduction.'

'Oh, for God's sake. Aren't you being a little pedantic?'

'I'd have thought a journalist would want absolute accuracy in their stories—if they were to be taken seriously, that is. Which leads me to another matter: your piece in this week's paper about the assault on one of my cops. Can I ask why you wrote it?'

'Because it was news.'

'Yes, but did you make any approach to our Corporate Communications department, to verify the story?'

'Of course.'

'And did they not expressly advise that this should be kept out of the press, as it was part of an ongoing investigation, and could jeopardise the safety of one of my officers?'

'They did.'

'But you still went ahead and printed it. *With* the officer's address.'

'Ms Cameron, my job is to seek out and write news stories, yours is to look after your officers. I can't help it if you're not able to do that properly.'

'I see. And I take it you intend to write about Mrs Maguire's disappearance too? Can I ask exactly what information you've gleaned, please? And where it came from?'

Lucy grinned. 'Chief Inspector Cameron. If your cops are really having that much trouble digging up leads, I'll be happy to pass on what we have. Anything to help your investigation. I take it we *are* in agreement now? I mean, there is actually an investigation, isn't there?'

They could skirt round this issue forever. Anna knew it and Lucy knew it. After today, maybe even later on this afternoon, Tom or the area detective super would have to make a decision about when and where a press conference would be called. Virtually everyone in the home had now been interviewed. Several spoke to seeing Cassie running on the landing most nights, draped in a variety of saris. It was her take-off strip, she told them. Someone always caught her, took her back to bed. They took it in turns, the nurses, to watch out for her, and Rob Macklin had had a stair-gate fitted, so she couldn't fall downstairs. It was an old one of his daughter's, but it did the job, and allowed Cassie to have her crazy way.

'A stair-gate?' she'd asked. 'Really? Is that standard old folks' equipment?'

'It does no harm. And she was terrified of being locked up, Anna. Told me she'd fly out of the window if I didn't let her run.'

'What about lockable bed-guards, sedation?'

His lips had pressed into a disapproving tilde. She saw her blurted, impatient words reflected in his face and felt ashamed. These were the very things she had castigated him for when they first met.

'Why not just give them a final jag and be done with it?' he'd said. 'Look, I thought it was a phase. To get it out of her system.' He breathed heavily. 'I didn't realise, though. I thought . . . Sometimes they go like that—just before the end. A last mad memory of energy. And . . . it's . . . well, what right do I have to deny them that?'

'Do *you* think Cassie's dead?'

253

He must have been so frustrated by what little activity he could see: the milling; the talking; the slow, methodical lack of action. The telly taught you that policing was all swift rolls over the bonnets of stripy cars, haring pursuits down alleyways, and an hour-long window of opportunity (or fifty minutes, if you counted the adverts) for the beautiful forensic scientist to uncover indisputable truths. But investigation was often a messy slog. Anna was glad she was rarely part of it. Proper, efficient criminal investigations could be a long and meticulous process. Your suspect, all the answers you crave, might be unknown and yet lie tantalisingly close for days, weeks, months. They might never be unmasked but burrow always like an ever-present toothache; or worse, they might be known, but remain untouchable. That was the most horrible type of investigation as far as Anna was concerned, and one that she had been involved in, several times in her statutory stint in Family Protection. Having to wait and collate, forbidden to intervene while a known abuser carries on living in his sordid home, unable to act because the evidence you have gathered is not yet sufficient for its task. Yes. That was the worst kind: impatient, complicit *watching*.

'I think she must be,' he'd said, finally, touching his lips. 'She couldn't have lasted this long without her medication.'

'And it definitely wasn't taken with her?'

'No, it's all locked away in the cabinet. Shit.' He closed his eyes. It was the first time she'd heard him swear. 'Maybe I *should* have locked her up.'

But he hadn't, so Cassie had been free to roam the landing in the night, the same as she would have been in her own house. And that was all anyone had seen—no unexplained visitors, no unlocked doors. The phone call the abductors made had been traced to a stolen mobile phone. The call had been made in Glasgow, and no further contact had been initiated since. If the Maguires could give the police nothing else, a major media appeal would need to be launched, and very, very soon.

Lucy Manning sniffed, bringing Anna back to earth. She was tugging a paper hanky from inside her sleeve.

'Well?'

The journalist blew her nose, the fingers lingering for a cheeky poke around. Didn't look into her hanky, but you *knew* she wanted to. Was definitely the type. Anna could just concede and let this woman write what she wanted. After all, it was a weekly paper; by the time it came out, the story would be old news anyway. But that wasn't the point.

'Lucy, does it bother you at all that you could be putting Cassandra Maguire's life at risk if you publish this story? All I'm asking is that you wait a couple more days. Then, maybe we could look at—'

'Look, I'm not stupid. You lot are never going to give the inside track to a local free-sheet. We get the crappy "cops running football tournaments" stories, and the cheesy photo ops.'

'Well, I'm going to have to speak to your editor then.'

Lucy stood up, shouldered her bag. 'You speak all you want, chuck. I'm only on a temporary contract with the *Sentinel*, and I'm firing freelance copy off left, right and centre to anyone who'll pick it up. Believe me, someone *will* pick this up. And if I don't write it, another journalist will.' She tapped her forehead with her notepad. 'Be seeing you, Anna.'

A brief respite, while Anna sat, considered what she was going to do next. Then the door opened and Rob came in. His face parched.

'Anna, I'm so sorry. I had no idea she was a journalist.'

'What did you tell her?'

Spectacles off. Rub, rub, rub. She wanted to seize his hand, stop the discs of glass from flashing.

'It was really her that did all the talking. You know, just chatting, saying what a terrible thing it was. I mean, she knew all about it already.' The suggestion of a hopeful smile.

'But you probably just confirmed it all, yes?'

'I suppose . . .' His face lost its animation.

Look at me again. Like you did when I came in.

'Did she speak to anyone else?'

'I'm not sure. Yes, I guess she must have—she was already here when I came down the stairs.'

Anna banged her head once against the desk. Let her cheek rest there for an instant, enjoying the cool, unyielding blankness of the wood. 'Right. We'll need to get a press conference set up now, before she files her copy to the highest bidder. At least that way we can control some of what's said. I'll phone Cruikshanks. And I'd better speak to Manju, quick.'

'Sure . . . Anna, I know this isn't a good time. But . . . how's your mum?'

She sat up. 'My mum's okay. Why?'

'It's just . . . I'd been making some enquiries.

There's a chap in Madrid I was at uni with—'

He was squeezing the personal into the space reserved for professional control. It *would not* do.

'Look,' she lifted her mobile, 'can we do this later? Please?'

'Yes, sure.'

She dialled Cruikshanks's mobile. 'Tom? Hi. Anna. Listen, have you got a draft media release prepared already?'

'Aye?' There was an echo.

'Where are you?'

'I'm in the bog,' he whispered.

'Oh. Sorry. Anyway. Have you got a format for the press conference too?'

'Yes.'

'Good. Well, you'll need to bring it forward. There's been a journalist nosing about . . .' She paused as Cruikshanks began his rant.

'How? Who let . . .? How the fuck did he get in?'

'I don't know, do I? But it was me that found her—she, not he, so stop bloody going on at me. Just get your arse up here and sort it, right? And no, I'm not playing at Kirsty Young—you can do your own dirty work.'

'Go on. You promised.'

'Did I buggery. Get Johnny; he's much prettier than me. And don't forget to wash your hands.'

Rob was still waiting, next to her, as she put away her phone, zipped her oath-filled mouth. At least she hadn't sworn direct at him; she didn't think she had. She felt visible, like he'd witnessed her in the shower. He was resting on the edge of the desk, one foot rubbing on the back of his other leg. His tie swung against his belt, his fingers spread on the wood, keeping him balanced.

'Look, just one other thing—' He brought his hands together. Some kind of announcement?

'Yes?'

'I . . . I've got two tickets here, for a dinner thing. I wondered . . . I know it's short notice, but it's on tomorrow night, and I wondered if you'd like to come?'

Did he realise he was twisting his wedding ring as he spoke?

'No.'

Anna flattened the word, pushing it tight and disapproving.

'No?'

'No. Absolutely not. I don't get involved with—'

She had been going to say married men, but that would have caused the very gods to reach from their clouds, slap her for her cheek.

'People at work. No, thanks, but no.'

A dark note in his expression, his face folding in. He seemed genuinely hurt. Flustered, Anna edged past him. 'I'll go and see Manju now. I'm going to need her next-of-kin details too, please.'

'Of course.'

*   *   *

Manju lay on her back, staring at the ceiling. Her hands were folded at chest height, on top of white sheets that could have been a shroud. Perfectly still, just a tiny rise and drop as evidence she was alive. Anna had asked to be left alone with her. She didn't want to be, but, if Manju was going to talk, the chances were that she would do so without an audience.

258

'Manju, I know you can hear me, and I know you know I'm here. I need to talk to you about Cassie.'

Nothing.

'Manju—she's your friend, and she's in trouble. Do you remember when I was here before? And you were singing, mind? The nurse told me that Cassie said there had been some men in your room. Were there? Did they come back?'

Trying to stay soft. No stridency, breathing gently. The smell here was the same as her mum's room: false, snappy perfumes; brown and damp beneath.

'Remember? Singing about the mighty Saracens? Big black men, Cassie said.'

Big black men.

To an old, confused woman, it might not be black. Brown could be black, could be all manner of unfamiliar hues.

'Manju—was it you? Were they after you, maybe?'

A fluttering lift, just a stutter of wrinkled hands, quick as a cough, then rigid.

'Were these men Asian?'

No response.

'Manju, if you don't help me, I've got nowhere else to go. You said I'd come back. Well, I did. I don't know what you mean, but I did come back, twice now. And I want to get Cassie back too; we both do. But you have to speak to me. *Please.*'

Anna lifted the old lady's hand into hers. It flopped, impassive, her eyes fixed high and distant. She waited and she waited, stroking those cold, still fingers, willing words to rise from somewhere. She had depressed the mute button once, why not this time, when it mattered? The seconds faltered, shifted, were lost. Gently, Anna laid Manju's hand on the coverlet.

'Fair enough. I'm going to leave you now. But I *will* come back, Manju. I'll keep coming back, till you talk to me.'

Even this close, Manju's face could be dim wax. Except for the glittering line, running diagonal from eye to ear. Anna wiped it away.

CHAPTER THIRTEEN

Tonight, it seems, she does want something more than the guard's blank and silent presence.

'Och son. Is it daytime outside? I know I couldny feel it. It wouldny heat ma toes or ma legs any more. But see if I could just see the sunshine. Just to know that it was there. Can you no do that for me son? Please?'

She does not know that he understands. Intent on scooping up her soft-rasped words, he does not realise how close their faces are, that she can feel his tears dripping on her face.

'Ach, you're feart, poor mite. Ssh now son. That's the boy. You curl up safe beside me.'

He lies on the floor as he is bid. And takes her hand.

'We've had a lot of lovely blethers, me and you. More than we've talked in a lifetime. Ach, you were some chatterbox when you were wee. Why is the sky, mammy? you'd say. Why is the sun? And I'd ssh you and gie you a jelly piece.'

He remembers when he last held his own child.

Then her breath comes again. Ragged.

'I wanted to answer you son. But I had to keep you quiet. Keep you safe. And then, when you got bigger, you kept me safe. Mind? You promised that son. No matter what.'

It is too much.

'I am not your son!' He rises, flees, and spills the water he has brought. The water that she has not yet drunk, but he will not go back down. He will not.

It will only be her heartbeat keeping her company in the dark. Her tongue out, trying to catch drips of condensation.

*   *   *

Queen's Drive was a dark dead-end, fringed along one side by the fat gnarled oaks of Queen's Park itself. This should have lent the street an open perspective of rolling hills and rural ripeness, even on the dankest days. It did not. It was as if the park itself was bursting out, too full of oily green to be sustained. Ornate black railings jostled against the tree trunks, some trees actually breaking through in places, their urgent root systems forcing pavement up and iron asunder, sap-blistered whorls which were riven by bowed metal. Two empty tennis courts waited in the rain, their nets sodden, and seagulls dived and cackled at litter bins.

This was where Manju's next of kin lived. A lady by the name of Carol Jenkins. Anna's flat was on the other side of the very same park, but it was nothing like this. There, flower beds skirted a Victorian glasshouse, broad paths led to a flagpole summit and breathtaking views. This end felt

261

slouched, like it wore a perpetual hood. The line of terraced Victorian sandstones facing the park had missed out on the cleansing scurries of their inner-city cousins. They had never been sand-blasted, never had new glass doors fitted in shades that were not dark purple or dark green. Of course, the buildings would have changed inside; everything does. Some had become flats, some dentists and opticians. A few remained as townhouses, while a whole chunk of the buildings had merged into a suburban hotel, three sets of stairs linked by matching, etched lamps. Dripping rooks took shelter below the angled glass. Pity the discerning traveller who decided to holiday in this hotel. Unaware of the 's' that should have been included in the sign, they would bowl up with their luggage, murmur approvingly at the park, and swing wide the door. Then quickly back away, as the smell of unwashed bodies and alcohol, the gaggle and grumble of half-cut voices and wholly cut heads spilled to greet them.

The hostel was a halfway house between prison and the streets; a stepping stone to getting a job, a Giro, a source of new mates, new drugs, or easy meat on which to prey, depending on your cash-flow, appetite or inclination. A couple of men loitered outside, their heads raised to follow Anna's passage; her scowl fixed full ahead to dissuade theirs. Carol Jenkins lived near the end of the row, this one, with purple pansies tumbling from an orange plastic barrel. Anna had thought of phoning ahead but, invariably, it was better just to turn up. That way, you got to see the whole, unvarnished picture; the face, the lips, the eyebrows up or down. The hands that wavered or the voice that caught. You could taste the genuine surprise, or sniff the subterfuge. Going by that principle, she should now be in Spain, confronting Teddy face to face.

'Any spare change, doll?'

Eyes down, keep walking. Another dosser was heading towards her from Victoria Road. You could tell by the filthy jeans and beat-up shoes, the rolling limp that came from one too many injections.

There was 'trendy distressed', and there was distressed.

Their shoulders nearly collided; the man wasn't for shifting course and neither was she. An edge of chin, of tilt-turned nose. Something about the defiance of a walk that once was buoyant made her halt, look round.

'No! Shelly?'

The man kept going. 'Michelle? Michael—is that you?'

He stopped, stayed small and tight. Unturning. Anna hurried back towards him, spun him round. Shelly from the fish shop where she'd got Alice. Her GBF, the Laughing Cavalier who'd turned out to be a money-lender.

'Michael! Michael, it *is* you! How are you?'

In her delight, she couldn't stop grinning, even as the image of their last meeting took focus: Shelly in the dock, and her in the witness box.

Shelly nodded, brusque. 'Officer.' Said loud enough that the other two men quickly dispersed around the corner.

She held his face, forcing him to look at her. 'Michelle, it's me, Anna!'

'I know. And it's no Michelle, it's Michael.

Michael Meek.'

'But how are you, how've you been?'

He tugged away from her hands. '*Since* jail you mean? Or how about during it? Oh, jail's fucking ace, thanks very much for asking. Didny take them long to sniff me oot at all. First week and I was getting it good style—'

'Shelly, don't.'

'Aye, but don't worry. I just got fucking fulla the junk. So that took the worst of it away—well, you canny really feel it after a while any road.'

'Oh, Shelly, Jesus.'

He was facing up to her. *Making* her listen, making her pay. 'Okay, maybe we should just talk about the trial. Mind that, *Anna*? You, firing me in, getting me to grass up ma own big brother.'

'Shelly, you did that of your own accord.'

'I did it for you, ya cow,' he shouted. 'And what did you do for me? What the fuck did you do for me?'

'What could I do? I'm a cop.'

'You could of fucking come and seen me. Just once.'

'But prisoners need to request their own visitors. You know that.'

'Don't gie me that shite. You're a polis, you could of come. You could of wrote me a note or . . .' He was sobbing, rage-filled hands quivering, and she drew him into her arms, held him as he squirmed and stiffened and grew still.

'Oh, Shelly,' she whispered, stroking his flat, sparse hair. 'Oh pal, I'm so sorry.'

Where had that light gone, the cheek and sparkle of him, his vigour for life? Shelly, with his glittery overalls, his tweezed, arched brows and coiffeured hair, smelling of Gauloises, of Gaultier, not of caked-in sweat.

'I lost ma house, ma shop. I lost ma family.' Wet words, breathed into her cheek. He pulled away, shaking still. 'I lost ma fucking cat.'

She seized him again, this time by the hands. 'No. No, you didn't. I went back for her, searched all round. Three nights on the trot on my bloody hunkers in that stinking lane, wandering up and down Woodlands with a tin of Kitekat.'

Shelly tilted his head, considering. 'For real?'

'Yes, for real. Giving it, "Here Julie. Yoo-hoo, Julie Andrews!"'

The merest glimmer of a smirk.

'I even . . .' she shut her eyes at the memory, 'I even rubbed myself in Alice's blanket before I left, in case the smell attracted her. You know, what with Julie being Alice's mum.'

Shelly was trembling again. His thin hands spasming in hers. She opened her eyes, realised he was laughing.

'Did you no think about skinning her and just pure tossing on the pelt?'

'For your information, it was very effective, actually. Because I found her.'

'You didny!'

'I did. Gave her to my pal Jenny—you know the policewoman I used to work with?'

'Tonka?'

'Tonka? Shelly, I thought you were gay?'

'Am are, but everyone called her that. "Big toys"—term of endearment, know? So—Julie! Where is she? Can I get her?'

'Oh Shelly, I don't know. I haven't seen Jenny for years. And you're not exactly well placed for keeping a cat, are you? I take it you're living here?'

'Aye, just for the now.' He sniffed, wiped his nose with the back of his hand. 'Till I get sorted and that, know? Get ma heid straight.'

'How long have you been here?'

He scuffed his foot along the kerb. 'Canny mind straight up. But I'm gonny get ma own place. Gonny get back on ma feet . . . aye.' His voice tailed off, the animation extinguished.

'Look, I'll see what I can do about Julie. I promise. But I think we need to get you sorted first, eh?'

'I'm great, me. Brand new.'

'I know you are. But maybe I can help, eh?'

There were a couple of charities Anna could contact. SACRO for one—they dealt with the care and settlement of ex-offenders. She could see about housing too, maybe find him a job. Shelly's whole body was jittering, even when he stood stock-still, like he was now. Hangdog, waiting to be kicked. Get real, Anna. No one would look at him until he was clean, in every sense.

'We could get you living somewhere a bit nicer for a start.'

Soft blue eyes, hopeful. 'Aye. I suppose.'

'And, here . . .' She stuffed some notes into his jacket pocket. 'You take that the now, alright? For food mind, maybe a clean shirt. *Nothing* else, you hear?'

A nod, another scuff.

'Look, I'm on my way to see someone just now, but here's my card. You can get me there any time—or leave me a message. I mean, I do go home sometimes.'

'Ooh—*Chief* Inspector, is it?' he read. 'Well,

266

thank Christ life's been kind to one of us. Take it you and Jamie Dreamboat bumped aff the wife and wean and set up home in a penthoose?'

'That's not even funny, Shelly.'

'Close but no cigar, eh?' His eyes squeezed thin. 'As Mr Clinton said to Monica.'

'Piss off.'

'So, no Mr Right after all?'

What did Shelly know about Jamie Worth? About what Anna had felt for him, how she dreamed of him, in some parallel existence, where they lived and laughed with their teenage daughter (it was always a daughter), fed each other champagne and kisses as they waited up for her to come home from yet another party. Because she was very popular their daughter; nineteen now, and beautiful. Anna was a super, and Jamie was . . . Jamie was probably still a cop, but they didn't mind, because they had twenty years of love packed inside. Her mum and dad, her *real* dad, were coming round for a barbecue . . .

The picture shrivelled.

And Shelly was greeting for a bloody *cat*?

'I've no got time for smart-arsed comments, alright? Just take the money.'

'Fuck you, *officer*.' He pushed her on the chest. It was only a Shelly-shove, hardly a whisper. 'And it's no Shelly—it's Michael, you hear me?'

'I hear you.' She seized his hand. 'Look. Do you want the money or not?'

His neck bent. 'Aye.'

'I will be in touch Michael, I promise.'

'Sure. Maybe we can go out on the town together, eh?'

A bitter imitation of a smile, then he limped

away, into the hostel.

She wished she'd never come here. The sad-eyed pansies at Carol Jenkins's door watched as she climbed the steps. Anna's gift of guilt-money had only made her feel more culpable; she relieved it by thumping sparks from the brass knocker.

A woman of around fifty answered. Thick dark brows and hair, with a vivid stripe of white at either temple. Her face was strong, sallow. The face of an all-weather golfer, or a tennis ace, perhaps, in her youth.

'Carol Jenkins? Sorry to bother you. I'm here about Manju Jaffar. I believe you know her?'

Anna was in civvies, had to show her warrant card before that first hint of revelation or concealment could swim to the surface. But the woman only looked perplexed.

'What's she done now?' Then a further slip of confusion, of genuine shock as police officer, female and kind-sad face all seeped to one obvious conclusion. 'Oh, she's not—'

'Manju is fine, Miss Jenkins. Can I come in?'

Straight into a panelled hall, then on to a polished front room. Beeswax and lavender, heavy, carved sideboard and deep green bergère suite. A plaster mermaid on the mantelpiece, with comedy breasts; all pendulous nipples and Beryl Cook proportions. An alabaster poodle either side of the fireplace, layered red then burnt umber, before fading into gold. The collar of one read 'Fire', the other 'Dogs'.

'Sit down, please,' said Carol. 'Can I get you some tea?'

Anna wondered if the woman was stalling. You'd want to know right away, wouldn't you?

What the police were calling for, what it had to do with you. But a drink was friendly, a little liquid bridge.

'Just water would be great, thanks.'

While Carol went off to the kitchen, Anna got back up, had a wander round the room. Nothing obviously Indian; plenty of rich colours, glitzy knick-knacks peeking like flowers from sombre undergrowth. A couple of photos on the wall. Black and white capture of a couple on their wedding day, the bride pale as her wartime gown, the groom taller, darker. Older. Gold frame for a toffee-eyed baby with chubby fists. Carol as a child? Next to that, a stunning print. Stunning in the sense not of finely wrought perspective, but of slap-you-round-the-face.

A *cri de coeur* on a pink background, stitched with letters and images like a patchwork ransom note. It was the yellow '40' that first hooked Anna's eye.

SHE WENT OUT LIKE A 40 WATT BULB

'Your water?'

'Oh, thanks.' Anna took the blue glass tumbler. 'Did you do this?'

Carol snorted. 'Wish I had. That's a Tracey Emin. Not an original, sadly.' She sat down on the couch. 'So. Manju?'

Anna opened her notebook. 'What's your relationship to Manju Jaffar, Miss Jenkins?'

'I don't actually have one.'

269

'Well, how well do you know her then?'

'Not very. In fact, I've never actually met her.'

'Can I ask then, how is it that you pay a sum each month for her upkeep at The Meadows Nursing Home in Newton Mearns?'

'It's not actually me, it's my father. Christopher Jenkins.'

Anna made a little note.

'Oh, I shouldn't bother trying to get in touch with him. He's dead.' Carol sipped her drink. 'Yes, has been many years now.'

Still addled from her encounter with Shelly, Anna just wanted this to be over. Then she could go home, open a bottle of wine, shut down her mind.

'Then how . . . ?'

'Manju was a woman that my father worked with. Reading between the lines, I think she got a bit of a crush on him. I remember when I was little, she used to sit outside our house, in the little park across the road, just staring in at us. All the time, in at the lounge, up at my room. We ended up moving actually, my mum got so upset.'

'So why did your family support her, if she was such a nuisance?'

'Manju struggled. There was some big furore at work, I'm not sure what. Before I was born. But it made her a little crazy, I think. I remember hearing my parents talking one day. My mum was on at Dad to call the police, but he wouldn't. My father was a great one for duty—he was a doctor, you know, always wanting to do his bit. Stray dogs, free consultations, you name it. I think my father brought Manju back from India, saved her sight or something. Then he must have got her a job, that's what my mother told me. Of course, we didn't realise he was helping her out financially too. Hadn't a clue, until the old man popped his clogs, and we saw he'd made provision for her in his will.' Carol drained her glass, clinked it back on the coffee table. 'I wanted to fight it, but my mother said let it be.' She glanced at the wedding picture on the wall. 'I know she was terribly hurt, though. When my mum died, well, I suppose I could have looked into it again then, but . . .' She clasped her hands. 'Didn't seem worth it, you know? They phone me occasionally, the home, to tell me how she's doing. And you never like to say, do you? I mean, it seems churlish to say "actually, I don't really care." That Mr Macklin phoned me the other week, in fact, to say there had been a bit of trouble. Oh,' Carol gasped, 'is *that* what this is about? I thought they found her under the bed?'

'No, they had, they have. Carol, do you know anything else about Manju, anything at all? Like where she came from originally?'

'No idea? India somewhere.'

'And where was it she and your father worked?'

'You know the Eye Infirmary, the one in Sandyford Place?'

Anna nodded. 'I think it's away now, but I'm sure I could still find records. Was she a nurse then?'

'Not sure. We *really* didn't talk much about her. She was . . . creepy, you know? Used to give me nightmares, that she'd come and get me. I'd wake up and she be out there in the dark, looking up at my window. Just standing, looking up. I mean, even after we moved . . . she still came back.'

'How do you mean?'

271

'Well, after we moved, I still used to come to Giffnock, for my piano lessons. And I'd often see her there, just sitting, staring at the house. You know, I'm sure I saw her years later too. The house had been demolished by then, they were turning it into—'

'Carol—you say you lived in Giffnock? Where exactly was your house?'

'Fenwick Road. Not far from the police station actually. We were right across from—'

'The little park?

'That's right.'

All those years. Her face was shrunken, her clothing less drab. But the eyes were still the same, Anna realised it now. Manju was Mad Maggie, who used to feed the birds. A tiny shift in the air, loose folds wrapping like damp cloth. Anna shivered, focused on the woman before her. 'And you've had no contact from her, or anyone else enquiring after her?'

'None at all,' said Carol. 'Can I ask why you want to know all this?'

Tom was preparing for the press conference imminently—it was the reason Anna had offered to come here: one, to be helpful, and two to avoid going anywhere near a bloody camera. So, it wouldn't matter what she withheld from Carol Jenkins, she would hear about it all on the news tonight anyway.

'The lady Manju shares a room with—a lady called Cassandra Maguire—has gone missing. We think she's been abducted, and I'm trying to find out if Manju is connected in any way.'

Carol's fingers at her face. 'Oh God. Poor soul! And do you think she is? Is Manju definitely

272

alright?'

'She's fine. Well, I mean, she's safe in her room, and obviously there's all sorts of security in place now. But Manju's not talking to anyone, I'm afraid, so it's really hard to tell how she is, or what she knows. I was kind of hoping you might be the key, but, if you've never even met Manju, it's unlikely you'd be able to get through to her.'

'No, but I could try though—if you think it would help?'

'I don't think so. Not at the moment. We're doing a press conference today, so we'll see what that throws up. But I'll bear your offer in mind, Miss Jenkins. Thanks.' Anna rose to leave. 'Here's my card. If there's anything else you remember about Manju—or if anybody, anybody at all, phones you, or asks you any questions about her, will you please let me know?'

'Of course. I do hope you find the old lady.'

'So do I, Miss Jenkins.' They walked back into the dark panelled hall. 'And thanks for your time.'

'No problem.' Carol Jenkins touched Anna's arm, compassion diffusing her hard, dark features. 'Look after Manju, will you?'

'I will.'

*　　　*　　　*

The press conference had generated all the headlines they had hoped it would—and several they'd anticipated too.

Forgotten OAP—police deny botch-up
Cassie Come Home: Gran lost—and nobody cares
Nursing home subject of enquiry

273

However, next day, the incident rooms were buzzing all the same; calls coming in, people scurrying out. A worrying development was when Robert Macklin had called to say that he couldn't actually find Cassie's medicine after all. He'd thought it had been locked away, Padma was sure she'd done it, but . . . well, the fact was, it wasn't there.

'But did you see it after Cassie had gone missing? Was it still there then?'

'I'm sure it was. Absolutely positive. I think.'

Anna passed the message on, in with all the other bits and pieces. Cruikshanks was permanently unavailable, but she'd gone ahead and arranged her flights to Spain. Slightly earlier than she had planned—next Thursday, in fact. She could find out Teddy's address when she got there, from one obliging gossip or another. Going so soon was not ideal, but her upstairs neighbour could only watch Alice until the middle of next week, and the Thursday flight was £150 cheaper than Friday or Saturday. There was another reason too. Mrs Hamilton had become even more draconian in her approach to granting time off. Claire Rodgers had just been complaining that one of her cops was refused a day to attend his own brother's wedding. By Anna's reckoning, she had more chance of getting away if she made it sound like an emergency. And it was, of a sort. Her mother hadn't improved one iota, so, using the logic that no improvement was the manifestation of a prolonged and sustained period of extreme ill health, you *could* argue that the situation was worsening. She'd wait until tonight, when she and Johnny were dining *à deux*, come over all tearful

274

after the pakora, and ask for time off then. Busy restaurant, quivering lip and a few nice glasses of wine. And a genuine, real need to see her mum. If Johnny approved her time off, then Mrs H would have to agree. Yes, they were busy, they were always busy, but people did have a life outside the police. Even Mrs Hamilton.

Fraser Harris was waiting for Anna, elbow on the uniform bar, car keys draped over one finger.

'We'll take my car, ma'am, yes? Less attention that way—I don't want a marked car turning up.'

Anna had already considered Fraser's sensibilities, had planned to take her own car. But his every angle and jut was radiating angry, forced concession; she'd no wish to antagonise him further.

'Sure. At least you know the way, eh?'

Not even a flicker. She tried to engage him on the journey, asking about his kids, his wife. Each answer just long enough to convey the information and short enough to convey distaste.

Holly and Sam.

Assistant manager.

At a bank.

Royal Bank.

A rasping sigh. *Buchanan Street.*

Fraser's house was lovely, warm russet sandstone, an Edwardian end of terrace. A fine sandstone church loomed near to the house; it was the first thing Anna had seen as they'd driven up Ormonde Drive and into the Crescent; a red Celtic cross on a hill. Heart of the aspirational suburbs this; old houses and new families, two cars for every house and lollipop lime trees in all the gardens. You could see the marks on the low

275

sandstone walls where metal railings had been sawn off for the war effort; young Germans killed by melted-down fences.

Parking was tricky, even at this time of day, narrow streets and broad 4x4s jockeying for supremacy. Any surveillance vehicles would have to stake out a space before they staked out the house, then work in a relay, one slipping out as one came in—otherwise they'd never get parked at the shift changeover. The Harrises had knocked part of their garden wall down, and taken end-terrace advantage by building a driveway on the thin strip of land there; but plonking a couple of hairy-arsed polis slap in the middle of the driveway would be slightly counterproductive to the element of secrecy.

Fraser's wife met them at the door, rich chestnut hair spilling on her shoulders, down her back. Where her husband growled, she grinned, a broad, happy face, still plump with the fat of the baby swaddled in her arms.

'Look Sammy. It's Da-da! And Da-da's friend Ah-na. Hello Ah-na.'

Anna shook the baby's tiny fist. 'And hello Sam. Mrs Harris, pleased to meet you.'

The girl shook back ropes of her hair, so greedily thick beside Anna's neat, weak bob. 'It's Maria, please. Come on in.'

She made it sound like a game-show host talking, singing out the words. Instantly, Anna liked her, liked the way she radiated joy as bold and bare as her grubby feet. A being to make you smile, in the same way Alice did. She suspected that, like Anna herself, nobody ever guessed Maria's job; for bank managers were dusty, dry things, just as cops were all crew-cut automatons.

'Where's Holly?' asked Fraser.

'At nursery, dummy.' Maria stuck out her tongue. 'Honestly, he's not got a clue. I run this house single-handed you know.'

'Shut it, you.'

He slapped his wife's backside as they went inside.

The lounge still had the original fireplace, an elegant wood and glass cabinet set into the alcove beside it. A swollen gold couch lay on either side of the fire, and a piano took up the far wall.

'Fraser, my love,' said Maria. 'Do you want to make some tea?'

'Not really.'

'Och, c'mon you grumpy bugger. Away and make yourself useful. D'you mind where the kettle is?'

'Funny woman.' But he went anyway.

'So.' Maria grinned, inclusive, like Anna was in on the joke. 'Fraser tells me I've not to listen to a word you say, but be very nice all the same.'

'Is that right?'

'Oh yes, but I've not to tell you that either.'

They both laughed.

'He's probably right,' said Anna. 'We just want to be really careful, so we're crossing all our Ts, you know? In fact, I'm sure we are overreacting, but I just wanted to be clear that you were aware, one, of what's been going on and two, what we're doing to keep Fraser—and you—safe.'

The baby began to girn. 'Ssh now, Samwise.' Maria shoogled him gently, but the crying got louder.

'Look, I'm sorry, but I think he's hungry.' She

began to unbutton her blouse. 'Do you mind?'

'Of course not—it's your house.'

'Oh, you'd be surprised,' said Maria, lopping out a fat white breast. 'Folk can get funny anywhere. I was in a café once, with Holly as well as Sam, and the manager told me I'd need to go into the toilets, 'cause I was upsetting the rest of the customers.' As she spoke, she rolled her nipple between thumb and the bent knuckle of her index finger, easing the flesh up and then in to her baby's mouth. She looked up at Anna. 'Sorry—he's not too good at latching on, I'm afraid. I need to kind of aim and fire. Ah, that's you, sunshine.'

A blissful lull as the crying ceased, wiped away by gentle smacking sounds.

'It's a bugger if you don't get them on right—but nobody tells you that. With Holly I ended up with a bruise like a gorilla's love-bite; had mastitis for a week.' She shuddered. 'You got kids yourself?'

'Um . . . no.' Anna smiled, brisk, clean teeth to show that it was fine, it was a conscious choice both made and reconciled with.

The baby's eyes were closed, instinct or smell directing his mouth to move and draw and swallow, while his fist unfurled, a bloom to pat his mother's breast. Nearly four decades alive, and Anna had never been this close to a mother feeding her child. Rhythmic, beautiful, curving love, and she'd never even seen it.

'So. Is Fraser in trouble then?' Idly said, Maria's thumb stroking the top of Sam's head.

'Honestly? I don't know. There's been the incident outside your house. You know about that, don't you?'

'I do now. Daft eejit wasn't going to tell me at

first.'

'Well, there's been that, and then there was a brick thrown through the office window, which we reckon was meant for him too.'

'Yeah—with the newspaper article attached?'

'That's right. And we know he's been followed from work a couple of times, but we're still no closer to finding out who.' Anna allowed the words to trail. 'I mean, would you have any idea who it could be?'

'Me? How would I know?'

Anna shrugged. 'Is there anyone you know of who's got a grudge against Fraser?' A little scratch, casual, at her arm. 'Or who Fraser might have a grudge against? Have you ever heard of a guy called Dougie Avalon, for instance? He's got a right bad reputation for violence—nearly choked a man he caught chatting up his wife.'

Not strictly true. Avalon had once been charged with assault, yes, but the charges arose when he thumped a man whose drunken carelessness caused a pint of lager to spill over Avalon's wife. And he'd never been convicted.

A clud of door on wall as Fraser came in with the tea. He slammed the tray on top of the piano, the swift crack causing the baby to jerk and start crying.

'Fraser!' said Maria.

'Right, ma'am. I don't quite know what you're driving at, but I think you've said enough.'

'Fraser, for goodness' sake, let the woman talk.'

'And do what? Scare you shitless? And this has got bugger all to do with Dougie Avalon either. If I had some big issue with him, I'm hardly likely to mention his name, am I? All that's happened here

279

is some anonymous neds have taken a dislike to me. Because I'm doing my fucking job.' This last was directed full and firm at Anna.

'Well, you won't be doing it for much longer if you speak to me like that, pal.'

'Meaning?'

'Meaning I can either recommend a period of sick leave, or suspension.'

'For what? For fucking what?'

'Fraser, will you please stop swearing and calm down?' Maria got up, baby still anchored to her breast. 'Look, Anna—I appreciate you coming and everything, but I think you'd better go. Let me talk to him, please.' An entreaty. '*Please.*'

Mouth pursed, a single nod. Anna's alternative was to hit Fraser about the head and body till he came to his senses. Or told her the truth. 'Fraser, I'll say to Inspector Rodgers I've granted you time off for the rest of this week. Don't argue with me, or I'll just make it longer. Maria, as yet, we don't know who we're dealing with, what they might do next, or what, exactly, their gripe is. But we do know that they know where you live, and so we've arranged for twenty-four-hour surveillance on your house for the next few weeks.' She put a little box on the table. 'I've also brought you a panic alarm. There's a jack there too—if you plug this in to connect with your phone socket, and set it for nine-nine-nine on the keypad, it'll go straight to—'

Fraser snatched up the box. 'I know how it fucking works.'

'Fraser—will you stop swearing?' said his wife. 'I'm really sorry about this.'

'It's alright, honestly,' said Anna. 'I realise you're both under pressure.'

'Only because you're creating a mountain out of a bloody molehill.'

'Well, we don't know that, Fraser.'

There was no point in prolonging this visit any further. The baby was crying, Maria's sunny face had dulled and Fraser stood with his back to them all, staring out the window at an empty street. It was only as the front door closed behind her that Anna remembered Fraser had driven them both here.

Ach well, it was a nice day for a walk back to Giffnock.

She headed from the Crescent on to Ormonde Drive, and down towards the main road. Faint scents of vinegared paper rose from the chip shop there. Four o'clock—they must be firing up the fryers for the teatime rush. Facing Ormonde Drive, on the other side of the road, was the entrance to yet another park. Not for nothing was Glasgow named the Dear Green Place. Over seventy parks breathed green light into Scotland's biggest city, but, like the portion of Queen's Park facing Carol's house, they could seem forbidding, with their heavy thickets of guard-dog trees. Once you ventured inside, though, and they opened out into glorious sweeps and undulations, that was when you realised their true beauty. A long, dark avenue of limes yawned a lethargic welcome into this one.

Linn Park, said the sign.

Halfway down the hill, fat globs of rain began to spatter, every single one of them aiming down Anna's neck. Bursting clouds, a sudden gushing, and a slither of water bounced from a broken drain inside the park gates, running down the sloping path. Licking like a thirsty tongue.

CHAPTER FOURTEEN

'The alcohol loves you, while turning you blue!'

Anna shrieked at the dressing-table mirror, arms out as she embraced the rising music. Guitar and drumbeat pulsing hard, a glass of Soave swilling in her dancing hand as her bare midriff jiggled slightly between matching bra and pants. *Purple* ones, with turquoise lace. See, folk thought she'd be beige through and through; she knew that, got her kicks subverting it—even if only Alice was privy to the secret. The cat sprawled belly-up on the bed, eyes half open, one paw behind her ear. Mottled, sink-your-face-in fur, and Anna breathed deep, took the plunge. As quick as her lips touched Alice's tummy, the cat sprung upright, twisting on her dignity and jumping from the bed.

'Och Alice. I'm not just here to feed you, you know.' She assumed a bad New Jersey drawl. 'I need somethin' from this relationship too, baby.'

Tonight, she was going to enjoy herself, irrespective of what lay before and beyond. Because, like the slogan said, she *was worth it*. One small, food-and-drink-and-maybe-a-little-romance-filled hiatus, she was allowed that. She would be good, very good. She would not shag her boss, she would merely flirt. *More wine, vicar?*

Her promise to Shelly lay on some brain-shelf, filed 'pending', not forgotten. Having something to love might guide him back to better days. By the look of him though, that was doubtful. There were a few possibilities for housing she'd already enquired about, but Shelly would need to put

282

himself up for interview. All Anna could do was knock a few doors—it was up to Shelly to choose to go through them.

What she would do, however, was phone Jenny Heath. Not that she relished the reunion. A right nippy sweetie who knew almost all of Anna's bad bits, and, like a wasp, was best kept at a respectful distance. They hadn't met since they worked together in the Flexi Unit; had only spoken briefly in, what, five years? Jenny was a sergeant now; she'd worked hard for it. A single mum with a lot of baggage. Anna hoped she was happy. She deserved to be happy.

She'd obtained Jenny's home number from Personnel, in anticipation of this very moment. It just hadn't been the right time, place or amount of alcohol to call her yet. One more gorgeous glug, as the singer pleaded *Awake me*, then she switched the music off. Found her diary, keyed in Jenny's number on the phone.

'Hey, Jenny?'

'Yes?'

'It's Anna Cameron here.' *Quick as you like, slide it out and keep talking because it's perfectly natural that we are having this chat and you don't scare me at all.* 'How are you?'

'Eh . . . fine. You?'

'I'm good. Listen. Remember Julie Andrews?'

'Star of song, screen and stage? You know, I don't think she's aged one bit since *The Sound of Music*.'

'I mean the cat.'

'Duh.'

'Have you still got her?'

'Of course I do. I said I'd look after her, and I

283

have.'

'No, I wasn't implying that you wouldn't. I just thought . . . well, she might be deid by now for all I know.'

'Well she's not.'

Belligerent already, and they hadn't even got past the pleasantries.

'Good. Good. It's just, well, her owner—you remember Shelly?'

'Shelly the mad old fruit in the fish shop, Shelly the Queen of the Bigot Brigade, Shelly the accomplice to murder, Shelly that went to jail? That the one?'

'Aye, alright. You've made your point. It's just . . . well, he's out of jail now, and he was wondering if he could see his cat?'

'You're joking! No way.'

'I'm not saying he'd take her back or anything, not yet at least. Just, if he could come and visit her maybe?'

A mirthless laugh at her ear. 'Are you for real? Piss off. I don't want some manky old junkie knowing where I stay.'

Bite your lip, Anna. Have some more wine. Lovely cool burning soaking her throat, soaking her spine. She swirled the liquid round her glass, ran her tongue across her gums.

'Could you not bring Julie to see him, then? You could borrow my cat basket—'

'Anna, will I buggery. The cat's mine. She's getting old, and she's settled. I'm not shoving her in a shopping trolley and wheeling her off to meet some raddled fuck-up who stood by while Mr Wajerski had his head stoved in. You forget—it was me that found the body, Anna.'

'Jenny, please? I really think it would mean something to Shelly. He's had a hell of a time.'

'Is this the guilt talking,' sniffed Jenny, 'or the drink?'

'No it's bloody not. Can I not just do something nice for someone?'

'I dunno. *Can* you?'

Well, this was going better than expected.

'Right, I'm sorry I bothered you Jenny—'

'No, wait. I'm sorry. Look, let me think about it, eh? It's just, you've phoned me up out of the blue . . .'

'I know. It was just a spur-of-the-moment thing. I saw him the other day—oh Jenny, you wouldn't recognise him, you know?'

'Yup. Prison does that to you.'

How's Jamie?

She wanted to say it. Not saying was like looking at a threadbare curtain. So thin she could see through holes, see moths and black things birling. *How's Jamie? You still see them; tell me don't tell me.*

'How's Cath?' she said.

'She's okay. They're up in Wester Ross, near Plockton. Got a wee croft—loads of fresh air and seaweed. Jamie's working as some kind of outdoor instructor too: climbing, biking, that kind of stuff.'

'Sounds good.'

'Yeah.'

Anna drained the last sharp drops of wine. 'Okay, so . . .'

'So—I've got your number, and I said I'll think about it. I promise.'

'Thanks Jenny. I really appreciate it.'

And she did, she appreciated it all. Quickly,

285

Anna finished getting ready. No more singing. She decided on a green dress, tight paisley pattern across the bodice, sweeping out to a chiffony skirt. Just enough cleavage to blink that expensive turquoise lace. So pretty, so not her. So she pulled on a pair of brown moleskin jeans to dress it down, or funk it up or whatever. To hide her up-and-down legs. Pointed brown boots and that was her done. As was the wine, but never mind. There'd be plenty more at Coriander.

*   *   *

Hand on brass doorplate, shadows chattering and tinkling through clouded glass. Anna walking alone into the unknown, along an open foyer lit with lines of turquoise candles. Johnny had made no arrangements about getting together beforehand; presumably they were meeting inside.

So.

She donned her subtle armour: pulling back her shoulders, sticking out her breasts. Chin high, skirt swinging, clip-on smile and in we go, to collide with a surge of perfumed spice, dark cinnamon lodging in her throat, a twiggy saffron smell, and Johnny, smiling, waiting for her at a big round table for ten at least. Most of the seats were already taken, but he'd kept her one beside him. Gratefully, deflatedly, she took her place, smiled round the rest of the table. She'd known it was a gala evening, and gala implied big brashness, clearly. She'd known, but she hadn't *thought*.

The room held well over two hundred, yet it still felt spacious, cool and high-ceilinged, even with the drapes of gold linen hanging there. Blocks of jade and fierce blue on the walls were interspersed with strips of mirrored gold, while one wall was a screen of ever-tumbling water. A mezzanine balcony oozed green ferns, behind which sat the DJ. Tumbling from the tented ceiling, fantastic chandeliers of hologrammed discs spun blue and violet flashes over the place settings on the tables. An army of waiters in electric green kilts, several wearing turbans, were circulating trays of champagne, juice and lassi, slick to the rhythms of hybrid bhangra'n'bagpipes. Anna plucked a glass of champagne, smiled again.

Straight into the face of Rob Macklin, over on the next table.

Thin, high cheekbones, straight dark brows. Blue-black eyes with dilated pupils, catching on the rise of her breasts, pushing needles under her skin.

It was a look that said she was beautiful. She shivered in the intense, bright flush of the restaurant. Rob nodded, at both Anna and Johnny, then turned his profile away.

This was going to be difficult. Worse still was the vision to Anna's far left. Mrs Hamilton, taking her seat, smoothing down a bile-green gown.

Anna whispered at Johnny, never losing her fixed-on grin. 'Thanks for telling me JC was coming.' A frugal wave for her boss, acknowledged by a slightly twisted mouth.

'Didn't know she was till today.' Johnny waved too, Mrs H actually baring teeth for him. 'Apparently it's a good idea, in the wake of the Aziz murder. Showing solidarity and all that.'

'Hurrah!' Anna drained her glass. Mrs H continued to glower at them, one hand scooping shovels of poppadom into the little salvers of lentils and bhel puri that dotted the table. 'Well, don't expect me to talk to the old boot.'

'Another drink?'

'Yes please.'

Johnny tapped her empty glass and a full one materialised by her cutlery. Blink and you hardly saw the waiter's hand. He was like that, Johnny. *Magic.* Anna shuffled slightly closer, keeping her voice low.

'And what about Robert Macklin? Can we talk to him, or is he still on Tom Cruikshanks's hit list?'

'For why? Because of the Maguire case? Sure, woman. Your doctor man's never a suspect.'

A little flutter-dance of relief; she was glad. For Rob, of course, and for the reassurance that you could be wrong about someone. Wrong at first, and then right. That was a good thing. A mature, reflective thing. It made her feel . . . luminous. And slightly drunk.

'Nah, if you're looking for some kind of a smoke-screen, my money's definitely on the family. We've got the SCDEA looking into Maguire's accounts and business associates right now. Apparently,' Johnny's burr slid even lower, a rumbling in her ear, 'it was quite a sudden move to their new house—a much bigger house, I understand . . .'

'God, yeah, I've been in it,' whispered Anna. 'It's huge.'

A rustle behind them. Mrs Hamilton was leaning over Anna's chair. How had she done that, scuttling unseen? Fingers splayed on the carved wooden chair-back, face pressed close and seething. Her back teeth were grey with fillings. Poor Mr Hamilton. If indeed there was one.

'Ho.' The impact of Hamilton's wheezy dhal-breath was augmented by the evidence of lentil on her tongue. 'I'm no much of a lip-reader myself, but that man over there is heidie at the local deaf school.' As she spoke, her eyes were wending their way round the room. 'All I can see is yous slinked up together like two cheeks of an arse. And so can everyone else. So, you're either talking shop, which isny on, or you're planning to slip off for a gruesome twosome in the lavs.' At this, she patted Johnny's shoulder. 'Which I somehow doubt.'

The wicked, insightful *cheek* of her. Anna was having none of it. 'Mrs Hamilton, I'm sorry, but that's totally out of—'

'Miss Cameron. Kindly keep your voice down. We are here this evening to socialise. Show our friendly faces. So get on with it, or I'll split yous both up. Councillor Nayar. How *are* you?'

One bosom swiped Anna's ear as Mrs H set forth towards the unfortunate man.

'You're gettin' it, big boy,' muttered Anna.

They sniggered like a pair of weans, then Johnny shushed her. 'Chief Inspector, do you mind? That chap's being lined up to be convenor of the Joint Police Board, don't you know?'

'No I don't. Should I?'

An abrupt seriousness, almost rueful as he broke off some poppadom. 'Damn right you should, lady. Politics is a dirty game. Almost as dirty as the polis. This place is crawling with councillors. Remember, our division straddles two fiefdoms—East Ren and Glasgow. That's a lot of *do-you-know-who-I-ams*? to keep happy. Look, there's your Education and Social Work chappie for Glasgow, your Govan Area Convener; oh, and

289

there's our lovely vice convenor for Community Safety, Old Man Heraghty. And see that one there? Brown? He heads Regeneration and Economic Development, so is, I suppose, guest of honour, seeing as he let the planning for this . . . confection go ahead without issue. Anyway,' picking up her empty glass, 'would you care for more wine, Miss Cameron?'

'Oh yes. I think it's going to be a long night.'

Before the food came the speeches, from a long top table of vivid-cut jewels. Men in traditional South Indian dress, long Nehru coats over churidars. The women more stunning than peacocks, pleated and strung in brocades and silk, thick loops of gold pennies glittering on necks and wrists. Councillor Brown, a dull cuckoo in the nest, spoke first, giving a clipped little address about regeneration and diversity and the council's efforts to promote both. Some polite applause, then another man, not at the top table, stood up. It was Councillor Heraghty.

'Well, I'd just like to say, in the interests of fairness, even though I'm only speaking from the body of the Kirk, so to speak, heh . . .' A low, brief titter, only from his own table, and even then, embarrassed. '. . . that we on the other side of the political divide are equally supportive of efforts to integrate and include *all* our citizens. Sadly though, I feel the gaps that cause our community the biggest problems are from a generational rather than a cultural divide.'

His language was assuming a more formal tone; an oration, not a chat, was in store. 'It seems to me . . .' Heraghty inhaled like a singer about to hit the high note. Anna saw several tables ripple out, the

290

spilling of unfed fidgets who can no longer sit at peace. Two women rose to go to the toilet, another threw her napkin on her plate, '. . . that our youngsters, *all* our youngsters, of whatever hue, are moving far away from the values we hold dear. They cleave less to family and more to friends, resulting in the kind of lawlessness and gang culture we see proliferating on our streets. I'm very glad to see various senior representatives from Strathclyde Police here this evening.' He dipped his head in the direction of Mrs Hamilton's table. Anna could see Hamilton's knuckles bulge as she gripped her empty glass. And still the man was not done.

'So, while we enjoy our wee bit dinner here tonight, let's not forget what's going on outside these walls. A young lad died not so far from this restaurant, a terrible, terrible tragedy for his family, and for all our youngsters. And it's incumbent on every one of us here this evening—community leaders, education professionals, law enforcers, whoever—to work together to combat the scourge of disaffected, angry youth, to give them other choices, a better future—and, most importantly of all, give them discipline and guidance. I ask every one of you who is a parent—do *you* know where your son or daughter is tonight?'

Abruptly, he sat, all energies expended. A rolling silence shifting, becoming noise, whisper, then chatter, before Heraghty's table started to clap. A haphazard gunfire of other claps peppered the room; just pockets, not cohesive. Not *sure*.

Johnny touched the bridge of his nose. 'In the name of the Wee Man. We're just here for some dinner.'

An elegant man in his fifties got to his feet, tinged a fork on glass.

'That's Mr Nayar, the owner,' whispered Johnny.

'I thought Nayar was a councillor too?'

'No, that's his brother—see the chubby one over there?'

'My friends. *All* my dear friends.' Nayar stared pointedly at Heraghty, who was munching on a handful of spiced nuts. 'It is my pleasure to welcome everyone here tonight.' He paused, opened his hands. 'Shuh. I say "my"—but this is a family business. As you so rightly—and unexpectedly—pointed out, Mr Heraghty, family is all; is paramount to our success and our well-being.'

His beam of benevolence encompassed all his guests, every one of them, but did not correspond with his eyes. 'And I couldn't have achieved all this without the help and support, first of my beautiful wife . . .' A stunning woman on Nayar's right lowered her bindi-ed forehead. 'It's her exquisite taste that has informed our exciting, innovative menu—which I know you are going to love. Also, my brother Balaji, whom I love, my wonderful daughters Anjali and Ramya and my son-in-law Jasveer. We have Jasveer to thank for the décor and the music—brought, of course, from his extensive experience in the nightclub industry. But why not? Who says an Indian restaurant must have flocked wallpaper and tacky carpets?'

White teeth flashing, he waited while the laughter died down.

'My friends, my fellow restaurateurs, forgive

292

me—of course, present company is excepted! Glasgow is justly renowned for her wealth of wonderful Indian and Pakistani cuisine, and indeed we are tipped, this summer, to win the UK's curry capital award once again.'

A cheer went up.

'Here, at Coriander, our menu is unique, so why should the surroundings not be likewise?' Nayar lifted his glass to the young man further down the table. 'We make an excellent team—Jasveer is the brains, while I am just the money!'

More laughter, then someone called out: 'Aye Jasveer. Well seen you've brains, cause you've no got any looks!'

A glimpse of anger on the young man's brow, only a brief flint striking steel, then it passed as he joined in the raucous laughter. For he was, indeed, handsome, in a too-fitted shirt and too-long hair kind of way. The young woman next to him patted his hand.

'So, no more talking, please, I beg you. Let's sit back and enjoy the manifold delights that await us—I give you Coriander, Glasgow's newest and finest South Indian dining experience.'

A surge of applause as the waiters marched in, trays aloft, to flashing lights and the drone of a piper. The girl next to Anna offered her a copper salver. 'Dosa, I think. They're fab.'

Anna took what looked like a rolled-up pancake, then a plate of curried lotus leaves passed from Johnny on her other side. More delicate dishes of mushroom stuffed with nuts and spinach, lime-zingy prawns, and other delicacies she couldn't even name, arrived.

Johnny flapped his hand over his mouth. 'Ooh,

hot, hot. Don't think we'll be needing chips.'

'Spicy, isn't it?' laughed the girl on Anna's right. 'I'm Kayleigh, by the way. I do all Mr Nayar's PR. Pretty much know everyone here too, so if you, like, want an intro to anyone, just give me a nod, yeah?'

'Cheers,' said Johnny. 'I'm Johnny, and this here is Anna. Mind, there'll not be that many wanting an introduction to us, and that's a fact. We're your local friendly constabulary, I'm afraid.'

Anna stiffened. No matter how pished she got, she would never tell folk what she did for a living first off. To do so was to invite immediate censure, or at the very least a retreat from casual friendliness, a subtle shuttering of features that would leave you no option but to give up and quietly eat your soup. Unless, that is, you got the alternative response—a prolonged and fascinated interrogation.

'Really? What, you too?' Kayleigh asked Anna.

'Mmm, me too.'

'Wow! A girl cop and a boy cop. And, so are you, like, partners then?'

'No—'

'Kind of, I suppose,' said Johnny. 'I mean, we both work in Giffnock.'

'Oh, God, yuh—that's where I know you from. You did that thing on the news, about that old lady going missing.'

'I did indeed.'

'Awful, isn't it? I mean, she's probably dead by now, but still. Urgh. And I feel so sorry for that poor doctor chap. See him, over there.'

Anna followed the bobbing of Kayleigh's chignon. She could make out the back of Rob's head, his shoulders dipping, shifting as he chatted.

'How so?'

Rob was sitting back in his chair, stretching one arm behind to remove his jacket. He wore no tie, the top button of his shirt was undone. Dark hollows at his throat, his clavicle, laughter edging his lips. A woman beside him was touching his arm.

'Well, all that bad publicity.'

Johnny had seized the opportunity to extricate himself from their conversation, and was now blethering to the man on his right.

'Publicity?'

'Yeah. People are taking their oldsters away from the home, you know. And he's been trying so hard to get things back together since his wife died, poor lamb.'

'His wife died? But I . . . sorry, I thought he was still married.'

'*No!*' She felt Kayleigh snuggle in for a good gossip. Ugly word, *gossip*, the smug, plump way it slipped out. Anna was still staring at him, couldn't stop.

'No, no. She died about three years ago. Knocked down—it was terrible. That's when he bought the nursing home. Better hours for looking after his wee girl, I guess.'

Kayleigh's hand was curved around her mouth, her hair so close Anna could smell the gel, see the kirby grips holding it all together.

'Is it true that he was involved, though? In the old lady's kidnap, I mean?'

'No, that's a lot of nasty bullshit.'

'Oh, thank goodness. Because it's such a shame, you know. He's such a sweetie—don't you think he's got gorgeous eyes? Look how blue they are.'

'I hadn't really noticed . . .'

'Oh, yeah. We all thought he was quite the dude. When I worked at the *Sentinel*, we were always doing, like, stories on him? He does a lot for charity, you know, for the home? Parachutes and fun runs and . . . stuff. Omigod, there was this one time, it was a sponsored swim, yuh? There's not a pick on him, right, to look at him? But you should have *seen* his abs. God, I sponsored him ten pounds, just like that. Well, I mean, they're always short of money.' She sucked thoughtfully on a tendril of escaping hair. 'That's why I thought he was maybe . . . yuh . . . well it could happen, right? Kidnapping them for the money?'

'Well, you thought wrong, Kayleigh. Oh look, I think someone's complaining about the food over there.'

'Where?'

'That lady that just bombed it into the toilets. She looked like she was puking up.'

'Oh buggeroonies. I knew they shouldn't have changed the fish supplier. 'Scuse me, Anna.'

Anna drained another glass. She was beginning to feel giddy, melting into the vibrations of this strident, colourful room. Could feel, too, someone watching her; some insistent pressure of padded air. JC was dead ahead, and wolfing chapati; it wasn't her.

She knew immediately who it was. The *widower*, not philanderer. Slowly, Anna turned, smiled. Rob inclined his head. She turned back. Not quite an apology, although she owed him one. All he'd done was ask her out, and that was not a bad thing. She sighed through her nose, the expelled air frouffing up the front of her dress. It felt nice. She felt . . .

weird.

Somebody laughed; that girl beside Jasveer. An exuberant peal, hungry, full of life. That's all folk wanted: to be happy. They didn't want to be lectured by Heraghty or be forced to gulp in all the shiteyness of life. They didn't want a window on a world they didn't have to see. God, they didn't want to know anything about what went on behind the scenes, all the bad things you had to do to keep them safe, keep a lid on it all. Anna watched the diners eating, enjoying the escape of creeping mellowness, this moment of being full and fed. Pleasant chat all around, Mr Nayar snaking between his guests, patting shoulders, receiving hugs. At length he came to them. Johnny half got up, Nayar's hand immediately on his back. 'Mr O'Hare, please sit, sit. Are you enjoying your meal?'

'Sure it's out of this world, Raju. Just fabulous. Here, can I introduce you to my new second-in-command?' A proprietorial arm grazed her. 'Raju Nayar, meet Anna Cameron.'

'A pleasure.' Nayar took her hand, draped it like a shepherd's crook, and for one corny moment she thought he was going to kiss it. Perhaps he had been, but she made a fist, shaking her way out of any awkwardness.

'I was just saying,' she improvised, 'this place is breathtaking.'

'You like it?'

'The detail's stunning. Those etchings for instance—they're beautiful.' Positioned at dado height, occasional slim rectangles of beaten copper depicted a series of leaves and plant designs.

'Ah, our "spice rack"! Yes—this one is

297

cinnamon, there you have ginger, and that, of course, is coriander. My daughter made them.'

'Wow.'

'Yes, Ramya is a graphic artist. She designed the chandeliers also.' He shook his head, gazing fondly at the woman seated next to Jasveer. 'She is a very talented girl.'

'And Ramya is Jasveer's wife, yes?'

Nayar frowned. 'No, no. Jasveer is married to Anjali, my eldest. Ramya is no one's wife. As headstrong as she is artistic, I'm afraid. Now, I must say good evening to your charming commander. It was a pleasure to meet you, Ms Cameron, a pleasure.' He lowered his neck, his voice. 'So beautiful.'

Anna stuffed a last chunk of lamb in her mouth. Chewing studiedly, avoiding Johnny's gaze, Rob's gaze too, if it was still upon her. She almost wanted Nayar to kiss her hand now.

'Smooth operator,' singsonged Johnny. 'I think Mr Nayar *likes* you.'

'Piss off.' She ate the meat, remembered her mission. Anna could no longer judge how much wine she had consumed, her glass perpetually filled by one charming waiter or another. But she had that fuzzed mistiness about her, the place where it is warm and damp and you are funny, exuding sex and sharp intelligence from the bubbles inside your blood. If she let one hand drift light across Johnny's arm, the shock of unexpected flesh on flesh . . . he would turn, would look with heavy eyes.

'Johnny, I need to ask a favour.'

'Hmm?'

'I need to take a few days off. My mum's taken a

298

turn for the worse . . .'

Let it curl, drift. He would catch it, do what was right.

'Jeez, Anna. I don't know. Mrs H is really cracking down on time off—you know she is.'

'Och, but Johnny, I really need to see my mum. I didn't . . . I wasn't sure when was the right time to ask. But you could speak to JC for me, couldn't you? C'mon.' She was walking her fingernails up his arm, him easing his weight away. Shiftless. Before he could answer, a spillage of glossy brown hair shook itself between them. 'Woo-hoo! Time to take out the hairpins and start high-kicking.' Kayleigh had a hand on each of their backs. 'They're about to start the dancing. Anna, can I borrow your hunky partner, please?'

Johnny held up a brace of fingers. 'Can you just give us two ticks, Kayleigh my sweet? You away and clear a space for us on the dance floor, eh?'

She blew him a kiss, shimmied off, in the direction of Rob's table. Another diner at the table lunged over to catch Kayleigh's wrist, and Rob . . . Rob fixed on Anna as he stretched, stood. She saw him coming, smooth and straight. Lowered her head, pretending to study the dessert menu.

'Room for another?' He slid into the empty seat beside her; thigh skimming the length of hers. Through the fabric of her clothes, an effervescence. Rob on one side, Johnny on the other.

'Hi Rob. Enjoy your meal?'

'I did. Can't actually feel my tongue any more, but still. It was all very nice.'

The hard edge of his haunch. Just there.

'Curry's just not your thing, is it?'

299

A bashful grin. 'Not really. Can you tell? Garlic's about as exotic as I get. Hey,' he included Johnny in his next question, his smile receding, 'I wondered if there was any more word on Cassie? I'm getting truly worried now, and your Mr Cruikshanks just isn't telling us anything—'

Johnny talked right over him, dunting Anna in the ribs. 'Look, there's Mrs H coming back from the bogs. Why don't you just ask her for time off yourself?'

Snapping shut on herself, on him. 'Oh cheers, pal. Thanks a lot. Hey, don't let me keep you from Kayleigh nae-brains. Clearly you'd rather go sniffing up a rabbit hole than help out a friend.'

Her words were slurring, she was aware of that, but still, she chose them with sober care, stressing *friend* and *pal* and then they could both pretend she'd never stroked his lovely bitter-dark-haired arm.

'Anna, I *am* helping you out. JC hates cowards more than anything. You want the time off, you go ask for it.' His lips brushed her ear before he stood up. 'And by the way—me and Kayleigh? Hardly. Anna, love, have you not got it yet? I'm as gay as get out.'

Watching her fingers on her glass, which was slipping, spilling, and she let it curve and bounce. It didn't break, just shuddered on its rolling contour, pale wine printing runnels on to linen cloth.

'Woah. Anna—are you okay?' She was aware of someone taking her hand, moving it from the wet place. Rob's hand, braided in hers, the long, clever fingers of a dead woman's husband. Then Mrs H was at her side, flapping a napkin, blotting the

300

cloth. 'For God's sake, Cameron. Get a frigging grip. You're a bloody liability, and I don't need that on my team.'

'Ma'am, I spilt a glass of wine.'

'You are pissed, you are embarrassing and I want you to go home.'

'*I'm* embarrassing? You're the one making a bloody scene.'

Rob's voice cut through the guddle of noise. 'Excuse me, but Anna's feeling a bit unwell.'

'No, Rob, I'm not unwell.'

She wasn't angry at him, he didn't mean to patronise. But *Hamilton*? Just standing there in her poison-coloured dress and her soggy napkin and all that anger, all that anger of the last few weeks came pumping like a muscle. Like an uppercut swinging high, yet she managed to keep her arms down. Not her voice, though.

'I'm sick, yeah, but that's different. I'm sick of being treated like shit for one, and I'm sick of being treated like an imbecile. I'm sick of being *lied* to and cut out of the loop. I'm sick of doing my best and having it rubbished . . . and I'm sick of being on my *fucking own*. Jesus. This job used to be about being part of a team—'

Anna felt Hamilton grapple with her upper arm, nipping the flesh in jaggy little nail-bites until Anna was rising up from her seat, her body, all the faces jumbling, staring at her and Hamilton hissing:

'*Get her out of here.*'

Then another arm, Rob's arm? One hand beneath her elbow, the other playing on her back. Music pounding. Him gently steering her above her feet, following a line of shimmering blue, lit

301

and dancing like a fuse.

*   *   *

It is dark, Anna is in her bed. She hears and she does not hear it; that whisper of late-night phone call. Cool plastic pressed against her ear, voices in behind the drumming, the stirrup and the nestle of fine-tuned bone. Because your hearing is the last to go.

Say it is not true.
Say it is not true.

'*Tu madre . . .*' the voice husks. And Anna will not open her eyes.

It is a dream, a dream. It is the same dream she's been having all her life, from that stinging distant moment when she first knew she was alone. Like playing tents beneath a dressing gown suspended over chairs, you think you're hidden, you're safe. You think you'll only come out when you decide, when you've had enough or it's getting stuffy, then some great hand comes from on high and rips it off.

And you are exposed.

She had been in her bedroom then too, when they came to tell her. The gown was her mother's summer one, rose-sprigged cream cotton, which let light slide through the fissures in its weave, freckling her toes and carpet, then the hand, the unknown face ghosting a smile as insubstantial as the pecks of sun dancing round her feet.

It's your mum, hen. She needs to see you.
It's your mum, hen. It's your dad, hen.
It's your mum, hen. She needs to see you.
Now, you be a big brave girl.

302

It's your mum.

'My mother?' Anna whispers.

'She has had another stroke.'

The woman breathes the words out, pushing them forwards and up inside Anna's head. Behind her brain, her tongue, her teeth. '*Grande*. You understand? A big one.'

'How bad is it? Is she conscious?' The words skitter in quiet desperation.

'I am sorry.' A respectful pause to temper the blow. Only the dark and the plastic pressing, and soft words spilling on her muffled head. She knows, she knows, steadies herself for the impact which, when it comes, is fine and firm and terribly small.

'She has passed.'

'I see.'

If she opens her eyes, it might be light outside. It only *felt* dark, like it should be dark, like when the sun died. The world is dark, lies are dark. Your dad leaving without saying goodbye.

'I see,' she repeats.

Your mum leaving. Same day, same way, in a lie that let you down.

'I . . . Thank you. I'll . . . I'll make arrangements to come out first thing.'

'*Sí.*'

'Was it, was she . . .'

'Your *mamá* was very brave. It was peaceful. And I was with her.'

A stranger, who was not her daughter.

'What is your name?'

'Isabel.'

'*Gracias*, Isabel.'

'God bless you.'

303

Then the voices stop. Just you and the silence and a long, fine hand reaching out in the dark. Across all the bitter miles and years it strokes your brow, which is sticky with fallen-up tears because you're still lying on your back. They run hot, splashing in your ears, and you try to sit up, eyes still shut, your bones all grinding wrong. Prising them open, your eyes, your bones. And you retch, hands tight round an empty belly.

A man, some man, is trying to give you tea.

CHAPTER FIFTEEN

Blossoms frothed from a scattering of twigs, early bees buzzing and drinking at sun-warmed flowers. All it would take was another sharp frost to kill these tentative buds; spring in Scotland was never a safe bet. Anna started to walk up the hill, like she'd done every Saturday as a little girl, skipping from her dancing class at the Institute. She'd made Rob park at the bottom; arriving by car would not constitute a journey. As soon as she began walking, her legs felt tight. When had she last been to the gym? Once the internment was done, once she was back at work, in some routine, she'd go again. She could even walk Rob's dog, she wouldn't mind. Anything that was moving. Moving, and being out and busy, that was all good.

The avenue ran the length of a long, sloping hill, with sandstone bungalows at the bottom, then some semis, and after that would come the row of terraced houses she used to live in. Anna hated her house when she was wee. She wanted a story-book house, with four windows, a chimney and a blue front door. Instead they had a car port, joined on to next door's car port, like a big hungry mouth, with her bedroom window forming an eye above. You went inside the house from the car port, and it was just stupid. Sometimes she thought that nobody knew the door was there. Important parties and invitations to tea would pass her by, because the postman couldn't find her letter box.

The slope was evening out now—they had lived on the crest of the hill—and she could see the whole terrace had been painted white, and, speeding up—this was silly—that was their house, there: three from the end, with the cherry tree in the garden. Quick dips of her head, as if she was trying to sneak up on something, someone, then, too fast, she was at it. Stopped right outside their front gate. And it *was* still their gate. Anna touched the metal, laughing with disbelief at its wrought-iron curlicues and three decades' more rust.

Thirty-four years since they'd lived there, but the house had never moved. Bricks and mortar, wood and tile. Same roof, same pebbledash, same place they had sat, the three of them, eating dinner in the kitchen, which was still there. How could inanimate structures remain, when a laugh or a voice could not? Caroline had touched all these walls, had scraped and papered them all herself. She'd carried her newborn baby across that same doorstep, which still had a chip out of the corner where Anna's dad had dropped a spanner or something. Caroline's form had sat by that window, fingers splayed on glass, watching as Anna dug in the garden, gouging out a hole to make a

305

pond.

Caroline had had to 'stay still' for weeks after Dad died. Anna remembered being left to her own devices, still not sure where her daddy was. Conscious that her mum was ill, short whispers, women in the hall. Piles of blood-soaked cotton, and closing doors. She had waited patiently, one day dragging a stool across to the sink. The stool was designed for a breakfast bar her dad had never built, and was as tall as she was, but she'd managed to position it. Holding on to the edge of the sink, she pulled herself up on the cushioned seat; first kneeling, then, slowly, slowly, like a tightrope walker taking to the wire, unravelling to upright. Craning her neck to reach the silver kettle. Mummy liked drinks out of the kettle.

Burny, burny, she scolded. That was what her mum always said. The stool wobbled as she stretched to reach a cup, put it down in front of her. Anna poured some stuff out, but it was the wrong colour. Mummy's drink was brown and this was just rubbish water, like Anna drank. But it was all that they had, and maybe it would still taste nice, since it came from the kettle. The liquid splashed on to the worktop at first, but she managed to aim it steady, one eye always on the door, until the water was right up to the brim. She crouched so she was as close to the floor as possible. It still looked a long way down, and now she had the drink to carry as well.

Daring it to smash, she held the cup in both hands and jumped to the floor. The water slooshed up the sides, wetting her hands and feet, but most of it stayed in the cup. Her grip was firm, like Daddy's, and she felt invincible. Tiptoeing up the stairs, creaking open the bedroom door, baby steps careful, careful, hardly spilling any. Putting it down gently on Mummy's bedside table, patting her face until she woke. Her mother, looking blank and empty, past her, through her.

Dull, flat voice saying *take it away*.

How could Caroline not be here? It was impossible that she was not here. Even now, flecks of her skin must freight the air, or lie in dust beneath the floorboards. If Anna walked inside that house, inside their wrong-way-round side door, the hall carpet would be maroon, the kitchen tiles blue and white. A tweedy orange armchair would be angled by the fire, and her mum would be knitting.

She held harder on to the gate, frightened for a moment that she might fall. Such a glittering inside of sobs that wouldn't come. But they were there, Anna knew that. She heard the car draw up. It would be Rob, her shadow of the last five days. Who had sat with her that night, who had phoned in sick for her that morning.

Say I'm ill, she had shouted. *Tell them nothing. Tell the bastards nothing.*

They'd had an argument then, Anna still pished. She remembered hitting him and him holding her, confining her arms. Saying stupid things like it would be okay and then wanting to use her phone again, and her shouting at him to get out. She'd heard him move about the room, putting stuff in her sports bag, saying, 'Do you have a suitcase?' and 'what about the cat? Anna, will I ask your neighbour?'; she'd heard her heart and the blood in her ears, him asking if she had someone that could go with her, would her neighbour go with her? and her saying where? and him going, *Oh Anna*.

She hadn't known, when he switched on her computer. Hadn't realised when he took his mobile into the hall, and his raised, sharp voice rang out: *'Well, that's what I'm doing.'* Had been unaware as he drove her to the airport, was grateful when he fetched her water from the kiosk, sat with her, told her it was time to go through. And then he was there, beside her, and it was the same dull feeling she'd had when she'd finished shouting.

Rob, a kind man who did not know her, had flown with her to Spain. He had hailed taxis, passed her forms to sign, held her hand. Rob had shifted blankets, pressed thumbs on eyes like a blessing, touched her mother's hand. He had cajoled and told the hospital staff what was to be done, and when and why. They respected him, he was a *médico*. Patiently, skilfully, he had managed Anna too, asking what she wanted, every step of the way, when all she wanted was for it to be over. Once she saw her mum, there was nothing more to feel, really. She asked him to go home then, to leave her alone with some excellent brandy and the golf club ladies who had promised to make sandwiches for the purvey.

Like migraine, Rob wouldn't go away. Somehow, he'd arranged a brief private cremation, agreeing with her that that was best. But had Anna said that? She couldn't remember, had vague recollections of standing in a chapel with her mother's gaggle of friends. No Teddy, though there had been an altercation at the door, Joan and Rob leaving her side, briefly, because she could remember swaying, then Rob was back, his solid hand there, and dreary music had begun. Anna cried then; she had told Rob to make them play 'All Things Bright and Beautiful', but he'd said they didn't know it here.

More angry whispers on his mobile phone a day or so later, and then they had come home. Rob and Anna. With Caroline, crated in a little urn which was bubble-wrapped and sealed for Customs, kept separate from real people until they arrived at Glasgow Airport. You could be the fattest, smelliest, most foul-mouthed oaf and still belch and shove your way on to a plane, but if you were quietly dead and causing no trouble at all, you were best kept secret.

'What do I do with her now?' Anna had asked. The shrink-wrapped box stared at her from the baggage trolley. Rob would have to pick it up.

'It's up to you, Anna. Where do you think she would be happy?'

A shutter closing, catching them both. Horses and gypsies and an orange scarf. A fist closing behind her ribs.

'With my dad.'

'Well, that's what we'll do then. You tell me where your dad is buried, and I'll sort it out.'

'Okay.'

This pattern had formed itself, Rob tugging, Anna being led like a goat. Not minding, but grateful for the respite—until they got back to Glasgow, and she saw Rob's daughter, waiting. *Then*, it felt absurd. Less than a week ago, Anna had been slurping curry at a table next to Rob's; now she had star billing in *Meet the Macklins*. The girl had stood in Arrivals, alongside the woman she'd been with at The Meadows.

'Anna, this is Laura.'

'Hey.'

Grave blue eyes and brown hair, which, in the glare of airport striplights, shone rich red bursts of sunrise. Laura had that halfway air about her Anna recalled so well—gappy teeth too big for your mouth, body poised between belly-fat and lanky, with your limbs and your breasts just tingling to grow. She was wearing black skinny jeans but uncool trainers, and a sweatshirt too long at the wrists, into which she buried her fingers.

'Hi there. I'm Anna.'

'I know. I'm sorry about your mum.'

And I'm sorry about yours.

But it would have been crass to say it.

'And this is my sister-in-law, Elizabeth. I . . . we . . . she helps me with Laura.'

The woman parted her lips, shook Anna's hand. 'Just as well I was off this week, or you'd've been having madam on your wee trip away too.'

'It wasn't a "trip", Liz,' said Rob.

'No, no. I know. You look tired, Anna. Shall we get you home? Laura, you get the lady's trolley, yes?'

Elizabeth linked her arm through Rob's and began an urgent exchange, which Anna only caught the start of.

'Rob—it's getting really bad. There's been four more withdrawals this week, and the place is still crawling with police. *And* someone's mislaid a batch of drugs—'

Anna hurried to catch up with them. 'Excuse me . . . Liz. Have they found Cassandra Maguire yet?'

Elizabeth pivoted slightly, a vague

acknowledgement of Anna, as if bemused she was still there.

'Eh, no. Although your Mr Cruikshanks is never away from The Meadows. Seems to time it perfectly for morning coffee or afternoon tea.'

'Liz,' said Rob, 'Tom Cruikshanks has been very good—'

'Well, we're going to have to think about closing. Like I said before, this really was *not* the ideal time to nip off with your new friend.'

Rob pulled his sister-in-law further ahead, leaving Anna and Laura to walk side by side, one hand each on the trolley. Caroline was tucked between them, in the little wire basket meant for hand luggage. Anna wondered if the child knew what was in the box.

'Are you my dad's new girlfriend?'

The trolley swivelled, sharp across Anna's toes. 'Ouch. No. Sorry, no, no way. It's just, when . . . when my mum died, your dad was there. And he's been really, really kind, really helpful.'

He has held my hand, held my head. He's wiped my eyes and run me baths, filled my days with words and food and silent back strokes, but never tried to kiss me. Not even the first night, before they phoned; not even when I was forcing my tongue inside his mouth while he stepped aside and laid me on my bed. And I can remember pulling my dress off, it being tangled in my hair, shrieking giggles as I was trying to be sexy. I think I even asked, 'Do you like my pants?' All he did was ease off my dress, pull the covers over me. But his hand brushed my belly and I was sober. I stopped trying to kiss him, because I knew it could wait.

Laura nodded, sage as a girl just into double

311

figures could be. 'It's because he's had to do it before.'

'Yes, I guess.'

'Lots of times, with all the old people at work.'

The car noise behind her had cut out, but the gate was still beneath Anna's fingers. She didn't turn round.

'Hey you.' The affirmation of his hand once more, warming the side of her arm. 'Time to go home.'

'I just wanted . . .'

He kissed the top of her head. 'I know.'

It felt good.

*   *   *

Anna could take seven days' uncertificated sick leave; she took them all. Some stubborn, irrational protectiveness kicked in, deciding on her behalf that she wouldn't mention Caroline to her work. The reason for her absence would remain as sickness: food poisoning, she decided. Far better that than endure a gauntlet of *Sorryaboutyourmums* blown reverently in your face, then a noxious backdraught of *doesn'tshe-looklikeshit?* trailing behind.

Anna phoned Johnny on the seventh day, the Friday, to tell him she was reporting back for duty. Kept it crisp and professional, as did he.

'Feeling better then?'

'Yup. Must've been something I ate at Coriander. I heard the fish was well dodgy.'

'Hmm.'

Was he waiting for a further explanation? She didn't oblige.

312

'Got it all out your system now anyway?'

'Think so.'

'Mrs H is gunning for you, you know.'

'D'you think I give a shit?'

'Anna, don't talk like that, please. You've a good career ahead of you. Look, you're not due in till Monday. Just take it easy over the weekend. If you feel you need more time, then I'll give you some buckshee days. You've only one meeting in the diary, a community council thing on Tuesday evening. I can get Claire Rodgers to go to that.'

'*No.* No, I'll do it. I remembered it was on anyway.' She had not. 'Any developments with Cassie Maguire?'

'Don't change the subject. I'm worried about you.'

'I take it that means no?'

'Actually, it doesn't. We've established that, over the last four months, Ronnie Maguire's bank accounts have seen a considerable influx of money appear—much of it unaccounted for. Ten grand here, five grand there. Appears he's paid off forty thousand pounds of his mortgage—in cash. They've also bought another garage out Lanarkshire way, and a part-share in a Chinese restaurant in Garnethill.'

'Yum yum. So what does that mean for Cassie?'

'It means there's a strong chance she's still alive. Especially now we know that there was insulin taken from The Meadows.'

'Definitely? When?'

'Fuck knows. But their records don't tally with what's been earmarked for disposal. Sure, this is absolutely not a random abduction. Cassie is being used as a pawn, or a bargaining tool. If we can find

313

out where the Maguires' money has appeared from, what it's linked to, then I reckon we can still find Cassie.'

'I take it the Maguires aren't co-operating?'

'Tight as a duck's arse.'

'Even Ronnie?'

'Yeah. Ronnie and Sheena have both been interviewed separately again, gloves off this time. We kept Tom Cruikshanks on bread and water for three days beforehand. Ravenous he was, ripped right into them both, but it's like they've had their tongues glued. Either they're shit-scared of whoever *has* taken her, or in it so deep themselves, they'd rather sacrifice Cassie than reveal the connection.'

'Let me talk to them.'

'You? I thought you didn't give a shit?'

'Well then, I've got nothing to lose, have I?'

'You'll need to clear it with JC first.'

'Of course. Can't have you soiling your pretty little hands by asking on my behalf now, can we?'

'Anna. Are you being homophobic?'

'Nah. Just wankerphobic. Cheery now.'

She hung up, lay back on the bed. Cassie was being kept alive, and Ronnie Maguire knew where. Good, that was good—and bad—in equal measure. But her response was anaesthetised, she knew it. She was observing it flat and from a distance, when before she would have been saddling up, all set for battle and saving the day. Yay Anna.

She could beat the truth out of Ronnie, she supposed, or she could shrug and walk away. Alice chirruped, launched herself into Anna's lap. Her fingers ran through soft fur. What difference would it make, in the end?

314

Alice purred, stretched long. There was a certain liberation in being genuinely at the end of your rope, strung so far out that you could explode or implode and never really feel it, just observe the shrapnel strike its mark, pieces flutter or stick as you ploughed on, impartial through the fallout. As far as work was concerned, Anna had scuppered any chances of being taken seriously by Hamilton, or Johnny for that matter. At Coriander, the worst had happened, and *then*, the worst really had happened. Her mother was dead. Nothing, nothing that occurred in G Division, in the whole of Strathclyde Police, could lessen the impact of that fact. The police was only a job, and, if she thought about it that way, kept it from spilling into everything else, then she could do what Jamie Worth had taught her years ago. Close down the sluice gates, so that work swilled in one compartment, Caroline echoed in another and . . . maybe warm washes of hope swelled somewhere else. Anna would let herself paddle there, become inured to all the rest.

You had to, you had to—when would she grasp that basic truth? Caring too much about stuff you couldn't change, letting it violate you from inside like you'd swallowed acid. Crime, that fathomless dark water she'd chosen to immerse herself in, was all a violation; its depth variable, dependent on who measured it, and why. Did *society* have the monopoly on defining moral turpitude? Society was wee shites like Gordo Figgis as much as it was High Court judges, or businessmen like Mr Nayar, or spent old souls in nursing homes. If Cassie's family didn't care enough, why should Anna? Why should any of them?

315

And then Anna thought of Rob, looking after her when he didn't have to. Or dear old Joan coming day after day to visit Caroline. That's why you did it. You did it because you hoped, one day, that someone would do it for you. Altruism came from some selfish desire to survive. If Anna was a lost old lady, she'd pray someone came looking for her. That was the trigger. She knew about loss; so did Ronnie Maguire. So maybe she could squeeze on some shared, painful tissue, see if that got a reaction.

But she took Johnny's advice, in part at least. Wrapped herself in the duvet for the entire weekend, did not answer the phone. Except when it was Rob, and even then she was selective, responding only to the messages where he said he might come over.

'. . . So . . .' the machine would go, '. . . I'll maybe just look in on my way—'

'Hello? Rob? Sorry, I was in the shower.'

'Again? You were in the bath when I phoned at lunchtime. I tell you, you're either very, very clean, or very, very dirty.'

She'd laugh and fob him off that she was tired, she was fine, she had a headache. He'd laugh too, a throaty, familiar sound, but he knew it was a firewall. He wasn't daft.

The times he didn't phone, she'd wonder what he was doing, rub her thumb across the phone keys. There were no barriers to liking Rob Macklin any more, and the Anna who'd rip coloured foil from chocolate, gulp handfuls in without tasting it, was scared. No longer caught in a crisis, no longer wrapped in a foreign daze, this was it: real life, hands out and open. And whenever she gathered

316

life up before, had started to run with it, feel it leap and thrill, she would always stumble. She would drop it, and it would smash.

*   *   *

Monday, back to work. A third of the day catching up, another third stalling. Then she forced herself to drive to Govan. Before Anna approached CID, she presented herself at Mrs Hamilton's door. It had to be done, and she had a potent sense of being bubble-wrapped, like poor Caroline was. Safe, inert. Beyond.

'Come.'

Hamilton's room smelled of wet fur. Something rustled in a wicker hamper under the window. Hamilton raised her eyes, closed the folder she was working on. It flumphed softly, paper belching air. Hamilton kept her hands atop the buff cardboard, flat and firm.

'Anna Cameron. Felt like popping back in, eh? How's the pain in your peenie?'

About as sore as the one in my arse, ma'am.

'I'm sore all over.'

'Amazing what a bad prawn can do, eh?'

'Amazing. Ma'am, I'd like your permission to speak to Ronnie Maguire. I think I might be able to get through to him, make him talk.'

'You do, do you?' Hamilton's palm seemed to be stroking the folder; rhythmic, covetous comfort-stroking. Ferrets and paper. Whatever turned you on.

'Feel like lending CID a wee hand now, eh? Meanwhile your own bloody workload just keeps piling up.' Hamilton's tongue poked the inside of

317

her cheek. Was this code for something? 'I'm very disappointed in you, Chief Inspector. I understand from Superintendent O'Hare that he had refused your request for unauthorised time off, almost immediately before you "went sick".'

A pop of padded plastic, a little red demon stabbing Johnny's inflated, handsome head.

'That's not true.'

'Well, that's what Johnny tells me. In fact, there's a variety of things Johnny's been telling me.'

Hamilton riffed the folder, a triumphant note. 'How he had to talk down a complaint from one of your bar officers, for one.'

'What?'

'Apparently you threatened the man with a free transfer to Arran.'

'Och, c'mon. That was just a joke.'

'So you admit it?'

'I—'

'And there's the wee matter of numerous phone calls to Spain. I mean, I wouldn't call it fraud . . . but you've certainly abused your position of trust—'

Pop-pop-pop. The bubbles all burst, just saggy polythene now, clagging at her mouth.

'My mother was ill!'

'Worst of all, though, it transpires that Claire Rodgers didn't actually omit to pass on details about Fraser Harris being at risk. She said you bullied her—'

'That's absolutely not true!'

Palpitations in Anna's chest, and she wants to lash out. How could Claire do that?

'I am genuinely disappointed in you, Chief

318

Inspector. And your little scene at Coriander was kind of the final straw. Actually being carried out by a doctor, I mean . . . it virtually makes your position here untenable, wouldn't you say?'

'I was not "carried out".'

'But you *were* utterly pished.'

Anna closed her eyes for a second, pressing out the room, the voice. This wasn't happening. Please. She couldn't process this.

'Still,' Hamilton continued, dangerously quiet, 'it's amazing what the drink makes us do, isn't it? Can turn us all irrational. Take Councillor Heraghty, for example. He'd obviously been matching you drink for drink, judging by the wee monologue *he* treated us to. Which,' flicking open the folder again, 'leads me on to this. Remember the chat we had before you went on holiday?'

'I wasn't on *holiday*, ma'am.' Anna's legs were trembling. The woman still hadn't asked her to sit down.

'Aye, well, whatever. When I asked you about the time Heraghty accosted you in your office—'

'He was invited.'

'. . . getting right stuck into what a disgrace G Division management was, etc, etc. *Nasty* wee bastard. Now, I asked you then if you thought he was smelling of drink.' A blank smile beneath thick-framed glasses. 'I'm not a vindictive woman, Anna. The reason I asked is that we've been concerned the pressures of his role are getting to Councillor Heraghty. Now, *you* know what that's like. And there have certainly been a few instances recently where Councillor Heraghty has appeared to be under the influence—'

'Like I said, he seemed—'

319

'Let me finish. Of course, I also asked Superintendent O'Hare about the meeting the three of you had, and, interestingly, he agreed with me. Quite obvious, he felt, that the man was inebriated. Coupled with the fact he was swearing at you both—'

'Ma'am, Councillor Heraghty never swore.'

Hamilton took her pen, pushed a sheet of paper across the desk, never touching it with her fingers.

'I think you'll find he did.'

Anna ran her eyes over the statement in front of her.

. . . I found his behaviour to be alarming and inappropriate in the extreme, and therefore decided to ask the councillor to leave. Mr Heraghty then became extremely agitated, waving his arms and shouting:

'It's a fucking disgrace. That fucking woman would rather eat her own ferrets than give me the fucking time of day.'

At this, I became alarmed and concerned for my own safety and well-being. When Superintendent O'Hare attempted to remonstrate with the councillor on my behalf, Mr Heraghty then shouted:

'Don't speak to me as if I was a piece of shit, laddie.'

She swallowed, trying to get the moisture back on her tongue. 'Who wrote this?'

Opaque glasses, the hint of dead-fish stare behind. Anna looked again at the page.

Witness statement: Chief Inspector Anna Cameron.

'Are you telling me you've verballed me?'

'Och, I wouldny say that. You weren't here, we had to act quickly. Remember the good old days? Standard procedure: your neighbour writes out

320

your statement for you, you sign it later. For the good of *everybody*, you understand.'

Anna balled the paper in her fist. That desire again, to strike flesh on flesh and make it smart. 'How dare you? I'm not signing this pile of shite.'

'Well now. That's a bit of a shame.' Hamilton waggled her pen against her teeth. 'If you don't mind me asking then, what *are* you going to do? Before I call Pitt Street and tell them to get you a move to another division, that is. I'm thinking Oban is lovely in the spring.'

'I'm going to do my job, *ma'am*. I'm going to talk to Ronnie Maguire.'

Move-and-door-slam, walk don't run.

'Are you *fuck*.' comes a roar through the flimsy door. 'You get your arse back in here.'

Don't run and scream and jump. First thought: confrontation.

Why Claire, why, when I never even asked you to?

A heart-stop shock, too fast, too slow.

I cannot deal with this. I do not know what is happening. I will not let it in.

Head down, metal segs on her soles sparking, Anna walked straight to the incident room.

'Ronnie Maguire still here?' she asked the nearest body.

'Aye.'

'I want to see him. Now.'

'Eh . . .'

'The divisional commander has approved it. You got a problem with that?'

'Right, ma'am. Eh, no ma'am.'

'He still on a voluntary, or have you Section Fourteened him yet?'

'Still voluntary.'

321

'Good stuff. Then you won't have to write anything in your wee log sheet, will you?'

Ronnie Maguire looked exhausted. His hair had fallen flat. Close to, it was revealing itself to be not a quiff, but a comb-over.

'Hey Ronnie. How you doing?'

'Shite.'

Anna shifted her chair round, so they were sitting next to each other. Concentrated only on him, his reactions, the way his body hugged itself quiet and still. Found herself mirroring his actions. 'It's hard to get your head round, isn't it?'

Her heart would not stop battering her ribs.

'Whit?'

'That you'll never see your mum again. You know, you think they'll always be there, that you'll be able to sort everything out, all the arguments you had, all the times you took them for granted. The times you meant to phone or say I love you. But you didny. Then one day,' she snapped thumb on finger, 'bumph—your mammy's gone. All the stories, the songs, the memories of *you* she kept safe, just vanished, and you can never, ever get them back again.'

A guttering of wet light in his eyes.

'But *you* can, Ronnie. Imagine that. You still have the chance to get your mammy back. To tell her one more time that you're sorry, and you love her. That would feel so good, wouldn't it? Stop you lying awake night after night.'

One tear joined another, Ronnie staring into the distance.

'Just tell us who it is you're involved with, who's been giving you all that money—and for what?'

He wiped his nose on his sleeve. 'I don't know

what you're talking about.'

'Who hates you that much they would want to hurt your mammy? Is it Sheena? Did Sheena make you do it?'

'Fuck off and leave me alone.'

Anna got out of her seat. 'Oh, you're a hard, hard man, Ronnie. You're all she's got, don't you understand? You're all your mammy has got, and, if you don't tell us who these people are, then you're leaving her to die.'

His face was still in profile; she walked round the table until he had no option but to look at her. Her body bent to meet his.

'I hope you can live with that.'

He fixed upon her a gaze of such malevolence that Anna's neck flexed back, instinctively seeking distance.

'You have no idea what I can live with.'

She knew then, it was time to go home.

Rob was supposed to be coming over, at last, to cook her dinner. But she needed to be alone. The world unravelling, she had to work out what was happening, what Hamilton was trying to do.

'Are you sure you're okay?' Rob had his consulting voice on, professional, doctorly.

'I'm fine. Just knackered after being back at work.'

'That bad?'

'Oh, you know. I'll survive.'

'You still holding the Maguires?'

'We're *interviewing* them, if that's what you mean.'

'D'you know Cassie's insulin is missing? From here I mean.'

'I heard.'

323

'I wanted to talk to you about it tonight.'

'Rob—I can't discuss—'

'I've no idea what happened to it; we always log and secure their medicines when a resident—'

She stopped him. 'She's not dead yet, Rob. Please don't say that. And if they do have her insulin, then it buys her a bit more time.'

'Aye, but *who* has it? Who came in to my nursing home and helped their fucking selves?'

He sounded like a stranger. An outsider who was holding up this soiled, small fact, making her view it through his eyes, not hers. Someone who was scared that they were implicated, who was angry they had failed. She had no history of his moods to compare this against, could only guess that he wasn't upset with her.

'We'll find out, Rob, we will. And no one's blaming you.'

'You don't know that.'

'Well, *I'm* not.'

'Thanks.' It was said sincerely. Quietly. 'I wish I could come over, Anna.'

One more nudge and she would cave.

'But I'll see you in the morning, yes?'

'Will you?'

'I thought you were going in late because you'd one of those community meetings at night?'

'So I do. I forgot.'

'And you said you'd walk the dog for me tomorrow? It doesn't matter if you can't, honestly—'

'No, no. Of course I can.'

He'd mentioned it yesterday, one small favour she could do for him. The girl who walked the dog had a hospital appointment, or the dentist's or

324

something. Anna must have said yes.

'No problem. I'll see you tomorrow, promise.'

'Take care.'

She was so tired. Take one cat, one bottle of Pinot Grigio and retire to bed. It is light outside, but you do not care. This is the only point at which there is a choice. After tonight, when tomorrow comes and you have to break out of this cocoon, you will have to do, have to *be* something. The rest of her career, her life perhaps, predicated on this single point.

Anna turned over in her bed, hugged her knees in hard, the muscle-brace of shoulder, neck and spine all taut and strong and stretching. Alice humphed, repositioned herself behind Anna's bent legs.

She had no idea what was driving Hamilton to destroy her, and maybe she'd never know. If Anna went back to work tomorrow, pretended nothing had happened . . . well, she couldn't. Hamilton would not allow it, for one. But if she did, she couldn't work as part of a management team in which she had no faith. And which had no faith in her. Not Hamilton, not Johnny . . . not Claire. Not even Fraser, whom she'd only tried to help.

What to do? Should she fight Hamilton, fight the system, keep fighting for Cassie and Fraser and boys like Aziz? Allow herself to be quietly shafted, moved to another division and left to lick her wounds? Go sick with stress? That death-knell which would be her shadow, forever defining her status and her capabilities, no matter how brief the time she spent off sick, no matter how loud and proud she acted when she came back.

Stress. She couldny hack it, see.

Or could she invent another illness, no stigma? A malady that would keep her safe beneath these sheets? No.

Stand firm and take out a grievance, then? Aye, aye, they'd say. Here she comes. When the going gets tough, she waves the international distress signal for 'victimisation':

I am a woman. You made me cry.

Take care. Rob was good, kind. An unexpected, unasked-for beginning, but it was not yet a relationship on which she could base her future. Anna had only her job and her pride. She had authored this herself, with choices about life she didn't really have to make. Now here she was, with this choice which would make or break her.

Baby steps, baby steps. Take each tiny thing at a time. One moment, her brain was whirling, alive with every option she could pursue. Then dim, shutting down block by block of coloured thought, until she could see nothing but the grey of self-preservation.

Would she fight or would she hide?

But I am already broken.

*   *   *

It is too far to run, he cannot run all the way. So the guard flits through the sliding doors of trains, steals under a tarpaulin-covered lorry until it stops, somewhere, and he can climb out. It has taken him to a place called Harthill. It is by a busy motorway, halfway to Edinburgh, and from there he can get to Rosyth. He knows Rosyth, after Rosyth comes Belgium; it is the way he came here.

Two fat pads sit beneath his jacket, panniered on

his hips. He should have taken more, but he was frightened. They won't notice these handfuls; he has taken them from separate boxes, resealed as carefully as they were split.

But will they notice him?

The cargo van comes every two or three days, sometimes delivering, sometimes picking up. It should be another day before the next visit: he has time, he has time. And maybe longer yet, for even when they are there, they rarely speak to him; they don't call out if he is in another room, or filling his kettle from the tap at the back. Boxes come and go; they leave him packets of food and tins. Never money. He has received no payment yet.

We will send it home for you, they say. His own money, the meagre remains of what brought him here, is gone.

They owe him. He is due payment for keeping secrets and doing his best. For creeping down in the dark and sharing his food. For pretending he has no English, that he couldn't understand; for what kind of a man would understand, yet still do nothing?

A man, a guard—what is he? He is nothing any more, he is a shadow. But a shadow that is very hungry. The café is cooking sausages; he can smell meat on the truckers who pass by, chewing rolls from greasy packets. He moves inside, takes a seat at an uncleared table. There is still some tea in the pot, a little bacon rind, some egg on the plate. Like an animal, he eats. Like an animal, he hunches small, is alert to every flicker. When three men walk in with a purposeful gait, it alarms him. When a fourth enters, and does not remove his shades, his belly leaps in elastic terror.

They are looking away from him, towards the

327

metallic counters of food. Slow, he slides his way along the long, grubby wall to the toilets. If he can . . . if he does not have . . . if he says he only . . . In desperation, he locks the cubicle, draws his legs up and tries to clamber through a broken space no bigger than a shoe box. It is an air vent, it is a space, why can't he fit . . . if he does not have . . . if he did not have . . . he rips the bundles from his thighs, stuffs them deep into the vent, then crouches down, his knees at his chin, feet on the seat.

At first, there is nothing. There is a glorious pause; he thinks he is safe.

Until the door breaks inwards. Slams once, twice, in shudders.

'Tut tut, little piggy,' says the slit beneath the shades. 'You know, you really should have stayed at home.'

CHAPTER SIXTEEN

Morning brought weak light and resolution.

Anna would not go sick. Anna would not face them and do nothing. She could not just cower, anticipating Hamilton's final boot-strike. She would walk Rob's dog because that is what she promised. After lunch, she would go into work as agreed. Do all the checks and ticks and processes that were expected of her, then drive straight to Headquarters and to Personnel. She would launch a grievance against both Hamilton and Johnny for harassment and victimisation, then she would sit back and wait.

Who would win? Anna Cameron of the dodgy

record and even dodgier rumours, who had never cultivated a sleek, useful network of well-placed friends and influences, or The Organisation, a beast in all its huge and armour-plated glory? The police force that men like her dad had served—the rough and ready family with a common morality and purpose she thought she shared—was gone. Perhaps it had never truly existed. Or, if it had, the only thing left was a shell, held together by bitter sinews and a resolute marching of on and up. Public service, honesty, integrity, the common good, all withered; to be replaced by targets, benchmarks, call centres, business processes. *Pace of change, pace of change*. Run faster, do more, care less. Cut the corners, serve up sound bites. Feed the all-consuming beast.

It was an unalienable fact of gravity: shit flows down. The beast would consume Anna, would shit her out and lumber on, and no one would see or remember what she was. All that would linger was the memory of a rotten smell.

Yet, surely, keeping the beast alive, in there somewhere, was a heart.

*   *   *

'Anna! Hi, you. You made it. Right on time, too.' Rob already had his coat on, briefcase standing by the door.

'Old Reliable, that's me.'

He kissed her cheek. She smelled his skin.

'Come in.'

The hall was long and broad, oak spindles on the staircase, stained-glass lilies filtering pastel sun through a narrow window. A painting of vibrant irises faced the archetypal Scottish hallstand, with its thin mottled mirror and chunky hat hooks. Training shoes, bags and brollies on the floor, and a spill of books lay over a crumpled pair of running shorts.

'Cleaning lady comes tomorrow,' he apologised.

'No, it's lovely. That picture's . . . lovely.'

'Amy did it.'

He'd alluded to his wife just once, while they were in Spain. Only in the context of loss and how it felt, not as a real person who had made things. Even deep in her own grief, Anna had felt he didn't want to talk Amy back to life.

Those days in Spain seemed unreal now. The easiness, the certainty that this was the only way it could be, that it was right and wholly unremarkable that Rob Macklin had seen Anna's naked guts, had faltered. She had waited too long and the raw momentum which had pushed them to that place had become the dusty, awkward pause where you don't know what to say.

'Really? Well . . . it's great.'

'Come on through into the living room. Can I get you a coffee?'

'No thanks.'

They stood, Rob's hands at his side, Anna's in her pockets.

'Laura at school?'

'Yeah.'

'So, where's this mutt then?'

'Oh, she's out the back. Hang on.'

He left her standing in the front room and the tension eased. She wanted to follow him though, to kiss his face and push him, press him so they did not have to talk, the way she'd straddled Alex

330

bloody Patterson, who did not matter, had never mattered, but whom she would let slip inside her on the basis of four gins and two pints of cider, and hardly even blink.

She exhaled. Brittle, cold air in the front room. She guessed it wasn't used much. The carved fireplace was dull, the sofas needed plumping. A table in the bay window was crying out for some flowers. Everything was waiting; an uncomfortable house, for all its space and polished wood, redolent with another woman's essence, her presence furled within the curtains she had put up, the paintings she had hung.

The door battered against the wall, and a fat golden Labrador charged into the room.

'Anna, meet Donna.'

It sniffed at Anna's groin.

'Donna? For a dog?'

Rob rubbed the back of his head. 'After Donna Summer. You know, the singer? Amy loved her.'

'Ah.'

Her name again, two sad syllables. A sigh like a stone, blocking the way so you could go no further, just nod your head quietly and keep your counsel. Anna had no business being in this house. She wanted to tell Rob what was happening to her at work, but where to begin? The dog panted, flopped on to the rug. It looked knackered already.

'I'm sure we'll manage.'

'There's a blanket in the porch you can put on your back seat when you take her out.'

'Can she not walk then?'

'I mean if you go to the park or whatever. There's a car park at the back of Netherlee Pavilion that's nice and quiet. But I wouldn't walk

331

her along the main road. She's not too fond of traffic.'

Another guillotine-slam, another conversation severed. Was Donna there, then, when it happened? Did she lie by her mistress's side, nudging her to move, or did she flee from the screech and smash and screaming?

Anna knelt to scratch the dog's ears. 'Don't worry. I'll look after her. We'll have a good time, won't we, Donna?'

The dog rolled over, tail beating time on the floor as a pungent meatiness spread across the room.

Quickly, Anna got to her feet. 'Has she just farted?'

'It's Laura. She keeps feeding her cheese and crisps and stuff. Oh, Anna—you couldn't do me another *massive* favour, could you?'

'Depends on what it is.'

Rob lifted a brown envelope from the sideboard. 'I need to deposit this—this morning if possible, at the bank on Clarkston Road. The overdraft's about to go into overdraft, and there's fees and cheques here going back the last two months. I've filled out the pay-in slip and everything; you just need to hand it to a cashier.' Over and back, over and back, folding the open flap into tight concertinas. 'Pretty much first thing, if you don't mind.'

'Nae bother.'

'Cheers. I'll leave it here. Look, I've got to go— the poo-bags are in the drawer beneath the sink, okay?'

'The what? No way, pal. That was not part of the deal. I'm not shovelling shit for anyone.'

'Can't hear you.' He walked into the hall, Anna after him. 'Right, I'm off. It's a meeting with the Care Commission, I can't be late.'

'I know.'

His tie was squint. It was the same mad purple one he'd worn when they met. 'Stand still a minute.' The silk loop loosened, made straight. Centred. Him swallowing, not smiling. The bow of his lips, the scattered darkness of the rough hair beneath his skin and the play of light on bright blue irises. To kiss him now, properly, would be like slapping a child.

'Things are really bad, aren't they?'

He moved back from her. 'Och, it's not me I'm worried about, Anna.' Picked up his briefcase, fiddling with the lock. 'It's Cassie, you know? I can't get her out of my mind. It's the not knowing; if she's dead, if she's conscious.'

'Rob, I promise you, we'll find her. Soon.'

He nodded, unconvinced. 'I'll be back by lunch, okay? A quick one, before you go to work.'

A momentary, shared glance. Lips upturned, him shaking his head at her dirty laugh.

'I mean a quick *lunch*. My treat.'

'You're damn right. But I was serious about the poo-bags.'

'I'm going now . . .'

'Well, go then.'

'I've gone.'

Donna bounded to the front window, placing two fat paws on the sill. The scraped paintwork and smeared glass suggested this was a regular haunt. Her tail wagged gamely until Rob's car had driven out of view, then it stopped, hanging low like her head. The dog gave a heave that was neither bark nor yelp, more like a human sigh, and curled up beneath the window, head on paws.

She seemed settled enough. Sleepy. Would the dog follow Anna if she took a wander round the house? Just to get her bearings. Back into the hall, a wee nosey in the kitchen. Of course, there was an Aga. Racing green and stylish, with polished rails and hotplates, and the dog basket nestling close by. Dining room next, with its long oak table and antique chairs. The table top was smeared, the candles melted to stubs. Not many dinner parties here for a while. Then upstairs—to the bathroom, if anyone asked, though it felt like delving below the belt, interrogating the private parts of a place that was not hers. Donna padded at her heels, waiting outside each room as Anna peeked inside. This must be Laura's room, with its lilac wallpaper and silver mirrorball refracting disco-daylight. Very tidy, all the bookshelves neat, the desk with pencils in one pot, pens in another. Posters of pop bands and pin-ups too young to register with Anna.

A faint breeze fanned her shoulder blades.

But that one did.

Move on, pretend it wasn't there. Of course it was, why shouldn't it be? More right to be there than Anna had. She made herself look again at the photo, the several photos; a collage of a red-haired woman with Laura's eyes. Standing head-on to the camera, holding up her baby girl. Clutching Laura on a trampoline. Blowing out candles on a birthday cake. All set in glass in a frame above the desk, so Mummy could still oversee Laura's homework, her drawings, her secret scribbles in the big pink diary. Exactly what Anna had done, defiant and brave, tucking her father's picture into the frame of her dressing-table mirror, persisting for years after her mother had removed all the ones from downstairs. Anna went back into the hall, shut the door. The master bedroom faced her, its door hip-width ajar. What if Rob kept a photo by his bed too? Donna scratched her ear with her back paw, eyes fixed always on where Anna was going next. Which was into Rob's bedroom.

Pine wardrobes, a dresser and a soft, sagging bed. Anna touched the covers, soft silk, a counterpane faded with years of morning sun and breakfasts in bed. She made a slow digest of each of the room's component parts. The bedside tables held books and tissues, a brass lamp on one, clock on the other. The dresser was also clear. Just a hairbrush, some loose change, bottles of aftershave and a vial of perfume.

Not meaning to, she picked the bottle up. Not meaning to, she squeezed the padded atomiser. Not meaning to, she breathed a buried woman into her head. As Rob must have done. Must still do. The scent was stagnant, she felt dirty, like a sneak-thief. Anna was so tired of being second best. She needed fresh air.

'Right you, dog. I suppose you'll be wanting a walk?' At the magic word, Donna jumped like a puppy, bounding on her hind legs, her front paws battering Anna's knees, tongue lolling like she'd just popped doggie Es. Anna feinted to one side, Donna tottered after, paws still high, face in raptures. 'Are you dancin'?' asked Anna. 'Are you askin'?' she replied, in a gruff voice. A wee top hat and a bow tie and they were away.

'Come on then. Let's go downstairs.'

She gathered all the accoutrements of the dog

walker: lead, Frisbee and ball. Poo-bags. Treats perhaps, in case Donna shunned her publicly and had to be tempted back to the car. But where were you meant to put it all? You could hardly yomp through the bushes with a handbag slung over your arm, and the pockets of her close-fitting fleece weren't built for bulk. A pooch-pouch, that's what she needed. Maybe she could patent it when she retired—or was sacked; sell it in the kind of shops that flogged designer dog-jackets, and crystal bowls for cats. A lightweight utility belt, similar to what she carried at work, with hooks for the lead instead of handcuffs, and little pockets for treats, poo-bags and . . . envelopes. She should take that with her too, deposit the money before she forgot. She stuffed the envelope in beside the ball and the treats. The pocket gaped too wide to zip, but it would do.

Anna loaded Donna and her blanket into the hatchback of her car. Rob had mentioned a park, but he didn't say which one. Newlands Park was the closest. It was pretty, but very small, just a pond, a tennis court and some flower beds. Twice round that would only take ten minutes, and Anna wanted to stay out of this watchful house as long as she could. She thought a minute, picturing the big map on her office wall. Linn Park wasn't far—and was huge, stretching from leafy Netherlee, where Fraser Harris lived, to semi-detached Simshill, from ancient Cathcart to the four-in-a-blocks of Croftfoot. The kind of park you could lose yourself in. There was a wee community pavilion, too, just behind the primary school at Netherlee. That must be the park Rob had meant. And the bank was on the way.

When she got there, though, the bank was closed for staff training. *Our nearest branch is . . . Clarkston.* Not that far, but it could wait until after their walk. Donna was making whining noises in the back, and Anna had just had the car valeted. She carried on to Linn Park, drew up at the side of the pavilion, noting the smashed-out security light, the new vandalism on the white walls.

Gordo 4 Aye.

We'll never forget you.

Busby Cumbie on tour.

And beneath, a swirl of S through Y, encased in a D: *Young Stampy Derry.*

What were these wee tossers like? Resurrecting bits of names from long-forgotten gangs, doodling their practised signatures on their neighbours' bought houses and two-car garage walls. High on boredom and money and too much choice, so they chose to play tough, scruffing up their designer trainers, knocking vodka from their mothers' cocktail cabinets. Joining their pals to run amok and stab a young boy's life away. Like it was performance art. Like they didn't have a choice. Take these kiddy-on hardmen to a scheme like Easterhouse, and they'd be flayed alive. Castlemilk even, just across the River Cart. Parachute the Young Stampy Derry into The Milk and see who blinked first.

The dog jumped from the boot, stretched. Her pouncing and grinning was an invitation to chase, and Anna did, safe in the knowledge that the park was empty. Spring had done another volte-face, returning overnight to stark, crisp winter, and it felt good to be pumping blood through her legs. They ran along the riverbank, further into the park, until they came out at a great, sweeping hill. Donna barked for joy and the hugeness of it all, then froze; gave two sharp sniffs, before sprinting off into the distance. This wasn't the capering playmate of before, but a frenzied, ears-down rocket-dog, who had some poor creature in her sights.

'Donna!' Anna panicked. If she lost the dog, Rob would never forgive her. Nor would Laura. She thundered after it, passing two young neds lolling on the yellowing grass. They were having a Glasgow breakfast—four cans of Special Brew each and a bottle of tonic wine. One of them thwacking a golf club on the ground, flicking his wrist like he was fishing.

'Donna. Come here!'

'Doner?' The two neds began wheezing. 'Haw missus—that a dug you've got or a fuckin kebab?'

She tried to ignore them, chasing harder and higher after Donna, who was sensing liberation and the sweet scent of what appeared to be cow crap.

Too late, Anna grabbed her collar as the animal bit deep into a pile of shite. 'Oh, for God's sake. Get away from there, you minging dog.' As she dipped forward to shove the dog's muzzle away, Rob's envelope fell out from her pocket, bursting open. While one hand fought to control the Baskerville hound, the other stuffed notes and cheques back inside. A sharp glance to the left as she crammed the envelope back inside her pocket, but the youths had returned to their carry-out; far more appealing than watching a middle-aged woman feeding faeces to a dog. Anna snapped the lead on to Donna's collar, dragging her away from

338

her prize.

'You really are a filthy animal. A cat would *never* do that.'

Up the long rise they continued, Donna pulling, Anna resisting, until they reached a line of trees at the top. It was the beginning of a wood, skirting the edge of the uppermost field. Two horses grazed there, ears rippling as Donna barked at them.

'So that's what it was—horse dung. Oh well, that's much more sophisticated, madam.'

A cheerful wag, and Donna was off again, tugging on her lead as she tried to reach another pile of manure. Anna took in the full-circle view: horses chewing, magpies dipping, far-off grey-slated houses and a rosy sandstone church on a hill across the way. It must be the one by Fraser's house. Far in the distance, the Campsie Fells trundled across the horizon, prehistoric humps that held Glasgow from bursting at the seams. Air like ice picks up here, cold and cauterising, sterilising her lungs. A trail led into the copse of trees, a small secret path, just dark enough to intrigue.

'Right, dog. You going to behave this time?'

Once they got inside the woods, Anna let Donna off the lead. She seemed less intense here, happy to root and snuffle, with the occasional dash towards imagined squirrels or day-old rabbit spoor. As they walked, Anna could see a golf course through the trees. That must be the one at the end of Old Castle Road, on the far side of the park. She didn't realise she'd travelled so far. To her left, rows of pine and birch clad a downward slope, undercut with scrubby grass and bushes. Anna followed Donna's progress in its stop-start zigzag through the undergrowth. As the dog galumphed towards an abandoned golf ball, a bundle of amber flashed in the greenery to her left. She moved closer, leaving the path to crunch over matted leaves. The foliage was thick here, growing close and tight. Glossy leaves of laurel and rhododendron spilt juice on her shoulders, and her face split a cobweb as she pushed through, fragile threads spinning loose in hair and air. She stopped about twelve feet away from the brilliant orange coil, hid her body behind a tree. It was a fox cub, lying inside mossed roots. Tiny breathing belly, and tail curled round tight eyes; it was the still but alert repose of a cat, not a dog. Anna stood a moment, watching its chest rise and fall. Above, a tired sun flickered, burnishing its fur.

She let it sleep, headed out before Donna came crashing in to find them both. As Anna made her way back to the path, she saw movement through the branches—two figures, a swing of silver shooting sparks of light. Golfers. She looked for the dog, in case Donna was the type to savage strangers on sight. No—there she was, away over to the right now, digging up the bunker by the sixteenth hole. Anna watched the golfers' progress. Not very well equipped—they only seemed to have one club between them both. Then she realised the people on the path were the youths she'd seen earlier. They were moving silently, heads sweeping in search. Must be looking for a ball.

She gave them a minute to carry on, so she wouldn't be walking up their heels. Donna seemed happy enough—oh, bollocks—she was squatting in the bunker. 'Donna!' Anna hissed. 'No! Come here

340

now.' Amazingly, she did. Anna didn't get too close, but the bunker looked crap-free. 'Right, you. Let's get a move on.'

They carried on following the path, which was narrowing all the time, barely enough room to push through the slapping leaves. Suddenly, a man's face appeared in front of Anna. Air jangling in her lungs; he was so close. Donna trotted past them both, her coat a melting shadow in the near-black bushes. The figure hesitated, and Anna moved aside to let him pass. He kept his chin into his chest, avoiding any acknowledgement. It was the same youth that had shouted at her earlier, the one with the golf club, but this time, he was alone. Vapours of sweat and cheap wine book-ended his passage. Anna waited to see if his friend was following, but when no one else came, she carried on.

'Donna! Donna!'

The dog reappeared to give her a wag, then hurried back to the undergrowth. This was the kind of day Anna loved, all dry and sharp-scented like a packet of good crisps. The trees closing, dense. Beginnings of rhododendrons that would offer a purple haze above. Then, so quiet you could almost ignore it, she heard a stuttering of leaves behind her. A padded footfall that was not her own. That youth had turned again. She knew it. He was following her. She could hear a laboured shuffling, sneaking like carpet slippers. How close, how many? A single crack of twig or ankle bone. A heartbeat pause. Only one, she guessed, which meant his pal was definitely still up ahead. Waiting somewhere.

Anna licked her lips. If she stopped, would the

boy behind stop too? Duck from confrontation, or circle the knowing prelude to his dance? And what of his hidden friend, flexing drink-fuelled fingers to commence a pincer movement. One pissed-up dipstick she could take. Maybe. But two? Anna reached slowly into her pocket for her mobile phone.

Which was in her handbag at Rob's house.

She could no longer see the dog, could see nothing but the tree in front, then the tree in front of that. If she had to run, she had no idea which way to go. A panic-fog became a rage. Just a woman, having a walk. Were morning parks forbidden now?

What was she thinking, going through a wood without an escort; enjoying peace and solitude in among the trees? Bold as brass—and in that tight fleece too . . .

Anna kept her pace, drew out her car keys. Slotted between her fingers, they might gouge a single eye, but they were hardly a sure-stop weapon. Although . . . The black key fob was square, big enough to notice if you held it at your ear. A half-cut arsehole with his eyes fixed on her back. Would he see her do it, though? Or was she already just a wraith to him, a form with no face or family or feelings? She had to time this right, let him get close enough that he could hear exactly what she said, but not so close that he felt cornered, with no option but to strike.

Anna shortened her steps, heard his tread get louder. Imagined heat from hands at the nape of her neck. Whispered as loud and slow as might be credible. 'Aye, Golf to G Golf. This is Operation Forester, within Linn Park. For your information, I am in close proximity to one suspect male. White, aged sixteen to twenty, around five foot nine, heavy build. Smells like a butcher's shop. Wearing red hooded top and dark jeans. Can you get stations to attend—'

Before Anna had finished the sentence, there was a scuffle and a thud. Then another, and another, as the youth's fat drunken feet took flight and the thuds grew fainter. Blood squalling in Anna's ears, pressing at her throat. Her choice now was to chase after him and his golf club, try to wrestle him to the ground and yell for help. Or carry on and surprise the other.

'Donna!' she hissed. 'Donna—here girl.' The dog emerged, Anna seizing her collar and snapping the lead into place.

'Okay, madam,' she whispered. 'You and I are going on a wee adventure.'

They left the path, delving through brambles that bit and nipped, Anna constantly looking behind, either side and then far, far ahead. She couldn't even be sure golf club guy had gone. It was hopeless. She needed to get up high if she was going to see anything at all. There was a wide-boughed tree over there that might do.

'Right,' she whispered to the dog. 'I want you to stay. Stay!'

Donna obliged, sitting to attention. As a precaution, Anna tied the lead to a bush, then swung her arms up to reach the first overhanging branch. A swift pull, a scrabble, then her feet found some nodules of bark. Enough to get some purchase, and push her higher into the tree. From there, it was easy to step on to the next layer of branches, and the next, until she was tens of feet

343

above the ground. Golf-boy had been wearing red—no sign of any red that she could see. The other . . . the other. She thought he had been in something white, a tracksuit top maybe. Many trees were not fully in leaf yet, bald gaps against spindly twigs, and she could see patches of forest floor, the glints of puddles.

And a vague floating of smoke about 200 metres to her left.

The wee shite was having a casual fag, waiting at a bus stop for his ride to come along. A little time out to regroup, before he smashed in her head, or ripped off her top. Experiencing the same frisson she got each time she laid hands on a ned.

Anna shimmied back down. Donna stood, tail spinning like a helicopter blade.

'Ssh. Ssh.' She fed her some of the treats she'd brought. 'Good girl.'

She led the dog a little further through the trees, closer to the hidden ned. Her belly sliding. The youth was clawing at his balls, sorting himself in that proud, proprietorial way men had. Normal women would run the other way. Or hunker down and hide until he'd passed.

'Do you want your ball?' she whispered, unfastening the lead.

Donna whimpered, mouth agog.

'Eh? Want your ball, Donna? Go fetch!'

Anna threw the ball as hard as she could, so it landed way in front of where the ned stood. She watched him jump, weasel-alert as Donna careered into his eye-line. At the same time as he was waiting for her to appear beside the dog, Anna was edging up behind him, nearer and nearer until she could see the yellow points of acne on his neck.

She wound the dog lead round her fist, raised her arm. Lunging at the same moment that he began to turn to where she was; but he was too late, Anna snaring him, dragging him sideways as she jerked her forearm into his Adam's apple and he began to scream as the dog launched herself on to his chest, thinking this was all a wonderful game.

'Get it off me. Get it off me!' he was shrieking, Anna rolling him on to his belly . . . One quick punch to the side of his flailing head. A precautionary blow, just so he knew.

'I'm feart fae dugs. Get it fucking off me!'

Anna clicked her fingers. 'Down, Donna. Down. That's a good girl.'

Using the dog lead to bind his wrists, she pulled the ned's arms high behind his back, his shoulder blades scything until his body followed suit. 'Up! Sit up, ya bastard. Now,' leaning him against a tree, 'listen, you wee fucker. You make one move, and my dog'll have your gonads.'

Donna wagged her tail.

'Right.' She let his arms relax, sitting as far to the side of him as she could, while still gripping his wrists. 'Maybe you'd like to tell me what the fuck you and your pal were doing?'

The ned's face was mottled with grass and fury. 'We werny doing fuck-all, ya fucking loony. I was just standing having a fag. Fucking loony cow, ya.'

'Bollocks.' She coated the word in cynicism, but, even as she was saying it, she realised the blunt truth. Anna had proof of nothing. Two men had gone for a walk, one had changed his mind. Then changed his mind again, whilst his buddy stopped for a fag. But Anna knew, she *knew* the youths had been following her. If it had been another

345

person—a nice quiet lady, walking her Peke; perhaps oblivious, perhaps growing uneasy . . . well, who would be lying face down in the grass now? What were you meant to do? Wait until they got you before you tried to fight back?

'Ho, ya fucking loony.' The ned kicked out with his foot. 'I said: what's this shite about?'

A twist in his eyes. If he and his mate ganged up, it would be their word against hers. Anna done for assault, and them off for a celebratory piss-up, then up for a rerun with a more compliant victim. They'd been *hunting* her like dogs. In the distance she heard a lilting whistle. A fellow dog walker, or the ned's mate, coming back to see what was keeping him?

'You got a moby on you?'

'Whit?'

With her free hand, she slapped his jaw. 'I said, have you got a fucking mobile?'

'Aye.' The ned's face was paler now, apart from the blotch where her hand had given him that wee bit of encouragement. He nodded down to the right. 'In ma jacket.'

Never taking her eyes from his face, she reached in to his jacket and pulled out the phone.

'What's your name?'

'Dunkey. Duncan Ritchie.'

Anna leaned forward again. This time, her hand reached out to his groin.

'Woah! Hey! What the fuck are you doing? Don't hurt me. Fucksake, missus, don't hurt me.' Eyes split wide, he was clearly terrified. 'Where's Spango? What have you done tae Spango?'

'Spango your big mate?'

He swallowed. Nodded.

346

'Don't worry. We'll scoop him up later. How come your fly's open?'

The ned looked down. 'I'd just went for a slash. How?'

'You one of those wee bastards that gets off flashing yourself to strangers?'

'What? *Fucksake*. No way, man. *Come on*. We were only gonny dip your purse.'

'Is that right? Well, Duncan Ritchie, I've got no proof of that. Luckily though, we do have proof of this.'

Anna pulled her sleeve over her fingers, made the gap at his groin a little wider.

'Oh, Jesus.' The youth closed his eyes. 'What you *daeing*, man?'

Just enough divestment to make it indisputable. Full foulness of sweating earth, queasiness rising at what she'd done, but still she did it, left him open as she keyed the direct number for G Division's Control Room.

'Hello? Dorothy? Aye, It's Chief Inspector Cameron here.'

'Oh for fucksake.' She saw the ned thump his head back against the tree.

'Yeah, that's right—no, no, I *am* off this morning . . . I've just made an apprehension in Linn Park. Could you send stations to assist please? We're on the footpath at the back of the golf course, about halfway along. Yeah. One male for indecent exposure and resist arrest.'

CHAPTER SEVENTEEN

One single tap to catch her attention. She thought she'd shut her office door, was just finishing up, about to drive to Headquarters. She'd dumped Donna back at Rob's house, along with two Bonios and a note saying something had come up, then gone straight to Giffnock office. Not even got changed. She wasn't sure why; it just felt safer to be here. A DC lolled against the door jamb.

'Duncan Ritchie?' he said.

'Mm?'

'Ma'am, we're questioning your body about a series of indecencies we've had in the division.'

'And?' Anna didn't look up from her PC.

'You know he's a juvey?'

'You're joking me—he's huge.'

'Aye, well, he's sixteen, but he's under supervision. Lives up at that home in Eaglesham. Anyway, he's going totally ballistic. Keeps screeching that he's no a pervert, and he was only trying to steal your purse. In fact,' the DC came full inside the office, closing Anna's door over as he did so, 'ma'am, I hate to say this, but he's spinning a whole load of shite, saying *you* assaulted him.'

'Well, I had to restrain him—'

'No.' He dropped his voice. 'I know it sounds stupid, but he's saying you . . . well, that you undid his flies and grabbed his dick.'

She glanced directly at him, held eyebrows high, mouth half incredulous. Then frowning, a little bit angry as reality dawned. 'Is that right?'

'The DS is having words with him just now, but I thought you should know.'

Anna stretched her arms behind her, holding her skull, before bringing her hands to rest on the back of her neck, elbows like chicken wings, vertically protecting her breasts. He wouldn't dare look direct at her breasts. Wouldn't see them rise and fall, rise and fall, faster and faster oh you stupid, panicky under-siege cow. She shook her head. 'Unbelievable. I thought I'd had everything that being a woman could throw at me in this job, but this is a classic. I grope wee boys in my spare time, do I, then tie them up and phone the polis, so my victims can grass me up?'

The DC was moving slightly from one foot to another. Anna wanted to tell him to stand still, but she was trying too hard to keep her gaze flat and level. Downright liar. That's where the phrase came from. Looking away and down to your right, where her shoulders were naturally twisting; it was the classic marker of deceit.

'I know it sounds daft, ma'am. But I . . . we're just worried that this might grow arms and legs, you know?'

'Well, don't let it, Scott.'

'It's just, other than your alleg . . . em arrest, we've got nothing else on him. I mean, he's got pre cons for crimes of violence, dishonesty and that, but nothing sexual, you know?'

'And my word isn't enough? Is that what your DS has sent you over here to tell me?'

'No, no, it's nothing like that, ma'am. But maybe you should come down to Govan. Have a wee word?'

'I'll have more than a wee word. I'll fucking have

349

the wee bastard. I'll find ten more charges we can stick him with and I'll sue his arse for defamation. Did you come up in a car?'

'Yes ma'am. Will I drive you down?'

'Yup.'

'I just need to uplift a couple of bags for the productions officer.'

'Fine. I'll get you in the yard in two minutes.'

After he'd left, Anna remained in the same position. A scrawny, scared statue at a chief inspector's desk. Then, for one slow moment, she let her hands cover her face. Retracing and recalibrating, and think, for God's sake, think. If Hamilton was aware of this already, Anna was lost.

There was little conversation on the road to Govan. The DC drove and Anna mithered. To retract her statement would be to ratify Ritchie's complaint. To plough on regardless would be to invite disaster. For the boy and her both. But what else could she do?

'That's us, ma'am.'

'Already?'

Whole swathes of road had trundled by unnoticed as Anna fought her thoughts, suppressed her conscience. The boy had been up to no good. She knew that in her gut. They passed through the barrier and parked in the side yard. Anna was always envious when she went to Govan. Purpose-built, and relatively new, you could fit about ten Giffnocks into Govan's yellow brick walls. Perched right by the motorway, the complex was home to the Fraud Squad, the Stolen Car Squad and the Serious Crime Squad, as well as being divisional headquarters for the south. It had also been built as a high-security holding station for the most troublesome of detainees. And none more troublesome than the youth seated right now in Interview Room Two.

The DS was waiting outside, arms folded, back against the door. 'Alright ma'am? Junior's calmed down a wee bit. Him and I have had a nice chat, about what can happen to little boys who tell big lies. And I think he may have seen the error of his ways. But he's insisting on speaking to you—if you don't mind.'

'Oh, not at all. I can't wait to have a wee chat with him.'

They all laughed together. But did they believe her? Was it: aye, you go girl and stick it to him, cos we're all mates together laughing, or was it: be polite and humour her, the utterly sick old hag?

'Will I come in with you, ma'am?'

'No. Thanks, but I'd rather do this on my own.'

He opened the door of the interview room. 'I'll wait outside. Eh, tape's off by the way.'

'Cheers.' Immediately, she wondered why he'd said that. Was he reassuring her? Did he think she was worried? Anna faced the boy, timing it so she could still be heard as the door was closing.

'Right then, you wee bastard. What's this all about?'

'What's this all about?' he shouted. 'You know fine fucking well what this is all about.'

Anna seized the neck of his T-shirt and yanked him up from his seat. His hands were still cuffed behind him.

'Never swear in front of a lady.'

The door was tight shut; no DS-shaped slumps pressing on the mottled glass. Anna spoke slow and quiet, close against the boy's ear. Each word a

351

brick to wall him in, each syllable a stab. 'I am fucking warning you. You ever repeat your totally unfounded allegation to anyone, ever again, and I will have you. I'll make sure you never leave this police office. Do you understand? I will parade you through the courts and have you put on every sex offender's list in the country.'

'But I didny fucking do it.'

'Didny do what? Didny stalk me through the woods? Didny wait to jump me, tie me up, do God knows what to me?'

Anna opened her hand, an angry star. Dropped him back into his seat.

'Do you know what they do to sex offenders in jail? Do you know what they do to pretty wee boys for that matter, Duncan? You're no a juvey any more, not when it comes to this. You don't go to the Children's Panel for indecencies.'

Not strictly true, but, then, the tape was off.

'Please miss,' he whined. 'You know I didny do it. I've got a girlfriend. She'll fucking kill me if she thought . . . please. We're gonny have a wean. I'm begging you. Look, I'm sorry we were following you—'

'We. So, who's we?'

'Spango. Samuel Reid. He stays in Croftfoot.'

'Good boy.'

The boy's features loosened. Not relaxed, just a little less terrified.

'Now,' continued Anna, 'the way it works is, I send a couple of cops to pick up Spango, we have a wee blether with him about how he might also go to jail—as part of a gang of would-be rapists, obviously—and, before you know it, he'll be telling us you've got a gimp mask and piano wire back in your room.'

'Please,' the boy whispered, 'don't do this to me.'

'Was that what you hoped *I'd* say? When you attacked me?'

'Miss, I hate pervs, I swear.'

The door opened, and the DS jooked his head round. 'Everything alright in here?'

'Yup, we're fine.'

'Ma'am, I need to have a word with you about something.'

'Just give us a minute.'

'Sure.'

He left again. She had to do something to get them out of this mess.

'Okay, Duncan. So, what kind of a deal are we going to strike here?'

'Deal?'

'Aye. What can you give to me that will make all of this go away?'

'You want a fucking bung?'

'No. I want intelligence. You're a bit of a player, so I've heard. You must have some juicy gen you'd like to share with your local constabulary.'

'You mean grass up my mates?'

'Doesn't have to be your mates, Duncan. What about local drug dealers, eh? Maybe the ones using ice-cream vans round the schools. Why not tell us where they keep their stash? Or what about all those housebreakings in Carmunnock—any idea who's been doing them?'

He folded his arms. 'Aye, but I'm no fucking telling yous lot.'

'Oh well.' Anna shrugged. 'I did my best. Right, what you will tell me is exactly where your pal

Samuel stays.'

'Naw, wait.' The boy was thinking, a ponderous chewing of the side of his lip. 'I *can* tell yous something. Plus, they're nae mates of mine.'

'Who aren't?'

'They boys that battered that polis. Mind, the one that was in the paper? Outside his own house? Ace, man! Fucking hole in one.' He stopped grinning, shook his head. 'Eh. Sorry.'

Anna's mouth went dry. This had better not be a wind-up.

'So. Tell me.'

'Well, I only know the one, really. Sparky the Darkie, he's called. Just started running with the Ubu Roi.'

'Sparky the Darkie?'

'Aye.' Duncan honked. 'Got dragged along by a stolen motor. He was trying tae climb in the window when they were driving—for a dare, like! He's mental, so he is. The sparks were pure firing off the segs in his boots.'

'And who is he, this Sparky?'

'I canny mind his right name, but he's a half-caste, miss. His maw's foreign, but his dad's white. I think. No long been down here. He was living with his maw in some pure *Deliverance* kinda place—Crieff or Crail or something. Dee-ding-deedle-deedle-ding.' Duncan mimed the actions of playing a banjo, pushing his chair back so it rocked on two legs. 'So. Will that do for you? Can I go now?'

'Oh, I need more than that Duncan. Why did they do it, for one? Who was Sparky working with, for another?'

His chair slammed back on four legs. 'Christ, *I*

354

don't know. I gied you a fucking name. They were just pure going on about it, total hardmen like.' He muttered something else.

'What was that?'

'I said: we still kicked their cunts, but.'

'So you fight with these boys?'

'I fight wi' everyone, miss.'

'Well, I'm going to have to check this out—'

'Jesus God miss, *please*.' The boy was shoving his fingertips hard in his face, reaching for bone. Thin pads of flesh squeezed up between the gaps. His was not the normal agitation of a caged-in ned, nor the indignation of wrongful imprisonment. Beneath the sheen of his faked bravado was a real and genuine desperation.

'I said I'll check it out.'

She would leave him here to sweat a little, get Divisional Intelligence to trawl their lists of known gang members and new arrivals. Then he'd think she was doing him a favour when she finally let him go.

'Ma'am?' The DS again.

Anna didn't need a babysitter. 'What is it?'

'I know you're busy, but DCI Cruikshanks really wants to speak to you. He says I've to haul you away from whatever you're doing—'

'Where is he?'

'On the phone. I can transfer it through here if you like.'

She nodded. Seconds later, the phone on the wall rang out.

'You no keep your moby on doll?' Tom's voice was a little disjointed, like he was moving. 'Some cop you are.'

'*Mr* Cruikshanks. What's up?'

355

'You jail a ned up at Linn Park?'

A flutter through her ribs. 'Aye?'

'Aye, well see when the troops came to pick you up, did some woman chin you about a slipper?'

'What?'

'Some mad jogger-woman started on at two of the uniform boys, asking if that was them finally investigating the slipper she found.'

'Tom, you need to keep taking the pills, pal. No, I did not see some mad jogger-woman raving about slippers.'

'Well, she was. And for your information, it was a burgundy velvet slipper to which she was referring.'

'Burgundy, did you say?'

'Aye. She was very specific. Burgundy.'

'Ho miss.' Duncan was wriggling in his chair. 'I need a pee.'

Anna held up her hand, discouraging the boy from speaking. 'And tell me, Tom, this excites you because . . . ?'

'Well seen you're no a detective, doll.' He broke off suddenly, and she could hear him shouting at whoever was beside him. '*Christ*, Norrie. Will you look where you're bloody going?' Then he was back. 'Sorry, I havny much time to gab, and I'm being driven by a one-eyed eejit on speed. Right, listen. The woman was out jogging in the park, and this van nearly knocks her down, so she hares after them, follows them up to the old house.'

'What old house?'

'I *telt* you, Linn Park. You know the old house that's getting made into flats? Right by there. Anyway, she sees these workies start carting a pile of junk out the van and into the house. Boxes,

356

tarps, that kind of gear. And while they were unloading, she's adamant she seen a burgundy slipper fall out the back of their van. He spoke the next words slowly, like he was translating for the deaf: 'A . . . single . . . burgundy . . . slipper.' The line crackled a little, his voice fading. 'Anna. It was the exact same night, same time as Cassie was abducted.'

Skin-crawling trawl of all the possibilities. A slipper could belong to a dosser, a bit-on-the-side in the back of the van, a cross-dressing workman.

Or it could belong to an old lady. Linn Park was not so far from Newton Mearns, and it was big and quiet and empty. This slipper was the same colour as the one Anna found at The Meadows. It could have been Cassie God please let it be Cassie.

She kept her voice steady.

'And when was it the jogger reported this?'

'Straight after the bloody press conference.'

'*Shit,* Tom—'

'I know, I know. I'm in the car now, on my way up. Thought you might want to come and all.' The line crackled again, then buzzed.

'Right you.' Anna ran to the door. 'Don't touch anything!'

'I canny, miss.' Duncan raised bound hands in a swallow dive. 'I'm fucking cuffed.'

She flung open the door, shouting into the corridor. 'Lenny! Lenny! I need a lift back to Linn Park. Immediately.'

The DS was leaning against the wall. 'That wee shite alleging something else now?'

'No, no. I think we may have established the whereabouts of Cassie Maguire.'

'Shit. You're joking?'

357

'Nope. Up at the old house in Linn Park, the one they're renovating.'

'Nae bother. I'll get you a lift. What about the boy?'

'Oh, he can go. Let's just put it down to a misunderstanding.' She pushed the heel of her hand against her temple. 'I mean . . . he *did*, you know, but in the light of, well, he could have been peeing I suppose . . . oh, shit, it doesn't matter. Just get someone to get me up to Linn Park now.'

Anna nipped back into the interview room, pretending to be professional.

'Okay, Duncan, you've been very helpful. How about we make out this afternoon didny happen?' She picked up his wrists, unlocked the cuffs. 'Let's just say you were taking a slash, eh?'

'Aye, cheers.' He sniffed, then shrunk his head into his chest. 'Ach, disny make fuck all difference. They're gonny take the wean off us anyway.'

'Who are?'

'The Social.'

'How come?'

'She's underage, miss. Ma burd, I mean.'

'I'm sorry.' Anna's fingers, pitter-patter against her trouser seam.

'Aye. You'n'me both.' The boy stood. 'So, I can go now?'

'Yup. Pick up your property at the desk. I'll let them know.' She manhandled Duncan into the corridor. 'This officer will look after you. I've got to shoot now—'

'Miss. See if you love someone? How come you canny just be with them?'

She paused, hand tense around the smoothness of the doorknob. 'I don't know, Duncan. That's a very good question.'

* * *

On a hill swept by oak, an old mansion house
sprawled, weathered and worn. Hefts of ivy and
moss might be all that stitched the crumbling
lumps together; that and the piles of scaffolding,
propping wall unto wall.

Cruikshanks, Anna and three detectives stood
outside. A vanload of Support Unit was in the
process of pulling up too, and Scenes of Crime
were on standby. There was no time to apply for a
warrant, and no need. They had sufficient
information to suggest that a human life was at
risk; more than enough reason to effect entry.
Cruikshanks had contacted the Duty Fiscal en
route, and they'd already had a quick scout round
to ascertain if the place was occupied. Nothing
apparent but desolation.

'It's owned by a company called Premier
Holdings, sir. We're running a check on all the
directors the now, but it appears to be a reputable
development company. We're trying to track down
a keyholder too.'

'Aye, well, we'll worry about that later.'

A woman in shorts and a sweat-patched vest
stood watching the proceedings. She shook her
head. 'Bit late now, don't you think? Twice I've
phoned about this already. *Twice.*'

'Madam,' said Cruikshanks, 'I've already
explained to you, with any appeal we have to
carefully collate all the information that comes in.
Now, if you'll excuse me—' he motioned to a
uniformed cop to come over '—we'll have

359

someone take you in to give us a full statement, okay?'

'*Collate?* Don't you mean ignore? When I phoned the last time I got some silly girl who didn't know *what* I was talking about.'

The cop ushered the woman back, began stringing up some cordon tape. The jogger's parting shot was directed at Anna: 'Those Indians nearly killed me, you know.'

Anna lifted a hand. 'Don't worry madam, we will fully investigate this, I can assure you. And thank you, so much, for all your efforts.'

The woman sniffed, nodded briefly.

'Indians?' whispered Anna.

'I'll tell you later. Right boys,' Cruikshanks was addressing the Support Unit crew now. 'We huvny a scooby who or what is in there, but assume the worst. The information that lady's provided ties in with the date and time Cassandra Maguire went missing, and I don't need to reiterate that that was nigh on two weeks ago. *So.* I want no time wasted, but I want every inch of the place scoured. Also lads, watch your backs—the building's getting renovated, so there might be nae light, rooms with nae floors, et cetera, et cetera. Mind and cover every exit too, in case someone tries to make a run for it.' He shrugged. 'Highly unlikely, I know. And remember, if our woman isny there either, she might well have been at some time, so I want any forensic evidence preserved, alright? Fag dowts, bits of paper, ginger bottles, pools of blood, the works.'

The Support Unit were used to this. An oil-sleek resource, they cruised round Strathclyde, well-equipped vans full of eager, fit officers who

360

could turn their hands to pretty much anything: public order, firearms, security searches, terrorist alerts—even chemical or nuclear response. Anna had been part of these specialists once; she knew they contained police search advisors and trained search managers amongst their ranks. Cruikshanks would know this too; his lecture was as much for his own benefit as for theirs, a verbal tick-list, in case there was anything he'd forgotten.

Anna mumbled. 'Remember she's an insulin-dependent diabetic too.'

'I was coming to that. Just to put you in the picture, Cassandra Maguire is a diabetic. We believe she may have some of her medication with her, but have no idea if it's been administered. So, we've also got a casualty surgeon heading out here. But . . .' He fumbled in his pocket. 'I've a Lion Bar here the now, if that's any help. For a hypo, like.' He turned to Anna. 'That's what you call it, isn't it?'

Her teeth, sinking into her lip. 'Yes. Can we just get on with it, please?'

They moved forward as one gradual wave, lapping the curtilage of the building, then the walls, then back door, front door, BOOM. A neat hand-held battering ram burst the lock, and the team piled in, peeling left and right into dusty rooms, torches on to augment light sliding in bars through scaffold-grids, through broken-boarded windows. Urgent rush of tramping boots filling overhead; coming down or up? A leap; a tremor, grabbing at her stick, then an out-breath, releasing taut knuckles; up. It was okay, the noise was the good guys spilling outwards, not the bad guys coming down. Anna wended through the ground floor; there but essentially useless, getting in the road as she followed at the coo's tail, kidding on she was 'overseeing'.

'Clear,' came an authoritative shout, then another, then another voice from the back rang out: 'Evidence of occupation here.' Anna and Cruikshanks scuttled through to a room where a thick wood door declared: 'Park Ranger'. An anglepoise lamp lay overturned on the floor, some empty tinfoil cartons from a carry-out beside it. Cruikshanks squatted stiffly, his belly visible between splayed legs. 'Pilau rice,' he sniffed. 'And a wee bouquet of lamb madras . . .?' He picked up a knot of cling-film. Traces of dried grass clung to the sticky, clear ripples. 'With a nice daud of waccy baccy for pudding.'

'Sir! Sir!' A frantic voice erupted beneath them, shining through knotted planks at their feet. 'Come down here.'

Out into the hall, find a back stair, where? Someone pointing, a man who was never a polis, too much hair, too beardy. 'Two of your lads just ran through there. I'm Doctor—'

'Great. Follow me,' puffed Cruikshanks, shirt weaving from his waistband, propelled by the pistoning of his fat, fast arms and legs, Anna nudging in front of him, finding a thin stone tread, then another, down into the dark but she had no torch. 'Ho! Someone shine a light up here', then it blinding in her eyes, feet one over other tripping, flat floor, faces, crouched faces and some shapes in a ring round a cover made of silk.

It was a sari, gleaming gold and painful red, too vibrant for this mildewed place.

And on the sari, shrunk like a foetus, lay

362

Cassandra Maguire.

It was her and it was not.

Her dead eyes dry and wide, face impartial. One hand had fallen open, balancing air, a tendril of dyed black hair spread in a comma to meet it. Anna knelt beside the old lady. Cassie's crown was haloed white, then the hair banded grey-brown and into black. Anna wanted to brush it back from her face but knew she could not touch a thing.

'For fucks . . . fucksake.' Cruikshanks was behind her, seeing what Anna saw.

Though her hands were free, Cassie's legs had been roped in a spancel, the way animals are tied. In the crescent of torchlight framing the body, Anna could make out the tight figure-of-eight, twined round Cassie's ankles. Not immediately obvious, because Cassie's lacerated flesh had puffed and folded over the ropes.

Anna was aware of Cruikshanks's bulk, wedged beside her. 'Jes-*us*. Trussed like a fucking donkey. As if she could've run far. Bastards.'

Anna could smell round, fresh sweat on his shirt and a sweetness of chocolate and she tried to filter it thin through her nostrils, the sweat and the chocolate and not the smell of death and shit. Cruikshanks cast his torch up and down Cassie's outline, settling once more at her ankles and feet. 'Here, look. There's something on her toe too. Anna, can you read that, hen?'

Careful not to disturb anything, Anna shuffled a little closer, her nose almost touching the pungent odours she was trying to avoid. A tiny piece of fabric or plastic, wrapped round the second last toe on Cassie's right foot. It had a grey-pink weave to it; an Elastoplast, one of those fabric ones. There was writing on it, just one word.

'It's a plaster, Tom. It says "none".'

'Nine?'

'No, *none*. As in nothing, nada, zilch.'

Cruikshanks scratched his head. 'Ri-ight. Well, that's helpful. *Not*.'

'May I see?'

Automatically, Anna moved back to let the casualty surgeon gain access to the body.

'Doctor,' said Cruikshanks, 'in advance of the PM, I need a cause and rough time of death.'

The doctor joined them on the floor; a strange, silent pow-wow. He made a cursory examination: look, don't touch. Scenes of Crime hadn't yet arrived to record every nuance and measurement and shred. If there had been any sign of life, someone would have tilted Cassie's neck to drop her jaw, enveloped her gaping mouth within their own, rocked clasped hands hard down on her heart, pushing and counting, pushing and counting, and bugger preserving the locus. But they had failed her. Nobody had saved Cassie, so all they could do now was save the crime scene.

'Well, no obvious contusions, no evidence of compression or suffocation. I believe this lady had age-related diabetes, yes?'

'That's correct.'

'Most likely cause, then, will be a hypoglycaemic attack. Possibly a myocardial infarction related to the diabetes, but we won't know until the post-mortem is carried out.'

'Fair enough. And time?'

Anna's grandad always said, the older you got, the faster time went. At the end though, when it all came to this, time was not calculated by the rushing of minutes or the hurry of hours, but simply by when it had stopped.

'Well, as you know,' said the doctor, 'the face tends to stiffen before the hands and feet, and maximal rigor develops in twelve to forty-eight hours, depending on the environmental temperature. As a diabetic, her circulation would be poor in any case, plus her age, plus the fact she has been maintained in an immobile position, lower limbs constricted. I mean, the myofilaments would have become locked in—'

'Doctor, you havny done this much before, have you?' said Cruikshanks.

'Well, no, but I can assure you I'm a highly—'

Anna found her voice. Surprised, when it came out, that it was firm and keen. 'Sorry, sir. No, what DCI Cruikshanks means is, we don't need to know all the technical stuff—just the time of death. Please.'

The doctor clicked his tongue. 'Well, my point is, rigor mortis is a temporary condition. It generally appears during the first day after death and then gradually disappears over the next several days, as the proteins in the muscles begin to decompose. So, really, the question is, what stage are we at here?'

Cruikshanks heaved himself to his feet. '*That's* what I'm asking you, Doc. No rush now, I mean, we've no got a murder investigation on our hands or anything . . .'

'Tom, shut up,' said Anna. 'Doctor, please go on.'

'Typically, as you know, rigor is first apparent in the small muscles of the eyelids, then the lower jaw and neck, followed by the limbs.' The doctor straightened up too. Just Anna and Cassie remaining, washed in torchlight. 'When rigor affects the levator muscles first, the eyelids open and the muscles stiffen. Judging by her eyes then, the fact we still have a degree of mobility in the right forearm, and the condition of the excrement, I'd say she must have hung on till about yesterday.'

Every day until the day she died, Anna would hate herself for that.

CHAPTER EIGHTEEN

From a quietly fading enquiry, Cassandra Maguire's investigation was reborn. The faint pall had ignited like gas, incident rooms billowing, teams doubling and tripling in size and fresh momentum. *Here* was something to get their teeth into; here was a body, facts, forensics. Here was real.

Anna stayed away. She took no satisfaction in seeing Cassie's waxen portrait at the centre of the whiteboards, and she wanted to avoid the posturings of Johnny and Mrs H and every other senior officer who hovered on the periphery, pretending they were invaluable, crucial; useful at least. Thoughts of Headquarters and grievances could wait, their importance ebbing.

Before she left Govan though, Anna sat in on the jogging lady's interview.

'She *likes* you,' said Cruikshanks. 'Disny like me. Try and mollify her, eh?'

He'd not enlighted Anna about 'the Indians'; they had barely spoken since the undertakers' shell

366

arrived for Cassie, and Cruikshanks was absorbed into mayhem and murder.

The jogger sipped her water. Her name was Valerie.

'It was still pretty dark; about five a.m.—'

'On the seventeenth?'

'Yes. I work shifts you see, so I just run whenever I can. But I always wear my fluorescent hat. And I have reflectors on the back of my shoes, so they *should* have seen me.'

'The people in the van?'

'*Yes*. I was in the park, jogging down the track that runs from the golf course, and this van screeches past, damn near knocks me over—but they never even stopped. No lights on or anything.'

The DC conducting the interview stopped writing. 'Terrible.'

'I know. So I chased them, all the way down to the old house. They had parked up right beside it, and were unloading all sorts of stuff.'

'What kind of *stuff*?'

She frowned. 'I've already told the girl in your incident room.'

'I know,' said Anna. 'I'm sorry. We just have to put it all down in an official statement. That way you can sign it, and it keeps everyone right.'

Valerie sighed. 'It looked like dust-sheets, and a rolled-up carpet. And there were some cardboard boxes. Quite big ones—sort of size you'd get a computer in. Anyway, I was going to give them a piece of my mind.'

'Could you describe any of these people?'

'They were Indians.'

'Yes, but could you be more specific?'

'Well, they were Asian, anyway. Or Pakistani.

You know. Three of them, all men.'

'Ages? Build?'

'Sort of medium, I suppose. Ages, I'm not sure of. I was kind of standing behind a tree, and the light was very murky.'

'You were behind a tree?'

'Yes, well, the closer I had got, the more I could hear raised voices. I didn't want to walk right in to a punch-up or something.'

'How far away were you?' asked Anna.

'Hmm.' She looked out of the office window. 'From about here to the other side of your car park, I reckon.'

'And do you think you could identify any of them again?'

'Oh, no. I don't think so.'

Again, the DC laid down his pen. 'What about the van?'

'White, maybe? I don't know, it was dark. Anyway, I was going to go up and say something, I really was. I mean, I was hopping mad. Next thing, I saw one of them lug what looked like a tool bag. One of those old, soft ones, you know? And, as he was lifting it, this slipper fell out.'

'This is the burgundy slipper you referrred to in your call to us?'

'*Yes.*'

'Did it fall out of the stuff he was carrying, or the van?'

'I'm not sure. I just saw it land on the ground.'

'And how did you know it was burgundy?' asked Anna. 'You're just after saying how dark it was.'

Valerie tutted. 'When I say dark, I mean greyish, like it was almost daybreak. But actually, I know for definite because one of them had a torch. He was waving it at the one with the carpet, so he could see what he was doing, I suppose. But I don't think either of them noticed the slipper; they were gabbling to each other, the one with the torch seemed angry. The light was all sort of bouncing about as he gesticulated, and I saw it flash, right on the slipper. And I remember thinking, oh, look Valerie, that's the same M&S slippers that you bought Mum.' She took another drink. 'It's not there now, of course—'

Anna interjected. 'Then what happened?'

'Um, I decided just to go home.'

'Not to speak to them?'

'No.'

'But you didn't think there was anything particularly suspicious? Not at the time?'

'No,' she shrugged. 'I just thought they were workmen.'

So Valerie had jogged on home and thought little more about it until Tom's press conference a week later. She'd been doing the ironing, had stopped when she heard 'that chubby detective chap' repeat the time and date of Cassie's disappearance.

'Hmm, I thought. That's the night I saw those men. And the detective had said she'd left her nightie and her slipper behind—it was the word "slipper" that caught my attention actually. Then I thought, ach Valerie, see you and your waxy ears. The man will have just said "slippers". It's probably nothing to do with anything.' She paused for breath. '*But*. You never know, do you?'

'No, you don't.'

Valerie had thought about it a bit more and then, like a good citizen, had phoned the incident

369

line. Two days later.

'Not immediately?' said Anna.

'Well, you don't like to cause a fuss over nothing, do you? And actually, I *meant* to go back up to the house myself and have a wee look first, in case I was wasting your time, but we were heading off to Portugal for a few days—for a friend's wedding—and I had a million and one things to do, and I thought, ach, someone else is bound to have seen them; then I thought, no Valerie, just do it, for heaven's sake, so I did, I called just before we were leaving. I told the young laddie what I'd seen, and he took my details and said someone would be in touch. And then I came back from Portugal and there wasn't a single message from the police, nothing. Well, *that's* when I started to get annoyed. You know, once you've made the effort, a courtesy call is only polite.'

Valerie had waited a bit longer, then phoned the incident room again. And was assured she was on their list, which she was. Just not marked 'priority' in amongst all the more pressing priorities.

'But it's not on, is it? I mean, if nothing else, you can let someone know if there's been any follow-up. Obviously, by this stage, I'm assuming that you've at *least* checked the house.'

The DC sorted his papers, Anna straightened her pen.

'And then, when I saw those two policemen today in their van, right at the park gates, I thought, enough's enough. I jogged straight over and asked if they were here about the van. Said I could show them exactly where it had been. But they just said that they were tied up with another call and that if I didn't have the vehicle's

370

registration number there wasn't much they could do. Think they thought I was on about road rage.'

'Did you not tell them it was in connection with Cassandra Maguire?' said the DC.

'Well no. They were so bloody offhand, I just snapped. Demanded the number of their most senior officer, and one of them sort of smirked and gave me a postcard thingy that had your headquarters' number on it. So, I jogged home, phoned immediately. After a bit of to-ing and fro-ing, I finally got to speak to someone in charge, and,' she opened her hands, then clasped them again, 'here we are.'

'Can I ask you something, Valerie?' said Anna. 'Tell me honestly. Why was it that you decided not to speak to the men?' She checked the notes the DC had made. 'You said you were "hopping mad", that you were all set to "give them a piece of your mind". So what changed?'

'This probably sounds daft.' Valerie scratched her eyebrow. 'But one of them looked at me. The one with the torch.'

'How do you mean: "looked at you"?'

'He just suddenly wheeched off his glasses and looked at me. I was sure they couldn't see me, I'd taken my hat off and everything, but this one stared straight over, to where I was at the tree. Like he wanted me to challenge him. Next thing I know, he's shining the torch right at me.'

'So you decided to keep moving?'

'Absolutely. I can't say what it was, I could only see shadows where his mouth and eyes would be, but I'll tell you this.' She leaned towards Anna. 'He gave me the absolute creeps.'

After listening to Valerie, Anna had gone

straight to The Meadows. Indians, Manju, Saracens; there had to be a connection. And she wanted to tell Manju about Cassie—Rob, of course, he should know right away, before he read it in some paper. Bugger Ronnie and Sheena Maguire; Cruikshanks would be breaking the news to them, right about now—hopefully while he was kicking seven bells of shit out the stupid, evil pair. Last thing she heard Cruikshanks yelling was: 'Fucking get them back in here. Now! I want warrants to search all their properties and businesses. And get me a double sausage supper.'

The Maguires may not have killed Cassandra, but they had let it happen, of that Anna was convinced.

The Meadows was as warm as ever. And just as noxious. She waited while the receptionist checked if Rob was free. The girl put her hand over the mouthpiece of her phone.

'I think he's just going into a meeting actually— oh, hello Mr Macklin. I have a Chief Inspector Cameron to see . . . oh. Fine. Will do.' She hung up the receiver. 'He says to go straight through.'

Rob stood as Anna came in. Hand outstretched, chin tilted forward.

'Hey you.'

She stayed on the other side of his desk. 'Rob, it might be best if you sit back down.'

'Why?'

'We found her. We found Cassie, Rob.'

'And?'

'I'm so sorry. She's dead. We did everything we could, but we were just too late.'

He let his eyelids drop, the shape of his face setting hard for an instant. She heard him whisper something; it might have been Cassie's name. A pause of air, a seal around them. His eyes, back on her. So weary.

'At least you found her. At least we . . .' He stared at the ceiling. 'Where was she?'

'I can't really say at the moment. It's still—'

'It's okay, I get it. So, what happens now?'

'Well, it's a murder investigation now. I guess everyone here will be interviewed again . . .'

'Oh great.' Rob pushed his index fingers into his temples. 'Sorry. Anna, I didn't mean that.'

'No, I understand. We'll try to be as discreet as we can.'

'It's not me I'm bothered about. Some of the residents have been here for years, long before I took the place over. If we *do* close . . . well, they'll have to start again, somewhere else. Can you imagine? At eighty-odd, when you can barely see or hear, but folk know you like to be called Miss Harvey, not Betty, and you know where the light switch is in your bathroom, and that Donald and Jessie sit next to you in the Day Room. These things are important, you know?' His voice grew duller. 'They help to keep you sane.'

'Rob, they're going to want to question you again too.'

'I know.' He kept circling the skin above his eyebrows. She imagined the pain he was feeling, her pushing it deeper, but she had to tell him the truth.

'We'll be looking at every possible motive. Revenge, greed . . . the fact this place is struggling . . .'

He nodded. 'I realise that. Greed I get. But revenge? What could Cassie have done to anybody

373

that would make them want to take her away and kill her?'

Valid questions, but ones they couldn't discuss. Rob was not a cop. She couldn't even tell him how Cassie had died.

'Ach, fuck. It makes you wonder, doesn't it?'

'Tut, tut. Not like you to swear, Doctor Macklin.'

A weak smile. 'Just wait till you get to know me. And it's bloody *Mister*.' He rapped his hands on his desk. 'Right. Manju?'

'You think she'll understand what I'm telling her?'

'I think so. Just go easy on her.'

'I have to ask about the men in her room again, Rob.'

'I'd really rather you didn't.'

'Cassie's dead, and Manju's the only person that may have seen who took her.'

'Can we just see how she is once you tell her, please?'

'Okay.'

A perfunctory tap on the door, then the matron walked in. 'Oh, sorry, Mr Macklin. I didn't realise you had company. Em, these just came in.' She passed over a clutch of brown envelopes. 'I think they're urgent. See that one, it's from Scottish Power. Now, if you remember, they phoned last week—'

'Thanks Jill. Just leave them there.'

'I really think you should—'

'Jill. Cassie Maguire has been found dead. I'll deal with these later, yes?'

'Oh! Oh my God! Oh poor Cassie. Oh.' The matron sought confirmation from Anna. 'Oh, are you sure it's her?'

'I'm afraid so.'

'Oh God, the poor old soul.' Fast-flowing tears, the tension of the last fortnight breaking, spilling.

'Perhaps you could inform the staff,' said Anna. 'And those patients you think need to know. I can't give you any details, but it'll be on the news tonight, so maybe you could prepare them?'

'Yes, yes, of course. Oh, God. Poor, poor Cassie.' She hurried out, wiping her nose with the back of her hand.

'You've some bedside manner on you, *Doctor*.'

'The woman's a pain in the arse anyway.' He dropped the envelopes, unopened, in a wire tray. 'Ach, sorry. I didn't mean that. Anna, I know this is a crass question, and it's hardly the time, but did you manage to bank that money?'

Her hand flew to her mouth. 'Oh shit. Oh, bollocks—I was going to, but then I got tied up in the search for Cassie.'

'Oh well. Too late now. Stand by for a slew of bouncing cheques. Where is it anyway?'

'In . . .'

Where, where . . . in her fleece pocket, which was hanging over the back of her office chair.

'It's safe, I promise. It's at my work. Look, let me see Manju, then I'll go straight down to Giffnock, pick up the money and take it to the bank. I'll tell them it wasn't your fault.'

That sad tightness in his face again. 'Don't think it matters if you talk to a person any more. It's all decided by computers now, isn't it? Anyway, come on and I'll take you up to Manju.'

They walked up the stairs in silence. Was it a good thing, so early on, that he realised he couldn't

375

rely on her? That her job made her inconsiderate and obtuse, taking her to places and people Rob would never want to know about? That it would consume large swathes of her life, and even the bits left over, those pieces that were exclusively her, Anna-with-no-strings, were often knackered and crabbit. At the top of the stairs, Rob turned suddenly and kissed her, the fierceness of it knocking her breath away. His lips imprinting ownership, absolution. She stared at his soft black hair and his lowered lids and the sweet dark angle of his jaw, then closed her eyes, didn't need to see it, could feel it was real, could feel the pressure of the banister at her back as she returned his kiss, his body against hers. Fitting.

Slower, slower, then stopping. Moving apart, but it felt like they were touching.

'I'm sorry.'

He traced her hair, her cheekbone. 'I just wanted you to know that you make all this bearable.'

Then, just as suddenly, he moved along the landing and into Manju's room. Anna went after him, each step resting lightly on the nylon carpet; that slight, padded buoyancy you get when wearing new trainers.

Cassie's bed was still there, made up with her pink donkey pyjama case glinting its false eyes at them. Manju lay quiet, prone. Someone had combed her hair, fanning it out on the pile of pillows. Her hands, though, were knotted under her chin, like a little rodent clutching nuts, and one leg appeared to tremble slightly beneath the blankets.

'Manju.' Anna sat on the edge of the bed, placed

her hands over Manju's twisted fists. 'Remember me? It's Anna. I was looking for Cassie for you. Remember?'

She was aware of the leg, jittering faster, but nothing registered on Manju's face. Anna needed to trigger some proper response this time, to unlock whatever pictures Manju held in her head. She glanced at Rob.

'She can still speak, can't she?'

'Padma says she hears her singing occasionally. But I've not heard her say anything since Cassie went away.'

'Manju. Remember the men? The ones who came into your room? Did they take Cassie? Squeeze my hand if they took Cassie. Please.'

Manju's hands lay motionless under hers.

'She can definitely still hear me?'

'I think so.'

Anna tried again. 'Were you scared of the men? Did they remind you of home, before you came here? Please think for me.'

'Anna. Go easy on her.'

The flesh she was touching felt hotter, igneous, as if fire was rumbling inside.

'Just give me a minute, Rob.'

'One minute.'

'Manju, I spoke to Carol. She told me a bit about you. And then *I* remembered you as well. You used to sit and watch the traffic, didn't you? In Giffnock, beside the police station?'

A fractured headspin, jerk left, jerk right, and she pulled her hands away.

'Hey, it's okay.' Anna stroked Manju's hair. 'Your hair was even blacker then. I always remember that. You had beautiful hair, and I was

377

dead jealous of it. Do you remember Carol? Dr Jenkins's little girl.'

The reaction to Jenkins's name was immediate—Manju flinging both arms wide, struggling to sit up. Low howling, like an animal baying.

'Jesus, Anna! Get away from her.' Rob slammed the call button. A nurse came running.

'Watch her while I run and get some Diazepam. I think there's some in my car.' He held Manju's shoulders. 'Ssh now, darling. Ssh, it's alright.'

But Anna had burst her, literally burst Manju wide and desperate. The wound was there now so she may as well keep going, before it closed and scabbed and sealed again and she kept shouting, God forgive her, but she did, over all the noise and tumult.

'Manju. Please talk to me! Cassie's dead, she's dead and we need to find out who did it.'

The crying stopped, instantly. Manju collapsed back on to the mattress, one fist in her open mouth.

'I *told* you to leave her alone,' said Rob.

'Look, we can't fanny about any more. I did that last time, and now Cassie's dead.'

Rob looked away from her, concentrating on the pulse at Manju's wrist.

'Just get out, Anna.'

'Rob, I'm sorry—'

'Just go.'

'Doctor's orders, is that?'

'If you like.'

*   *   *

378

It was like a ghost ship at Giffnock. All available manpower had been pulled into the second wave of interviews, focusing on anyone with connections to the house in Linn Park: the developers who owned it, previous owners who could be traced, contractors who'd been there to quote or deliver, the architects who'd drawn up plans and the council officials who'd checked them, the parks employees who cut the grass or emptied the bins or fed the nearby horses. And the public appeal to all park users—the dog walkers, joggers, mums and weans—would throw up hundreds more lines, all of which would require to be recorded, checked, prioritised, actioned. Somewhere in there would be the nugget: they just had to pray it wasn't buried weeks down like the burgundy slipper had been.

Anna's office door was unlocked, her fleece still draped on her chair. And, yes, the money was all there too. She counted it, carefully, making sure it tallied with the number and denomination of notes on the deposit slip. Seeking comfort in the automatic, not thinking about Cassie dead and Robert hating her, putting the tens in one pile, twenties in another. More money than cheques, which seemed odd. Surely everything was done by credit card or bank transfer nowadays? Or were half of the residents true to stereotype, keeping biscuit-tin stashes beneath their beds? Every so often, she'd stop counting, flick through her emails, deleting and archiving all but the most essential. Seven shagging hundred at least from Mrs H but she couldn't bring herself to look at them now. You had to be sharp to take on a ferret, and Anna was blunt, blunt, blunt. But she could count and make neat heaps of money.

Eighty, one hundred, hundred and twenty, hundred and forty.

Quick two-finger typing to the intelligence manager, the email headed *re. Const Harris*. She gave him the name Duncan had furnished her with, saying only that it had come from an anonymous source. It appeared to have gone quiet on the we-hate-Fraser-Harris front. Maybe having an unmarked car outside his house had scared whoever it was. Good. It was doubtful there'd be any more financial elastic to continue with that surveillance, now they had an ongoing murder enquiry. Tracking down this Sparky would put the final nail in the coffin—particularly if it turned out he worked for the charming Mr Avalon.

Sixty, eighty, two hundred.

In her paper-breeding in-tray, brown buff files, unopened envelopes, orange internals . . . this to Inspector Cameron, Easterhouse P/O. A memo, come to her by mistake. She scanned it; yes, it should be the new inspector at Easterhouse dealing with this.

Subject: Long service and good conduct medal

Owing to the prolonged sickness absence of the above-named officer, who, having served 22 years within Strathclyde Police, is due to receive his long service and good conduct medal, I would be obliged if you could make arrangements to contact said officer and enquire as to whether he wishes to attend the forthcoming ceremony, or have the medal forwarded to his home address.

Forty, sixty, eighty, three hundred. All present and correct.

She looked at the name on the memo again. *Constable Stuart Wright.*

Stuart of the hangdog face and scary wife. She pushed the memo away. The shifting air generated by the movement flapped a pile of twenties, dealing them squint like a hand of cards. She went to push the pile together again. Noticed something strange.

ADG948226

And the next one: ADG948226. And the next, and the next, all repeating the same serial number along the top and down the side. She rubbed the paper, felt the ink. Felt exhaustion overtake her, hand covering her face.

'Oh Rob. Not you. Please not you.'

Two slow breaths. A sore, studding sensation as she picked up the phone. Cruikshanks would still be in the incident room. Cruikshanks would be *living* in the incident room for the foreseeable future.

'Tom. I've just come across a load of your counterfeit notes. About three hundred quid's worth. Really high grade, but the serials are all the same.'

'Anna, my sweet, that's great news, so it is. All adds salt to the pot. But I'm a wee bitty distracted the now. You might not have heard, but we've a thing called a murder enquiry erupting.'

'No. Really? Would that be to do with the dead body I found for you?'

'Nah, not connected at all. Look just put the notes in the safe at the bar for now. I'll get someone down to uplift them when I can—I know for a fact the Fraudies are all at an away-day in Saltcoats.'

'Lucky them.'

'I know. How's your mum by the way? I meant to ask before.'

She's in a box, Tom. Ground up grey, finer than coffee. But it smells more like tea actually, kind of . . . ashy. You see, my mum is the literal embodiment of a piece of advice a very good friend once told me: Keep your life in boxes. *And any time I don't listen to that advice, I get a wee bit burnt too, and slip further into ashen. Not* ash *you understand, but pale and wan, a thin reflection of myself. The kind you catch in an unlit bathroom mirror.*

'Yeah, fine,' she said. 'What do you want me to do with these notes, though?'

'Well, if you could attach a wee statement, outlining who why where and when, and the cop's contact details too.'

'Tom, they've come from The Meadows.'

'Ah.' There was an intake of phlegmy breath. Then a lot more puffing. 'Ah. Ah, ah, ah.'

'Are you having some kind of seizure?'

'No yet, doll, no yet.

'You understand what I'm saying? They came from the doctor, Rob Macklin.'

'Aye aye. *Your* doctor.'

'How d'you mean, *my* doctor?'

'I heard he flung you over his shooder at Coriander, and gied you a fireman's lift to his car. You need to choose your pals more carefully, hen.'

'It might not be him though? Don't you think? I mean, he said the money's a mix of fees, bills and wages. There must be some log to record income and expenditure . . . If we can see who paid what—'

382

'He'll need to be questioned, but. Best if he's brought in too, I'd say. *In* the circumstances. Then my lads can speak to him first. But I canny spare a living soul to pick him up. A couple of your troops'll need to go. And if they could ask nicely for any financial spreadsheets, files or paper invoices too, that would be awfy good. Failing that, get a cop to stand by at The Meadows, take root in the office so nobody touches anything till I can get a warrant.'

'Tom, I've virtually no one on the street as it is. You've bled us dry.'

'Aye well, tell it to the violin player, doll. Place is like Bedlam here. I've got the detective chief super fae Pitt Street doing his dinger at JC not sixty feet away.' He spoke very quietly. 'You're no gonny believe this, but the frigging Maguires have done a runner.'

'What? But how?'

'Daft bitch watching them telt them the good news about Cassie being deid, then "gave them a moment" to be on their own. In a bloody lounge with French doors to the garden, the garage, the back bloody lane. Her "moment" was sufficient to smoke a fag plus phone her boyfriend. They were long gone by the time she "thought it prudent" to go back in. Prudent? I'll give you prudent . . .'

'Look, Tom, I'll just go back up myself.'

'Well . . .' His hesitation unfurled slowly, like he was picking through tangles that still perturbed him. 'Aye . . . okay.'

'Don't sound so bloody grateful.'

'No, no. That would be grand. You're some kid. You sure you don't mind?'

'Nah, just stick a brush up my arse and I'll sweep

383

the floor too.'

Nice and gruff and grudging, but really, she was glad of the excuse. If it was Anna who first approached Rob, rather than some CID tosser with his sharp-creased suit and even sharper tongue, then at least she could temper the blow. Show him the banknotes and either watch his composure crumple, or his face pucker in confusion. It would be the latter, of course it would; how could she even doubt that?

It would also let her gauge exactly how things stood between them, in the calm light of middle-afternoon, with Manju sleeping soundly and him mellowed to some degree of understanding. Surely. When he was in his métier, barking orders as a patient squirmed in cardiac arrest, some professional aggression must flow too. You had to invoke it, to make the whole thing work. Force folk to listen and do what they were told. Rob would understand that.

'Take someone with you doll, eh?' Cruikshanks was saying. 'Even if it's the lollipop lady fae Giffnock Primary. I want everything corroborated—just in case.'

'In case what?'

'Just keep it all official. Anna, I've got to go.'

'Are you implying it somehow wouldn't be "official" if I went alone?'

'Two ticks, ma'am. Be with you in two ticks—okay, one tick. Anna, I'm protecting my investigation and I'm protecting you. That's all I'm saying.'

The dull throb of a dead line, humming in her ear.

Et tu, Pieman?

Ach, it was only Cruikshanks being paranoid. Probably something he ate.

That's right. Keep it light, keep floating above the surface, remember that feel of your feet on the floor. When Rob kissed you and soft pads of joyful air cushioned everything; your senses muffled and acute at once, so forensically aware of the blunt tips of bristle on his chin and the grain of the wood and how your skin was thinner where he'd touched it. Hang on to that.

Give yourself a chance.

Traffic was building in a teatime rush. She wondered where the Maguires were headed. In a city of over 600,000—easily rising to a couple of million when you counted all the suburb-dwellers, the commuters, the tourists and the shoppers; with a six-lane motorway thrusting busily down south or off to the east; hundreds of back roads wending quietly to towns and villages, and miles of coastline offering ferries and escape—the options were abundant. The snake of traffic Anna was in grew ever more sluggish as it approached the roundabout at Eastwood Toll. A dark-coloured hatchback was edging forward from a side street, indicating left, but she didn't stop for him. The driver was in his mid-sixties, with a pinched, fretting face, his collar too wide for his neck. She watched in her rear-view mirror, slowing to see if someone else let him out. The car behind her obliged, and she relaxed. Put on a Johnny Cash CD, playing live at San Quentin Prison.

Even thicker on the Ayr Road, the traffic jostled and hooted into place, two lanes merging into one—and an empty cycle lane. Who'd be mad enough to pedal their way through this? The

385

congestion spaced out at the next roundabout, most cars peeling off to join the motorway link, and Anna carried on through old Mearns and the vestiges of farmland beyond, singing herself hoarse with a variation on San Quentin.

Strathclyde Polis, I hate every inch of you.

When she got there, it looked like the staff and residents of The Meadows had just launched a school sports day. Groups of old biddies milling in the car park, nurses running in all directions. Two with blankets, charging round the back—was this a variation on the sack race? A stout woman in an overall bashed against Anna's arm as she thudded past.

'Hey, what's going on?'

But the woman didn't stop, didn't even look her way. Anna followed her to the rear of the old farmhouse, feet crunching on the cinder path, round to where all the action seemed to be. Heard a male voice yelling: 'Get an ambulance. Dial 999 now.' She felt fine hairs rising on her arms, smelled the faint, metal-earthiness of blood. A deep-knotted crowd stood below an open upstairs window. The curtain inhaled and exhaled, free to dance in air where it had part-torn from its pelmet. The fabric was bold, brave umbels of floral greens and orange. A horrible, dry-mouth déjà vu as Anna made her way, firmly, professionally, through frail, woolly elbows and slippered feet. She could hear wails and sobs, a woman singing, soft crooning in a foreign tongue. Padma was kneeling on the cinder pathway, singing Hindi lullabies to a dark head in her lap. Beside her Rob folded swathes of sari, bright tears streaming as he pressed desperately against an open head-wound. Another nurse,

386

shouting into a mobile, 'Please hurry. It's very bad. She's fallen from a window', and Manju, Manju's sad, small face staring vacant at the line where earth and sky merged into one.

CHAPTER NINETEEN

Loud music pushes at the walls. It is thudding on the guard's back, through the polished curves of the radiator to which he is strung. The heat no longer sears him, the pain refined to unremitting white.

Strobes of luminous colour dance at the gap between door and floor. Light and noise in the next room, laughter, a roar of applause. Palate raw, he has no strength to lift his head.

'I've a pal same colour as you,' she had said. 'Smooth as toffee. You widny think it to look at her mind, she's aye that calm and gentle, but, och, the life that poor soul's had. Makes mine's look like a bloody picnic.'

It was the first story she had told him. He thought she offered it as currency at first. But then the story took over, took them far to a river running, sun streaming. To the heat, and all the women by the water, stretching loud colours over flat-baked rocks, laughing and gossiping and pointing at the stranger.

'Aye, she was in love with this man. A white man, he was a doctor in India, same as her. I think he was her tutor. Telt her she was the cleverest, most beautiful student he'd known. And it wisny a front, know? He even came to see her, in her village. Telt her he'd take her home with him. But he didny, the bastard. Well, they never do.'

387

She had cried a little, then.

'But she was that brave, ma pal. She upped and followed him hame. Across continents and oceans, to prove how much she loved him. To bring him their baby. Can you imagine that, son?'

She had sighed, and the sound rolled out like the sea. 'Aye, all that way, and then he only takes the wean. No her, poor lamb. No her.'

And still, the guard had kept her ropes on.

His ropes burn into him now. He tries to flex his fingers, realises the juddering, the music has stopped. Someone is screaming. 'The snake! Watch the fucking snake.' Then there is more cheering, a cry of 'He's got it! C'mon the Big Man!'

And the music starts again. Louder, more frenetic, there is a rhythm of the East about it as the door unlocks and the Mirror Man enters the room.

From the waist up, he is naked.

Anna was still required to take Rob back to Giffnock with her. Once the ambulance had been, then the cops, then the statements, she'd had to slide the box labelled 'Manju' to one side (directly on top of the one called 'Stillborn Romance' in fact, and slightly to the left of 'Mother: Dead (disposal pending)'—there was no particular order of priority for any of them; they were piled up any old how), sit him down with her hard-bitch hat on and say, 'The reason I came was . . .'

She didn't like to remember how his sad face buckled, but he complied with everything, getting her all the ledgers and invoice folders he could find, arranging for disks to be made of spreadsheets. It was almost like he wanted to keep busy too. There were no low words of anger or reproach, no recriminations. That would happen later.

Yes. If nothing else, Anna could always say: Robert Macklin came quietly.

Cruikshanks was not pleased to see her, squawking about *more dead bodies* and *you'd better pray this isny another murder* and *are you a bloody jinx, Cameron?*, but she delivered the goods anyway, then went quietly home. Alice slept well that night, for Anna watched her, stretching and rasping, her back legs springing straight, then all curled tight again. Anna beside her, feeling cold.

At six twenty-eight a.m., her landline rang. It was Mrs Hamilton.

'Do not go to Giffnock this morning. Come straight in to see me. First thing, you understand?'

And that's where she was now. In the ferret-fragrant surrounds of JC's boudoir, reading the newspaper. Not with croissants and a coffee, just a quivering finger thumping an inside page. Hamilton seething: *'Read it!'*

Soon as she saw the byline, *Lucy Manning*, Anna knew it wouldn't be good. And this wasn't even the local weekly, it was a national daily, hot off the press. It would appear Lucy had finally got her big break.

TOP COP CONNECTED TO MYSTERY DEATH PLUNGE

An elderly Asian woman died in an unexplained incident at a nursing home in Glasgow yesterday afternoon—only hours after being visited by a senior officer from Strathclyde Police.

Horrified onlookers saw the unnamed

woman fall to her death from a second-floor window at The Meadows Nursing Home, in the affluent Glasgow suburb of Newton Mearns. One resident, who didn't wish to be identified, said, 'It looked like she was diving from the windowsill.'

This second shock death comes less than twenty-four hours after another Meadows resident, eighty-two-year-old Cassandra Maguire, was found dead in a derelict mansion house in nearby Linn Park. Mrs Maguire had been missing for nearly two weeks, and extreme concerns have been voiced over security at the nursing home.

It is believed the patient who died had been visited earlier in the day by a senior female police officer, who questioned her regarding the disappearance of Mrs Maguire. One unnamed nurse said: 'The cop was really aggressive with her, she was in a right state after.'

The cash-strapped Meadows Nursing Home is run by forty-two-year-old consultant geriatrician Robert Macklin. In recent weeks the home has been haemorrhaging residents as families continue to express unease about safety and management practices at the home. In a bizarre twist, Mr Macklin—a widower with a young daughter—and the female officer in question are rumoured to be romantically involved, reportedly going on holiday together just before Mrs Maguire's body was found.

And there it was, there it really was in all its

tacky glory: a fuzzed paparazzi shot of Anna and Rob, coming out of The Meadows, his hand on her arm, their heads bent close.

Police deny that this second death is in any way attributable to police involvement. A spokesperson said: 'We are confident that our officers have acted in a professional and appropriate way throughout. However, we take any suggestion of misconduct extremely seriously, and a full enquiry into the circumstances of the lady's death is under way. At this stage, there is nothing to suggest foul play is involved.'

Police have also strongly denied that there is any suggestion of racism connected with this incident. A spate of racist gang violence in the area has already led to the death of one Asian youth, Sabir Aziz, although decisive action by the local divisional commander ensured a rapid arrest and conviction. However, a police insider indicated that the female officer concerned has a history of controversy, on one occasion being denied a top job in America due to inappropriate comments made in relation to women wearing the veil. Strathclyde Police have refused to comment on this allegation.

Anna had rushed on with the reading, as if the act of hurrying would brush the text clean, troublesome syntax and innuendo swept from the margins. Galloping to the end where it would squeal *April Fool! We're only joking!*

'I take it you spoke to them?' It was all she was

able to say.

'I wanted to speak to you first,' said Hamilton. 'See how much of it was true.'

'No. I mean *before* the thing was written. I take it you spoke to the reporter, then?'

'Sorry?' Hamilton's vowels had gone nasal. 'Are you insinuating *I* had something to do with this? That I would want my division rubbished so resoundingly in the public eye?'

'How else would they have got that information? About the bloody UN, for starters?'

'You tell me. You shoot your mouth off a lot. Maybe you were boasting about it somewhere public. You know, one of those times when you get drunk and make a tit of yourself in public. Oh, and I've just noticed the piece mentions you went on holiday with Doctor Death. I *do* hope not, seen as you were off sick at the time.'

'My mum died! My bloody mum *died* and I went over to Spain to sort out the funeral. Satisfied?'

Fighting it, fighting it; she could feel the swell in her shoulders, then the angry shudder as her body humiliated itself, thin salt water stronger than layers of civilised constraint. Tears more wilful than Anna, who could only shout: 'Dear God, what do you *want* from me? What the fuck have I done to *you*?'

Head in hands, awaiting sentence. But none came, not a word. The silence swelled to a boom, long and resonant, until it became impossible to speak. Anything that came now would be an admission of defeat. She scrubbed at her cheekbones.

'Or are you one of those bullies that doesn't even need a reason. Just get your kicks out of making lassies greet?'

She looked up. Hamilton was smiling, a fat, patient smirk.

'Anna. You're clearly not coping. I think you'd better do the honourable thing, don't you? Right now, just go off sick with stress and give us all peace.'

'Or what? You'll suspend me?'

Hamilton folded the newspaper neatly, running her finger over and over the same crease, until dark ink smudged her nail. 'Kind of looking that way, isn't it?'

'On what grounds? On what *substantiated* grounds?'

'That I think you're unfit for duty? Screaming at me like a harridan—I might have to . . . I don't know . . .' Hamilton sniffed. 'Have you maybe been at that bottle again? All-night session, was it?'

Anna screeched her chair back, ready to jump up. 'If that's what you're alleging, let's go down to the Intoximeter right now. C'mon, let's you and me go down and you can breathalyse me.'

'You really do need to calm down, Chief Inspector.' Hamilton walked carefully round her desk, skirting wide of Anna. What, did she think she was going to lunge at her? Bite a big chunk out her arse?

Hamilton opened her office door as wide as it could go, spoke loud and proud and obvious as a megaphone. 'Now, for the sake of your mental health, I'm *ordering* you to go home. We'll make you an appointment for Occupational Health, see if we can get you to some kind of head-shrink.'

Anna stared at her knees. To go upwards would involve engaging her quads, hamstrings and glutes, tensing her Achilles tendons, placing palms on thighs and pushing. Dropping forward would be so much simpler; she could just ooze out on her belly. She inhaled, realised she felt quite calm, in the same, still way it must be when you're poised at the sucking gap, parachute on your back, thinking *Dear God I'm going to die*, and the pit of your belly dreads that next, essential step. And then you take it, maybe without even noticing, and you fall, all the spread of the globe rushing up to meet you, and suddenly the fear goes away. You find you *can* move. You are falling, certainly, but by making yourself fall, by fighting every rational instinct that tells you not to, you've at least initiated movement. And chosen your direction.

Which was: up and out, in more glorious silence. Hamilton shouted after her, something about getting her a lift home. Anna kept walking. Her intention when she arrived at Govan was to go and see Cruikshanks too, ask what the true position was with Rob. But now, her natural suspicion was kicking in, a need to act with absolute circumspection.

Back to the wall, nobody was more sleekit than a cop.

She drove her car out of Govan yard. The Palace of Art faced her, an Art Deco remnant of Glasgow's Great Empire Exhibition of 1938. Now a sports centre housed inside Bellahouston Park, the elegant building had seen a handy, neon-lit curry shack built right next to it, serving lamb madras and poppadoms to the health conscious of Glasgow. It was rumoured Hamilton had a special order every Friday lunchtime, for deep-fried whole chillies and chips.

After this, Anna could expect a full-scale witch-hunt. Far too late to take out a grievance now. It would just be perceived as sour, retaliatory, trampled-on grapes. She should have lodged it when she had the chance that someone might believe her. A weird confection about undrunk councillors and oppressive shoe-cleaning and mean Irish men who turned on the charm while sharpening their daggers would have been tissue-thin at the best of times.

She fed the wheel fast through her fingers, changed gear with a satisfying grind. Gathering evidence was problematic when it got embedded in emotion rather than actuality. How stuff made you *feel*, the implicit threats behind innocuous or unproven actions. That's when you had to invoke the Moorov Doctrine, a canny principle of Scots Law which allowed evidence from one lone witness or victim to corroborate the evidence of another— even though they were victims of two separate offences. Of course, the circumstances of each incident had to be closely linked, and refer to the same accused. It was normally used in sexual offence cases, had evolved because bullies strike in stealth and isolation. Chances are Hamilton had worked on Claire too. Why else would Claire jeopardise her own position by telling lies?

Anna slammed the accelerator, spun sharp along Mosspark Boulevard. Well, by telling a large portion of the truth, actually, but it was all relative. Perhaps she *should* talk to Claire Rodgers, rather than avoid her as she'd been doing so studiously.

In all probability, Anna would never prove a thing. But what could *they* prove, exactly, about her?

Make a list, Anna. That's what you usually do.

She dropped a gear as she passed a speed camera. Okay. What would they say? That Anna, in the midst of receiving shocking news about her mother, had forgotten to pass on an important instruction.

Tap.

That as soon as she remembered this, Anna had made efforts to rectify same—she would have her mobile records, they would show she phoned Claire Rodgers from Spain. No, better still, Claire had, voluntarily, phoned *her*. If she had contrived to coerce Claire into covering for her, where was the plan and subterfuge there?

What else? *Tap.*

That Anna had got a bit pished at a night out? Guilty, but it wasn't a hanging offence.

Tap.

That she'd gone to Spain because her mother had died? Well, there was a cedarwood box somewhere in Rob Macklin's house that could be the production for the defence there.

Ach, there were probably a hundred and one things they could 'get' her on.

Back to the wall, nobody was more sleekit than a cop.

When Anna returned to Giffnock, she'd check through every piece of correspondence in her basket, send home any files or emails they might twist to use against her, so she could plan out some defence.

Tap, tap. A tiny point, insistent through the shell.

That Anna had driven an old lady to jump to her death?

Ah.

396

In prison, when she'd visited Jamie Worth all that time ago, that was what scared her most: his reluctance to accept any help; masochistic almost in his wish to embrace punishment. *I killed that girl. She had as much right to live as you and I.*

She pulled up at Giffnock office, parked her car next to Johnny's empty space. Good. Probably out receiving his instructions to shoot her on sight. Unless they actually found enough reason to formally suspend her, this was going to be a war of attrition. Anna was going nowhere.

Indeed.

She beamed warmly at her bar officer, the whinging little shite who'd fired her in. 'Morning, Constable.'

As she turned, she tripped over a wad of files which had toppled from a cardboard box. Piled up by the door were several boxes, and a maidenhead fern that she recognised from Johnny's room.

'Boss off on his holidays or something?'

'Eh, have you not heard, ma'am? He's been made up to acting deputy commander. All his gear's going up to Govan.'

A hot-cold helix twisted through her.

'Oh, and ma'am, there's a woman here to see you.' He nodded through to the public foyer.

It took a minute, seeing her out of context, out of her white dress and flat white shoes, for Anna to recognise Padma, the nurse from The Meadows. She jumped from a blue plastic chair as Anna opened the connecting door.

'Please. I need to talk to you. It's about Manju.'

Anna clocked the bar officer's antennae creak, honing in on their conversation, and she ushered the woman inside. 'Let's go to my office.'

She half expected a sentry outside, or ribbons marked 'Do not Cross' taped across the door, but the door was just the door, panelled wood with its little brass plaque. They were barely in the room before Padma shoved a sheet of crumpled white paper into Anna's fist.

'I took this note from her hand.'

'You did what? From Manju?'

Padma nodded, licked the side of her mouth.

'But why?'

'I don't know. I was frightened.'

Anna smoothed the paper out on her desk, noticing red spatters on one half of the page. The writing was beautiful, looping and ornate; the language like a poem.

I fly from this life to a new one. It is my choice, the only one I have the power to make, and I go in peace and supplication. To my friend Cassandra I leave my finest sari, the peacock blue that she loves. If you wrap her in it, then we will recognise each other. Please will you ask the men to burn her? She does not wish to be buried. She fears the dark.

To my daughter I leave my ring. It was her father's, and she should have it. I have kept it safe for her. It was all I had.

To God, I leave my soul.

Anna blinked her eyes against the starkness of the full stop, of the dark head on blood-damp ground, but the picture followed her inside, monochrome.

'This is definitely Manju's writing? It's very ornate. And lucid, come to that.'

Padma scowled. 'Manju wasn't daft, you know. Just because folk don't talk disny make them stupid. I've got other stuff too, if you need it, some verses she wrote, some old letters too.'

'No, it's fine. I believe you.' Anna read the note again. 'You realise this proves that she meant to do it? It's suicide, not an accident. Or murder.'

'Yes.'

'Well, it has to go to the enquiry. I'm sorry, you'll have to take it to DCI Cruikshanks. I don't understand why you didn't just hand it in yesterday.'

Padma fiddled with a paper hankie. 'See if you're a Hindu . . . och, it's hard to explain.' She sighed, started again. 'You've got to understand, what we strive for is *mochas*, but you can only achieve that after hundreds and thousands of births.'

'Musk . . . ?'

'*Mochas*. By being reborn again and again, we can jump to higher planes—even immortality. But, to commit suicide—well, it mucks up the cycle of death and rebirth, brings bad karma. I mean, it's no for *us* to decide the time. For Manju to have killed herself, it's like rewinding the clock. It's very bad—it means she's got to go back, further than before, you know?'

'Hiding this note doesn't change the facts, though.'

'I know that. It was just . . . ach, I thought I was protecting her.' She blew her nose. 'Then I thought about it, and I realised the best way of helping Manju was to come and see you. She wouldn't

399

want you to be blamed, like they're saying in the papers. She liked you.'

'She did?'

'Aye. She said you brought her food once, or a drink? Years ago? She thought you were kind.'

Anna cast her mind back twenty years, to a thin, eager probationer, with soft hands and a softer heart. Faint memory of a cold day and a warm flask of soup. She'd had loads left after piece break, it would've been a shame to chuck it. That's right; she'd taken paper cups from the vending machine and handed it out to the dossers on her beat. Just a bit of leftover soup.

Padma shook Anna's wrist. 'Look, it wasn't your fault. I know why Manju killed herself.'

'Why?'

'Because she missed Cassie. Pure and simple. I was the only person Manju ever talked to properly; even then she hardly spoke. But, every day, she would ask me "Where is my *mitra*. Where is my friend?" And when you told her Cassie was dead . . . well . . .'

'So it *was* my fault.'

The sentence fell, a dull, flat disc.

'No. It's the fault of they bastards who killed Cassie.' Padma was shredding the hankie into snow, little tufts like dandruff floating. 'All you were trying to do was help. Manju understood that, I promise you she did.'

'Did she ever say anything to you about these "men"?'

'Yes. That's what I wanted to tell you. Only the once, right after you left her yesterday. I sat with her till she fell asleep—that's how I know she was alright. She'd calmed right down, started praying

400

for Cassie. Just before she fell asleep and I left her, she was mumbling about *jawans*—soldiers— coming into her room. She said they had come back, but that they didn't want her, just Cassie.'

'Soldiers?'

'Aye. She had been sedated, mind.'

Anna chewed the edge of her fingernail. The taste was silvery. 'Could be any men in uniform. Male nurses?'

'We don't have any. The only men in uniform are Mr Macklin and his locum, but she said the soldiers were in black. Which just leaves all your polis that've been buzzing around—and the security guards.'

'Security? I thought they didn't come inside?'

Padma blushed a little. 'A few of them come in for a wee cup of tea on the night shift. There's some good-looking boys, you know.' She tugged the remains of the hanky in half. 'It gets lonely at three, four in the morning. Mr Macklin is never around at that time; he wouldn't know.'

'And how do they get in?'

'Chap the back door. Sometimes, if we're busy, we just leave it off the latch.' Padma studied her hands. 'I know you were looking into the security firm before.'

'We were, but they checked out fine. Especially as we were assured they only had access to the perimeter of The Meadows.'

'Aye, well, we should of said then. But no one wanted to get into trouble.'

Anna thought for a moment. 'But what makes you think they have anything to do with Cassie? You're just after saying Manju was sedated. And no matter what you say about her calming down, she still jumped out a second-storey window that same afternoon.'

'I know. But *someone* had to sneak Cassie outside in the middle of the night, didn't they? And it's not fair what they're saying about Mr Macklin. Security *isny* shite—not from *inside* the home it's no. They're making out folk can just get up and wander around.'

'But if the nurses leave the back door off the latch, that's exactly what they can do.'

Padma flung the bits of hankie on the floor, stood up. 'Och, look, you do what you like, okay? But, I'll tell you this—my . . . I know someone who works for All Star. Very low down, but he sees things. Gets told to move stuff at night. You know the thing: do this, keep quiet and get an extra tenner.'

Delicate prickles up her spine. This was more like it. 'What kind of stuff?'

'Boxes. Heavy boxes. He never knows what's in them, never asks. But it's something dodgy. Maybe I'm being paranoid, but I'm so bloody . . .' She broke off, scrubbed at her eyes. '. . . angry, about Cassie, and about Manju. They didn't ask for much, you know? They were happy playing at birds and pleating hair. Just wee kids really.'

This was all good. Padma would have no idea that Valerie the jogger had also mentioned boxes.

'Right, sit back down. I want you to give me the name and contact details of your pal at All Star. Let me speak to him.'

An emphatic shake of her head. 'No way. I can't. He . . . he isn't supposed to be here.'

'I'm not with you.'

'He's an illegal immigrant? This job is all that

402

keeps him from living on the streets.'

Anna grabbed a pen, started to make some notes. 'Well, that's something concrete we can get them on then—it's a start. If All Star Security are giving jobs to illegals, we can pull them in for that, see what else squirms out in the wash.' She clicked the biro on her teeth. *Tap*. 'Work it right up them.'

'No way!' Padma came round Anna's side of the desk, got as close as she could. 'Please. I have to trust you. If my . . . if these "illegals", as you put it, get arrested, they get sent back home. Get put in jail. I can't give you any details.'

Anna put down the pen, rested her fists on the underhang of her chin. It felt soft there—and worryingly loose. 'So how's that supposed to help Cassie? I'm like a journalist, Padma. Nothing's off the record. Once you tell me something, I can't unknow it.'

'Even so, I . . . canny say anything, and I won't. I'll deny I even mentioned it.'

'*Jesus*.' Anna blew across the surface of her knuckles, funnelling air until it almost whistled. 'Right, well, what if I gave you my business card? It's got my work line, and my own mobile number on it. Could you at least give that to your friend? Ask him to get in touch with me?'

'I don't know . . .'

'Padma, I promise it would be completely confidential—I don't even need to know his name.'

'What *would* you need to know then?'

'Everything that he does.'

'I don't know,' she repeated. 'All I can do is ask him to get in touch with you. *If* he wants to. I canny force him. But I don't know how much use he'd be anyway. I'm telling you, all he does is patrol old

403

buildings and shift the odd box.'

'Aye, well, sometimes it's the nothing people, the ones who know how to be small and grey and unimportant, that see the biggest of pictures. Here, take this. Please.'

Padma slipped the card into her purse.

'Can I ask you something?' said Anna.

'What now? I'm no doing anything else for you.'

'Do you believe Manju's at peace?'

Padma shook her head. 'She canny be. She has to remain here, as a bad spirit, until the time she was meant to live to has passed. *Then* she'll go to hell.' She smiled. 'We're nothing if not thorough. Only after she's suffered there can she come back and finish her previous karma.'

Falling, falling, watching all your life rush by, then the one before, then the one before that, all rungs you couldn't grab on to, and never wished to see again. God, Anna's *one* life would be bad enough to repeat.

'One other thing,' said Anna. 'She talks here about her daughter? I didn't know she had one.'

'Neither did I. She never mentioned her. Ever.'

CHAPTER TWENTY

Dark outside. Smudged, incessant rain catching on pitted glass. She had always planned to replace the old casements, never had. Only one slid up, the other two painted shut years ago, by some other person. Maybe even when this was a whole house, and a family lived here instead of two sealed-off women with separate front doors.

Anna lay back on the knubbly tweed of her three-seater, Alice arching to meet her trailing fingers.

'Hey gorgeous. Can you not sleep either?'

The cat squeezed her eyes, furry cheeks puffed in a smile, then slid away. She sat, paws folded, by the door, her tabby body turned grey and stone. No lights on in the living room, just open blinds and the soft mute shapes of Anna's cat and her furniture.

'If I let you out, you have to come back, understand? No all-night wanderings?'

Alice looked away, already out in the wind, expectant face and glittering eyes absorbing the rising storm, which would scour out small creatures, flood nooks and burrows, make the earth bubble with damp-fresh scents of fleeing life. Her hackles tufted, patience thin.

'Oh, alright then. You're just like your mother. She was a dirty stop-out too.' Anna rolled off the couch and shoved the door. A glow from the hall lamp spilled cheery orange over the edges of her safe, shrouded room. Alice had a cat flap, but Anna kept the kitchen door shut at night. It gave the cat the run of the house, but stopped her from accessing the back door—and total freedom. A small, but important control, and an assurance of someone in the morning.

She padded down to the rear of the hall, Alice stalking at an independent distance, and opened the kitchen door. 'Bye then. Don't bring me back anything dead.'

Tomorrow she would ring Jenny, ask if she'd reconsidered hosting a cat reunion. A single shriek of wind penetrated the gap, the kitchen window

405

rattling in its loose-fitting frame. Anna hoped Shelly was still ensconced at Queen's Drive. The next stop after places like that was usually the pavement; huddled in a pissy doorway or wrapped in newspaper beneath a bridge. She yawned, remembered she'd not eaten since breakfast, hadn't been shopping since Godknew. But there were always essentials, squirrelled away in the fridge: cheese, half a dozen eggs, couple of bottles of Soave. She tucked a wine bottle under her arm, stuffed two packs of salt and vinegar crisps in her dressing-gown pocket. Better take a glass too.

Outside, the wind slapped at trees, their skittery, bending yield flashing streetlights into Morse-code shadow. Anna rested her forehead against the living-room window, sipped from her glass. Nice and cold, inside and out. She jumped when her doorbell rang; hadn't seen it coming though she'd been staring, vacant, into the street.

It was Tom Cruikshanks.

'You still up? Good.'

'Well, I am now.'

'Ach, don't gie me that.' He stomped wet feet in the vestibule, shrugged off his sodden anorak. 'You were so, anyway—I seen you mooning out the windae.'

'I was not mooning. I was . . . pondering.'

He closed the front door behind him. 'Aye, well. You've a lot to ponder, lass. Am I getting a glass of that or what? Nice goonie, by the way.'

She tugged the belt on her purple velour dressing gown. Underneath were her lucky bra and pants, the ones with the turquoise trim. Of course Rob would not come near her, not after being questioned and held to account, and why would she want to see him anyway? His business was in trouble, he was handling counterfeit notes. Which was foolish or criminal, or both.

'Help yourself.' Anna switched on a lamp, handed Cruikshanks the wine bottle.

'Jesus, things that bad, hen? Do I no even get a straw?'

'Sorry. I'll—'

'I'm kidding you on. I'm no stopping, any road. Just on my way home . . .'

'At this time?'

'Aye. Thought I'd see how you were doing.'

Like a gruff, malodorous bear, he heaved forwards, wrapping gloved mitts around her startled frame. 'Anna, I'm that sorry about your mum, my love. I only just heard. How d'you no tell us?'

'I . . . I didn't want any fuss.' Her mouth was squashed against his shoulder. A wash of relief, buffeting her. Here was a friend, he must be a friend or he would disdain her too. She was grateful for a friend.

'Tom, I'm sorry. I should've said.'

Cruikshanks released her as abruptly as he'd grabbed her. 'Ach away. You've had enough to worry about. I take it you've seen this pile of shite?' He chucked a newspaper on to the coffee table.

'Aye.'

'It's a lot of bollocks, and it didny come from me, Anna. Not one shitey word of it.'

'I know that. I reckon it was JC.' She sat down. 'Hamilton is trying to stitch me up, Tom.'

And then she told him; about Johnny, Heraghty, everything. To pass the torch, share the load off

407

her chest, her head, her heart, felt edifying. Small kindnesses and courtesies implicit in the sharing; Cruikshanks being outraged, then soothing. Making her tea, even breaking open a packet of chocolate buttons he had stashed somewhere near his trouser waistband.

'Disny surprise me really, doll.'

'But why?'

He slurped some tea. 'Folk like Hamilton don't always need a reason. Could be she disny like your face, your hair. God knows. What I *will* tell you is that she's angling to get that ACC's post when it comes up. You know—Community Policing?'

'You're joking?'

'Naw. And the worrying thing is that the Chief seems to think it's a good idea—woman in a high-profile job and all that.'

'But she's not a woman. She's no even human.'

'You know that, and I know that . . . Anyway, that's no all. You know how the convenor of the Joint Board isny well, and they're all jockeying for position there?'

'I thought that Councillor Nayar was a shooey-in.'

'So did a lot of folk. Perfect gentleman, so he is—a former JP 'n all, which is no bad thing. But apparently Heraghty's well-quoted for it too. He asks lots of awkward questions about the polis, and that seems to be the way certain board members would like things to go.'

'And Heraghty hates Hamilton. Who loves Johnny and hates me.'

'Smart lass. I know—deputy divisional commander, and O'Hare just a sprog as far as I'm concerned. Aye, life can be shite, my pet. *Any*

408

road,' he thumped her knee, 'much as I enjoy chewing the fat with you, that's not why I popped in. I thought you'd like to know—they counterfeit notes? All appear to have come from the Maguires.'

'Not Rob?'

'Ooh, *Rob* is it? Dr Rob-can-I-flog-your-log Rob. That yin?'

'Piss off, Tom. Was Macklin knowingly passing counterfeit currency or not?'

'Not.'

She felt like punching air, but hugged her knees in instead, just rocking to the beat of the small warm pulses at her wrists, still paying attention to Tom. Hearing it sparkling and clear.

'Aye, we were able to cross-reference everything with the nursing home's books—last three payments from the Maguires have all been in cash. All fifty-quid notes. And, you'll never guess how they paid the deposit on their new garage.'

'Fifty-pound notes?'

'Aye. Guy remembers having to count it all out—twenty-five thousand pounds' worth of them.'

'And he never noticed the serial numbers?'

'Well, we don't know if they were from the same batch or not, but no. I guess when you're looking at that amount of cash, you don't check the small print, just that it all adds up. Particularly when cash-in-hand helps avoid the taxman. But, the best of it is, the manny also tells us that, less than a month after the Maguires bought the place, they were chapping at his door again, asking if *he'd* like to buy it back.'

'What?'

'I know. Claimed they'd overreached

409

themselves, offered him it back with a ten per cent discount, but he telt them to get hunted.'

'And would that have been after Cassie was abducted?'

'Aye, it would.'

'So, what next?' Anna pulled on her bare feet, bending her knees so her feet slid under her backside. It was coming closer; the shaking, then the settling, seeing where pieces would fall. Her toes were cold. Thank God she'd not been wearing her cow slippers when Cruikshanks arrived. Black and white cartoon heads with goggle eyes and pink comedy tongues, they'd been a present from Elaine. *Seen as everyone thinks you're a cow anyway. It was that or old boots.*

That was funny, so funny she could laugh aloud; her veins were filling up with brightness.

'Well, we find the Maguires,' said Cruikshanks, 'detain them under Section Fourteen, and have a good old six-hour chinwag with them each. Find out where they do their printing, how they distribute it, and—most importantly—why it got their mammy killed. And,' another thump, this time on the couch, 'listen you here to me, girl. There's absolutely *no* suggestion of Cassie's death having any link with Manju—apart fae the obvious: i.e., that Manju missed her. As far as I can see, the poor old soul had just had enough of life in all its crapness. I've spoke to Dr Macklin too, sorry, *Rob*, and—'

'How was he?'

'Hard to tell. Very sort of closed off, you know? No as friendly as before. Eh, speaking of which . . .' Cruikshanks flapped the newspaper again. 'It's none of my business, hen, and I'm no your dad—

but do you think it was a good idea, you and the good doc going off together like that?'

Anna sighed. 'Probably not Tom, no. It wasn't planned. It's just, he was there, when they phoned about my mum, and I kind of . . . went to pieces, you know? I have to say, he was brilliant. Booked flights, got me on the plane—I hardly even noticed he was there for the first few days. Why?'

She fixed on his eyes, trying to catch his true expression before he clouded it up with ambiguities. '*Do* you think he was at it, Tom? He didn't, I mean . . . we're just friends. Nothing happened.'

'Like I say, none of my beeswax, my love. It's just how it looks, you know? You don't want to be giving Hamilton any more excuses to shaft you, do you? Look, I know I'm saying the dodgy notes arny his, and I'm ninety-nine-point-nine per cent certain Cassie's abduction isny down to him either, but lump it all thegither and it's no a pretty picture, is it? So, unless this really is love's young dream, I suggest you stay well away from Dr Macklin.'

No, he wasn't her bloody dad.

'Don't gie me that face, you.' Then it was Cruikshanks's turn to sigh. 'Ach, just be discreet, yes?'

'Don't worry. I don't think I'll be on his Christmas card list any more.'

She finished off the wine in her glass. Tea just kept you awake. 'Who interviewed him anyway?'

'Eh, Bullbar.'

They both winced. Bullbar was named for the thickness of his hide and the density of his approach. No, it was unlikely Rob Macklin would ever look with fondness on a polis again.

411

'Oh, Tom—I nearly forgot. One of the nurses came to see me today—Padma. Did you get the note Manju left? I told Padma to pass it straight to you.' Anna ran her thumb round the rim of her glass. 'Didn't even want to touch it, in case I got the blame for something else.'

'Aye, she did. Like I said, the note just confirms it wisny anyone's fault—'

'Yeah yeah, but did Padma tell you about the security guards? Apparently one or two of them *do* come in on the night shift. For tea—and possibly more than biscuits.'

'Way ahead of you there, doll. I've arranged a wee squad to go back out and see Mr MacLeod of All Star Security tomorrow. See if he disny know the Maguires after all.' Cruikshanks chucked the last of the buttons into his mouth. The happy smack of his lips when he caught them made Anna think of seals and fish. 'I thought about just huckling him at his house, but I reckon it will be far more persuasive if we visit him in public. Especially if we have to blitz *all* his various offices at the same time.' He gave a tiny burp. '*Pardon*. For efficiency, obviously.'

'I don't suppose you've found out if there was a security firm in operation at the park?'

'Anna. *Anna*. What do you take me for? Unfortunately, security for Linn Park Mansion is provided by a bunch called Pinnacle, not All Star. And very cursory security they were at that. Don't actually seem to have visited the place much. Their gaffer tells me they were really employed for later, when all the builders' and decorators' gear would be on site. So, pulling Mr MacLeod again is all we have at the moment I'm afraid.'

'Or . . .' Anna poured more Soave into her glass. It curled and glugged like a friend. 'What if I told you to wait one day more, do a wee bit of surveillance on All Star instead? Seen as I've got a contact on the inside, who's going to do a bit of rooting around on our behalf.' Half-true, half-hope, but her dying swan act had continued long enough. She had to redeem herself with some illusion of added value.

Cruikshanks's scowl rippled into a slow-moving beam. 'Ah, Anna. See when I finally murder the wife—will you marry me?'

'Aye, but who's to say you wouldn't kill me too? There's a reason I live alone, Tom.'

*   *   *

Clotting mouth and nostrils, sucking cloth, not air, trying to wake, she was awake, couldn't breathe. Her duvet was over her head. Anna unwound herself, wriggled free and up to clean, cold air.

Daft cow. Her heart, panicked, then laughing at itself. A little lighter, the night softening into still-wet dawn.

The counterfeit notes were nothing to do with Rob. Surely he would be relieved by that, not furious? She punched her pillows upright. Was it incumbent on Anna, his jailer, to make the next move? He'd want nothing to do with her, would be sheltering somewhere, a little bruised. How readily the system could strip you, the very act of taking you to a police station you did not wish to be in. Oh, they call it voluntary, tell you you are 'attending the police office on a voluntary undertaking', but by giving the process a name, and forms and *procedures,* by making you sign your name to *prove* you are a volunteer, by committing words tossed on air to permanent paper or tape, they give it confining, sinister status that is anything but voluntary. It is a date-rape. Afterwards, you want to scuttle home, shower thoroughly and wrap yourself in comfortable fleece. And wonder how this could have happened, how you got there, and what you should *do*. Then you realise you will do nothing, for you feel stupid and angry all at once, and then it's best just to leave it be.

Would Anna just embarrass him now? She looked at the blue stare of her clock. Too early to get up, too late to go back to sleep. Pulled herself on to her elbows, listening to the sheets of rain that bled and bled all night, and grew the Scots into a dour and crabbit race. A race with lovely skin, mind. She could do sit-ups, she supposed, or read for a while, pick one of the books teetering on her bedside table. Before she could decide to flop back down and do neither, her mobile gave its own dawn chorus: 'Ride of the Valkyries'. First, an unknown number, then a garbled, thick voice.

'Please. You are police?'

'Who is this?'

'Please. We need help. The air is . . .' the man coughed, 'wrong. Please. We can't get out.'

Anna could hear other voices in the background, high-pitched panic, women screaming, men shouting. If this was a hoax, it was elaborate.

'Who are you, and how did you get my number?'

'I have,' he coughed again, retching hard, '. . . the daughter of my father's aunt . . . Padma . . . please, you have to help us!'

'Padma? Padma gave you this number? You work for All Star?'

'Yes, yes, I . . .'

'Look, what's happening? Where are you?'

'Man came with ferter? To make the crops grow strong but it is wrong. We cannot breathe, I cannot turn my key. You must help, please!' He screeched this last, a terrible, rasping burn across the night, that made Anna leap from bed and pull on clothing, anything that was heaped at the foot of her bed, still talking, still keeping him talking.

'Okay. You can't breathe. Is it a fire?'

'No,' he panted, 'no fire.'

'What is your name?'

'Dilip.'

'You must tell me where you are, Dilip. Are you in Glasgow, in the city?'

'Yes, yes.' It was a whisper now. 'I am at the window, but I cannot get out.'

'What can you see?

He sobbed. 'I see a bus.'

'Good. A main road. Anything else?'

'We are in big place. Windows all brick, but this little one. Too small to get out.'

She grabbed her car keys from the mantelpiece. 'Can you remember what the place looks like from outside? When you came in, what did you see?'

'There is a cross. Your Scotland cross. And little trees.'

'Is there a park?'

'No.' His voice was very weak, breathing laboured. Anna could no longer hear the screaming behind him. 'Trees coming from the building, from the roof.'

A brick building, disused, with a Saint Andrew's

cross.

'Dilip!' she shouted. 'The bus you saw. Did it have a number on it?'

Barely a croak. 'A six and a six. I am sorry . . . my eyes . . .'

'No!' she yelled. 'You hang on, you hear me? I know where you are. You're in the old printworks—it's very close to where I am. You hold on—I will get you out. I am going to phone for help on my other phone; you keep this connection open. I will keep talking to you and I will come and get you out. You tell the others, Dilip.'

Silence.

'Dilip, please. You tell the others. You stay strong for them, yes?'

A whisper, dissolving as it was uttered. 'Yes.'

She stabbed nine nine nine on her landline. 'This is Chief Inspector Anna Cameron of Strathclyde Police. I want police, fire and ambulance to go straight to the St Andrew's Printworks at Eglinton Toll. It may be a chemical leak or explosion of some sort. Persons believed trapped inside—I don't have numbers, I'm afraid.'

Dilip had talked about crops. What crops would you grow in a locked up, run-down building, which was meant to be empty? Which needed to be guarded? The operator was asking if persons were injured; Anna interrupted: 'Affirmative. Breathing difficulties at least. But, this is important. Please advise all emergency personnel to approach with extreme caution—the building could be booby-trapped.'

'I'm sorry?' said the operator.

'I think it might be a drugs factory. Look, I'm en route to the locus now.' She hung up, ran out into

416

the rain, the blue-grey sky like a churning sea, washing her, rinsing her eyes as she fumbled with the car keys, clicked the lock, and *in*, and *drive*, phone under her chin. 'Dilip, are you there? Are you still there?'

'Yes.'

'How many of you are there?'

'Four.' Words scratched from a razor-blade throat. 'I cannot see—it is burning my eyes.' She could hear weeping again, either from him or someone close by.

'Dilip, lie down on the floor. The air might be fresher there. I know it hurts to talk, but I will talk to you, okay? I live in Shawlands—it's only five minutes away from where you are. In a few minutes, five at the most, if you look out of the window you will see my car come down the main road—it's a silver Audi. I'll be turning into Pollokshaws Road in a few seconds, and . . . it's raining outside—chucking it down, we call it.'

Her tyres were slipping on the rain-spinning road, whorls of water exploding on the windscreen. Even full blast, her wipers whipped and struggled to break the deluge, steam rising inside the car from her frantic commentary and her sweating skin.

'Yeah, it always bloody rains here, Dilip—and you never get used to it. Every summer, you still hope the sun will shine, you still buy your barbeque food and parasols to keep the nonexistent heat away.' She scrubbed the windscreen with her sleeve, seeing only unmisted rivers of rain, the smear of grubby streetlights, a red light—bugger it—turn right, the wind catching her, twisting her gently in a skid; she let the wheel thrash through

417

open hands, resisting the urge to brake. It was slow and it was fast, still gibbering, 'I'm nearly there, pal.' She caught the wheel, reined it in, correcting the skid, declutching. Smelling wet dirt and burning rubber, past a stonemason's yard, neatly lined with unmarked, patient gravestones, through a bus gate and she was there; the building's bulk dominating the flooded pavement from which it rose: the old Glasgow Corporation printing press.

Dilip was right. Thin trees grew out of it now, cracking through the slates, dancing in the wind. The press was a leftover from the days when paternal provision was a good thing, and every brochure and report and sign and school jotter the city fathers would ever need was typeset and rollered, blocked, printed, cut and bound in-house, in one vast hall. Big enough to be a bus garage, it was a fortress of sheer red-brick walls, with darker bricks filling in the space of high-arched windows, three triangular pediments with stone urns stuck ridiculously on top. The carved crest of St Mungo above the boarded-up main door, and a faint, peeling painting of the cross of St Andrew, white on blue, and she had already parked the car and was battering on the door. Hair saturated on her neck, shouting down her phone. Into nothingness.

A flash of blue light, one fire engine, two, trust the polis to be bloody late, and she was running round the building, trying to find a way in, another door, a yard—a fire door. It was pushed slightly ajar, and she was shouting at the fire crew to hurry up, and there was Cruikshanks—was the man permanently on duty?—at her back, asking questions, *I don't know,* trying to prise the fire door open, both trying, a DC joining in, the rain

418

slapping in her eyes, down her front, licking at her breasts because she had no bra on, some fireman gone to get the bolt cutters, for the door wasn't stuck, but chained.

Two great loops like Marley's penance wound round the 'press-down' bar, the sharp stink of swimming baths and bleach, but as coughing-thick and viscous as the unctuous gunk you smear round drains. A little inch, a precious inch, and a hand fell out. Anna stared at it, the palm cupped in supplication or to catch the rain, yanked harder, the fireman clipping, chewing metal through metal, and the door swung forward. Open eyes like pearls. More hands behind, bodies all piled up and desperate.

Desperate and dead.

CHAPTER TWENTY-ONE

Harsh ammonia had faded into sickly sweet. They stood, a disgruntled huddle of them, in the tropical dampness of the printworks. The heat was unbearable, even in this vast hangar. 'Over a hundred degrees in here, I reckon,' said the senior fire officer who was leading them round. The firemen had done their best to leave the scene as they found it: no fire, therefore no need to switch off electricity. In fact, positively dangerous to do so, Anna had been told. 'One click of a switch, and the whole place could go up.'

The building was still technically hazardous, but the residual airborne gases had been diluted with jet after jet of water, and the Council's Scientific

Services people had been through the building with their testing equipment, deeming it safe enough for the impatient polis to get inside. Anna and the other cops had spent the last few futile hours standing soaked on the pavement outside, watching firefighters in decontamination suits roll out cylindrical tanks and fat hoses, breathing like beige Darth Vaders. Then sipping pale, paper-cup coffee and sheltering in the police incident caravan when it was set up at a safe distance. Three-way conversations, with Control fielding feedback from officers dispatched to the four winds, wrapping up the messages, passing them back to Cruikshanks.

Premises no longer owned by the City Council.

'Well, who, then?'

Stand by.

The City Chambers gatehouse staff ask: can it wait until office hours?

'No, it bloody canny.'

Relentless updates from the hospital. *Dead. Dead. Dead. Dead.* Anna was eavesdropping, not on duty, not official, only her own mobile which told her nothing.

Premises was sold to someone called Adair Holdings. Am tracing contacts or keyholders now.

And the media, oh the media, squealing up in cars and wagons. They reminded Anna of that film *Ghost*—the one where, at the onset of death and despair, ectoplasmic demons would drag from the shadows, grunting their way to the hub of the horror, consuming what they found. The journalists swirled and broke in eddies, men with cameras, arcs of light, furry beasts on sticks. Cowled shapes setting up, making notes, checking exposures, or doing nothing much at all, like the sallow producer in absurd sunglasses who just stood to one side, surveying his camera crews. Then a raincoated woman, with an accent like broth, was waving to Anna. 'How many dead? Was it an explosion, Chief Inspector? We understood this place was unoccupied.'

Anna tried to move away from Lucy Manning. She'd only come out of the caravan to get some fresh air. The morning sky was a grey lid over Glasgow, the rain softer now, soothing. It fell like gentle breath, the kind of drops a child would catch on her tongue.

Pushed right in her face, a soggy notebook, Lucy's long-chewed pen.

'You'll find out what's happened if you go along to the official press conference,' said Anna. 'Which you've already been advised of.' She had nearly made it, swept by on a crest of moral superiority, because her job gave her more right to be here than this woman's did, when she flicked one stupid, splashy kickback. 'Not that you'll write the truth anyway.'

'Oh, I think you'll find I always write the truth, chuck. It's the stitching together of it that's the real art. Now, come on, give us a little snippet. We've heard it was illegal immigrants inside.'

'No comment.'

'Or is it just that you don't actually know? I mean, you're only uniform, aren't you? In fact, why is it you're here, actually? This area isn't covered by Giffnock. Do you just turn up at everything?'

'What, like you, you mean?'

Lucy dimpled, flashing gappy square teeth. 'Yeah, but at least I'm not a spare prick at a wedding, trying to ingratiate myself.' Oh, she was good, opening Anna up with jab, jab, jab, moving straight to the punch that would burst her. 'So, was it arson, then?'

'No, it wasn't arson.' Anna was aware of her voice getting louder, pushing her face close in, like she controlled the breadth of air between them, the persistent curve of Lucy's cheek annoying her more than she thought possible. 'It wasn't arson because we don't have "arson" here, we have fireraising—wilful or malicious, depending on the type of property involved. Because this is *Scotland*. We are a separate country, we have a common law and a separate legal system, going all the way back to the jurisprudence of the Romans. We don't have manslaughter and we don't have burglary, we don't have coroners, and we don't have GBH. You can't just superimpose all your English guff on to us— you should learn that if you want to have a future in journalism here.'

'Ta for the lesson, Chief Inspector.' Lucy flipped her notebook shut. 'I'll be sure to quote you next time I'm writing up an Anna Cameron special. Which there seems to be quite a market for, I must say.'

'Aye, and while you're at it, why don't you go look up hamesucking and stouthrief as well, eh?'

What a ridiculous note to end on, a kind of syntactic baring of her arse cheeks. But it was worth it, for the wash of befuddlement on Lucy's face. Anna hurried back inside the caravan, stayed there until a fireman popped his head round the door, told them they could return to the printworks.

She was grateful to Cruikshanks for allowing her to come to this dismal viewing party at all. *Ach, it's*

422

only fair, hen. She had followed at a respectful distance from the main group, of Cruikshanks, the detective super who had arrived on scene, two DIs, assorted other detectives desperate to prove their worth, the unshaven slump of some Drugs Squad officers, and a team of Fire and Rescue bigwigs. It felt like a wake, but a watchful one.

On a patch of bare, concrete floor sat a couple of mattresses, a few ashtrays, a portable TV. A sad little bundle in the corner, of men's jumpers, socks, a brightly coloured dress, all scatterings that would never be reclaimed by their owners. The rest of the floor space was covered with plastic mats, blues and yellows and grimy-white, which squelched when you walked on them. Tins of fertiliser and pesticides were stacked in queasy pyramids, gleaming in the glare of rows and rows of lamps, roaring out forty degrees of heat.

All spotlighting a jungle of cannabis plants.

Umbrella-splayed leaves motionless in thick, toxic air, some reaching up to Anna's shoulders. Five garden gazebos, the sort of thing you'd get in B&Q, were ranged at the far end of the factory, lined in tinfoil.

'That'll be their hot-house nursery there,' said the Drugs Squad inspector. 'A wee bit TLC for the superskunk.'

'Nae traps then?' asked Cruikshanks.

'Don't think so. We've had a good look round.'

Some drugs factories had electrified doors, or poisonous liquids poised to splash on unsuspecting heads. Even mediaeval spikes under windows. This one had had a security guard. A young boy called Dilip, whose scarlet, flayed face may have once looked a bit like Padma's. A guard who was a jailer, who would hold the only key for this damp, hot death camp, would control access and keep his fellow workers incarcerated. People like him, who had left home in search of new and better things, not realising they were new-wave slaves.

'Tom.' Anna caught up with the rest of the group. 'Did you ask someone to check if there was a name or a logo on the uniform the guard was wearing?'

'I asked young Chris already. Haud on and I'll ask again—he's at the infirmary now.'

The response came back almost immediately.

Confirm. Security guard was wearing a uniform from Pinnacle Security, not All Star. Repeat, not *All Star.*

'But Padma definitely told me her cousin worked for All Star—the same firm that does security for The Meadows.'

'DCI Cruikshanks to Control. Tell DS Ramsay to run a check on all directors of, or references to, both All Star and Pinnacle Security firms—find out if there are any links at all.'

Roger.

A DC clutched his stomach. 'I feel sick.'

'You shouldny have ordered the tandoori mixed grill then,' quipped another. The snort of stifled laughter, not missed by Cruikshanks.

'Right you. Oot.'

'But sir . . .'

'You heard me. Away and piss off. Help wi crowd control or something. And you,' he scrutinised the sick DC, 'you're probably getting high just breathing in the spores. Not to mention your septum getting chewed up by the acid.' Cruikshanks fussed at the young lad's neck, pulling

424

at his shirt. 'For God sake, pull your bloody jaicket over your nose or something.'

Of course nobody was wearing masks or protective clothing, being the polis, who were immune to acid, drugs, bullets, knives, mental breakdown and all the ordinary laws of the universe. However, lecture delivered, Cruikshanks, who was wearing a zip-up cardigan over his shirt and tie, secured the zipper as high as it would go, and burrowed his own nose and mouth deep into the folded woollen collar, although his entire head was already red and sweating from the heat of the room.

A constant *drip and splat, drip and splat* fell from the network of pipes and showerheads clanking above the cannabis plants. It was the factory's makeshift irrigation system, which had been sluiced clean with foam and chemical concoctions.

'That's definitely the source of the exposure.' The fire officer pointed up to where an ugly brown hole on one of the pipes had caused the metal to buckle and split. The pattern was repeated at several joints and bends across the system. 'You can see where the pipes are all corroded. The system runs off a tank, not the mains, so we were able to preserve samples of the contents, like you asked. That's where the chemicals were introduced in the first place.'

'Cheers.' Cruikshanks's voice was muffled.

The detective super spoke. 'So, what you're saying is somebody put chlorine into those drums of pesticide. Just those ones there?'

'Yes, they seem to be the only ones. But they didn't add it—we believe they replaced the fertiliser *with* hydrogen chloride.'

425

The super drew his hand, again and again, over his Adam's apple. 'You said someone delivered them, Anna?'

'Well, the guard said they had delivered fertiliser, but I guess he meant this.'

'No descriptions?'

'Nothing. Just "man", that was all.'

'Well, whoever the "someone" was, he presumably told the poor sods in here that these new drums had to get mixed into the irrigation system first. Then jammed the door shut for good measure after he'd left.'

They had established some kind of resin had been poured into the lock of a side exit, the only door that hadn't been boarded up or otherwise secured. It would appear that the side exit had been the sole point of entry and exit for the factory. The rear fire door had definitely been chained from the inside, and for some time, judging by the weight and rust of the chain. Designed to keep the occupants *in* as much as to keep others out.

Cruikshanks crouched to read the label on the drum of pesticide. *'Noo impooved formla, ma arghse.'* It sounded like he was at the bottom of a bucket.

'That's how it would appear,' said the fire officer. 'As soon as the chemical mixed with the water in the sprinkler system, it turned to hydrochloric acid. Lethal if you breathe it in long enough—and in strong enough doses. But what's compounded it is . . . see, if you look here and here . . .' he climbed up on a chair so he was closer to the pipework, 'it would appear that there's actually been a series of explosions. Combination of the

426

heat and the water, I'd say. So what's happened is that they've been struck with the shrapnel from the pipes, *and* the acid, which they've then ingested through the eyes, mouth, skin.'

One of the DIs passed the super a green cardboard folder. 'Here, boss. The initial medical reports suggest they had at least a twenty-five minute exposure—there's evidence of chemical burns to the skin, damage to the mucous membranes, eye ulceration . . .'

'Jesus. So they suffocated *and* got eaten by acid.' The green-about-the-gills DC swallowed. 'But I still don't get it—it's usually Vietnam these folk come from. You know, the snakeheads and that. But all they bodies were Indian.'

'How?' snorted Cruikshanks, tugging down his jumper. 'D'you think there's some kind of special job centre, matching up illegal immigrants with their cultural criminal stereotype?' He shoved the collar up, then instantly pulled it down again. 'These folk are desperate, son. They'd go anywhere, do anything, just about, to get by. And there's aye plenty willing bastards to exploit them.'

'Boss, you know how there's a bus gate on Victoria Road?' said one of the detectives. 'And nae cars are allowed through?'

'Aye.'

'Well, I'm sure the Traffic had one of those mobile cameras on it recently, to monitor all the drivers who thought they'd take a short cut. I know it's probably clutching at straws, but, if it was still there, it would give footage of any cars driving down here tonight.'

'*If* they came down Vicky Road,' interjected another.

'Aye, I *said* it was a long shot—'

'And if they came by car . . .'

'Well, they're hardly gonny push they big cans here in a pram are they?'

'Em, I don't know if this is any help,' interrupted the fire officer, 'but I'm pretty sure there's also CCTV at both the petrol station at Eglinton Toll, and the bus garage on Butterbiggins Road. We've been having a lot of trouble with wee shites setting fires against the petrol pumps, and I know one of your lads was looking at tapes for us.'

'Brilliant, pal. Cheers.' Cruikshanks turned to the DC who first mentioned bus gates. 'Okay, Bobby. Away out and find me tapes wi bad men on them. And failing that, find me some wi dirty women. *Boom boom*.' He wiped his arm across his forehead. The heat and thick, sweet smell was unrelenting; Anna was starting to feel sick too.

'Sir! Sir! We've found something else up here.'

Two firemen, another DC and a Scenes of Crime officer had been systematically working their way through the premises, the firemen showing the police where they had been and what they had moved. The DC emerged now from a stairwell, close to where they had come in. He was beckoning, eyes wide and eager. 'Wait till you see this.'

'Well, there's a man who's happy at his work, eh?' Cruikshanks shuffled after him.

Anna pressed her temples. *Not more bodies, please.*

Tucked away on a landing was a square-shaped room, maybe twenty-five feet by fifty. At its centre, an old boardroom table, the wood ring-marked, with a paper guillotine and two computers sitting on top. Linked to one computer, a four-colour high-res printer, some ink cartridges at the side, still in their boxes. On the floor, wired up to the second PC, was a scanner. A steel shelving system to the rear of the room held around fifty cardboard boxes; they seemed full, the decrepit metal sagging with their weight.

The super nodded at the boxes. 'Take one down and open it, Alan. *Carefully.*'

The DI shoogled out a box from the lowest shelf, moving it gently from side to side, keeping the base in contact with first the shelf, then the floor. It wasn't sealed, the lid simply folded one flap under the other. Tentatively, he ran his hand beneath one edge.

Control to DCI Cruikshanks.

'Go ahead.'

'Eh, sir?' The DI raised his head from his task.

'Stand by Control. What is it?'

'You might want to look at this.'

Anna pushed her way to the front of the murmuring, shoulder-shoving men. Same height as some of them, smaller than others, she found her gap, edged in. The box was full of uncut banknotes.

'All tenners. I'd say several hundred thousand pounds' worth, easily.' The DI fingered the edge of a sheet. 'High-grade quality, feels right. Like cotton.'

'Whoah, whoah—check out this box.' The cops pounced like kids beneath a Christmas tree.

'Quit pawing everything, lads. We need to get the experts in now.' 'Aye but sir, sir. See this box—it isny even British money. It's bloody pink.' 'Let me in there, you.'

Slowly, tongue protruding, Cruikshanks peeled off one sheet of paper, held it up. Anna could make out a purple-pink landscape, the words: *Reserve Bank of India*. It was a 100-rupee note.

'It's a fucking printing press!' Cruikshanks shook his head. 'Hidden inside a printing press. Jeezo, you've got to hand it to them. I like their style. This has got to be Maguire's place, surely?'

All Anna could see were some computers. 'But where's the plates, where's all the engravings?'

'Don't need them any more.' The detective super was keying furiously on his BlackBerry.

Cruikshanks walked around the table, gazing with unalloyed wonder at his prize. The sugar which would take away the bad taste of multiple murder.

'Aye see, it's all gone electric now. See, with a scanner, you can just take a digital image of the note, then manipulate it on your PC. I'll bet when we get the boys to trawl through all the files on this baby, they'll find some lovely sharp photies of big fat fifties with Her Majesty's regal phizog on, and more with Mr Punjab here, and God knows what else.'

'Why would you want to manipulate the images if you'd copied them?' asked Anna.

'Well, you can white out security features, sharpen up the lines—change the serial numbers even. Then you fire it on to your printer and Bob's your uncle. Oh, mammy. Foreign notes too—we could be talking state-sponsored counterfeiting here.'

State-sponsored counterfeiting was a recent innovation, something the Fraud Squad chap had mentioned the day he came to Govan. Run usually by overseas criminals, these gangs were rich and well-connected enough to access the same type of equipment and craftspeople that made the real, genuine banknotes in their respective countries. There had been suggestions that a Pakistani government printing press in Quetta was churning out large quantities of counterfeit Indian currency. The rupee notes then got smuggled into India, allegedly as part of a plot to destabilise the Indian economy—or to fund terrorist activities.

The DI was shaking his head. 'I hate to burst your bubble, boss, but I don't think we're talking that big. I don't even think this is thon ring the Fraudies were after.' He tapped the printer. 'Where's all the high-tech equipment to make the holograms? Even the printing, I mean: look. You canny use a photocopier and an ink jet to produce shit-hot notes. All they wee dots of ink show up under a magnifying glass. Now, if they had an intaglio printer, you'd get those continuous fine lines.'

'You can get intaglio presses from bloody Hobbycraft,' said Cruikshanks.

'Naw, but those guys were using the real thing, boss. Treasury standard.'

The detective super beckoned them over to another, smaller room Anna had thought was a cupboard. Barely big enough to house the smart black machine that hummed there, slick with the sheen Alice had when she'd just licked herself clean.

'You mean a printer like this?'

Cruikshanks's face grew redder and redder with a joy so unconfined Anna was frightened he'd erupt. 'Boys, I think we've found our professionals

431

right enough.'

Control to DCI Cruikshanks. Are you ready to receive your update yet?

'Oh, sorry hen, sorry. Aye, on you go now.'

Roger, obliged. For your information, MD of Adair Holdings is one Raju Nayar.

'Well,' said Cruikshanks. 'Bugger me.'

*   *   *

After lunchtime when Anna made it into work. She should be knacked, but she was buzzing. Probably didn't need more coffee, but she made a cup anyway, drank it while she was reading her emails. Among them, one curt missive from Jenny Heath:

Anna. Cat has got vet's tomorrow. Getting stitches out (long story). They will be sedating her because she bites like buggery. Will need to be picked up at 5, but I have prior appointment with the Sadie Simpson School of Dance (don't ask). Vet is in Govanhill, so not that far from you. If you still want junkie boy to see her, why don't you pick cat up from vet's, take her home/to junkie's pad and he can see her then (will leave her basket at vet's). I will make arrangements to collect her from you later that evening.
Jenny

Anna replied right away.

OK. Ta. Send me details of address. Take it I don't have to pay vet bill??!

432

She was surprised there had been no contact from either Johnny or Mrs H. Were they pretending she didn't exist? A strategy, perhaps, to isolate and corral her into making more mistakes? With Johnny up at Govan now, Anna presumed she was meant to run the whole of Giffnock office. Fine, she could do that standing on her head, but it would be nice to have been told to what degree she was free to make decisions, or if she was required to filter everything back and forth to Govan, awaiting Johnny's permission before she ordered more pens for the stationery cupboard.

Then again, that was Anna being as arrogant as Alice, assuming she was the centre of everybody else's world as well as her own. The senior management at Govan were no doubt too diverted with recent developments to give any thought to Anna Cameron. Mr Nayar had already been brought in, as had Callum MacLeod. Of course MacLeod had interests in more than one security firm: All Star for mobile patrols, Pinnacle for on-site guards and escorts. He appeared as outright owner for All Star, and as a security consultant for Pinnacle.

'He couldny even spell the word,' Cruikshanks had grumbled. But dig down far enough, and MacLeod's money was in both firms. It was not, however, in Adair Holdings.

'I just canny see it.'

Scuffing his feet across the dirty printworks floor, Cruikshanks had not been at all convinced. 'Raju Nayar—the guy's loaded in his own right, with his businesses, his properties, his restaurants. Not to mention his brother's position—you know, the councillor. Why would he want to risk all that?

Plus,' Cruikshanks oozed despair, 'he was meant to be sponsoring the SPRA angling competition.'

'There's loaded and there's loaded, boss,' said the DI who'd first opened the box of notes. 'You add up all the sheets of cash in here—bearing in mind that's just what's stacked on the shelves, multiply it by the production line they've probably been churning out in the two months or so since the Fraud Squad were first alerted, and my guess is you could be talking millions. Notwithstanding whatever overseas scams they're also involved in.'

'I know, I know. But Nayar? He just disny seem the type, know? I canny imagine him sullying himself wi dodgy money. The guy's got too much class for that.'

'Aye, and how cheap does class come?'

'So, are you gonny be telling me next that he's been doing dodgy business deals with wee Ronnie-call-me-Elvis too? Because the Maguires are definitely part of this—I bloody know it. And if they are, so's poor old Cassie.'

'Well, it's an interesting angle,' said the detective super. 'And a worrying one too. We need to find the Maguires asap. If the same person or persons who abducted Cassandra Maguire have just deliberately asphyxiated four more people, then who's to say the Maguires aren't next in this vendetta? Tom, you say neither of the Maguires has any previous convictions?'

'None.'

'And have you gone right, right back? Checked everything about their backgrounds, family feuds, jailbird fathers, any child protection issues—'

'They've nae kids.'

'No, I mean with regards to themselves, when

Sheena and Ronnie were younger. The fact it's Maguire's mother who was abducted lends itself to that avenue of enquiry, does it not?'

'Aye.'

'And?'

'And, *boss,* we've already done all that. Did it days ago, in actual fact. Sheena Maguire née Galloway. Born at Bridgeton Cross. Parents Alice and Patrick. Attended Our Lady of St Francis School in Charlotte Street, went on to College of Commerce . . .'

'Aye, alright Tom. Alright.'

'Ronald Xavier Maguire. Born in Gallowgate. Parents Cassandra and Alfred. Attended St Mungo's Academy—'

'I said alright.'

'There *was* one point of interest here. Maguire's father, Alfred, was the subject of a sudden death enquiry in the Sixties. Family had been camping, up at Loch Lomond, and father and son had taken a wee dinghy out on the loch. Short version is, they got into some trouble, and the father drowned. Wee Ronnie was recommended for a bravery award.'

'What age would Ronnie have been?' asked Anna.

'Twelve, fourteen I guess.'

'Shite age to lose your dad. And see it happen too.'

In that context, Ronnie's mother-love made a bit more sense to Anna. Funny how families evolve. Once a part is excised, other pieces shift and loosen, harden and ossify over the wound. They may cling together or float apart, but they'll never be the same.

The detective super had massaged his throat again, the drip, drip, drip of the sprinklers stabbing like little knives.

'Tell me, what lines came up when your guys did enquiries into the Maguires' customers?'

'Did? Are still doing, more like. Maguire runs two scrapyards and six garages, each garage with their own car-hire office attached—have you any idea how many invoices and customers we're having to wade through? Every limo out on a hen night, a school prom, a wedding—it's a nightmare. Not helped by the fact the gruesome twosome have done a runner, so canny give us any pointers. And that Sheena is a right wee scrubber, as it happens.'

'Ho, time out.' Anna had clapped her hands, sharp as a schoolmistress. 'I'm sorry, but—'

Cruikshanks dunted her in the side. He had right jaggy elbows for a fat bloke. 'Cool your jets, doll. She runs a cleaning firm.'

'I know that, *doll*.' She dunted him back. 'I was joking—you already told me. *Ha*.'

'Ha, yourself.'

Normal service resumed, she could get back to business, balanced in the banter of being big tough guys.

'Thank you, Punch and Judy,' said the super. 'Well, okay, but let's be a bit more targeted now. Don't waste time interviewing each of their individual customers—look through all their invoices for any links with Nayar's businesses instead—and with MacLeod too. Has he ever worked for Maguire, or has Maguire done business with him? I mean, what about vehicles—has MacLeod ever used Maguire's cars? Or catering? Maguire hires out vans too—maybe Nayar's used

436

him for something in connection with his restaurants. Or Sheena might even clean some of Nayar's premises.'

'Or why don't I just ask Mr Nayar when we bring him in?'

'Or why don't we do both, Tom?'

The super had smiled. Cruikshanks had not.

And Anna had returned to Giffnock. Back in the suburbs and out of the loop. She had no real desire to work in CID, but it annoyed her when the door was literally shut, and you could see talking heads through the frosted glass, but couldn't hear them, couldn't join in. Being a cop gave you a licence to pry, and it irked to have that licence revoked by men in suits and too much hair gel. She yawned, glanced back at the screen.

Meeting at . . . blah
Request for . . . blah
Memo to . . . blah

Anna should go and see Carol Jenkins. The Meadows staff would have informed Carol that Manju was dead, but Anna wanted to tell her how sorry she was. She truly, truly was. It was a spontaneous thought, a kind one—and one instantly revoked. Madness to consider visiting Carol, with Lucy Manning stalking Anna for signs of a guilty conscience.

She called up a new Word document. A letter would be safe though; no face to face, just a finely typed sheet of her deepest sympathies, because she'd already seen Carol's eyes cloud at the presumption of Manju's death. And who else could Anna say sorry to, anyway? Aye, a sheet of incriminating outpourings, that could be cut and pasted to make any quote you wanted.

437

Do you want to save the changes?
No.

It was only when she'd read through all her emails that Anna realised the computer had been switched on when she entered the office. Anna never left it on; it was her nod to being green. That and saving newspapers in a teetering heap she never managed to recycle. She remembered, absolutely, that she had turned the computer off last night. Neither had she left her in-tray in such neat, small bundles either. And her chair had been adjusted, she could feel the backrest lower, her feet more flat on the ground. Had a wee Brownie been in and tidied up?

'Oh!'

Anna's door swung open, firm like it had been kicked. A woman stood there, hands full of papers, a cellophane-wrapped sandwich held in her teeth. It was Claire Rodgers, and she had gone all blotchy. The marbling started on her neck, visibly spreading like a virus, up her throat, along her chin.

'Hello, Claire. Can I help you?'

'I . . .' The sandwich dropped. 'I thought you were off sick.'

'Did you?' Anna clasped her hands, on *her* desk. *Her* desk. 'Well, clearly I'm not.'

'No . . . I . . . sorry, Mrs Hamilton told me you were off sick.'

'So you just thought you'd move in? Keep my seat warm, maybe?'

Too far, Anna.

Claire was retreating, not physically, but on the defensive, the tight lock of her features like the sound had been turned down, curtains drawn.

438

'The divisional commander told me it was likely you'd be off long term, and that I'd be acting up for the duration.'

'I see. Only problem is—no one told me that, Claire. So, much as I'd like to help you out . . .' Anna raised her eyebrows as she took in all the room, then got up, out of her chair—*you're milking this now; yeah, well, if I don't, she will*. Finishing with hands flat on the desk, the appearance of firmness, and a conspiratorial whisper: 'I think you're fucked.'

'You don't need to be rude to me.'

'Don't I? Don't I, Claire? Is that me *bullying* you again, eh?'

Small and neat, like a child ponderously carrying her cargo, Claire continued into the room, placing the papers on Anna's desk.

'These will be for you then, ma'am.' Her eyes were averted, face pale, drawn-in as a polis geisha.

'Don't worry, Claire. Mrs Hamilton's told me how upset you were.'

'I—'

'But *why*? Why did you set me up like that?' Anna would nip away now till she reached bone.

'It wasn't intentional, I promise. She— Hamilton—just . . . guessed.'

'What, she guessed that I "bullied you" into covering for me?'

'No, I never said bullying. She kind of implied it.'

'And you didn't bother correcting her?'

Claire met her, stare on stare. An honesty there that was appalling. 'She kept going on about how well I was doing, what a great career I had ahead of me. I—'

'It's alright.' Anna felt the wrong-shaped back on her seat rub as she sat down. A fullness in her throat, a nasty taste she recognised.

'You know, I'd probably have done the same, at your age and service. Because you do, don't you? You keep thinking that it's just this once, and it's for the greater good after all, and if you don't *carpe diem*, well, someone else will instead.'

'It wasn't like that. She made me think . . . well, maybe I'd been a bit rash. I mean, I do respect you, Anna, but—'

A flat smile. 'But, when you come to think of it, I'm a bit of a lame duck, eh? Not really someone you should pin your star to. I understand, I really do. Good luck to you; I reckon you'll make an excellent chief inspector, Claire. But not in my office, and not today.'

'I'm sorry.' Snap, snap of the papers being shuffled into hospital-corner order. Claire's slim fingers flashing wedding ring, engagement ring, a clean star of diamond.

'Good for you. Now, was there anything else?'

Claire opened her mouth, then closed it again. She gathered the paperwork up to her breast. 'I finished the report on Fraser Harris. You know, the one Mr O'Hare asked me to do on all his recent arrests.'

'And?'

She hates this. The stillness of their bodies saying everything is fine, that they are two women in an office discussing business. Calm air, which hears no evil, speaks no evil, the cheat of it, when what she wants to do is punch Claire's chisel-perfect face. See the façade smash like Anna's window did, then brush Claire up in little, bright

440

lumps, send her tinkling into trash.

'Two things. Firstly, we've traced this chap Sparky. His real name's Kasim or Christopher Murray. Not long moved to Glasgow, lives with his mother in the council scheme in Busby.'

'Anyone spoken to him?'

'Not yet. I was going to send a cop out, until I noticed this.' Claire leafed through a couple of pages, then laid them back on the desk, turning them round so Anna could see. 'Mr O'Hare asked me to check right to when Fraser was in the Support Unit. Took forever, but I went back six months at least. Ran each name that came up through the PNC, checking for aliases, any known associates.'

Of course you did. Thorough beyond belief.

'And then I saw this. Couple of months ago now, Fraser arrested one Alan Murray, for joyriding and possession.'

'Murray? Same as Sparky? Shit, it's the same boy, isn't it? Just giving different aliases.' Anna leaned back. 'Well, there you go; there's your motive. Fraser jails Sparky, Sparky starts stalking Fraser.'

'*No,* ma'am. Just *look.* Look at the alias that came up when I fed Alan Murray's name in.' Her pointing finger covered the actual bit Anna was supposed to be seeing.

'Claire, can you mo—'

Caught up in the excitement of her own revelation, Claire motored on, oblivious. 'It was never on the original report to the fiscal. Typical Support Unit: scoop 'em up, bash out a quick résumé then roll on to the next Dodge City.' She gave a wry smile, the corners spreading as if she

441

was trying to include Anna in the joke.

'Claire, can you move your finger please?'

One slim, manicured nail shifting. One printed line becoming clear.

ALAN MURRAY/Also known as ALAN SABIR MURRAY/Also Known as SABIR AZIZ

*   *   *

'*Did I tell you how much I hate disobedience?' The Mirror Man unrolls a nylon stocking, begins to stretch it over the guard's face. 'Almost as much as I hate stupidity and greed.'*

It has gone beyond fear, now.

'*Cruelty . . . well, cruelty is another matter.' His hands are on the guard's raw and blackened shoulders, massaging flesh. Through the mesh of nylon, the Mirror Man licks the guard's ear. His breath is perfumed, not unpleasant. Drawing lips from teeth.*

'*Cruelty's actually quite honest, when you think about it. It's just saying what we all feel. That is the truth of us, isn't it? Rage.'*

'*That's the truth of it, son.' He hears her whispering, although he knows she must be dead. 'See all what you do, what you think even? You canny ever run away fae it, no properly. The monsters aye follow you.'*

It is worse to hear her than to suffer this. The guard watches himself in the Mirror Man's sunglasses. Can see the fibres contorting his features, nose flat and spreading like a boxer's. He remembers that it is broken, that there is a shattered V there, shaped like a beak at the top, then it is all he can feel. Through the numbness; this biting, cloudy pain.

442

The Mirror Man strikes him across the back of his head. 'And I am so fucking angry. So angry now, you wouldn't believe.'

The force of the impact sends him reeling, sends them both reeling, the guard half from his chair, but his arm is still attached . . . to its shoulder and to the cuff. He tries to see his son's face. Does he have a son, he cannot visualise one.

The Mirror Man collects himself, rights the guard so his back is firm once more, into the boiling radiator.

'Let's be honest.' His hand is stroking the guard's cheek. His hand smells of sex. 'For old time's sake, eh? For Auld Lang Fucking Syne. Ssyne.'

He hisses the Ess in a string of angry sibilants. Goes horribly, appallingly guttural. 'Does that no piss you aff? It really hacks me aff, when they pronounce it like a zed. It's an Ess, it's a fucking Scottish Ess.'

The Mirror Man is grabbing some lump at the back of the guard's neck; it is the gusset of the nylons they are tights not stockings he thinks and the Man is using the gusset like a handle, like a dog-lead, forcing the guard's head to nod vigorously in agreement. 'Yeah. You feel it too, I can tell.'

He swings the guard's face into the wall. An agony, an explosion as his nose erupts in blood.

'Can you fucking feel it?'

'Yes!'

'Do you want to die?'

'No.'

'Say it louder, little man. Say it louder.'

'No!'

'Would you do anything to live? Anything at all?'

'Yes, yes,' he sobs. It is gone, all gone his will, his self. He is only blank and rawness and the strike-

443

smash of head on brick.

'You will do me one more task, then I'll let you live. Do you understand? I will let you live and I will let you go.'

He smashes him again.

'Would you like that, little pig?'

'Yes.'

'And what do we say?'

A final smash. 'What do we fucking say, little thief?'

'Thank you.'

'Good man.' The Mirror Man leans in to whisper to him. 'You know, I might even let your boy live too.'

CHAPTER TWENTY-TWO

The lobby smelled of cumin and fried fish fingers. It was small, but smart, with pale grey carpet and lilac walls. A wooden picture hung above the phone, the clear blues and pinks of a gold-bedecked man, his bowed head wrapped in cloth, hands clasping a book.

'Mrs Murray?'

The woman was small, about Anna's age. Shadows for eyes, and dark, damp curls as if she'd just come from the shower. Her complexion was caramel, glowing, and her baggy T-shirt read: *I love New York.*

'If you like.'

An ambivalent accent too. Glasgow, certainly, but the posh south-side Glasgow of elocution lessons and private school, worn slightly frayed by the passage of life, and with a diphthong-lilt Anna could not place. She couldn't place the connections either. If Sabir Aziz had also used the name Murray, the same alias that Sparky used, then who was this woman to him? An aunt, a friend, a random name stolen from an associate in his gang? To a lonely boy, maybe a pretend family was better than none at all.

'I'm sorry. I'm Chief Inspector Cameron, from Giffnock Police Office. I'm looking for Kasim or Christopher Murray. Does he live here?'

'You'd better come in.'

The woman led her into an equally tasteful lounge, at odds with the shabbiness of outside, the dog-shit and the graffiti and next door's weed-strewn drive with its two cars up on bricks.

'Have a seat. I've just made tea. Do you want some?'

'Sure, thanks. Just milk, please.'

Squeaking into the leather couch, raking the room for photographs, football boots, some evidence of a teenage boy. There was none. A gas fire hissed three bars bright, too hot for this small, close room. It was warm outside too, though you'd only know by standing there, in amongst the weight of the air. It was not the light, sharp warmth of spring, but of a brewing. All day it had been muggy, sky tempura-washed, eggshell over pulses of grey. More storms were due.

'Here you go.' The woman passed over a long, thin Mockintosh mug, burning at the lip. Anna blew on it, tried to sip, then let the mug rest on the muffle of her knees.

'Shortbread?'

'No thanks.'

The woman helped herself to a piece, put the

445

plate by the edge of the fire and took a bite. She chewed, waiting.

'I'm sorry to bother you. Like I said, I've really come to see . . .' Anna braved a guess: 'Kasim?'

'He doesn't live here.'

'Oh.' Her tea was still too hot. 'I understood that he did.'

'Not any more.'

'Can you tell me when he left, then? And where he is now?'

'Can you tell *me* what this is about?'

Four times she'd tried to get hold of Cruikshanks. *In a meeting. On the phone. Unavailable.* The appearance of the counterfeit notes, the quiet echoes of Cassie's murder and four freshly dead bodies in the mortuary meant he would be thoroughly engaged for the foreseeable. Driving here, Anna had wondered if she should get in touch with O'Hare instead. Hard, hoick-it-out-with-a-spit O'Hare, not round, soft Johnny any more. But Johnny was an arse, and he was Hamilton's lapdog. Fraser was Anna's responsibility.

'It's about an assault on one of my officers. We believe Kasim may have been involved.'

Mrs Murray creased her already heavy lids, as though a light was shining in her eyes. Considered Anna as she took another bite. Every sway and dip of her, slow and definite.

'You *are* Kasim's mother, aren't you?'

'You're that policewoman in the paper, aren't you? The one they said killed that old lady.'

'Mrs Murray, I'm not here to—'

'I read about the veil thing, too.'

Anna wished that she could find some reason to

lock up Lucy Manning; jail her and her lie-typing fingers.

'You're wrong, you know,' said Mrs Murray. 'To slag it off, I mean.'

'I didn't—'

'It keeps you safe, the veil. Preserves a woman's modesty, protects her from stares.' Mrs Murray lifted her mug. Sniffed the scent of hot tea in a hot room, then put it down without drinking. 'It's probably the only time I felt truly relaxed and comfortable. Walking down the street, people looking at you . . .'

'Look, can we get back to—'

'You can see it two ways.' The woman's gaze drifted to the window. 'It's either a complete subjugation, to God or to your husband. Or it's a proud symbol.' She nodded at Anna. 'Like your uniform, I suppose. I mean, what does that say, those horrible trousers and your bullet-proof vest? That silver nonsense on your hat? It says: This is the respect a woman demands.' She wiped some crumbs from her jeans. 'I tell you, I felt very dignified when I wore the veil. Very respected.'

'Mrs Murray, your son?'

'My son. I have to keep reminding myself of that, Chief Inspector. Son, not sons. I always talked about the boys, but you can't say "the boy", can you? It's not . . . friendly like "boys" is.'

'I'm not with you?'

'When I saw you at the door, I thought you were here about my other son. Sabir.'

'Sabir is your *son*?'

That had been her next question, to ask if Mrs Murray knew Sabir Aziz, if he was connected, related in some way to her son. But not this; never

447

this.

'*Was,* Chief Inspector. Was my son, until a gang of boys stabbed him.'

'I'm truly sorry . . . I didn't realise.'

The sensation of something emptying inside, and she was back there, on her knees in the lane. The night like a blindfold, her jacket, a useless gag catching the blood that was frothing from his mouth, his tears on her hands as she watched him struggle. Confession pounding up, drumming through her ears and out in a roll of clangs and snare-drums.

'I was there when Sabir died, Mrs Murray. I found him, I . . .'

Mrs Murray lurched forward to catch her hand, knocking her cup from table to hearth. It split in two, the half with the handle bouncing on the carpet, staining brown over grey. 'You found him? Did he . . .'

'He didn't suffer, I swear. He was very peaceful. It could only have been moments after . . . the gang had just run away when I got there, and Sabir was lying on the ground.'

'Was he conscious? They never told me, and there's been no trial yet, so I—'

'No, no. It was just like he was sleeping. Hardly a mark on him.' A delicate fabrication. 'I held his hand and he just slipped away.'

'Thank you.' Mrs Murray was kneeling before her. 'Thank you.'

Anna could see the pores on her nose, the grey wires in her hair singing with the electricity that hummed, hidden, in this hot room. Shifting in drifts, a song through her head.

Immortal, invisible God only wise.

448

It was the same song she had sung to Sabir as she held him. It was the hymn from her father's funeral.

Don't take her, Caroline. She's only little. A funeral's no place for a child.

But I need her.

Her mother had said those words. In clear staccato chimes.

'Thank you.' Mrs Murray was weeping down *I love New York*. Anna said nothing, what could she do, other than a gentle tapping on the woman's back? Watching the birds wheel outside as the heat of the fire burned on and on, her right leg getting singed.

Afterwards, more tea, only Anna made it this time, put in extra milk to make it cool and drinkable and let it stand a while on the worktop so she could tear off a piece of kitchen roll, wipe stuff away.

'There you are.'

She sat beside Mrs Murray on the couch, ready to catch if the cup fell again.

'Thank you.'

'Would you like to talk about Sabir?'

'Not really. I . . . it . . . each time I say his name, I see the baby he was. Do you have children yourself?'

Anna shook her head.

'Then it's hard for you to understand. You look at this man, and it's like you see all the layers he ever was—like ghosts. He was my boy, my little man. Walked at nine months, ten teeth by the time he was a year old.' She was rocking slightly in her seat, the tea swishing in her cup. 'You know, this is what I don't understand. The thing with Sabir was

449

that he had many white friends. Well, you'll see by the way he picked and chose his name, that he flitted quite happily from one to the other. My younger son, Kasim—now, he's more confused. Sometimes, I think he hates his whiteness; other times, he'll only answer to Chris. Yet,' Mrs Murray turned her cup, 'he's chosen to go home to India.'

'Really?'

'Well, I helped him. Paid his fare, bought him some new clothes. You see, I know Sabir was up to bad things, but Kasim is a good boy.' She put her cup down, untouched. 'Or he was until his brother died. Then he started to get in tow with that stupid gang—'

'Ubu Roi?'

'Yes.'

'Mrs Murray, do you know why Kasim would attack one of my cops? I think he followed him home, kicked him to the ground—him and another boy.'

'I'm afraid I don't know any of Kasim's friends. Not since we moved here.'

'From India?'

'No. Crail. How come everyone thinks I've been living in India? It took your lot two days to even let me know my son was dead.'

Anna frowned. 'I'm sorry, I'm not really involved with the case. I think it was Sabir's neighbours . . . I mean, Sabir never stayed here with you, did he? We don't have him listed at this address.'

'No. When his father and I . . . well, Sabir chose to stay with him. I—me and Kasim that is, only came back to Glasgow recently.'

'And why was that?'

450

She reached for her cup again. 'To keep an eye on Sabir. I know he was a grown man, but his father had moved down south—'

'I thought his dad was dead?'

'No, no. Just buggered off to follow his latest wee tart. Sabir didn't let on for ages that his dad had gone. I don't even know how he was paying the rent . . . Well,' she sighed, 'that's not strictly true. I knew he was up to something. I knew he was in trouble too.'

'What kind of trouble?'

'Well, you'll know better than me—gangs, petty crime, drugs. But it was more the people he was working for. I think he was scared of them. He'd done something wrong—wouldn't tell me what, but he said it wouldn't stop at being sacked.'

'What wouldn't?'

'I don't know. He never told me.'

'Was it to do with the boy that killed him? Gordon Figgis? He lives quite near to you.'

Mrs Murray frowned. 'No, I don't think so. That's what Kasim was so angry about. He kept saying that Sabir had been stitched up. He swore neither he nor Sabir knew this Figgis boy at all—I mean Sabir lived in Pollokshields, he was hardly ever here. Kasim tried to talk to Sabir's friends, you know the ones who said Sabir had a knife that night, but they wouldn't have anything to do with Kasim. Just told him to leave it, or he'd "get the same".'

'And what did you and Kasim take that to mean?'

Mrs Murray's toes were moving up and down in her slippers, little frantic bumps. The cup going round and round in her hands. Anna wanted to press her still in her seat, force it up to her lips. *I made you tea, good tea. Drink it while it's warm.* But the jittering was a necessary precursor to warming up her answer. Anna must be patient.

'I thought it meant that he'd be killed too?' Then, more decisive, sure of this at least, 'That's when I decided to put Kasim on a plane back home.'

'But not you?'

She finally stopped fidgeting with her cup. 'I'm not so welcome there. I chose to live in a different family, unfortunately. My mother was right, as usual. Ach, but you never listen to your parents, do you?'

Anna smiled, a neutral nothing of a smile. 'So,' she said, 'the sense you got from Sabir's friends was that they didn't want to talk about the incident, that they maybe had something to hide?'

'I think so.'

Anna needed to speak to Cruikshanks again. She'd always had a bad feeling about the apparent resolution of the Aziz murder. Nobody concedes defeat that easily, especially not a stab-daft wee laddie like Gordo Figgis who would relish his day in court. All that fame and notoriety, yet another forum in which to strut his stuff. Nah, kids like Gordo would *want* that; they had no common sense to prevail. And yet Cruikshanks had been virtually promised by Figgis's lawyer that a charge of culpable homicide would be acceptable to all. Anna would make Cruikshanks re-examine the Aziz file, in the light of what Mrs Murray had told her. He wouldn't like it, the prising open of something he thought was done and dusted—but tough.

452

'One thing I should have told you.' Mrs Murray spoke quickly, all the words sliding like they were running downhill. 'A day later, after Kasim had come back from seeing Sabir's friends, he got a phone call. He didn't tell me who it was, but he rushed out of here like a bat out of hell, didn't come back for hours. When I asked him, all he would say was, 'Business.' And that terrified me, the thought that he might be getting drawn into whatever Sabir had been involved with. But I remember when he was dropped off, I looked outside. It was some black car, and I'm pretty sure it was a white boy driving. I was so relieved that he wasn't Indian, because then I thought that it couldn't be anything to do with Ubu Roi.'

'This white boy—was he blond?'

'Em . . . maybe. It was hard to tell.'

'So that reassured you? That the driver was white?'

'Not really. Hey, I'm an Indian mother—we're worse than Jewish ones. I still wasn't convinced, so I snuck out Kasim's mobile phone while he was asleep, looked at the calls he'd received.'

'And?'

'I was too scared to phone. I just wrote the number down—he'd had two calls that day, both from the same number. I don't know why I did it; I mean, I've done nothing with the number. It was just in case, you know? I wanted to have it in case anything happened to Kasim as well.'

Mrs Murray's toes were crabbed again. Anna could see bulges rearing through thin velour.

'When was this, Mrs Murray? What night was it when Kasim got dropped off in the black car?'

'Em . . . I think it was a Thursday or Friday. In

453

fact . . . yes, I know exactly when it was, because I'd been at my friend's that day for lunch, for her birthday. So it would have been the Thursday, then. Thursday the seventeenth of March.'

Same night Fraser was attacked.

'I don't suppose you still have the phone number?' Anna asked.

'Of course I do.' She heaved herself up, pushing at some invisible weight, for she was only spindle-thin herself. An old-woman shuffle across the room, her sharp efficiency of earlier all washed out. She went to a drawer in the sideboard. 'I'm not stupid.'

It was a Glasgow number, the 0141 code giving it away.

'Do you want me to phone it? You can speak, though. I don't want anything to do with them.'

Anna took the notepad from her. 'No, I'll use my mobile—just in case they do 1471.' She keyed in the numbers, let it ring. Convinced it would be the Tammy Lin pub, and Frankie's dulcet tones that greeted her. Eventually a bored female voice answered:

'Hullomandyspeakin. Lap It Up for the best time in town. How can Ah help yi?'

Anna pressed the red button, cut the call.

*   *   *

Govan was not the obvious choice for a lap-dancing club. Not city centre, not glitzy, not *known*. It was a land of proud memories, of ancient faith and hog-backed stones, of shipyard workers and philanthropists who bequeathed parks and libraries and hope to the poor. It was a land of

454

unemployment, of blue and red-brick Ibrox Stadium; half of Glasgow's footballing Old Firm. It held the city's only Country and Western music hall, the occasional stranded restaurant, forgotten streets and squares of grimy sub-let Victorian townhouses waiting to be rescued, and a glorious town hall, boarded up and left to crumble. This was a burgh, a town in its own right that had been eaten up by Glasgow, the bones picked clean, discarded on the south bank of the Clyde until the city decided it was hungry again. And it was; it was Govan's *turn* again. Or the beginnings of it at least. The futuristic Science Centre gleamed like a silver hill, the BBC had forsaken the douce sandstone of the West End for a postmodern box with an empty belly and a Govan postcode, and a jaunty new Squinty Bridge linked south to north—which was just as well, because the Beeb folk still had to cross the river to get their deli sandwiches.

It was 'a hauf and a hauf' place right enough. So why not young girls in patent boots and sad, eager breasts, employed to dance in a dingy, thin townhouse that looked on to Elder Park? In their fag breaks, the girls could gaze over to the statue of Isabella Elder, a woman way ahead of her time, who dedicated her life and fortune to promoting the advancement and education of Glasgow's females, freeing her sisters to be doctors and teachers and hot-to-trot babes.

The door to Lap It Up was, of course, locked. From the steps, Anna could see inside one of the property's bay windows. Flaking paint, grubby nets and a lounge of sorts, with comfy chairs, a desk and a phone. Moody uplighters in unimaginative red. A girl sat behind the desk, head down, finger moving up a list or book of some sort. A sharp rap on the glass made the wee lassie rise, her ponytail bobbing as she peered out, grimaced. Anna rapped again.

Eventually, the girl came to the door. As she opened it there was a pulse of thumping music, a glimpse of figures on the stair.

'Aye?' She tugged on the pelmet pretending to be a skirt.

The day was brooding, but still mild, so Anna had left her lurid yellow jacket in the boot. Other than that, she too was in full uniform: black trousers, black T-shirt, black stab-proof vest. Natty bowler hat, solid and reinforced, far better than the squashy white vinyl of yesteryear, but *still*, a bowler hat—a round, fat thing for song and dance, for Charlie Chaplin and soft, southern business types. Not the stern, handsome, gloss-peaked cap the male cops wore. Were women's heads a different density, a different shape? Her hat itched like buggery, an unyielding rim which was migraine-tight. Still, she kept it on, kept staring back.

'I want to speak to your boss.' She moved up a step.

'Why?'

Anna could see a wodge of pink gum rolling in the girl's mouth.

'None of your business. What's your name?'

The girl popped her gum. 'Eh, none of *your* business. Whit's yours?'

Anna took her by the elbow, propelled her, gently enough, through into the shiny pink hall. You could *feel* the music here, throbbing floor and walls in dull, wild roars. 'Don't even think about

being cheeky to me, dear. Now, I'll ask again—
what is your name?'

'It's Althea.'

'Okay, Althea, well you totter off and tell your
boss that there's a Chief Inspector Cameron here.
And I want to see them, now.'

The girl regarded her, all angles and folded
arms, gum going off snap-crackle-and-pop. Her
legs were bare, badly tinted, the tan a tie-dye until
it got to the ankles where it gave up altogether,
ceding to a nasty bruise on one leg and a swallow
tattoo on the other.

'Boss is busy.'

'Althea, I'm warning you—'

'Naw, seriously. Won't be long but.' The twinkle
of a sidelong grin. 'You can wait if you want.'

'I planned to, anyway.'

Althea sniffed, wiped her nose on the back of
her hand. 'Through here, then.'

The girl led her up one flight of stairs, and
straight to the heart of the noise. A broad black
and pink den that was alive with bump and bass
and thud, silver studs of fractured light spinning
cats'-eyes from a mirror ball, all sweat and scent
and tom-cat sprayings. As her eyes became
accustomed to the flashing dark, Anna could make
out low tables, chairs grouped in semi-circles,
leopard-skin divans round the wall. Girls in
matching leopard-print or zebra-stripe pants—
that's all they were, just pants, pants on legs with
vertiginous heels and matching animal-skin ears,
serving drinks to the men sat on the chairs and the
divans, some who were sprawled, made only of
eyes and crotch, others laughing, others flushed.
One or two with uneasy grins, one flat out and

457

pished as a fart. Talking, swilling, munching crisps—and gawping at the stage. Anna scanned the room—no sign of Avalon. She would remember his pockmarked face. If he wasn't in this stinking shit-hole, then why had the girl brought her in here?

Anna turned to ask, but Althea was moving through the throng, closer to the stage. It would be insane to follow. The girl looked back to see where Anna was, held up her hand. Was Anna to wait by the door? At least she was in some kind of alcove, barely visible in the gloom. She took off her hat; pressed herself deep into the fabric wall. God help her if the lights went up at any point. Anna shouldn't even be in the club. She should have contacted the Deputy SDO at Govan, and asked him to send a cop up. *Two* cops. And before, even, she had done that, she should have written one of her nice, planned lists. Thought through exactly what she wanted to ask Avalon, and why. Did you get my cop beaten up? In fact, see while we're at it—did you procure the murder of Sabir Aziz? She should have done some research on Lap It Up, got back-up, run the whole thing by Cruikshanks and Divisional Intelligence. In fact, she wasn't even sure if Avalon *did* own this place. She'd just barrelled out of Mrs Murray's and driven straight down, assuming everything but the address of the club, which she had checked en route.

Anna leaned further into the wall. Ach well. Apparently she had a 'history of controversy'. She'd wait and see who Althea brought forth, and take it from there.

A guy at the bar took advantage of the lull as one song faded and another revved up. Cupping

458

his hands round his mouth, he bawled at the stage: 'Ho! Get on with it, doll! Am needing hame for ma dinner!'

Anna hadn't realised at first that anyone was there. The girl on stage was crouched low, cobra-flicking what looked like a tail; a long, pale straw and bushy thing. Humping empty air, writhing so her bethonged backside winked at every aspect of the room. No one could say that Lap It Up didn't give good butt. Then she arched her back, her arse, rolling carefully up like they tell you in Pilates. First your waist, then your shoulders, unfurling so your head comes up last and, as it did, she flung her hair away from her face, tresses cascading down her back in hanks as dirty-yellow as the tail, which she was drawing between her legs, rubbing it back and forth, the music booming louder, and then she pulled it, hard, so the tail broke off. With it went her G-string. A cheer of approval flared, a grown man jumping to catch the tangle of animal hair and shiny net. She writhed a little more, gyrating and crouching, a flapper-dance of legs; and now it was the turn of her bra, two spangled triangles which she stretched round an old boy's neck, his nose pressed full to her cleavage, her bare arse being slapped by a guy at the next table. A wriggle, a twirl and both were free, the old man triumphant, the stripper blank, striding back to the low stage as the music slowed. Her timing was impeccable. Posing hands on hips, she fluttered eyes painted blue, gold and green—but the most shocking colour was her pink hairless groin. The woman stood completely still, smiled for the first time, and blew a kiss. Then slowly, slowly, she snaked a single finger from her lips to her breast to her belly to her crotch. Anna's mouth went dry as the woman paused, then slid her finger through her labia, like a slow transaction on a credit card machine. She made circles with her hips as the crowd showed their appreciation.

'Get it up ya, ya hoor!'

'Come and sit on me, doll!'

The woman pouted, then flourished her hand aloft. As she walked naked from the stage, she traced the soiled digit across the face of an admirer, who, dear God, tried to suck it. Anna was still holding her hat. If push came to shove, she could puke into that.

Rather than going backstage, the woman seemed to be making straight for Anna, Althea scurrying at her side, whispering. Anna started searching desperately for an obliging hole to open up (not *that* one again, dear God, no). A naked woman walking through a room of randy drunks, the whiteness of her skin a spotlight, swivelling every head to follow her luminous passage, which was directly aimed at Anna.

'Oh ho, boys—we're getting a polis wumman next.'

'Magic. Wanna see ma truncheon, doll?'

'Way-hay. Show's your sussies, hen!'

The stripper drew level with Anna, spat words from the side of a thin, thin mouth. 'There's nae frigging backstage in here. Follow me oot when Charlene and Avi come in.'

'Who?'

The door opened, 'Walk Like an Egyptian' blared, and two dark-skinned girls bobbed forwards in a cloud of veils and clashing gold discs. One of them wore a stole which wound loosely

460

round . . . Anna looked again. The stole had just moved. It was a snake, yellow eyes fixed on Anna, face to scaly face as she squeezed herself out of the door, back into the peace of the hall.

'In here.' The stripper stood in an open doorway, shrugging on a robe. Althea had disappeared.

'Why?'

The woman put a cigarette to her lips, cracked a match down the door frame and held the flame to her mouth. Two puffs and a blow, red tip and narrowed eyes against the smoke. 'Althea said you were wanting the boss.'

Up close, the stripper was older than Anna had realised. Wearing well enough, but cellulite dimpled her skinny thighs in pockets the texture of tripe. Her teeth were yellowed, skin thin and creasing round her eyes and mouth, set with a hardness that was baked-on, which no amount of scrubbing would ever clean. Sometimes, when it came to interviewing women, you could go for the sympathy vote, claim a common alliance that would open doors and invite garrulous responses. Anna would get nowhere with a woman like this.

'Nah, I'll just wait, thanks. I'm looking for the organ grinder, no the monkey.'

'Fuck you, doll. I *am* the boss. So it's me or it's cheerio.'

Her gown was loose at the front, a nipple peeking disconcertingly close to Anna. The stripper was tall, must be six feet in her heels, and wore her body like a favourite outfit.

'If you're the boss—why were you up there . . . dancing?'

She grinned. 'I like to keep my hand in. And it's

461

a good stress-buster. Straight up. Better than yoga any day.'

'I'll take your word for it.'

'You should try it, hen. Work out some of they worry-lines you've got. I tell you, nothing freer than dancing bollock-naked with a crowd of tossers bursting their flies for you.'

'If you say so . . . Miss?'

'Lori. Lorna MacLeod.'

'Okay, Lori. I'm Anna, and I'd like to ask you a few . . .'

Lori had sprawled into a chair, one leg draped across the arm, the tautness of the silk gown causing the cord to unknot, the gown to fall away.

'Sorry—would you mind doing up your dressing gown?'

A broad smile. 'How? Never seen a grown woman naked? You get undressed in the dark or something? This is my work gear, doll—an I'm at ma work. You were saying?'

Anna kept her eyes above waist height. She knew her face was hot, felt stiff and clumsy in the weighted vest and non-stretch cargo pants, the pockets in all the wrong places.

'Does Dougie Avalon ever work here?'

'Frankie? That creepy wee cunt? No way. He's barred fae here. Absolutely, a lifetime bar. He's got mair hands than an octopus, him.'

'But you do know him?'

'Who disny?'

'Okay then, do you know a Sabir Aziz?'

'A what?'

'Young lad, goes by the name of Sabir Aziz.'

'Never heard of him.'

'Also known as Alan Murray. Good-looking lad,

aged about nineteen. Black hair, brown eyes?'

Carefully, Lori pulled the gown across her body, masking herself in shiny satin. Brushed the wrinkles smooth all down her elevated leg. 'Nah. Don't think so.'

She reached for a glass of wine that sat on the fake-teak trolley between them, the kind of Sixties affectation you would wheel in to serve drinks from, usually accompanied by maraschino cherries and an ice bucket in the shape of a pineapple. Beside the glass was a little carved box, full of business cards. Anna took one out.

Lap It Up dance club.
Asian Babes a speciality.

Cards that Anna had seen before somewhere, had held, had read.

The name sprang, ringing and bold as sales on a toy cash register. Anna caught it, sharp, before it sank back down and was lost.

'And what about Jazz? What's his involvement here?'

'Jazz.'

'Aye, *Jazz*. Jazz Chaddha. I understood he owned this place?'

That was what Fraser had said—and it looked like he'd been right. Pink blotches spread across Lori's cheeks. She took another swig of wine, set the glass back down.

'Well, it's a kind of joint arrangement.'

'How do you mean?'

'Jazz is . . . eh, helping us out with a wee cashflow hiccup right now. But he's very much a . . . a sleeping partner.'

463

'Is that right?'

'Och, piss off. No way would I touch him with a bargepole.'

'Why's that then?'

'Cause I'm a happily married woman.' She crossed her legs, swinging the draped one down and over in a gesture of respectability. Unfortunately, the movement let her breasts escape again. 'You married, Chief Inspector?'

Anna leaned forward. *Those tits don't scare me now, doll.* This close, you could see the shelf, the unnatural fullness of silicone, a sore stretching of puckered flesh. It must hurt, heaving two plastic bags of jelly straining in a hammock of your own, thin skin. Not clever, not clever at all. Just big.

'To go back to Jazz,' she said. 'He has an investment in Lap It Up?'

The business cards; it was all pouring in now, splashing bright as a penny dropping. Thinking on her feet, thinking as she was speaking, the one feeding the other. The person Sabir worked for, the person who had been angry with him, was *Chaddha*. Sabir had been stopped in the car by Fraser, Sabir had led Fraser to *Chaddha*. The person who had got Sabir killed, who was still trying to punish Fraser for who, for what? Was *Chaddha*.

Damping her lips with her tongue, beginning again. 'Jazz got these new business cards printed up when he took over, and Alan—or Sabir—worked for him. In fact, it was Sabir who delivered these cards to the club, wasn't it Lori?'

'Huvny a clue.'

'Och, c'mon. You must know the name. Poor boy was murdered only a few weeks later.'

'Is that right? Canny say I heard.'

'So where can I get hold of Jazz, Lori? I'd really like a chat with him.'

Lori lifted her arms above her head, straight and stretching. Doing that subtle-gulping thing with her mouth so that a yawn would come. 'Dunno. He sometimes pops in here for a drink on the way hame. Takes a very close interest in the welfare of our girls, so he does. Failing that, you could try his hoose, I guess.' A mobile phone began to trill, faint and distant. 'I've really got fuck all to do with him. He's a kind of necessary evil at the moment, that's all.' She picked up a brown, squashy handbag. ' 'Scuse me, I'd better get that.'

Once Lori was finished with her call, Anna would ask if there was a back way out. Slip away before the club got any busier, run to Cruikshanks and spill her guts. Now the sand had shifted, and she was sinking a little deeper in, it was obvious this had been a stupid idea, coming here on her own. The dressing room had a long window, covered only by toile. She shifted the material to see out into the street. It was fairly quiet; a woman walking a little dog, a taxi passing. A glossy BMW pulling up across the road. If she nipped out now, even at the front—

'You're joking me.' Lori jumped from her chair, caught Anna's shadow, and fell silent. Began to whisper urgently as she made for the door. 'Don't say a fucking word. Tell him *I'll* phone the lawyer.'

Anna pretended to be engrossed in the street, ears straining for every last syllable. She watched the driver emerge from the BMW, saw him unfold something slim and black. Clocked him slide on daft sunglasses in the twilit street as he shook out

465

his too-long hair. A Govan superstar, wearing shades in the dark. Flashing like fireworks beneath the streetlamp.

Sabir had been stopped by Fraser, Sabir had led Fraser to Chaddha and Chaddha—this man who was striding towards Lap It Up like he owned the place, which indeed he did, was the same man who had sat by Nayar's side that night at Coriander. Chaddha was Nayar's son-in-law.

CHAPTER TWENTY-THREE

Anna could hear Chaddha coming up the stairs, grunting orders, demanding food. The reverberating music had stopped, air poised as the whole house held its breath. A strong smell of pies or pastry was curling under the door, right through the cracks in the plaster. They must have stopped for an interval. Seriously. Too much joy to bear if you had to cope with a hot pie *and* a naked woman at the same time. 'What d'you mean, the fucking polis? See if her man's said anything, I'll bloody kick her cunt in.' A pause. 'Still *here*?'

This was never what she had planned. It was too soon to do or say anything; her thoughts were still slotting into place even as he was thumping along the corridor and Lori was muttering down the phone, the stripper's face twisted, one eye always on Anna, frightened to leave her, frightened to stay. If Chaddha was Nayar's son-in-law, then this whole thing could be, must be, connected with the printworks. Was that what he was afraid of, that Sabir might have led Fraser to a drugs factory? A counterfeit ring? Anna could feel the wall behind her, only tired, peeling paper, no hidden escape routes. This was huge, too heavy for her to carry. They had to gather substantive proof, build a case, find witnesses, and here was Anna waving a big flag and going 'yoo-hoo! The polis is on to you, big boy. But we're giving you plenty of notice, so you can hide all the evidence and jet off to Honolulu.' If she let him go now, that's exactly what he would do.

Lori was in the death throes of her conversation, nodding: 'Yeah, yeah, I've got to go,' inching towards Anna, to do what? Show her out, lock her in? Overdressed and out of her depth, Anna felt her body clenching, felt real, deep fear creeping, that delicious, gut-flipping thrill of hide and seek inside the wardrobe, one finger hooking the door shut, a chink of light, the movement of shadow. You are an observer, but you are not safe; you feel it, slipping velvet on your back, that growing sense of doom, the held-in breath, the creeping silence. Knowing that your back is literally up against it. Nowhere to go but out or wait.

Waiting is worse.

Anna flung open the door. 'Ah, Mr Chaddha.' He had passed the dressing room, was making his way towards the . . . what would you call it? Theatre? Showroom? She knew he had heard her, the shocked brace of his shoulder, the almost-hesitation and then there it was, that other step, the step that said *this* is the way I will play it.

'Ho. Chaddha. I'm talking to you.'

His hand was on the brass plate of the door; she could see the rigidity of his jaw, set in a half-turn.

'Nobody speaks to me like that.' Chaddha tilted

467

his neck further, no longer in profile but full on to Anna. Black shades still hiding his eyes, but she could feel a darkness run up, and down, and across her body. He smiled. 'And certainly not a woman. No even you, gorgeous.' He kept walking, let the door swing back in her face.

She charged after him, seeing a shimmer on the door, the walls, knowing this was a lure, it's what they did, the clever ones, unfurl a red rag, mocking until you were confused, saw mists. Did things you shouldn't do.

Inside it was still busy, men milling at the bar, tits-out women caressing bald spots and offering refreshments, but the lights were a little starker and, with the music off, it was curiously mundane. Especially with the metal catering trolley parading the route that Lori had taken, this time dishing out things that were actually edible. Pies and sausage rolls and nice green peas. She was aware, too, of conversations crunching as she made her way through the room, of Chaddha still walking ahead, shaking the odd hand, patting a pert cheek. Could feel bodies press in on her, separating her from Chaddha, pushing her sideways. A firm hand at her elbow, jostling her towards a wall; someone knocked her hat off, if she bent to retrieve it, they would just knock her head. A second, you only got a second to seize control or sink, and she did sink, slightly at the knees, but only to get some purchase. A breath, a *Fuck you* and she rammed her elbow backwards, stabbing into the belly of the person holding her. As her arm swung back she seized her baton, cracking it open and long. Struck one, maybe two limbs that were nearest, raised a voice from her belly.

468

'Get BACK! Everybody get back now. Anyone lays a single finger on me—in fact, anyone opens their mouth to me—and they will be arrested for obstructing a police officer.'

A shifting, a lull as the sweaty patches and the suits, the dimpled bums and glitter ebbed slightly back, her stick conjuring a moat of space round her and Chaddha.

'Right, I want you all to collect your belongings and walk out of this establishment. Now.'

What was she doing, what was she doing? The crowd stared on, mouths slack, eyes troubled. Were they waiting for her to dance? Anna smashed her stick along the top of the trolley, peas and pies skittering, plates crashing.

'Fucking *now*! Do you hear me?'

She pointed her baton tip at Chaddha's chin. He had frozen midway across the room, his back still to her, fingers twitching. Anna reached for her radio with her free hand, held her magic wand high with the other. 'Chief Inspector Cameron to Control. Request stations to assist at Lap It Up dance club, Elder Park, Govan. Urgent assistance, I repeat, urgent assistance required.'

If not to arrest, she has enough to detain him, surely. In her head, it is very precise, a slow-motion play of when dice crack green baize, clattering high and tumbling. She lets her radio fall back on to her breast, lays hands on Chaddha's shoulder and swings him round. 'Jasveer Chaddha. I'm detaining you under Section Fourteen of the Criminal Procedure Scotland Act.'

One arm lifts, and she goes to strike it, realises he is removing his shades. His eyes are on hers, *inside* them. Brown with amber flecks, joining hers

469

dot to dot; the dot dilating, his iris a black hole through which her own light passes, and he would drain the strength from her knees, buckle them neat as a belt. Anna's eyes consider wavering, but she does not blink; instead she gouges her stick in the crook of his elbow, the handle cracking his funny bone. She forces his arms up his back. Hard.

'Any other of you fuckers still here by the time I've finished cuffing him will be getting the jail and all.'

At last, they start moving out.

*　　　*　　　*

'But what the fucking fucking *fuck* did you think you were doing?'

Johnny O'Hare's hands kept running through his hair. Cruikshanks looked as if he might actually weep. Anna had only seen an expression like that on him once before, recounting the tale of a ten-pound trout that got away.

'I'll tell you what she was doing.' Mrs Hamilton spoke quietly, her bosom swelling in and out. Not looking at Anna, or the two men, but fixed on her ferret wall of fame. 'She's doing her damnedest to wreck this investigation, wreck this division's reputation and wreck my fucking career. Not only are you no on my bus, Cameron, you're no even on the same bloody road, in the same bloody town, in the same bloody country.' She pushed her specs up the bridge of her nose, 'Well, it'll be a walk in the park to get you punted after this. That's if you retain your job at all. Where d'you fancy? Traffic Greenock's very nice this time of year.'

'Ma'am, this maybe isn't the time?' Johnny

murmured.

Let them all expend their energies. Then Anna would reiterate her case.

'But how did you not think to come to us first?' said Cruikshanks. 'We're in the middle of interviewing all the security firm staff just now. Plus we've been liaising with the SCDEA—we're setting in place arrangements to have all four directors of Adair Holdings put under surveillance.'

'Including Mr Nayar?' Anna glanced at Hamilton.

'Of course Mr Nayar. And we would absolutely have added Chaddha to the list too—if only you'd bloody telt us, hen.'

'I tried to phone you several times, Tom.' She put on her pious I-was-only-doing-my job voice. It didn't win you many friends, but it sometimes kept you safe.

'The situation accelerated really quickly. (*Another good phrase. 9.8 for artistic endeavour: officious, yet heartfelt, with a hint of vulnerability.*) I had no idea when I went there that Chaddha might be tied up in the counterfeit operation. I'd gone there to interview him in connection with Fraser Harris—you know, the assault outside his house. But,' Anna hesitated, knowing the onslaught it would invoke, 'I'd also got a tip-off that Chaddha might have been connected with the Aziz murder.'

'Oh, for fucksake. Now she's lost it completely.' Hamilton spoke very loud and very slow: 'Gordon Figgis killed Sabir Aziz. He's all but confessed to it, you stupid, stupid, cow.'

'Yes, but I have reason to believe Chaddha may have ordered the killing.'

471

'You are in total fucking La-La Land, you are.'

'Ma'am—would you at least look at my notes, please?'

'I want nothing more to do with this nonsense. It's bad enough we had to detain Raju Nayar—all the poor man's done is own a derelict property. I mean, anyone could have prised their way into that building: it's been lying empty for years. And now we're beating up his son-in-law and trashing his premises for good measure.'

'Ma'am, I was surrounded. Things were turning nasty.'

'Things aye turn frigging nasty when you're around, Cameron. Well, guess what? Four witnesses have said that *you* went for Chaddha. That you went, and I quote, *absolutely berserk*.'

O'Hare's hand on her shoulder. It felt like the Inquisition. 'Anna, Anna. What were you doing, going in there without any corroboration?'

She could think of no adequate response. Paid great attention to the edge of Hamilton's desk until O'Hare finally moved away. The structure pretended to be solid mahogany, but the corner was starting to curl; an inviting little beckon like dried glue when you were a child, a skin just begging to be peeled.

Cruikshanks breathed deep into his hands, held them for a moment, supporting his head.

'Look, Anna, I take on board everything you've said. And let's set the whole can of worms that is now Sabir Aziz to one side. I need a bottle of malt and a double sausage supper before I can even *think* about that one. But, regarding the rest of it, as it stands at the moment, there is nothing *at all* to connect Chaddha to the drugs factory, or the

472

counterfeiting ring—other than the fact his father-in-law is one of three directors of the company who own the derelict premises.'

'But I think he was there!' Anna blurted. 'Chaddha, I mean.'

'Where?'

'In the crowd at the printworks. Once all the media had arrived.'

Slipping on his shades and watching us.

'And did you note this at the time,' said Hamilton. 'Bring it to the attention of the senior investigating officer?'

'No ma'am, I didn't. I've only just realised it was him.'

A pitying smirk. 'Just after you've Section Fourteened the man for sweet Fanny Adams? My, that's convenient.'

'But I did see him, I'm sure of it. Hanging about in the crowd—Tom . . .'

Cruikshanks gave a tiny shake of his head, the fingers of his left hand splayed in a stop sign.

Anna tried again. Tried not to sound like such a tit. 'Okay, okay. I take your point. But can we not . . . I don't know—search all Chaddha's businesses, seize his computers—there's bound to be designs for notes, files sent from India . . . I don't know.'

'On what possible grounds would we get warrants to do that? Cause the nasty man wouldny stop and talk nice to you when you asked him? Je-sus.'

Anna picked at the edge of the desk.

'The only possible, solid way in we have at the moment is the security firm—the fact their man Dilip was employed at the printworks, that he died there—they canny deny that,' said Cruikshanks.

'Of course, we'll put it to MacLeod that we think Chaddha might be involved, see what he says . . .'

The name triggered a shimmy of wobbly bums and flashing breasts. 'MacLeod?' said Anna.

'Callum MacLeod: owner of All Star and Pinnacle. Mind I telt you?'

'That's right. And what did you say his wife was called again?'

'Lori. Aye, the lovely Lori.'

'That would be the same Lori MacLeod who part-owns Lap It Up with Jasveer Chaddha?'

'So it would.' Cruikshanks looked at Hamilton. 'Ma'am? There's a connection there.'

'We still have to let Chaddha go. He's been detained for three hours now, refuses to speak, and we have absolutely bugger-all concrete to hold him on.'

Anna again made to tempt her with the sheaf of notes she'd written. 'But what about the fact that Kasim Aziz received a call from Lap It Up the night Fraser was attacked?'

'Aye, from Lap It Up—no specifically Chaddha. Unless one of you wants to hop on a plane to India at your own expense—cause I'm no frigging paying for it—and ask Aziz yourself, then we're on a hiding to nothing with this one.' Hamilton unfastened the chain around her neck. It was gold wire, like lots of paperclips had been crushed and twisted together, and she used it to keep her specs in check.

A little moment while they drifted, each in thought. Unravelling here, patching there, Anna nearly skimming off the top layer of veneer. Noticing, too late, that a fragment of chipboard was now exposed. She looked up; no one else seemed to have noticed.

'And where do the Maguires fit in to all this, anyway?' asked Hamilton.

'Are we still sure they do? Why would the Maguires be involved with a cartel of Indian businessmen?' said O'Hare.

Motive—it was the defining factor of every Sunday night crime drama: work out the reason *why* your crime had happened, follow that twisty fibre back through the maze, and you will find the exit, the perpetrator holding the end of the string, head patiently bowed, waiting for his mask to be whipped off. In real life, that was bollocks. Prove *how* it was done, who did it, then—sometimes— you found a why. But the sad reality was that often there was none. And truly, it didn't matter. What did matter was the evidence, the physical fact of a thing—an unbreathing body, a dropped cigarette. A print that said *I was here.*

'What? D'you think the Maguires got all those bum notes in their change or something?' Cruikshanks rubbed his eyes. 'Ach, I'm buggered if I know anything any more. But, I tell you this, I wish we could trace wee Ronnie and Senga to find out.'

'It's Sheena, not Senga,' said Anna.

'Aye, well, she looks like a Senga to me. MacLeod claims he's never heard of the Maguires. But I'd been warming him up nice. I was just about to show him pictures of Cassie on the slab when I had to break off and come down here to this palaver.'

The bloody corner wouldn't stick back down. Anna moved her unwanted notes to cover it. This counterfeiting gang had rarely made mistakes.

Each banknote was beautifully crafted, passed in sufficiently small quantities that they'd never been traced. Had barely even been noticed as they floated into the tide of general currency, washing far into the distance and away from their original source. Until now, when the Maguires had got their profligate mitts on them . . . and there it was. A motive, right enough.

'What if the Maguires aren't part of the ring at all?' said Anna. 'Well, they are, but inadvertently.'

'Meaning?'

'Meaning that they knew about it, that perhaps they helped themselves to some of the proceeds on the QT—but they weren't actively involved with it.'

'Aye . . .' Cruikshanks was playing with a button on his shirt. 'And that would certainly give someone a motive for abducting Cassie, wouldn't it?' He laughed. 'Classic, in fact. If someone's stole your money, you just steal their mammy till they gie it back.'

'Only they'd spent it all,' said Johnny. 'Which would explain why they tried to get that guy to buy his own garage back.'

'So, wait, wait,' said Hamilton. She was looking *at* Anna this time, as opposed to through her. 'Are we saying that whoever we finally pin for the drugs factory and the notes at the printworks also abducted Cassandra Maguire?'

'Yup,' said Anna.

For a second she forgot the ma'am; they were all just people in a room, solving a puzzle and on a roll, pieces flying in, being caught and lobbed and placed, a chain gang of problem-solvers. This was when she loved being a cop, when the team was all and you were part of some great, proud creature that thought with a single mind, that would carry you along with the liveness of it, closing ranks, lifting you up until you were a purer, better version of yourself. It was exhilarating.

Until you remembered the creature was full of shite.

'But I'd go further than that,' said Anna. 'I'd say that that's why the printworks operation was destroyed. Because—'

'. . . Because it was done to get back at whoever killed Cassie.' Cruikshanks grinned, raised a broad, freckled hand in the air. 'High five, Ms C.'

'High five yourself, Mr C.'

'High frigging nothing, the pair of you. How the fuck do you arrive at that?'

And there it was, normality resumed.

'Come on, Sherlock. Who would be getting back at whoever killed Cassie? Ronnie Blue Suede Shoes and his good lady wife? Aye *right*.' She snorted. So like a pig, it was uncanny.

'Exactly that, ma'am.'

It wasn't ridiculous, not really. Not when you thought about it, and when you recalled a fury the potency of which you had never encountered before. The rage that someone could hurt your mum, that was present even now, as soon as you thought of that infantile, ursine name. *Teddy.* You could feel it like sucking air, rushing through you, in you like a gasp. Pared essence, pure instinct. Always there; just a single breath away.

'I think Ronnie loves his mammy so much that he'd kill for her. And I think, possibly, that he's done it before.'

'His da, you mean?' Cruikshanks's voice was low.

477

That deadness in Ronnie's eyes when Anna had spoken to him. 'I bet when you interview him, or you go back and . . . I dunno, speak to old neighbours, friends, relatives, maybe even Sheena, you'll find that Ronnie—Cassie too—had a shitty life. At least until his dad died. And how did his dad die? Alone, on a boat, with the teenage Ronnie.'

Mrs Hamilton was shoving all the scattered paperwork over towards poor Tom. 'Ho hum. All very speculative. But we'll prove none of it unless you find the Maguires, Tom.'

Ah. There is no 'i' in team.

Anna wanted to go home. She'd lost track of the time, the cat would be eating the cheeseplant and the stink of Chaddha still clung, ripe like onions. She wanted to get away from here; needed to shower and sleep. 'Look, I know this is a daft question; but has anyone tried Liverpool? You know, the place where they found Cassie—or alleged they did. The house is empty, apparently, it's on a really quiet street . . .'

'Aye, that *is* a bloody daft question—'

'Yes, Mrs Hamilton,' said Cruikshanks, 'but it's a valid one. And no, Anna. I don't think anyone has.'

'Well, I've got a pal in Merseyside who'd be only too happy to check it out for you.'

'No, no, we need to keep this tight. I'll get one of the boys to drive down the night—just sit and keep an eye on the place for a wee while, see if our wee chickies come home to roost.'

Hamilton clicked her spectacle case shut. 'Well, I canny afford any more overtime.'

'Ma'am, come on. This is really important.'

478

'You'll just have to take someone off something else. I've got a budget to balance.'

'Ma'am, I'm running five murder enquiries at the moment.'

'Well, what about Fraser Harris?' said Hamilton.

'Send him? Nah. He's no experience.'

'No, I mean those two lardy-arses who've been camped outside his house for the past two weeks, watching the dog walkers forget to scoop their poop. Use them.'

'But we still haven't established who attacked Fraser,' said Anna.

'According to you it's a wee lad who's now in India.'

'Yes, but we're not sure why he did it—or exactly who told him to.'

'Well, if it *was* Chaddha, he knows we've got him in our sights. He'll no be stupid enough to do anything now, will he?'

'Are we putting him on the list for surveillance too, then?' asked Johnny.

'I think we should, ma'am,' said Cruikshanks. 'Anna's given us a lot to chew over.'

'Aye. Given me bloody indigestion, more like.' But there was a grudging lightness in Hamilton's tone. Was Anna being slithered from shade into sun? Off the intensive care list?

'Happy then?' said Hamilton. 'We watch Chaddha instead of your boy, thus freeing two men to go down south.'

'I'd still prefer it if we could keep an eye on Fraser's house too.'

Hamilton hadn't seen Chaddha's face, the blank menace of his eyes. Even after Anna had cuffed him, and he'd stood, solid and uncomplaining, there was razor-wire craziness spiking from every limb, catching her like teasels.

'Oh, for God's sake. I've had enough of this,' sniffed Hamilton. 'Just do what you're told, the lot of you: get Chaddha hunted, get they two lads to Liverpool, and get out my office, now. I've got Mr Nayar and his brother coming to see me in two minutes.'

'Ma'am, is that wise? Can I remind you, Raju Nayar is still not off the hook? We're going to be combing through his background, his businesses, his family . . .'

'And can I remind you, DCI Cruikshanks, that I am your divisional commander, and I need your approval for fuck all?'

'*Ma'am.*'

Cruikshanks and Anna left the office together. She was aware of his knuckles hitting off his trouser seams, bouncing as he strode; Anna caught his fist.

'Slow down, tiger. You'll give yourself a heart attack.'

'Like Sangster? No wonder he keeled over like that. She is a twenty-four-carat cow.'

'Tell me something I don't know.'

The mobile function on her Airwave set began to vibrate. An incoming call: someone was ringing her ISSY number. 'See if that's Hamilton . . . 'Scuse me, Tom.'

Tom raised his hand in farewell. If a hand could look exhausted, this one did, drooping in mid-air, bumping off his jacket as it wilted down. 'I'll speak to you in the morning. Night, night.'

'Sleep tight.' She pressed 'receive', carried on walking downstairs.

'Chief Inspector Cameron?'

'Yeah?'

'It's Fraser Harris, ma'am,' said the disembodied voice. 'Can you talk?'

'Aye. Where are you?'

'I've just come on duty. Night shift.'

'Jeez, is it that time already? I didn't realise.'

His voice was wheezy, strained like he was running. 'I heard you've arrested Jasveer Chaddha—is that right?'

'Afraid not. He'd only been Section Fourteened, and the div com's just put a stop to that too. But, look, we need to talk about this. I'm strongly of the opinion that it's Chaddha that's been threatening you—'

'Fuck. I *know* it is, ma'am.' It came out like a sob.

'Fraser, are you okay?'

'Yes. No. Look, I need to see you. Are you still at Govan? They said you were at Govan.'

She was and she wasn't. She had worked something like thirty-odd hours out of the last forty-eight. She would get no overtime. She could still smell the flesh of four skin-stripped bodies, their eyes weeping pus, with that look of mild puzzlement the dead often wear. She was running on empty—no, beyond that; she was running on the muddy sump below empty. Her brain had no spare capacity to cram one more thing in. Bed, sweet bed, was calling.

'Not any more. I am out the door and heading home as of this very minute.'

'Please wait. I'm just outside, I'm at the bottom of the steps.' He sounded desperate.

'Okay. Okay, I'll wait, Fraser. Are you at the

front?'

Anna opened the glass door into the public atrium. Positioned to be viewed as you came in from the street was a framed sepia photograph: rows of stern Edwardian officers, some in pillboxes, most in helmets like the English still wore. With stiff, high collars and almost uniform moustaches, they were the original Govan Police Force, roughly a hundred in number—and scary as hell. They stared out into the Govan darkness, still watching the streets they used to patrol. The outer door flipped, and night fell in, Fraser with it. No hat, half-uniform, his face like a brick wall.

'What is it?' said Anna. 'What's happened?'

'It's not enough he's trying to frighten me.' Panicked words bouncing, furrows cracking his brow. 'Look what that bastard put in my wee girl's bag. Fucking bastard. I went in it tonight, before I went to work. To put her playpiece in—a Penguin, she always gets a Penguin biscuit. And I found this . . .' He slumped against the glass wall, started to slide. Anna had to get him inside. People would see. But she had the notion he would break clean in two if she touched him.

'Fraser, slow down. Who put what in your daughter's bag? Let me see.'

He shook his head, uncrunched his fist to show an A4 sheet of paper, crush-lines webbing the page. Anna took it from him and tried to smooth it with the back of her hand. No point in worrying about incriminating fingerprints now; it had been in Fraser's damp palm. The heading was done in childish crayon, *Went to Market* in green and red and blue, and under it was a Polaroid of a wee girl carrying a wicker basket. It looked quite cute,

482

shades of Little Red Riding Hood off to see granny.

'Is that your daughter?'

'Yes.' His voice broke. 'He's been at her nursery, her bag's always on her peg at nursery. He's been there, and he's taken a photo of her—and stuck it on to this . . . this filth.'

Anna looked again. It was a child's body, at least until the waist, where a magazine cut-out of a basket of groceries had been stuck. The basket trembled slightly; just one side of the cut-out had been secured to the page, hinged with tape. If you lifted up the basket, a woman's spread legs leered out, her naked, shaved vagina folded purple the way Lori's had been at the club.

'Oh my God. That's disgusting. Oh Fraser, I'm really sorry.' She squeezed his fist, still clenched where he'd held the paper. The veins on his neck were twisted blue, tears pooling at the corners of his eyes. 'Right, let's get you inside. You're in no fit state to stand out here. Come on.'

As they moved back into the building proper, Anna could see two men coming from the cell area. She realised one was Chaddha, rolling from the hips as he glided forth, accompanied by a charcoal-suited wide boy who had to be his solicitor. Too late, she was aware of Fraser's shadow, the force of it scudding by, too fast for her to catch.

'Fucking cunt. You fucking, mental cunt.'

A flux of grabbing, other bodies appearing, moving out from the rooms and warrens of the police office. An automatic conditioning—shouting meant movement, you ran towards the shouting. But there was no need to intercept

483

Fraser. He halted, not quite skidding, but abrupt, his energy filling the gaps, keeping them all away.

Chaddha, too, bulked up, his shoulders and chest swelling. Only he chose to smile as well. 'Fergus, isn't it? How's your sore face, pal?'

'I'm no your fucking pal. You're shite. You're nothing but neddy fucking scum.' Fraser gripped the lapel of Chaddha's leather jacket. 'You keep away from my family, keep away from my life, you hear me?'

Chaddha stared pointedly at Fraser's hand. 'I'm sorry, but I have absolutely no idea what you're talking about.'

'Fraser.' Anna prised his fingers away from Chaddha. Being so near to Chaddha, touching him again, made her feel sick. It was his stance, the wide thrust of it, the appraising eyes that stroked your hair. 'Fraser, come with me the now. These people were just leaving.'

'Excuse me,' said Chaddha's solicitor. 'Is this part of an official police interrogation, or just a common breach of the peace—and assault?'

'Och, let's just say we've all had a long night,' said Anna. 'I'm sure your client is anxious to get home. Aren't you, Mr Chaddha?'

Chaddha wiped an invisible smudge from his jacket, drew his hand down to rest inside his trouser pocket. 'Unless you'd like to detain me further, Chief Inspector.' His jacket was open, the groin of his trousers stretched tight. Did he think Anna hadn't heard him in the club, effing and blinding in coarse-rasped tones? He was adopting another persona entirely, the sexy businessman, the mildly amused bon viveur who had wandered into a jolly jape.

'You intrigue me,' Chaddha continued. Who was this for the benefit of? He had no audience, save his solicitor. Did he really believe his own PR?

'This piece of crap I'm not disposed to chat with—but you, now, *you*—'

'Don't you talk to her like that. We're the polis—have you not got that yet, you stupid bastard? I'm the fucking polis,' shouted Fraser. 'I *own* you!'

Chaddha's eyes flared. This time, he *was* going to hit someone, and this time, so would Anna. And she doubted if she could stop. Thank God there were no public in the station to witness this. But his bloody lawyer was. A circle of cops was positioned round the foyer. Hamilton was bound to hear too, to sense the spasms in the fibres of her web.

'Fraser, I want you to move back now. I want you to go with Sergeant Jeffries there. Go and get a cup of tea and I'll see you in the refreshment room.'

Jeffries moved forward, took Fraser's arm. Instantly, the young cop creased; very neat, very quiet. Let himself be led away.

'Now, if I can ask you both to leave the building, gentlemen . . .'

'That was better.' Chaddha parted his lips. Not pleasant, more a sign of hunger.

'Pardon?'

'You asked me much more politely than you did earlier.'

Creep, creep, creep. Alone, she would handcuff him again. Tie him to a locker, remove his trousers and his underwear, invite every woman in the building to come and mock him.

Call that a prick, son? I've seen better on ma mammy's poodle.

Then get JC's ferrets to join in the fun.

Behind her, Anna heard a deep, rich voice. 'Please, what is going on here?'

Jesus God. This place was like *Family Fortunes*. It was Raju Nayar, coming in to see his son-in-law surrounded by a posse of stick-twitching cops.

'Jasveer, I came as soon as I heard. What are they doing to you?'

'Nothing, Papa. We're all good.'

'Anjali tells me you have been imprisoned here for hours.'

'Ssh, it's fine, Papa. Everything is cool.'

'*You.*' Nayar eyeballed Anna, no longer the urbane sophisticate from Coriander. He was a lion defending his family, a good and noble thing, but not when the beneficiary was Chaddha. Yet it made her believe that Nayar knew nothing; his outrage was convincing. 'I will be speaking to Mrs Hamilton about this, in the strongest of terms. As will my brother, when he arrives. My son-in-law is a good boy, a very good boy. He works hard, feeds his family—'

'And the sun shines out his arse, is that right?'

'How dare you.'

Chaddha's eyes sparkled. He was loving this.

Anna took a gamble. 'Mr Nayar, your son-in-law may indeed be a respected, upstanding citizen— but did you know he owns a lap-dancing club?'

'Of course he doesn't.'

'Well, that's where we detained him. The Lap It Up in Govan—"Asian Babes" a speciality.'

'*No.*' Nayar glared at his son-in-law. 'What is this? Does my daughter know?'

486

'It's just a recent acquirement.' Chaddha showed his teeth. 'No biggie. It's a business deal, that's all. We buy it up, we make it profitable, we sell it on.'

'Jasveer, I don't give you my money to—'

'Papa, it cost next to nothing.'

'But I know nothing about this.'

'And you don't need to.' Chaddha smiled again, gums visible. 'Let's just say it's in settlement of a bad debt and leave it at that.' He made to move past his father-in-law.

'Jazz. Wait. I want to discuss this further. You'd better not bring shame to my door. You hear me?'

Chaddha continued walking.

'Jasveer. I told you to wait.'

Chaddha shoved the door open, held it to let his solicitor go first. '*Gaand mara*, old man.' Then he went out into the yellow-lit dark, cold air sucking as he left.

'What did he say?' said Anna. 'What did that mean?'

'My son-in-law has just told me to fuck off, Chief Inspector.'

CHAPTER TWENTY-FOUR

Fraser was waiting by the microwave. Pinging the button on and off, watching the white light spin.

Anna nodded at Jeffries. 'Cheers, pal. Let me speak to him on his own.'

She sat at the long mess table, swiped some crumbs from the marbled Formica. Watched a muscle in Fraser's close-shaved neck indent each time he pressed the microwave switch. Anna only had the one management technique—ask once (reasonably nicely), then resort to shouting, usually laced with a vicious quip or some veiled threat. They gave you courses at Tulliallan, asked you to analyse your personality, your own 'emotional intelligence', to consider how staff below you related to it, and how those above you nurtured it. *By pissing on me, normally*, Anna had said. The messianic trainer flown in from down south had not laughed. Red bra shining through her white blouse, she had frowned slightly, then carried on showing them her creative techniques, using colours and flow charts and video clips.

There had been other courses too, the ones where they ask you to consider the best motivational tools to use for 'an individual's needs', where you would do *case studies* and form *syndicates* and *feed back to the group* but, as soon as you got back to base, it was all forgotten. Because the police force does not run on consensus and debate. It runs on orders, on hierarchies, on knowing your place and quite how far you can stretch that. And most of Anna's subordinates knew it wasn't very far. But that was fine; they were all comfortable with that. Touchy-feely disturbed her, she didn't know how to do it. She would walk over hot coals for her troops, of course she would—but only if they weren't looking. Involved in practicalities, Anna could zing and ping. The doing of *things*, tangible progressions and points to be ticked, that was where she shone. But you couldn't see emotion, couldn't sort it. It rose like a big hungry snake, feinted, tricked you, and then it bit. And it scared her.

This, all her, was just a big act. Strip her of her uniform, and Anna was nothing. That was why she had not been in contact with Rob. That was why, truly, she could not go back to Carol Jenkins's house. She had no purpose there now, no end product of information to obtain or advice to give. She would only be saying she was sorry, and what right had she to do that? To intrude where she wasn't wanted, be a nuisance, get *in the road*? *You're in the road, Anna*, her mother would say. *Stop skulking round me like that, Anna.*

And here, now, with Fraser, his every inch of skin proclaiming *leave me alone,* she was meant to intervene. How? Was she to say the *right thing*, to hold his hand, burn that hideous picture? God knew. She banged the seat beside her, watched him jump.

'Fraser. Sit your arse down here and talk to me.'

Dead man walking, he obliged.

'What is going on? *Why* would Chaddha do this? And why would he be doing this to *you*?'

Many of the answers she knew, or assumed she did. But she would let him tell this straight; it would be cathartic, it would help order things in her own mind, and it would give her time to think.

'Why is Jazz Chaddha pulling your strings?'

'He's not, he's fucking not—I'm pulling his, okay?'

'Alright, alright.' She poured some water from the cooler. It gurgled and bubbled, and she wished it was gin. 'Here—drink this.'

'I don't want—'

'Bloody drink it.'

He took the cup, hands jittering. She could see the whiteness of his knuckles bloom as he

489

compressed the plastic, misting the sides with his body heat.

'He knows I know what he's up to.'

'Explain.'

The heaviest sigh, as if something was rammed in his gullet, and he had to breathe round it.

'I'd need to start at the beginning then.'

'Always the best place.'

'Fine.' He closed his eyes, began to speak. At first, Anna found it disconcerting, that he would not look at her. Then it relaxed her, freeing her from the nods and sympathetic murmurs he might expect.

'When I was a young probationer, this boy came to me. He was in a gang, just a kid, mucking about like all the kids on his street did. I'd been in at their school in Govan, with Recruiting, to do some daft career thing—you know, shiny new probationer raving about the job. Anyway, he came up to me at the end, asked if he could have a word. He looked like shit, you know? The gist of it was that this older boy in the gang had been harassing him to sell drugs, really applying the pressure, saying if he wanted to be a true member of the gang, etc, etc. So,' Fraser's eyes screwed tighter as he grasped for the right words, 'so, the boy asked me what he should do, and I told him he should just say no. Better still, he should say no and'—his finger wagging in a parody of a lecture—'tell this lad that if he ever hassled him again, he'd go straight to the police. *Come to me*, I said, and I'll sort him out.' His eyes opened, staring at Anna like it was her fault. 'Because I had seven months' service and I knew everything, you know?' He took another sip of water. 'So, the boy says thanks, and he goes away—even took a leaflet on joining the police as I recall. And, one week later, his wee sister gets raped.'

Down into the bottom of his plastic glass, he was peering, searching like it really mattered.

'She was thirteen I think. Name of Bel. Family never reported it—I only found out from another lad, who was a tout for my neighbour. Great source of information, could tell me everything.' He blinked, focused again on Anna. 'And d'you know the boy that was hassling him? The boy who raped his sister?'

'Chaddha?'

'Yup. I went to see the family of the girl, but they wouldn't let me in. Said everything was fine, fine. I went to the Family Protection Unit too; they tried to speak to her. Next thing we knew the family had done a moonlight flit, and that was that. No complainer, no suspect, no trial. And I had to watch Chaddha strut about like he owned the fucking place. He was a rich kid anyway, from a good family. Private school, the works. This . . . this was all like a hobby to him, the gang, the drugs, the power.' Fraser got up to pour more water for himself. 'You want some?'

'No thanks.'

'I only worked there for another six months or so, then I got moved. And you know how it is, upwards and onwards, more shite takes over. It's not like in the movies. I mean, I didn't launch a one-man crusade to make Chaddha pay or anything. But I *do* know my neds, and I did hear he was building a nice wee empire. So, it's always a pleasure to bring them down a peg or two when you get the chance.'

'Hence you stopping his motor when you saw it?'

'Yeah. Back in my old stamping ground with the Support Unit, well, it was like a gift horse, you know?' He ran the tumbler along the edge of his lower lip, his jaw sharp. 'Christ, I didn't think I'd be kicking off all this, but.'

'All what exactly?'

But she knew already. If not the exactness of the sequence, the sense of what he meant, at least. No matter what plans or goals you make, it all comes back to this: you are not in control of your life. Chaddha was not, Fraser was not, she was not. It is the tiniest, most random pivots and pinpricks of chance that send you spinning; you have no choice.

Fraser put his cup down, but stayed on his feet, walking as he talked. 'That it would lead to Sabir Aziz getting killed. I mean, it didny even cross my mind until I saw his photo in the paper—the one that got chucked through your window, ma'am.'

'Sabir's photo?'

'Yes. The one I'd seen before was just a school photo. Different picture, different name—I never clicked at all. But the photo in the *Sentinel* was the exact same face as the boy I'd pulled in Chaddha's car. Then the fact he'd been murdered a short time thereafter, the speed at which the culprits were found, the lack of resistance, the confession from Sabir's own gang mates. Well, it all smelled like shit to me. Total and utter shit. It smelled like Sabir was working for Chaddha, Sabir had ballsed up by borrowing Chaddha's car, and going for a wee drive with a bag of superskunk in the glove box. Sabir had brought the polis to Chaddha's door, and Chaddha had him "punished".'

492

'By killing him?'

'No, by getting someone else to do it. That's the way he's always worked. How do you think he's floated so far off the radar until now?'

'I know, I've checked his pre cons. It's all pishy stuff.'

'That's because he rules by fear and money, ma'am, and he's so bloody smart that he extricates himself from any shady deal he's solicited. And now that he's married into a good family, he's got connections everywhere, a whole veneer of respectability. But shite still stinks, no matter how much perfume you spray on the toilet.'

'Very profound.'

'Thank you.'

'But you're still making a lot of assumptions here, aren't you?' She would play devil's advocate, test her own theories as well as Fraser's. 'Just because Chaddha was an evil wee shite when he was a teenager, disny mean he's a murderer now, does it?'

Fraser sat down again. 'That boy Gordo—I've been asking around. He owed Chaddha money, quite a bit of money. Unpaid drugs debts, I think. It wouldn't have been beyond Chaddha to offer to wipe the slate clean if Gordo did a wee favour for him: i.e. getting rid of a troublesome employee, and making the death look like a straightforward racist gang attack. Ergo, a few years in jail with your credibility ratings soaring, as opposed to a blade through your spine and a wheelchair—or a permanent limp at best.'

'Great theory. You got any proof?'

He shook his head. 'I've been to see Gordo's father, though. Asked him if he'll get his boy to request I visit him in the jail. I thought if I could speak to him . . .'

'Do you think that's likely?'

'Probably not. But I thought it was worth a shot.'

'But why the Lone Ranger crusade? Why not just pass everything you had to DCI Cruikshanks?'

Very astute, Anna—and not remotely hypocritical. If only she'd known, Anna could have lent Fraser her own wee black mask. Given him a shot of Tonto too.

'I thought if I could gather sufficient evidence first, you know, present it like a package rather than a vague idea . . . Look, I've seen Chaddha walk from a brutal rape. Why would murder be any different? So,' Fraser sipped his water, 'I just kept working away, subtly. Kept my ear to the ground, talked to a few of my touts.'

'Sorry Fraser, this still doesn't make sense.'

'I know, but Chaddha's slippery.'

'No.'

She didn't want to say this, but, when your brain is raw it can be at its sharpest. That point for which swamis deprive themselves of food and water, why shamen inhale weird barks and moss, fasting, sleepless for days. To reach enlightenment. And they didn't have to cope with a caffeine-induced migraine, either.

'What I mean is that I don't believe you. You're telling me you suspected nothing about Chaddha's involvement in Sabir's murder until you saw the article in the *Sentinel*.'

'That's right.'

'But, if that's the case, how come you were getting hassled by Chaddha's goons long before that? We'd already received information you'd been followed home, you'd already been warned off—let's face it, had your head kicked in outside your house. So what, exactly, had you been playing at up till then?'

Fraser stood up. 'This isny a fucking game.'

The photo of his daughter still rested on the table between them, beaming a happy face up to the sun. Hair curly like her mum's, wide eyes oblivious. Anna felt like shite for doing this, but, hey, she too was a necessary evil.

'Ho you. Don't you ever use language like that to me again. Sit down and answer the question. You've got someone so wound up, so warped, that he's implying he would sell your child to a paedophile ring. I'm sorry, Fraser, is that not clear to you? You're damn right this is not a game. Now sit down. You—get out,' she bawled at some unfortunate cop who was inching his way to the sink.

'Can I just fill the—'

'Use the tap in the frigging toilet. Out!'

Fraser dropped back in his seat. Lidded eyes anchored on the microwave as though it was the television.

'If I'd known . . . Christ, I was just playing with him, alright? At first, before I realised what Chaddha had done to Aziz, I was just winding him up. I lied when I told you we'd had lots of run-ins. The truth is, Chaddha scared fuck out of me when I was a probationer.'

He was pulling on his fingers, clicking them one by one. The noise grated, bone on bone, but Anna let him be.

'After the wee girl's family left, I . . . I went to see Chaddha. On my own, off duty. Stupid, I know.

495

Thought I'd administer some summary justice. Got him in a lane outside a club he was DJ-ing at. And guess what? He beat the shit out of me. Pure laughing while he was doing it. 'Like that, white boy? Like me fucking you over, white boy? Maybe I'll fuck your arse too—just like that wee girly.'

You could see it was happening to Fraser now, his face flickering, mouth braced against the pain. This was when normal folk would say: *It's alright, son. You don't have to tell me any more.*

'Go on.'

'Then he smashed his head against the wall. His own head. I think he broke his nose. He told me his dad knew my super. One word from him, and I'd get kicked out the job. Said he had four pals who would all say I'd beat him up, called him a Paki bastard. I was still in my probation . . . I felt like such a prick. So . . . I just crawled away, and that was that.'

He burrowed down further in his seat, shrinking his body small and tight.

'I kept my distance after that—I'd seen what Chaddha could do to folk who crossed him. See the God's honest truth, ma'am—I didny even know it was Chaddha's car when I stopped it. Just some flashy motor, with a jumped-up ned inside. Then I PNCed it, and, bingo! *Jasveer Chaddha.* I mean, I'd heard of him since then. Knew he was running nightclubs and that, but our paths had never crossed. No reason to, no desire to. Like I say, he's a very clever, careful, mental man. But it all came flooding back, and I thought, what goes around comes around, you bastard. Here's my chance to scare you back. Shiny car, well-off businessman, and here's me still pulling padlocks and chinning neds. *But I remember you, and I remember what you did*. And I'm bigger now, I'm braver. I can mess with your head too. You know?' He looked at Anna, seeking what? Acknowledgement? Encouragement?

'I wanted to hold it up to him, to show him that his past was still there, and that it could come back and bite him.' Fraser laughed. 'But you know, he didny even recognise me. That *really* pissed me off. As I was leaving his office, after he'd sacked Sabir Aziz, I asked him. I'd played it so cool up till then, waiting to see who'd blink first, if some look would pass over his face as he realised who I was. But it never came. So, I said, "Do you remember me Jazz, cause I remember you? Mind the back of Nico's, our wee contretemps?" And, do you know what the bastard said?'

'What?'

'He goes: "I'm afraid you all look the same to me, officer." '

In and out, in and out, the plastic cup being crushed then released. The same noise as fire crackling.

'Then I went: "Remember wee Bel Goli? Do you still see her face, her body all rolled up and crying?" He pretended not to know what I was on about. Well, I'm no a wean any more.'

He tossed the cup on the floor. 'So I went back. The next day and the next day. Just sat outside in my car—'

'Your own car?'

'Yeah. I was off duty. Look, I know it was insane, but I wanted him to know that I knew. That I'd always known. I wanted . . . I suppose I wanted a reaction from him.'

'And then he started watching you back?'

'I guess so.'

'And now this?' Anna turned the paper round so Fraser would look at it. 'What day did you visit Gordo's house?'

'Yesterday.'

'And this appeared today?'

'I guess so.'

'Good news travels fast then, eh?'

Anna tapped her finger on the crayoned scrawl, cold wax slick and separate from the page. *'Went to Market.* Why does that ring a bell?

'This little piggy? I'm a cop, she's a cop's daughter. He's a sick fuck.'

She took Fraser's hand, an involuntary response, but it felt right, so she did it. Pressed down tight. 'Fraser, I believe everything you've said, alright? I believe Chaddha had Sabir killed.'

And I also believe he had Cassandra Maguire abducted and left to die, but I'm not telling you that.

'Let me take all this to Mr Cruikshanks, as a matter of urgency.'

He nodded. 'What'll I do now?'

'I think you should go home.'

It was the same thing Anna did when she found CID empty. First though, she scribbled a big, long note for Tom, the jist of which went: *FH threatened again. V imp info come to light, need to interview Gordon Figgis. Phone me first thing—or else. Anna.* Then she sleep-drove home, possibly through a variety of red and amber lights, but she made it, a kind genie guiding her straight to the perfect parking space, directly outside her door. Nothing short of a miracle in an area where you were loath to go out in the evening, fearing you'd have to park

498

six streets from your house when you returned. Once, she'd even tried using a police No Waiting cone to reserve her space, but that had been treated with the same contempt as School Keep Clear markings or double yellow lines.

The storms of the last few nights had broken through the mugginess, sharpening the air, bringing clean, soft rain that smirred but did not soak. She switched off her wipers, her lights, her engine, and summoned up the energy to lift her sports bag from the passenger footwell. It was stuffed full of kit, because she'd planned to go to the gym, she really, really had. Opened the door, eased her tired limbs out. Her segs struck flint, a high, clear ring in the empty street. It must be well after midnight, not a soul about. Dog walking stopped at eleven here, curtains drawn at ten past. It was a quiet street at night, no pubs, not a thoroughfare to anywhere but home. Anna felt for her keys and found an envelope instead: *Fao Michael Meek.*

She'd meant to hand it in at the hostel, just a wee note to say about Alice. There was still time. Vet day was when—tomorrow? Tomorrow, which was now today. If she dropped it in on her way into work, Shelly would get the message when he woke up. Plenty of notice. It's not as if he'd have many previous engagements. Once things had calmed down and she had married a rich man/murdered Hamilton/was working as a sergeant in Traffic, Anna would get Shelly sorted. Buried under the envelope, a wad of tissues and some Extra Strong Mints that had spilled from their packet, Anna found her keys. As always, she threaded them through her fingers. Number one tip when she lectured on personal safety. *Have your keys ready before you reach your door. Stops you rummaging on the step—plus they make a nifty wee knuckle-duster if required.*

It wasn't paranoia, it was being careful. Anna slammed the car door shut, beeped the lock. Crossed the yard or so of pavement that bordered her front gate, each crisp step a triangle tinging. She liked the sound. It was brisk, *tough*, like soldiers. One hand reaching for the gate, a rummage of hedge at the side of her. She froze, sensed a rapid movement of air. The stomach-thud of knowing what was coming, as cold palms pressed into her eyes.

'Guess who?'

CHAPTER TWENTY FIVE

He watches the woman press the red button, and the TV shrinks to blank. The baby's bottles are made up, the little girl's clothes have been laid out for nursery school. She has even filled the kettle, for her husband in the morning.

She is a good wife. He is vile.

He can hear her talking, on the phone.

'No. I mean, it used to bother me, at first. Locking up, setting the alarm; felt like I was shutting him out. But see now, I quite like it.' She pauses, then adds, 'I know! Two episodes of Sex and the City *back-to-back, a bowl of cornflakes, and then a diagonal sprawl across a double bed. It's brilliant! No scratching, no snoring. Until the wee man wakes, that is.' She laughs, then there is a '. . . damn. I better go.*

I've still got a washing out. Fraser's police shirts. I know. I'm always worried someone nicks them.'

She waits a moment, he can see her nodding her head, large mocking gestures like this is a story that she has heard before. Beautiful copper curls, the guard has forgotten beauty; it feels tender, like a bruise. Her laugh rises and he cannot draw breath, he cannot draw breath, he is a man not a monster.

'Och, don't you start. It's getting ridiculous. He actually said I've no to answer the door any more, unless I check who it is. I tell you, cops stationed outside the house—like I'm in a bloody zoo. Aye, maybe I should get one of them to bring the washing in. They're doing bugger all else!'

This cannot be done. Her hand is on the back of her head, scratching. He senses she is impatient to come out and his body tenses. It stiffens, and he is repulsed. He can feel it flow like mercury, the lurching quicksilver that is life, that will seek to survive no matter what. All moisture draining from his mouth, rising to his eyes.

'George Grant?' she is saying. 'No, I'm not sure who's on tonight. I've not even noticed the car to be honest . . . Yes. Yup, I will do. If I see him. Right Tanya . . .'

Stop up my breasts. It is the Mirror Man, deep inside his head. He melts back, away from the sliver of unlocked patio door that he has worked and loosened as instructed. It seems he will not have to use it.

Into the kitchen she comes, yawning. Opening the back door, tucking the basket under her arm. The heat sets hard now. Hard. He has been beaten into flint.

She stands at the threshold to the night-swept

501

garden, screened by trees and a six-foot fence. Walking into shadow, the light at her back.

Pale and snappable as bone.

The crunch of pebble path as she crosses the lawn to the clothes line. Faint flapping of textiles, dark in the dark. The unpegging of cloth and the absence of birdsong. Tiny blue bow on the collar of the baby's sailor suit. Her husband's black T-shirts, empty and dry.

She shakes one out, begins to fold. The crunch of pebble path, but she is no longer on it. The brittle-quickening of the instant of perception, then the clunk to dread and terror at the hands; his hands, on her face, on her mouth, pushing round, forcing down, her face skewered on the grass and his beside her. He will not look at her face, but he can see her open door and her children are inside. The grass is green, he can see every blade, can see her mud-scratching nails, green spikes and lattices and his hands are on her.

In her, and she cannot even scream.

Her children are inside. He is vile, he is vile.

And his child is far away.

*   *   *

'I'm really sorry.' Rob held the pad of witch hazel across the slashes on his cheek. 'I thought it would be a nice surprise.'

'At midnight?'

'I'd been waiting since the back of ten. Brought you a carry-out, too.' He raised a white polythene bag, the bottom stained and seeping saffron-yellow.

'Here. Give me that. You're dripping all over the floor.'

Anna laid the congealed food on top of the ceramic hob, where it wouldn't mark anything.

Rob's hands had nothing to occupy them now, except to squeeze the cotton wool. She found she was shivering; her head on one side, regarding him standing in her kitchen, feeling the quick bursts of her heartbeat nudging, the furry wrapping of Alice as she wove a charm round Anna's legs.

'Anna, I didn't know what else to do. I waited two days for you to get in touch.'

'Likewise.'

She let the tension ripen. Not for gain or cruelty, but because she didn't know what else to do. All her life, a constant searching for something beautiful, making things right, trying to see colours instead of the grey, just one colour that could be hers. And now, she could see far past the spectrum, her mind shrieking ahead of itself on fast forward and she couldn't stop the rushing.

'What was I supposed to do?' Rob chucked the pad into the sink. 'Last time I saw you, you had me brought in for questioning. Seized all my financial statements, and dumped me in an interview room. Far as I know, I'm still some kind of a suspect.'

'For what?'

'I don't know,' he shouted. 'You tell me. Printing dodgy money? Killing Manju, killing Cassie? I don't bloody know what to think, or what you think of me any more.'

But she couldn't say, couldn't say anything except mumble the obvious. Terrified of the answer.

'So why did you come here tonight?'

'Because I had to see you. My whole life is falling apart—my business is going down the tubes, my professional reputation is in tatters, my name's getting rubbished in the papers, and all I can see is you. Everywhere: you. Do you not understand? I love you, Anna. I love you.'

The answer is exactly right, it is perfect, it is hers; all she has to do is say it back. Instead, she gathers up the cat in an undignified bundle, not able to bear this, because it would go wrong and a cat cannot speak, only offer up noises that you can translate as you wish.

'Why?' Her whispered thought comes out aloud.

'Oh, Anna. There's your answer, right there. Do you not think you're worth loving?'

Alice was fighting to get down, arched back demanding to be wanted on her own terms, not plucked without asking from where she was happy and quiet.

Rob was smiling at her, a soft, slow warmth that was intoxicating. The creases round his eyes were sunbursts, grinning fit to ignite.

'I want to keep you safe. I want to feed you healthy dinners and rub your toes when you come in. I want to be the man who breaks your heart open and makes all that sadness pour out and tells you how beautiful, how brilliant you are. Anna, believe me. I know how crap life is. And I also know how wonderful it can be—if you let it.'

Rob loved her. The fact embraced her, softened her iron-clad, careful world; the force of it scaring her. She could cope with sex, not love. An unambiguous coupling that leaves you both intact.

'Rob, please. I can't do this right now. I'm not . . .'

'Anna. Do you love me?'

'What?'

'When I kissed you, I know what I felt. Did you

504

not feel the same?'

'Rob. I can't. I have too much . . .'

'Anna. *Anna.*' He pushed his fingers through his hair, and she wanted to snatch at them, stop them from fretting. But her own hands remained tucked into Alice, who was incandescent with rage, and would—later—make Anna pay.

'Life isn't something that happens next, once you've got your head together and everything's sorted. This *is* life. Now. We're living it, and I want to live it with you.' He folded his arms, leaned back against the worktop. 'Okay. I've said it. Now what are you going to do?'

'Do?'

'Yes, do. Put that bloody cat down for a start.'

She shook her head.

'Anna, she doesn't even like you. Look at her— she's ready to rip your head off.'

'Thought you said I was loveable?'

He leaned forward, tugging at the belt of her coat. 'You are. Come here.'

And, as if by magic, Alice jumped down, the world disappeared, and all she could see was him. Not here, in this cold kitchen, with the smell of curry dripping and the key-scratches wet on his face, but filling her head, his mouth breathing into hers. 'You don't need to do this on your own.'

Holding on to his hand, a soft chord rising in her head. She knows this, wants this. Wants *us*.

*   *   *

'Good morning.' A chink of coffee cup, a lamp clicked on. A gold, happy light.

'Hey.' Anna stroked Rob's face. 'What time is

505

it?'

He was already dressed. 'Really early, I'm afraid. I didn't want to say last night, but I've got a conference to go to.'

'When? Now?

'Uh-huh. That's how I had an all-night pass. Laura is at her auntie's. I was supposed to be at the conference last night . . . but,' he moved down to kiss her, 'I couldn't go without seeing you.'

'Well, I'm glad you didn't.'

How glad. She stretched her body, fingers wide. Smelled his body on hers, the air still volatile around them.

'I made you breakfast.'

There was a tray resting on her bedside table. Round flat muffins, spread with . . . she nibbled an edge . . . honey. Did she even have honey? Or muffins?

'Did you bring breakfast with you?'

Rob took a bite from the muffin in her hand. 'Well, you know. I thought I might get lucky. Reckoned you were a bit of a hing-oot really.'

'Honey, muffins, but no johnnies? You're either an inveterate romantic or a dirty, devious . . .'

The plate went flying. He held her wrists, covered her mouth with his and she wanted him inside her again, tugging her arms down, pulling at his zip, at him; she didn't deserve this; her heart would burst with filling up.

Later, when the flavour of honey is still humming at her throat, the radio clicks on. Time to get up.

Rob lay on her breast, stroking the nipple. Small frissons radiating in her belly.

'Did I tell you I loved you this morning?'

506

'No.'

'I love you this morning.'

'Good.'

'Do you love me this morning?'

'Might do.'

Rob struggled up on his elbows, hair all mussed. She wanted to groom it flat.

'Might do?'

Anna pushed him back down. 'We'll need to see. How long are you at your conference for?'

'Just the one night, then I'll be back. It's only down in Peebles. Hey—want to come?'

'I can't. Duty calls.'

Wads of it. She stretched. Just as well she was awake so early. She could catch Tom Cruikshanks before anyone else did, convince him of the urgency of locking Chaddha up—immediately, and bugger Mrs H. Anna would fit up Chaddha with a flick knife if necessary, just to get him off the street.

These problems, this mess, it was all still there, but it felt different now. It felt surmountable.

'I'll phone you when I get back.' Rob heaved himself from the bed and reached for his jacket, kissing her on the forehead first. His shirt was still undone. 'Maybe you could come over?'

'Yeah, I'd like that.'

'We'll need to talk to Laura when I get home.'

'Really?'

'Well, yeah. I know she likes you, but I don't want her hearing about us from someone else. Anyway, I want to show you off.'

Anna stretched again, her limbs feeling slim and long, like flesh and bones you'd be proud of.

'And,' Rob leaned in for another kiss, 'I know

507

you don't want to, but we could maybe talk about your mum too. If you're up to it.'

All the muscles in her feet clenched.

'I've been in touch with the crematorium, and they can do an interment of ashes any day next week.'

Anna pulled the covers up. It was cold. 'Oh, that's too soon.'

'Too soon? Och, Anna, c'm here.' He sat on the bed, held her. 'What do you need to plan out? The men make a hole, we go to the hole, the men put the box in the hole, we go home. What do you need to prepare for that?'

'Me.'

His head on one side, appraising. 'Fair enough.' Then kissed her again, one of those chaste-on-the-brow pecks, but she pulled his face down until it met hers, full and soft and safe.

*　　*　　*

Was she walking on air, or drunk with stupidity? The only way to find out was to keep on going. Anna licked the corner of her mouth as she drove through the sunrise, all her veins full of humming, buzzing honey. The sun was pale and clean, pink-gold washes on yellow sandstone. She stopped the engine, wound the window down. She loved this pause in the morning, the moment before Glasgow wakes and you see that a city is a sum of all its parts, and that it does really belong to you. That moment at the end of a night shift, with the streets bereft of people, and the sky drawn slowly back, tracing the orbit of earth. When you feel you've been protecting something vital—unseen and

508

unacknowledged, but you've been there all the same.

Anna closed the window, got out of the car. She noticed Carol Jenkins's house no longer had its purple pansies outside, just a ring of dry earth where the pot had been.

The hostel looked shut, but she knew there would be a night-bell. Always some sentinel who was sober, dozing with one eye half open— otherwise the residents would choke on their own vomit, or steal the front door on the way out. She tried the handle anyway—it was open.

'Hi.' Anna smiled at the heavy-lidded man behind the desk. His gnarled hands were working on a roll-up, an intricate contortion of arthritic fingers shaking fragments of tobacco into paper that spilled at one end as rapidly as it filled the other.

'I know it's a bit early, but can I leave this note for Michael Meek please?'

'Who?' Tongue out, not looking up from his task.

'Michael—em, he's sometimes called Shelly? Wee, skinny guy, curly hair?'

'Junkie or alkie?'

The entrance hall to the hostel was a once-grand space, cluttered now with filing cabinets and noticeboards, posters for addiction services and giving up smoking and psychiatric counselling and mentoring, a dead pot plant, and this man's desk. A wood-panelled staircase had been glossed in institutional beige, and the rug she stood on smelled of damp and barely digested alcohol.

'Michael is a homeless person,' she said. 'I think you get some of them in here from time to time,

509

don't you? Probably what keeps you in a job.'

The man plonked his feet up on his desk, smoothed the edge of his uneven cigarette.

'Aye, well, I think you'll find ma job is tae keep undesirables out of this establishment, doll. So, shut the door on your way out, eh? You'll have tae see your boyfriend at a more reasonable hour.'

'He's not my boyfriend. He's just a friend, and I'd like to leave this message for him, please.'

'I'm no a post office.'

'And I'm no very patient. *Pal*. I'll ask you again, do you know a Michael, a Shelly or Michelle who's been staying here?'

'Might do.'

'Would it help if I gave you *my* name? It's Chief Inspector Cameron.'

'Chief inspector? You a poliswumman then?'

'Aye.'

She was wearing civvies this morning. Her uniform had a cling of sourness about it; she'd hung the trousers up over the shower rail to air.

'Aw, I mind your man now.' Yellow tooth-stumps on show as he began to laugh. 'The wee poof, you mean? Michelle ma belle?'

'Yes! You know him?'

'Aye.' The man flicked his lighter. Puffed, then puffed some more. 'Aye. He's no staying here, but.'

'Since when?'

'No idea. One night they're here, one night they're no. And that's fine by me, cause there's aye some other bugger wanting a bed.'

'Well, see if he comes back, could you give him this?' She laid the envelope in front of him, although all it said was to meet her here, tonight, and she'd take Shelly to the vet's to see Julie

510

Andrews. Not much use to Shelly tomorrow or next week, but she had written it, and she'd come down here, and she'd *arranged* this. At least he would know that.

The man blew two perfect rings of smoke.

'Just tell him Anna left it for him.' She slid the envelope closer to his feet. 'Oh, maybe you'd look out your hostel operating licence for me while you're at it. I take it you have a multi-occupancy licence? Fire safety too—I'm pretty sure that smoking isn't permitted—'

'Aye, aye I do mind now.' He sat up, stubbed out his fag. 'It wisny that long ago he left. Only a couple of nights ago, sure. He left *you* a message an' all.'

'Is that right? What did he say?'

The man picked a bit of tobacco from his teeth. Looked at it, then popped it back into his mouth. 'I canny mind exactly. He was pure mincing out of here because some lad had stole his hairbrush or something. Squealing: *I'm gonny kick your cunt, so I am!* And he goes tae me as he was flouncing out: *See if some stuck-up poliswumman comes looking for me . . .*' The man raised his crumpled roll-up, 'That's no me, hen, that's just whit the boy said.'

'Go on.'

'So he goes: *Gonny tell her this? Tell her: "Thanks for all your help."*' He chuckled. 'Then he goes: *Aye. Ma fucking arse.*' The man shrugged. 'Or words tae that effect.'

'That it?'

'That's it. Cabaret over, and off he goes.'

'Right.' She nodded at the man, turned to go. 'Right. Thanks anyway.'

'Here—what'll I do with this letter?'

511

'Just bin it.'

Anna carried on out the stinky, shitty door.

'I take it you're no wanting tae see my licence,' he shouted after her.

'Nah, you're alright. You just keep on doing a great job.'

She texted Jenny at the first set of red lights she came to. 'Can't pick cat up. Sorry. You were right about Shelly. Anna.'

An early delivery van was rolling up at the newsagent's at the top of Victoria Road, a few folk gathering at the bus stop to head into town and begin the daily grind. Stupid, really, but she looked for Shelly's curly head amongst them. He wasn't from the south side though, he was a Maryhill boy and would have hopped across the Clyde, no doubt. Or got on a bus to London; melted into the flotsam and jetsam of King's Cross or Hampstead Heath, where his accent would mark him as exotic, and thus, desirable. At least he'd shown a bit of fire when he'd stormed from the hostel. Maybe he'd got his flounce back. She hoped so. Wherever he was, she hoped he would keep on being Shelly.

Anna picked the sleep out of her lower lashes, tried to regain that sense of lightness that had woken her. Up over the hill, past the Langside Monument, with its barley-sugar pillar and sad lion staring, down over the River Cart and into sunny Giffnock. Rob would be on the train now, heading off to his conference. Miles of land speeding between them, and she tried to picture him, imagine what he would be doing: was he thinking of her, too? His long, long fingers would be lifting a scalding paper cup, blowing on it. Perhaps a wicked light was moving as he thought about

512

Anna's breasts. She prodded one with the flat of her hand. These breasts, which were mundane and a little lacking in pertness, but were new and wonderful to him.

The early shift had just come on when she arrived at the office. Well, you called it early shift, but there was no such thing any more. The new Variable Shift Agreement meant that cops had staggered starts, staggered days even, so coverage on the street was maximised to the nth degree. It also meant that no one knew where they were or who they belonged to any more. Good for squeezing the very last drop of polis-juice out of the squeaking pips, but pretty crap for morale.

She unlocked her office, hesitated at the light switch. Through the upper reaches of her window, a little corner of sun was creeping into Anna's room. Such a rarity, to see it roll across the dullness of the walls, that she thought she'd leave the light off. Yes, it was still a good day. It was a wonderful day, all the signs were there—breakfast in bed, bruised lips, blue skies—and an unexpected bottle of Prosecco, sitting on her desk. She circled it, once. A poisoned chalice from Hamilton? As soon as she touched it, a camera would flash, and she'd be done for drinking on duty. There was a yellow Post-it stuck to the neck:

Come up and see me, make me smi-i-i-ile!!! Tom x

A glow inside, to match the sun. It had to be good news—MacLeod had spilled his guts and confessed to killing Cassie, or they had found Chaddha, papering his downstairs loo with hi-res

513

scans of ten different worldwide currencies.

She dialled Tom's number.

'Hello—is that the CID? I'd like to report a very unusual incident. Someone has left an unopened bottle of alcohol on my desk.'

'Ah yes, madam. That would be the pished piskies of the wee small hours. There was a bit of celebrating going on, and we didny want to leave you out.'

'And what were we celebrating?'

'We, missus, have found the meandering Maguires!'

'Brilliant.' But part of her wished it had been Chaddha they'd incarcerated. Yes, yes, he'd keep, perhaps—but for how long?

'I know!'

Anna could hear the glee in Cruikshanks's voice. He might not be the smartest, most innovative detective on the block—but he was diligent. Cruikshanks was a big, determined, slightly fishy-smelling Lab who would just not relinquish his ball. Ever. And now he'd been handed a huge great Bonio biscuit. 'Just waiting on them getting brought down the road. From Crieff Hydro, would you believe? Here we are with an all-ports lookout, and they don't even go two hours beyond their own front door.'

'How d'you find them?'

'Cop from Tayside was in having an anniversary celebration with his wife; thought he recognised them from the photies we punted round all the forces. So, he very kindly nipped into his office early to confirm. Tayside officers have not long apprehended them and . . . and—it gets even better, dollface.'

514

This was it, the exhilarating rush to certainty. 'Is this going to take long? Should I open my sparkly wine?'

'They were driving a small white van, same registration as a van we've noted appears on CCTV, heading through Eglinton Toll on Thursday morning. Five a.m. to be exact.'

Not long before the security guard had phoned Anna. A red light began to flash on her phone, indicating that some other eager beaver who was at their work for seven thirty was trying to get through.

'Forbye all that,' continued Tom, garrulous with *joie de vivre* and sleep deprivation, 'even before we'd tracked the wee bastards down, I was apprised of a very interesting fact. What kind of an organisation would use gallons of hydrogen chloride as a legitimate part of their business?'

'No idea.'

'Scrap-metal dealers. Apparently they use it to strip zinc off of galvanised steel.'

'Arise, Sir Smart-Arse.'

Funny line, funny girl. But Anna's palate felt sticky; there was a waxy aftertaste in her mouth. Angry, brittle Ronnie had indeed poisoned those four souls at the printworks. Which made her revenge theory pretty much fact—and brought her no consolation at all. What a brutal way to get revenge. All that collateral damage, which was not scorched earth, not next door's smouldering ruins, but *people*. Tearful Ronnie, who loved Elvis and Sheena, who could love his mammy so much, who could let human beings burn in acid. And Anna had heard them burn. *This* was why you didn't take your work home with you, why you showered it off

515

and moved on, because the more you tried to rationalise the blackened heart of man, the less it all made sense.

The phone light continued blinking: a little, urgent beacon.

'Well, we've still to interview the pair,' said Cruikshanks, 'but, yes. I think you'll find they 'fess up to the dirty deed. Thank you and goodnight, Mr and Mrs Maguire. Ronnie's greeting already, according to the Tayside boys, and all they did was ask him to confirm his name. Ah, murder virgins.' Anna could hear him swishing his hands together. At least, that's what she hoped it was. 'All ripe and ready to burst.'

'You don't know that Ronnie's a murder virgin, though. Did you find out any more details about his dad's death?'

'No yet. Oh for fucksake, you always look for the negative, don't you?'

Maguire's rage about his mum would be expended, she guessed. If it had fired and fuelled the atrocity at the printworks, it would have burnt itself out by now. He'd either be drained and silent or, better yet, full of contrition—perhaps with a helpful dollop of relief. All that waiting and worrying ripped the edges of your nerves. Folk would be surprised about the number of criminals who don't flee the country or grind off their fingerprints after they'd committed some foul deed. Who thought if they sat small and quiet and tight as a mouse, acted normally, did nothing, then it would all go away. And Ronnie had been doing that for over forty years, she was sure. Like the bogeyman under your bed, though, your mind won't let it go; waiting, waiting, hiding in the dark, the terror building until some kind policeman opens the door, and you rush out, crazed and thankful, your confession on your lips. That bloody red light was annoying her.

'Listen, Tom,' said Anna, 'did you get my note about Fraser?'

'Aye—'

'So, can we bring Chad . . . sorry, hang on a minute.' Anna put her hand over the mouthpiece. Cruikshanks could get his arse kicked for discussing all this over the phone as it was. Now she had an audience. The bar officer was hovering. 'Sorry ma'am, but I've an urgent call for you.' He was in her space, too close, too pushy.

'Well, tell them I'll phone back.'

'Ma'am, I really think you want to take this message.' A glaze across his face, his features locked. He stood on, a big solid wall that was evidently going nowhere.

'Sorry, Tom. I'll need to phone you back. But don't go away.'

The bar officer pointed at her phone. 'If you just pick up line two, ma'am.'

'Thank you. I had worked that out. Hello, Chief Inspector Cameron. Who's calling?'

'Hello, ma'am. This is DC Lesley Grant, from the Family Protection Unit. I . . . em, this is a bit awkward. I just wanted to make you aware that I'm dealing with the alleged rape of a female in your subdivision. Em, her name is Maria Harris—I think you know her?'

Anna's guts igniting. Wild rushes of adrenalin with nowhere to go. The girl kept talking.

'Happened some time last night. Her husband says he discovered her when he got home. I believe he's one of your cops—Fraser Harris?'

'Yes.'

'Well, Maria's not very coherent at the moment. I think it'll be a while before we're clear on what happened.'

'Where is she now?'

'With me—at the Victoria Infirmary.'

'And where's Fraser?'

'I'm not really sure, ma'am. That was one of the other reasons I was phoning you. I only spoke briefly to him—he contacted us direct, told us to come to the hospital. But he wasn't here when I arrived.'

'Does Maria know where he's gone?'

'Don't think Maria knows what day it is, ma'am. It's—he's been pretty brutal.'

'How did Fraser sound when you spoke to him?'

A fractional pause. 'Like someone I wouldn't want to meet.'

*   *   *

Anna was at the Vicky in under ten minutes. Lesley, the DC, would hate it, think Anna was there to compromise her investigation or tell her what to do. But all Anna wanted was to establish that the assailant was neither Fraser nor that sick nutter they supposedly had under surveillance. Of course she wanted to see Maria too, but Anna's pointy face inspecting Maria's hurt, humiliated one would not help the girl any; ascertaining who did it would. Might. And you couldn't help a victim if you went all weepy on them, and if you let it get personal then you might blame yourself for agreeing to remove surveillance on the Harris

518

house, for assuming too quickly it *was* Chaddha and thinking of no other risk than that.

Inside a private cubicle they were in the dying throes of the initial interview, the DC scooping up brief bullet points of information, no notes, just talking. Enough to be going on with for now. Both went rigid as Anna came in.

'Maria. Hi, it's Anna—'

'I know. Fraser's boss.'

Avoid direct contact with the eyes, keep it all professional. Anna registered Maria's voice, hesitant, sore, like bare feet walking on gravel. Her hair was dull and matted, her skin smeared in mud. Cheeks and chin striated with dried blood, indicating that she had been held face-down. Her left eye swollen, her temple blue and red and gold.

'Sorry, please go on. Don't let me interrupt.'

The DC sighed. 'Is that alright with you, Maria? If you'd rather no one else was here . . .'

Exactly what Anna would have said. *Good on you, girl. This is your investigation, not mine.*

'I don't care.'

'On you go then. Just take it slow.'

Maria tried to swallow, began to cough and shake. 'Can I have a drink?'

'Can you wait two ticks? Just until the oral swabs are done? Soon as we're finished up here.'

Maria nodded.

'So, you were saying?'

'Yeah.' She frowned, searching in her tight-curled fingernails for an exit or a reason. 'And . . . after he hit me the first time . . . I was aware of him standing up, I think. Standing over me. I thought at first it was raining . . . but it was . . . warm, you know? Then . . .' she looked up at them both, 'then

519

I realised he was pissing on me.'

She fell silent, rubbed her middle finger on her eyebrow. It was a gesture Anna could imagine Maria making at work, in the bank when she was counting notes or working something out. Both cops waited for the rubbing to slow down, but it didn't, slight fragments beginning to flake from her brow, the skin reddening, pulling. Gently, Anna went to take Maria's hand.

'This okay?' she mouthed at Lesley. The DC nodded, she must have had samples taken from her hands, her nails already. Anna flanked Maria's hand with her own. She didn't register, her finger still working, pulsing against Anna.

'After . . . after he was . . . done . . . he crouched down again. I thought he was . . . I thought he was . . .'

Again, the gap, between sense and insanity, speech and comprehension.

'It's alright, Maria,' said the DC. 'Take your time.'

Maria spoke as if half the sentence had been uttered in her head. 'Not my mouth . . . No. He . . . when he'd finished, he wiped himself on my hair.'

Three women, sitting in a hospital cubicle. Outside, Casualty is jumping, as it always is. This is Glasgow; it doesn't matter that it has just gone eight thirty a.m. Kids come in with broken wrists, with beads stuck up their noses; workies reel with concussion or clutching half-on fingers; old ladies shuffling on to trolleys after tripping on their slippers and falling down the stairs. Then a sudden siren will jump the queue with rush and blood and panic. And folk will moan, and shuffle and move up and the three women will still be there, always there, with that admission hanging, bright and awful. And what can you say?

What can you say?

'Did you see his face?' asked Anna.

'No. He . . . my face was on the grass, he kept it down . . . then he went . . . I felt him between my legs . . . his hands . . .'

Maria retched a little, into her cupped palm, only then seeming to notice that Anna held her other hand. She tugged it loose. 'I'm okay, I'm okay.' Inhaled through gritted teeth, the air resting, shuddering slowly outwards. 'Then he picked me up by the hair . . . there's . . . we've a wee rockery at the edge of the lawn. I tried to get up, I did . . .' her anguished face, searching them both; it was important that they believed her, 'but I couldn't. I felt this pull on my hair, then he swung me—I think he maybe smashed my head on the rockery? And then I don't remember . . . Not until Fraser found me.'

'Maria, I have to ask you this,' said Anna, taking her hand once more. 'Is there any chance it was Fraser who hurt you?'

'What? God, no.' She tried to sit up on the bed but her arms would not support her weight; they buckled, she skidded on the paper-topped vinyl beneath. 'No! No. How can you say that?'

'I'm sorry, but I have to ask these things. And Fraser was very upset, last time I saw him. Where is he now, Maria? Do you know?'

'I don't know . . . to get the kids, maybe?' Recoiling from Anna's grasp, trying to hunch in the corner of the trolley. 'God. How could you say that? How could you say he would *do* those things?'

Anna could sense the DC was preparing to forcibly eject her from the cubicle.

'Are you sure you didn't see who did it?'

'Ma'am. I really need to—'

'No. I told *her* already. It was pitch black.'

'Was it just one person?'

'Yeah.' Silent tears brimming, slipping down the dirt. Livid, clean streaks like flame on her face.

'Just the one. You'd think you'd have a chance, wouldn't you? With just one person? I always thought that. Knee them in the balls . . . I don't even think he had a knife . . . Nothing. I just . . . I just . . .'

'Maria, did the man say anything? Anything at all?'

'Ma'am, can this not all wait until I get her statement down?'

'No . . . it's okay. I don't care.' Obedient and flat again, Maria replied to Anna's question. 'Yeah. He kept saying to be quiet, telling me this was a message. Did I understand that this was a message? And,' tugging on the thin paper that she sat on, 'when he . . . near the end, before he knocked me out, he whispered right in my ear:

'*I* own *you. Forever. You understand?*'

Fear sliding from Maria's brow to her eyes to her mouth. The same stricken look that old man had given Anna, when he realised he had soiled himself.

'I can't get that out of my head,' she whispered. 'It's like he's still in there. Like he'll never go away.'

Chaddha. It could only be Chaddha.

One last pat of her, and Anna handed Maria back to the DC.

CHAPTER TWENTY-SIX

'Well, where the fuck is she?'

Anna and Cruikshanks were standing in Hamilton's office, but the cupboard was bare. No ferrets, no specs and no sign of JC.

A fluster, a spin, touching a filing cupboard, the blinds, Anna did not know what she was doing. There was no focus to her anger, just obscenities fizzing sherbet-sharp on her tongue and a disproportionate sense that she herself was being stalked, that some malevolent creature was locked on her and would not be shifted from its course.

'Why the fuck wasn't Chaddha put under immediate surveillance—I thought that was a condition of him being released?'

'So did I, doll.' Cruikshanks was rummaging through Hamilton's three-tiered desk tray. He drew a manila folder from the pile, flicked it open. 'Ach, Jesus God . . . There's your answer there, hen. She's no signed the bloody permissions yet.'

'You're joking! Despite everything we told her, she just let Chaddha skip off into the sunset?'

'Looks like it.' He handed her the file. 'She's raised it up to RIPA level, mind—but she still needs to pass it on to an ACC.'

RIP(S)A was the Regulation of Investigatory Powers (Scotland) Act, used to sanction covert surveillance, and it should have been implemented immediately. The UK-wide legislation, RIPA, augmented these powers, allowing for more intrusive interceptions like the seizure of data, the interception of emails and phone calls. So Hamilton must have thought they had a convincing line of enquiry, had actually decided to increase the level of intervention. Yet, still, she hadn't bothered to raise pen to paper and fire it off.

Disgusted, Anna chucked the folder back into the tray. 'Can we get Johnny to deal with this?'

'Aye, but it's a bit late now.'

'Should the whole thing not be getting handled by the SCDEA anyway?'

'That's what both me and the detective super advised. No way should we be co-ordinating an investigation like this. It's no really Hamilton's call any more.'

'So why's she just sitting on it?'

'You'd like to hope it wisny to protect Mr Nayar, wouldn't you? Maybe JC just wants all the glory for herself.'

All this energy funnelling up. It had to come out, go somewhere, do something. Mauve veins flicking in Anna's wrists . . . Maybe your blood really did boil. She had never noticed it before, this furious, wobbling concave on the bracelet-lines, but she felt if she took a blade and opened up her veins, surely gas would flow.

'Fuck that for a game of soldiers. How quick can we get warrants?'

She must have shouted it. Cruikshanks's shoulders flurried, he wiped his mouth. He was aye bloody munching something, that man.

'For what?'

'Well, if we're going to start turning all Chaddha's properties and known haunts looking for him—which we are, aren't we . . . ?'

'Aye . . .'

'. . . Then we should be seizing any evidence of counterfeiting activities at the same time. Because now Hamilton's given him a head start, he could be hiding bloody everything. I want to roll this all up and really shaft the bastard.'

'Anna, love, I hear you—'

It was crisps. He was grazing on a bag of cheese and onion, trailing crumbs and salt all over Hamilton's carpet.

'But I havny even interviewed the Maguires yet. We still don't have proof that Chaddha's actually—'

'Tom. *Jes-us*. Chaddha has just raped a cop's wife.' Anna grabbed the packet off him, sent it hurtling groundwards. Like buttered toast, it spun mid-air to land face down, scattering a hurricane of crunch. Neither spoke, just watched the crisps fall. Listening to the sad, slow crump of Cruikshanks finishing what was in his mouth.

Anna pressed her wrists together, knuckles at her mouth. *Count to ten count to ten count to ten.* 'I *know* it was him. Look. If nothing else, I want to get to Chaddha before Fraser Harris does. So how much can you scrape up so far to justify raising warrants for the other stuff—and who can we get to sign them?'

'Well . . . we need to show credible evidence of suspicion. So, the quicker I get to grips with the Maguires . . . how's wee Fraser doing, by the way?'

'Don't know, can't find him.'

She didn't want to dwell on Fraser, couldn't envisage how she would structure that initial, tiptoe conversation or if she would simply stand and take the full blast of rage and anguish, soaking it up in mitigation. But, whether she wanted to or not, there was a pressing need to find him, quickly,

525

before Fraser found Chaddha.

'What about the security firm?'

'We had to let MacLeod go. All he's saying is that the security boy at the printworks didny work for him, that he'd never seen him before in his life. Spouted some shite about a load of uniforms being stolen. But we've seized all his company's vehicles anyway—fae both different firms. The Scenes of Crime boys are working their way through them as we speak, looking for any forensic matter that might indicate Cassie was ever inside one.'

'Well, bloody lie! Go back and tell MacLeod that we've found some forensic traces, tell him we've got Chaddha, and he's saying it was all Callum MacLeod's idea. Do something, for God's sake. Jesus, I thought your bluffing skills would be second to none, Tom. Make him think he's being shafted by Chaddha, and MacLeod will shaft him back.'

Anna would never make a proficient detective; she knew that. She didn't possess the patience. She was a beat cop to trade. On the street, in uniform, it mostly happened *pow-pow-pow*. You get a call, you go, you deal. You take statements, you warn, you report, jail or write off. Or you stumble across a situation played out before you, which you cannot back away from and must instantly sum up—but, even as you're taking stock, it accelerates, takes wings as you take sides, nail it down or ramp it up. In any case, your actions are immediate, a reflex almost, but one tempered with all your wits and experience and your knowledge of the law. Whatever it is, you sort it then and there. Yes, you might have enquiries and follow-ups and checks, but unless it is something like a complex fraud or a

526

housebreaking—which the CID would most likely steal if there's a hint of a decent body—a beat cop rarely does much genuine investigation. Not the careful piecing of layers and tatters of truth, not the slow toil of drawn-out dead-ends, the looping tangles of a true detective's craft. Which, give him his due, Cruikshanks did.

'Cool your jets, hen. I canny handle a case of spontaneous combustion on top of everything else. Look, I'll speak to the CHIS Manager, see what he's turned up.'

It sounded indecent to Anna, but a CHIS was a Covert Human Intelligence Source—the touts of old, who were handled and managed at a divisional level. Far more professional than the wink and quick bung of days gone by, when the margins between fact, fiction and friend were often blurred.

'He was already putting out some local feelers for me. If there's even a sniff from the street about Chaddha at all, whether it's as a source of superskunk or red-hot money, I'll pad it out and puff it up. You'll get your warrants, and I'll get Councillor Heraghty to sign them too.'

'I didn't know Heraghty was a Justice of the Peace.' It was hard to remember she'd only been in this division a month. Some days it felt she was cemented into the sandstone.

'Aye, but we hardly ever use him,' said Cruikshanks. 'JC's orders. So Heraghty will be only too happy to oblige if I hint that she's been dragging her heels. Doubt he'll even read the warrants that closely.' He crouched awkwardly, dusted off his bag of McCoy's. There were still one or two crisps at the bottom.

'Right, I'll dig out the list of Chaddha's various

premises, his home address—but you, my love, are going to have to find the additional manpower to go chapping on all they doors.'

'Tom, I've got no one on. Seriously—there's about three cops mustered this morning.'

'Look, I've just detailed my very last available body to go wake up Gordo Figgis in the Big Hoose. If we can get him to testify the Sabir killing was at the behest of Chaddha, then we're laughing.'

'Okay, okay.' She thought a moment. 'What time do the Support Unit start again?'

'Think it's nine o'clock.'

'Then I'm just going to make a quick call.'

If it had been anyone other than Alex Patterson who answered the phone, it would have been fine. Anna had her spiel all prepared, how it was urgent, vital. Fraser was an ex-Unit man, they would be coming to the aid of one of their own. But Anna's voice, combined with, *I'm on for a really big favour*, led only to silence. She didn't blame him, not really, seeing as she'd treated him like shit. Thoughtless, cavalier, because it was her buddy Alex. Just a bit of fun, so it shouldn't really have mattered. But that's what made it matter all the more. She battered on anyway, telling him everything she thought was relevant.

'So,' she finished, 'I was wondering if you could help?'

'Fraser Harris, you say?'

'Yeah. Hoover? Do you know him?'

'Aye.' She could hear breath sucked through teeth. 'Bastard did it in their own back garden?'

'Yup.'

'How's Fraser's wife?'

'How do you think?'

528

'And Fraser?'

'Disappeared.'

He sniffed, or was maybe drawing on an illicit fag. 'We'll be there in fifteen. How many do you need?'

'Many have you got? I really want to hit everywhere at once, so he's got no time to think, and nowhere to run.'

'I'll call out as many of the backshift as I can as well.'

She didn't want to quell his enthusiasm, this oncoming gallop of outrage which she shared, and needed to harness. But the fiscal reality was stark. 'Thing is, I can't really sanction any overtime payments.'

'Fuck the overtime. *Ma'am.*'

*   *   *

A horrible, horrible day. One of the worst of her career, ranking up there with Billy Wong being murdered, or Jamie Worth going to prison. And yet, there was a twisted poetry to the thing, the skirl of tackety boots, the low murmur of soft-focus rage in gathering faces, sticks and storms. Anna had informed Claire Rodgers, since she was Fraser's line manager, and she in turn had recalled half her shift. Even Johnny put in an appearance, aligning himself, briefly, with the good guys, protecting Anna and Cruikshanks from whatever wrath might come. He was the most senior officer in the division, and he was now seen to sanction this.

Hamilton, they had established, was down in London, although nobody was supposed to know.

529

Who cared? She was probably taking her monthly dip in the gore of fresh-slaughtered bulls. Cruikshanks briefed them all, at least forty cops, milling about the room. They were to detain Chaddha on sight, and were also in possession of a number of warrants granting permission to seize any implements, articles or other evidence that could reasonably be believed to be involved in the manufacture and/or supply of a controlled substance and/or the procurement, manufacture, custody, control or distribution of items relating to forgery or counterfeiting.

'There.' Cruikshanks breathed deep after reading the full substance of the warrants. 'That should be enough to be getting on with, eh? We're very grateful to officers from both the Drugs Squad and the SCDEA joining us here this morning. We'll try to have one of each available in all four sectors, so, if in doubt, gie them a shout.'

The plan was to split Glasgow into four—north, south, east and west. The city lent itself to this kind of division; for the most part her streets flowed in neat, square grids, bisected north and south by the Clyde and bound either side by hills. The bulk of the raids would take place in the south side and city centre, where Chaddha had most of his businesses, but they'd managed to extend the parameters to include all of Nayar's and MacLeod's premises too, and would have also tackled the Maguires' remaining establishments, but for one glorious good-luck gift. Within twenty-five minutes of being ensconced at Govan Police Office, Ronnie Maguire had, as predicted, burst.

A used-car salesman and scrap dealer to trade, Ronnie was an East End boy made good. He'd done well for himself—very well, in fact—but it seemed that wasn't sufficient for his good lady. Through various intermediaries, Ronnie was introduced to Jasveer Chaddha, a fellow local businessman, just a wee bit more upmarket than him. Jazz offered to invest in Ronnie's various enterprises, and Ronnie, flattered, never thought to ask why. And so it came to pass that Chaddha's various companies began pumping money into Ronnie's Motors and Sure Fire Scrap, using the businesses as a front to launder drugs money—and probably floating the odd forged note as well, trying them out for size.

After a while, when the trust had solidified and the claws been embedded further, Jazz suggested that Ronnie use some of his hire cars to do a wee bit of delivery work for him. Ronnie admitted he thought it odd that Chaddha preferred a steady stream of different vehicles to do his bidding, but, like before, just smiled and pocketed the cash.

Hadny a clue, Mr Cruikshanks. That's the God's honest, know?

He did know, however, where the deliveries were coming from—the old printworks at Eglinton Toll—and he knew where they were headed: various disused premises to which Chaddha had access. Some of these premises would turn out to be Chaddha's; some, it transpired—embarrassingly—belonged to Chaddha's father-in-law.

Eventually, a person as dumb and avaricious as Ronnie would click that it might be worth opening a parcel or two. Now, the drugs he could take or leave. His Sheena's nephew had 'got in an awfy state with they funny cigarettes. Ended up injecting all his dole money straight into his arm.' But boxes of money, boxes of crisp-inked pages that fair crackled and whispered as you freed them from their cardboard prison; that was an altogether more beguiling sight. At first, Ronnie would just take a wad or two from the middle, or the bottom. If Chaddha ever noticed, Ronnie planned to blame it on one of the drivers—a mix of scowling, voiceless men who belonged to Chaddha, and some of Ronnie's own lads, who were mostly dimmer than him.

But the funny thing was, Mr Cruikshanks—naebody ever seemed to notice.

And that was when Ronnie got greedy, siphoning off more and more, until, one day, he liberated an entire box. He knew it was bad, knew it was dangerous but, like a man trying to give up cigarettes, they were there, he was weak, and he'd resist it all next time. Quick fluff of air with his hand and all the smoke would be blown away.

You know, I reckon he knew I was at it fae the start, Mr Cruikshanks. I think the bastard was playing with me.

You think so? Bastard.

Shortly thereafter, Ronnie was told Chaddha no longer needed access to his hire cars.

Far as I know, that was when Jazz started using thon security firm to do the deliveries instead.

And also when Chaddha liberated Ronnie of a mother's tender love.

We didny know it was him at first, Mr Cruikshanks. Then he got in touch again, telt us to wind our necks in, and we'd to kid on we'd found her. Tell yous lot that. If we hadny he would have 'butchered' her—that was what he called it—right then.

But we had taps on your phone.

Aye, no ma mobile, but.

Ronnie had seemed proud at this. *That's how we'd communicate. Christ, he even let me get ma mammy's medicine. I thought . . . I know the score and that, but I thought she'd be alright, you know? And then, when yous wouldny let up, he started threatening Sheena.*

Threatening? How so?

Asked me if she took it up the arse. Fucksake—ma mammy or ma wife. What would you do, Mr Cruikshanks?

That would be the same wife who had watched too much American TV. Perfectly composed in the interview room, she thought she'd take the Fifth Amendment, and Ronnie seemed content to let her do so.

She'd nothing to do with any of this shite. Wisny even in the van when I went to the printworks.

So—you're admitting you were there?

There? It was me put the fucking acid in the sprinklers. Hit him where it hurts, eh? Well over a million quid's wortha waccy baccy in thon place. Plus I knew it meant yous would find the printing press.

Ronnie had looked a little puzzled then. Squinted from under his drooping quiff. *How . . . is that no why you've jailed me?*

It is now.

I must caution you that anything you say . . . Anything you say. Don't they listen? You tell them as soon as you lay hands on them, you ask them if they understand. You note it down, and then you start to chat. A wise detective will eschew the good cop bad cop routine. It is old, passé, although, when all else fails, it still has its place. Much better to introduce an element of surprise, particularly with the newbies. So, you don't shout or jab with pudgy fingers. You don't wheel out that fierce white spotlight, which doesn't actually exist. No, you offer them a coffee, tell them you understand. That it wasn't their fault, that life is tough, that they were driven, driven to do something they didn't mean. You sweeten and you soften, en route from cell to interview room. Then the tape starts and you're already their friend, you've offered them hope and a listening ear. You encourage that proffering of rebuttal or defence or alibi or justification, because without these threads you cannot weave your rope, the rope with which they will, hopefully, tie themselves up in knots. And, parcel thus wrapped, you can deliver up your gift.

Even though it's stolen property.

—And so you didny know there'd be anyone inside the printworks, Ronnie?

No really.

Not even the person you handed the 'fertiliser' over to?

I thought he was just there to lock up, know?

So you just thought you'd be damaging Chaddha's property, was that it?

Aye, aye. I thought folk would smell the chlorine, call the polis, know? I mean, if I'd huv torched the place, there would of been nae evidence, would there?

True, true. And you've never hurt anybody before in your life, have you? You're not that kind of guy Ronnie, right?

Maguire's brief must have wondered if they'd

534

swapped roles.

No me, Mr Cruikshanks, no.

No even your dad, eh? How did that feel, when you seen him, seen Alfred, day after day, punching your mammy, slapping her, kicking her?

Don't you talk about my mammy. You know fuck all about it.

I know your da used to duff her up. Didn't he, pal?

'I'm sorry.' Ronnie's brief was a soft, beady man, like Mole from *The Wind in the Willows*. 'I can't see how this is a relevant line of questioning—'

—Did that no make you want to hurt someone, Ronnie? When your dad done that to your maw?

Ma father's deid.

Oh we know that, Ronnie-boy, we know *that*.

'DCI Cruikshanks, are you trying to imply any—'

—So how did you feel when you heard what they men had done to your mammy? How we'd found her, all alone. Did you feel the same way then? Were you furious—

'Detective Chief Inspector, I really must object . . .'

Did you Ronnie? Same as when your da was beating your mammy, making you so angry that you wanted to kill him. You did, didn't you? You wanted to kill him and you wanted to kill Jazz Chaddha.

The swiftness of the burst was stunning. As Cruikshanks said later, it was like lancing a dirty great boil.

Aye, I did. Alright? I wanted to rip his fucking heid off. I knew that Jazz would be there. He's aye fucking there; early doors, Thursday. That's when he sorts out the deliveries—

'DCI Cruikshanks, I must insist we curtail this immediately—'

It's no ma fault he wisny there, sobs Ronnie. *It's no ma fucking fault.*

*   *   *

Cruikshanks finished his address to the waiting troops. They were all silent, fixed on him, this plump, red-cheeked man with grease-stains on his tie. 'So, stay focused, stay professional—and give these buggers nae quarter, right? If there's no more questions . . . let's go shopping, folks.'

A single, dark scream, they surged from Govan Police Office, a cop on points stopping traffic, waving them out of the yard and on to the dual carriageway. Initially moving in a cortege, the vehicles and vans began to peel off, some to the motorway, some heading into town. Chaddha's home was around five minutes from the office, and that was where Anna would head, in a transit with three Unit men, stopping en route to visit two shops that Nayar owned. First, a carry-out restaurant and food store combined, two teams taking an entrance each, breezing through like wind over dust, rocking shelves, upturning desk drawers. All the while, random pop songs played in Anna's brain, chunks of tunes that followed her all morning. It was what she did when she was at the gym: head down, tune out, get on with the job in hand. Any tune would do: the last thing you heard on the radio, the first single you bought as a kid; anything as long as it had rhythm and a beat, a syncopated beat that you could bash and crash and breathe to.

Next stop, a DVD emporium, boxes and boxes of discs—Godknew what was on them, just seize them, seize them all—aye, and the manager too if he disny shut up. Like the gym, once you'd started, it ceased to be a chore, became, instead, exhilarating, and she was riding on a wave, and they were bantering in the van, crude jokes and too-high laughter, mind that motor, ho—do you no stop for red lights, *Constable*?

And then they got to Chaddha's house.

Anna watched the cops knock once, quietly, then kick in the front door. Chaddha was not there. Only his wife and kids at home, two terrified weans who would, from this point on, forever hate the police.

But what could you do, except your job?

'How many computers does your husband have?'

'Only this one, in the living room. But my son— he needs it for his homework.'

'Tough. And guys, there's a garage out the back. Check it too, just in case.'

Chaddha's wife was petite, fretful. In her hand, her sari twisted, slippery satin with a small child clamped to one end. A little girl of two or three, thumb in mouth and eyes full on Anna.

'I'll ask you one more time: Do you know where your husband is?'

The woman shook her head.

'Do you have Jasveer's mobile number?'

'Yes.' She recited the number, then added, 'But he won't answer it. He never does.'

Anna keyed it straight into her mobile, fired it off to Cruikshanks. 'That's okay.'

With Cell Site Analysis, all they needed was the

537

number. That should be sufficient to track Chaddha's passage, and Cruikshanks had specifically asked her to try and get it.

'Is that the only mobile he uses?'

'I think so.'

Anna looked up. 'When did you last see him?'

'Yesterday.'

'When yesterday?'

'When he left for his office.'

Your house is being trashed, your most private of possessions being raked and pawed by strangers, and you are being interrogated by this thin, presumptuous woman, who speaks only in barks and monosyllables, offering you no courtesies or explanations beyond that which she legally must. Your children are crying, the baby clinging to your knee, your son bristling and half grown; you have to hold his shoulder to keep him from hitting out. Your instinct, your natural dignity, demands that you order these intruders to leave, but the profound reality is—you have to stand and take it. This is a democracy, and you have done nothing wrong.

'And which office would that be?' asked Anna.

'The one in Grantley Street.'

'You do know Jasveer was taken to a police station last night?'

'No.' Mrs Chaddha seemed surprised.

'He didn't come home then, after we released him?'

She lowered her head. Only the children watching Anna. 'No.'

'And that didn't worry you?'

'Jasveer often does not come home at night.'

'Is that right? Do you know where he goes these

538

nights you never see him?'

Mrs Chaddha made a loose gesture with her arms, like sowing seed. 'Sometimes to his nightclubs, I think.' She mumbled something else beneath her breath.

'Sorry?'

'I said, sometimes, I also think he goes to my sister's.'

Without any intentional searching, without even recalling that she witnessed it, Anna sees, immediately, the scene at Coriander. It has been there, germinating in her skull, but now it blooms, the bracks of cinnamon catching in the folds of Anna's throat, the peppery clarity of one hand reaching for another, a touch of ownership.

'And where is your sister's house?'

'Ramya has a flat, in Pollokshields. It's quite near the Sherbrooke Hotel; I can give you the address.'

'Will she be there now?'

'Probably. She works from home.'

'What is it she does again?'

'She's a graphic designer.'

Pollokshields was on the same side of town. A garden suburb of Victorian and Edwardian tenements and townhouses, it was laid out in tree-lined streets and open spaces. Nithsdale Road was not on their list, but it wouldn't stop them from calling. Common law and a glib, gallus tongue opened all manner of doors. Anna detailed two of the cops to start knocking on the neighbours' doors, while she and the one remaining officer went to call on Ramya.

Ramya Nayar had the air of someone who'd just woken—hair tousled, sweatshirt inside out. Her face, at first, seemed swollen with sleep, but Anna could detect a ribboning of colour on her cheekbone that hinted at a brewing black eye.

'Yeah?'

'Hope I'm not disturbing you. We'd like to talk to you about your brother-in-law—Jasveer Chaddha. Did he come here last night?'

Keep talking before they know what's hit them, and, even as you're machine-gunning it out, you're up that step and your foot's on the doormat.

'*No.*'

With her eye half closed up, Ramya was already keeping a secret, but the speed of her denial underlined this. It was too emphatic to be true.

'Can we come in anyway?' said Anna. 'Cheers.'

Anna and the cop followed Ramya into her open-plan apartment. The girl thumped down on a bed settee, glowered at them. Again, no queries, no 'why are you asking?' or 'what's happened, is he okay?'.

'If you don't mind me saying, I think you're lying, Ramya.'

'Well, I'm not.' She hugged a cushion into her belly, legs curled up on the seat-pad. 'Why would you think he'd come here?'

'Because your sister told us.'

Quick as baton-twirling, her mouth twisted. Anna had thought Ramya's sister might have called her before the police arrived, but clearly not.

'Anjali said that?'

'Yup. Give her a call if you don't believe me.'

Hands working the cushion like a cat, the girl was going to cry. 'I never thought . . .'

'Your sister's not stupid, Miss Nayar.'

540

It was time for the formal stuff now. In the switch from the familiar first name, you offered some respect, let them think there was now a barrier behind which they could crouch and feel safe. Then, two seconds later, you'd just tug it all away.

'Yeah, your sister's not as fucking stupid as you are.'

'I beg your pardon?'

The girl was too busy staring at Anna to notice the cop moving out to the edges of the room. They had no warrant to search this place, but that didn't preclude the casual glances, the fingering of objects.

'Getting in tow with an arsehole like Chaddha— what were you thinking of? You wouldn't believe the charges we're racking up against him. There's the counterfeiting, obviously.'

She shot a glance at the girl, to see if there was any reaction. Ramya was intent on her cushion. Anna knew this was a gamble, revealing every one of her cards so soon, but time was pressing, and she wanted to pile it on, show this daft wee lassie exactly what she'd been shagging. 'And the drugs, of course. But now . . .' she went closer to Ramya, so the girl would have nowhere else to look but at her, 'well, now we're maybe talking murder.'

Ramya held her eyes down, held herself totally still, but a ripple passed through her; nose and brow in the slightest flux. You could take it as the reined-in response of a consummate liar, or absolute, bleaching shock.

Anna took the chair opposite the settee.

'Ramya. See when Jazz came here last night— was he in a bit of a state? Bit dishevelled, not his

541

usual self?'

'I told you. He wasn't here.'

Defiant, scowling. Scared.

'Did it frighten you a bit seeing him like that? I mean, you clearly like your men dangerous.'

'That is none of your business. Excuse me, what are you doing?' Ramya turned at the noise of china clinking, the cop lifting ornaments on a shelf. 'Can you put that down, please?'

'But sometimes,' continued Anna, her voice low, comforting, telling a tale as familiar as a bedtime story, 'Jazz goes beyond that, doesn't he? When he gets that crazed look.'

'I'm sorry, but I don't have to listen to this. I'd like you to leave now. Both of you.'

Anna shuffled to the edge of the chair, but remained sitting. 'Fair enough. But before I do go, I'm going to tell you something I didn't tell your sister. I didn't think she could handle it. She's really frail and delicate-looking, isn't she? She's your big sister though, yes?'

'Yes.'

'Bet she looked after you when you were wee. She looks the type. Kind; the sort of person you could rely on.' Anna gave an oblique little smile. 'Anyway, when Jasveer Chaddha left here last night—and I don't know, maybe he was all fired up, maybe you denied him his wicked way—and you're right, it *is* none of my business, but whatever it was, he went from your house to the house of another woman he knows. Well, they've never actually been introduced, but he's watched her from time to time. Out in the garden, playing with her kids, taking her wee girl to nursery. And when Jazz saw her, last night, he decided the time was right to introduce himself. Properly. Do you know what he did, Ramya?' Anna's knees, earnest and tight, hands prim and pleading on her lap.

No words. Only a head-shake.

'He dragged her to the ground by her lovely long hair, and then he raped her. I won't go into details, one because I can't, and two, because I don't think you could bear to hear it. But he raped her, Ramya. I'm utterly positive of that.'

At last, the tears fell.

'Come on, you saw him last night, didn't you?'

'Yes.'

'Speak up.'

'*Yes.*'

'What time did he leave here?' Anna was talking to the top of the girl's head, Ramya's hands meshed in her hair. Even sleep-twisted, her hair was gorgeous, a blue-black lushness that coiled with a mind of its own.

'I don't know—after midnight. He was only here for half an hour. I didn't . . . I didn't want him to stay.'

'You have a fight?'

Nothing. Just the sad droop of shoulders and a growing trembling in the girl's right knee.

'Did Jasveer hit you, Ramya? Did he do that to your eye? At the moment, I've got two cops going door to door in your building. What do you think? Will any of the neighbours say they heard your fight? Shouting maybe, a door slamming? I mean, it'll be pretty embarrassing if you lie to me now, knowing what I've just told you, and then we find out the truth. I won't really be able to help you then . . .'

'I told him to leave, but . . . he wouldn't . . . he

543

wanted to . . .' She raised her head, the remains of last night's make-up bleeding black. 'He told me that he owned me, that he could come here any time he liked.'

'What did you do?'

'I told him to go take a running fuck to himself.'

Brave lassie.

'That when he belted you?'

'Yeah.' Proper weeping, bone-shaking sobs, into her hands. 'Does my sister really know about us?'

'She knows.'

'Oh God.'

Anna signalled to the cop to leave. All he was doing was rearranging the decor anyway. She waited, letting the crying expend itself until it was nothing more than whimpers. It was never pleasant to witness another human being in despair, but it wasn't Anna who had made Ramya cry. It was different with true victims; the randomly plucked. You had to feel for them, otherwise you yourself were beyond repair.

But, when you're simply the mirror that society holds up to itself, you are as non-stick as glass. You're just a witness to the tears and recriminations; you show that which it is, transferring the emotion back on to the unfortunate you're reflecting. You have to concentrate, but you do it.

Seven years' bad luck if you break a mirror.

'So. Do you want to tell me where Jasveer might have gone?'

Ramya wiped her eyes, laughed. It was unnerving. 'He told me he wanted one last shag for old times' sake, because he was heading home. I mean, he arrives here, unannounced, I'm already in my bed, drops that on me, then starts to get undressed.'

'Home? You mean Govan or India?'

'I was glad, to be honest. I thought I could get my life back to normal, and Anjali would never know. I knew she'd be happy too.' Ramya caught Anna watching her. Didn't look away. 'She doesn't really love him, but he looks after her, pays for everything. She doesn't have to lift a finger. Not like me. My own father doesn't even subsidise me any more.'

'Ramya, are you telling me Chaddha is going back to India?'

'Yes.'

'When?'

'Today, I guess.'

Anna spoke quietly into her radio mouthpiece. She never wore the headset—it looked like an embarrassing ailment, some kind of face-calliper, and it worked just as well if you held it in your hand. The whole operation had been put on a separate, secure channel, with immediate talk-through if required. Radio traffic had been revving quietly all the time she'd been in Ramya's apartment, updates and queries and requests for this and that, but you learned to block it out while, at the same time, keeping a watching brief, responding only if it related to you.

'CI Cameron to DCI Cruikshanks.'

'Go ahead.'

'Get on to K Division personnel at Glasgow Airport, circulate subject's photo and details. I believe he may be headed for the sky.'

'Balls,' crackled Cruikshanks.

'You said it. Can you get someone to start

545

checking if he's booked on a flight to India, dunno where—or London even. I'm not sure if you can fly direct from Glasgow.'

'London? Bloody hell, there's a shuttle there every five minutes. Ho—Lennie. Did you catch that?'

'Affirmative.'

'Well, get on to it—now.'

'Excuse me.'

Anna blanked Ramya's voice. 'Any update from Claire Rodgers, Tom?'

Claire had been dispatched to verify Fraser's kids were with a neighbour, as suggested by Maria, and to oversee door-to-door enquiries around the Harris's house.

'Aye. Found the kids with a neighbour; they're both okay. No trace of Fraser, but a—'

'Excuse me,' said Ramya again.

'What?'

'Jazz booked his flight from here.' Ramya had pulled a laptop off the dining table, was tapping on the keyboard. 'That's why he came here, to use my computer.'

'Can you get into his emails?'

She shrugged. 'No, but I think he just booked it through mine.' Her laugh was desert-dry. 'Jazz and I have no secrets from each other.'

Within seconds, Ramya had called up the confirmation email.

Mr Jasveer Chaddha. Glasgow to Bangalore, India via Heathrow, London.

British Airways depart Glasgow at 10.30 hrs. Arrive Heathrow 12.00 hrs. Depart Heathrow to Bangalore 13.50 hrs.

It was 09.55 hrs now.

CHAPTER TWENTY-SEVEN

'Ma'am—why are we driving so fast?' asks the cop in the passenger seat. 'He'll be at the gate by now anyway. They'll just send an airport cop to intercept him before he gets on board.'

'Because I want to see him when they do.'

Her radio is calling her, and still, she has no earpiece on. She nods at her passenger.

'Get that for me, eh?'

It is Claire. She has found Fraser Harris. Thank God, thank God. He was sitting in the dark, in his bedroom, in his house. Claire let herself in with keys from a neighbour, walked quietly through the house until she found him.

'I'm taking him to hospital now.'

Anna takes her radio from the cop. 'Roger. We're en route to Glasgow Airport, so can't attend. Stay with him, Claire.'

'Will do. Has subject been apprehended?'

'Not sure. Hoping they'll wait till we get there.'

'Ma'am?'

'Yeah?'

'If you see him, give him one from me.'

She wants to ask how Fraser is, really, but not over the air so his colleagues can hear. They sympathise, are angry for him, yes. All wearing their hearts on their Gore-Tex sleeves and their anger on their booted feet, but this is private.

'Claire, phone me on my mobile, yeah?'

She does, almost immediately, and Anna asks how Fraser is coping. One hand spinning the wheel, phone pressed beneath her chin, she sees the cop in the passenger seat wince, sees him feel for the edges of his seat, hold tight, look dead ahead.

'Can you talk right now? Is Fraser there?'

'No. He's gone to sort some clothes to take in for Maria. I think they'll just keep her in the one night, for observation.'

'How is she?'

'I think Maria's more together than Fraser. It was really weird when I found him. He had the duvet round him, like a cloak. Just perched on the end of the bed, with the curtains shut. Oh, hang on a minute, would you? I think there's someone at the door.'

'Claire, wait.'

What? What is it? She is not sure herself. Claire knows not to interrupt.

'Be careful, eh? We've still to confirm that Chaddha is actually at the airport.'

'Och, away. You don't think he'd be mad enough to come back here?'

Anna weaves through morning traffic, which is neither rush-hour slow nor I've-slept-in fast. Cars and lorries are trundling off to Gourock or Irvine or on to the single-lane roadways that lead to the Highlands. Fifteen minutes from here, you can be on the side of Loch Lomond, gorging your senses on wide, glistening water. A sensation of gliding, of air elevating her tyres, then Claire is back.

'Anna, are you still there?'

'Mm-hm.' Anna is feeling remarkably calm. She has a man, a good man, who says he loves her; she has unpicked this most troublesome of tapestries, seen the knots and crosses behind the pretty

548

picture, and Claire has come back to the phone.

'It was just the postman. But, Anna, Fraser's car's not there.'

'*Shit.* Have you checked the whole house?'

Claire sounds as if she is running. 'Am doing that now.'

'Did Fraser hear that last broadcast?'

'I don't know.'

'Was he still in the room there, when I said I was going to the airport?'

Claire speaks in monotone. 'No. No, he went upstairs ages ago. Before I phoned you.'

'When you were with him, did you have your radio on? Could he have heard me talking to Cruikshanks?'

'I can't . . . yes.' Her voice is muffled for a minute, then comes back. 'His hat's gone too. His polis hat and stick were on the hall table.'

'Claire, did he overhear your radio?'

'He could have . . . Yes, I remember hearing Mr Cruikshanks telling you I hadn't found Fraser yet, but I *had*. I was with Fraser when he told you that, but I was too busy to shout it in. I had to keep talking to him, you know? I'd just got him down into the living room. It was like coaxing a kitten down out of a tree . . .'

Anna drops the phone on her lap, Claire still squawking. *Stupid cow.*

She flies above the sewage farm that marks the turn-off to Glasgow Airport. Wide bowls of slurry washed by long rotor arms lie far below them, under the bridge on which they are speeding, doing far more than the forty miles allowed. As well as the phone, Anna is holding the laptop on her knees. A precious, precious cargo, jettisoned by

549

Ramya at the very last, as they were running out the door.

'Just take it,' she said, thrusting the computer on Anna.

'It's alright, I took a note,' she replied, thinking Ramya meant to give it for the flight details.

'No.' The girl's eyes closed. 'No, you'll need it later, when you charge him.'

She let her arms drop; she folded them so Anna could not hand the laptop back.

'The prototypes are on it, for the holograms. And there's some disks . . . I . . . I'll look them out for you.'

'I'll need to come back then.'

'I know.'

Ramya tapped her painted nails on the silver casing.

'Some of my best designs, you know. Shame, that.'

Anna had phoned Cruikshanks to tell him, as she was running to the car. Laptop under one arm, keys and phone in her fist. It went straight to voicemail.

'Tom. Ramya Nayar designed the notes. I've all the originals here.'

Back came a text a minute later, with a wee smiley face attached.

Ramya? Hologram Ram! Ur my main man!!

What a tube. She won't contact him now, won't even say to the cops who are swinging and clinging in the van, one beside her, and the two in the rear—who are pretending not to look worried every time she glances in the mirror. They'll have heard enough, anyway, to work it out: that Fraser is now their target, not Chaddha. A blast of an irate horn, into the airport car park, skirting the ridiculous width of the roundabout, the switch of lanes, the smooth, fast burn right up to the front door. In two years' time, men will drive a Jeep laden with explosives into this space, will ram the glass doors and set themselves on fire; but for now it is a happy place, an open door for comings and goings. They get out, she says nothing. A traffic warden approaches, and Anna flings the keys to her passenger.

'Deal with that.'

Flitting through people, she is searching for two men, two men who must not meet. She entrusts the laptop to the second cop, tells the third to come with her. Up the stairs towards departures, passing businessmen and families, she is back in Spain. Rushing to see her mum, her heart packed into her mouth, pushing through people who have no right to be there.

'Ma'am, will I broadcast a lookout for Fraser?'

'No. No lookouts.'

She thinks this will protect Fraser, keep it unofficial. As long as she can find him first. Everywhere on the first floor, shops. A Boots the Chemist for mosquito repellent and diarrhoea pills; a Dorothy Perkins for last-minute sarongs; Celtic tops and Rangers socks and See-you-Jimmy hats—all that is wrong about Scotland beside smart leather luggage and sparkly pumps and scarves, toffee, tablet, shortbread and whisky, cashpoints, bureaux de change and spend spend SPEND! You might not ever be back here! You may not get home alive!

'You stay here,' she tells the cop, 'and keep an eye out for Fraser. Shout me if you see him.' She looks at the departure screen. It is 10.22. 'I'll head

551

for the gate.'

She avoids the ground staff, showing her warrant card and speaking discreetly to the plain-clothes cop who lurks on the sidelines. It takes one to know one, and he lets her through; yes, quite a few cops through already. Take it this is something big?

The corridor is long and empty. Anyone who is planning to go somewhere is already at the gate. She walks briskly, does not run, sees Chaddha in the distance, sees first the blackness of his glasses, the bigness of his hair. Imagines him and Ramya, vying for the mirror, while his own wife, Ramya's sister, brushes one hundred times and goes to bed alone. She sees a surge of dark-suited men, a single uniform with them. Sees Fraser in the background of that surge, in full uniform too, moving nearer. These men in suits don't know him, one nods, acknowledging Fraser as they go to lay hands on Chaddha. Anna does not shout, doesn't want him to run, doesn't want to make him do anything. Detaching her brain, she is fast-walking on eggshells, watching a strange ballet as the cops nod and move and whisper, an unchoreographed dance with no discernible score.

Chaddha swings round; his eyes fix on hers even as his arm is pulled back and a heavy-set plainer speaks to him. She sees Fraser's hand go into his back pocket and she is gliding forward and she is there, right up against him, her hands gripping his wrist. It is cold and soft as lead. She holds him, low, firm, her thumb on his wrist, in the little concave that throbs by the bracelet lines, that she feels beneath her own skin and she strokes in circles, like how you hypnotise a snake—or is it lobsters?

Some useless piece of trivia she picked up from the telly. Fraser does not see her, he sees nothing except Chaddha. Hatred and Chaddha are imprinted like tyre tracks through snow, like fossil footprints on a pale clay undertow of prehistoric sand.

A suited man speaks. She knows him as a DI from the SCDEA, and he knows her. 'This definitely him?'

Sweet, sweet satisfaction as the handcuffs come out. Chaddha, who is a piece of property. Chaddha, who is a piece of shit.

Anna nods, stroking Fraser's hand that will never be still. Wordlessly, the men lead Chaddha away.

CHAPTER TWENTY-EIGHT

'Anna Cameron, you old slapper. You been on the sunbeds?'

Anna closed the door, gave a little bow. 'Ta-Da! Cheers, Tom. I was actually going for 'bronzed and refreshed'.

'Aye, naw, naw. You're looking good. Put on a wee bit round the middle too—suits you.'

'So I'm a fat perma-tanned old crow is what you're saying?'

'Not at all. You look very . . . comely.'

'Up yours.'

They had just returned from Disney World, a place Anna was sure she would hate on sight. Why go all that way for plastic castles when you've got real ones at home? But it had been a brilliant holiday, just her and Rob and Laura. It had been Anna's idea. She'd three weeks' leave lying, and she'd asked Laura where was the one place she'd most like to go in the world. *Disney* came the breathless reply. So Anna had gone ahead and booked it. They'd been talking about a holiday anyway, but Rob wanted it to be just the two of them, on some luscious, foreign island.

'D'you think that's a good idea?' Anna had said. 'We've just told Laura we've got together, then we bugger off and leave her.'

Being wedged out was unbearable, no matter what age you were. If this relationship was going to balance, then it was a shape of three. Different weights at different times, but a tripod.

And so they had dogged school, dogged work, and gone to Florida, Anna and Laura sporting absurd hats with ears. Rushing through darkness on unseen rails, not knowing where you were, where you were turning, what would happen next and you didn't know if you were going to go faster or drop down, if you were terrified or exhilarated. Eating too much fried food and squealing when dolphins rose distant in the sea. Only yesterday, Anna had stood on Turtle Beach, looked over all the wide fathoms of the ocean. The shhh of the breaking sea was murmuring still, in her ear. That, and the fact it hadn't popped yet from the flight.

Govan Office had struck Anna as very quiet when she came in, and up here, it was worse. Deserted almost.

'Ach,' Cruikshanks smacked his ample thigh. 'That's what it is: you're in lurve.' The flesh kept quivering, long after the impact had struck. '*Up yours* indeed. See before, you'd have just telt me to

554

fuck off.'

'No, no. I'm keeping that in reserve.'

'And how is married life?'

'Tom, we've only been going out for a few weeks.'

'Aye, but take it fae an old man who knows. You're *glowing*. Look—there's Rob coming now!'

'Where?' She spun round, but there was no one behind her.

'Ha. See. Just say the man's name and your nips pure stand to attention. I could hang ma coat on them.'

Thank God the incident room was empty. They were in the central office; no longer a hub, but a husk. Cases closed, overtime dried up, the circus moved on. And Anna, taking a massive beamer, blushing like a lovesick schoolgirl—but there was no one to see it except a gleeful Cruikshanks.

'Tom, your daughter's in the job now. D'you think she's to put up with such sexist crap?'

'Ach, she's like you—gives as good as she gets. Sink, swim, or fucking splash; that's what I've always telt her. Now, I take it you'll be wanting an update on Jazz the Spazz, or did you just come to give yours truly a big sloppy kiss?'

'Eh, no. I'll just have the update, ta.'

Anna sat herself up on a nearby desk and shuffled her bum until she got comfy. Most of the extra chairs had already been repatriated, but desks were harder to spirit away.

'Your choice, doll.' He adjusted his trousers, letting his belly rest more easily on the waistband. 'But, I tell you, I'll no wait forever.'

He walked behind a long trestle table, stood proud as a shopkeeper displaying his wares. 'You

555

right?'

'Aye. On you go.'

'Well, for starters, Chaddha's remand, obviously.'

'Duh.'

There were five separate piles of paperwork in front of him. Cruikshanks plumped his hands on each pile as he referred to the contents. 'First of all, Chaddha's been done for the abduction and murder of Cassie—we've got the Maguires' evidence, and Callum MacLeod's admission, helped along by the forensic we acquired from one of MacLeod's vans. MacLeod himself, and two of Chaddha's sidekicks, bundled up Cassie while All Star's in-house Romeo was chatting up the night staff.'

'Bastards.'

'Oh yes.'

Cruikshanks shifted along to the next pile. 'We also have Chaddha running the cannabis farm and counterfeiting set-up with person or persons as yet unknown, but that's really the SCDEA's baby now.'

'Was MacLeod involved in that as well?'

'Don't think he was "involved", as such, in anything. MacLeod's just a thick, greedy half-wit. Chaddha offered to help MacLeod out with his cashflow problems months ago; then, before MacLeod's finished picking his nose, Chaddha ends up owning two-thirds of Lap It Up. Poor old Callum finds the interest rates on his "business loans" keep rising, and next thing he's embroiled in plans for a granny safari too.'

Cruikshanks skirted over another cluster on the table, not of paperwork, but shiny wrappers, cellophane and tinfoil in Kit Kat red and Flake yellow. 'Cleaning out my tuck drawer too,' he muttered. 'You know, I wouldny be surprised if Chaddha approached MacLeod and offered him a loan in the first place, just because All Star had the contract for The Meadows. Chaddha's a very strategic thinker for a raving bunkernut.'

Anna smiled.

'Anyone that's dealings with Callum MacLeod has got to be a bunkernut, eh? The boy's got nae hair and only one eyebrow. Oh, nae offence, by the way. I mean . . . I don't mean your doctor man's a bunkernut . . . you know, at face value, All Star look as professional as they come . . .' Cruikshanks fiddled with his hoard of sweeties, sorting them into rows. 'Eh, how's Rob's business going anyway?'

'It's fine. There's a Care Commission report to come out, but he's allowed to continue trading in the meantime.'

The Meadows was still surviving. If he could, Rob planned to rebuild it, taking NHS patients as well as private ones. It would be far easier for him to simply serve notice on the remaining residents and close the place—he was still a consultant geriatrician, with a steady hospital wage. Instead, he was going to remortgage the house in Newlands, use his own money to reinvest and make improvements.

'Well, good luck to him. He's a nice lad . . .'

He was indeed. Last night, when Laura was in bed, and they were ensconced in a lounge that could swallow Anna's entire house, they had talked about the future. Her belly was skittering, she was worried about her job, his job, this family she appeared to be knitting. Head on Rob's lap,

557

voicing her fears while looking at the ceiling. Then Rob's face had filled her vision, and all the chuntering stopped. Quick-diving into light and calm. This morning, when she woke, the feeling was still there.

'What about Ramya Nayar?' she asked. 'What exactly is she speaking to?'

Cruikshanks grinned. 'Done a wee bit of jiggery-pokery there. Ramya Nayar will testify against Chaddha in return for a reduced sentence. Say that he coerced her into doing the plate designs. She's given us a few names too, which we've passed on to the SCDEA. The lassie's a first-time offender, fae a good home . . .'

'I take it that means Mr Nayar's in the clear?'

'Nothing to stick on him at all. Poor guy's a wreck, actually. Family scandal, daughters at war . . .' Cruikshanks sighed, shook his head. 'I don't think he'll be sponsoring our fishing trip now.'

'You're all heart, you.'

'And here, in this big pile, we have statements from three of Sabir Aziz's "mates", who would say their ain granny had a blade if Chaddha telt them to; one from Sabir's brother—'

'So was it Kasim Aziz who was following Fraser?'

'Aye. Chaddha told him it was the polis who were behind his brother's death; some shite about how Fraser arresting Sabir kicked off the whole gang-war thing with Figgis.'

'And Kasim believed him?'

'He's an angry young boy who'd just lost his big brother.'

'But why go to Chaddha in the first place? You see, I don't get this. Kasim and Sabir were Muslim,

Ubu Roi seems to be all Muslim, yet Chaddha must be a Hindu, eh?'

'Must he?'

'Well, he's married into a Hindu family—that's what the Nayars are.'

Cruikshanks's beam was dimming. 'I canny keep up wi you some days. Away and have another holiday.' He scratched his head. 'I dunno. Chaddha disny strike me as a particularly holy type person anyway. I think Jazzie-boy's the kind of man who can be anything you want him to be. Anyway, can I get back to my statements please?'

'You may.'

'So. These are statements from the Aziz boy's mother, you and—crucially—young Gordon Figgis.'

'Was Fraser right then?'

'Would you stop bloody interrupting me? I'm totally losing my flow.'

'But was he?'

'Aye. Absolutely. That cop's shit-hot, so he is. Soon as we telt Gordo that Chaddha was going down anyway, he opened his poor wee heart up. Kill or be killed, that was how Chaddha presented it to him.'

'Well done. Next!'

Cruikshanks shimmied a little to the right. 'And next, we have the minging Maguires. Ronnie is taking full and sole responsibility for the four deaths at the printworks. Says he only meant to draw our attention to the clandestine activities going on there, that he never dreamt folk would die, but bollocks to that, I say. And so does the Fiscal.' He threw Anna a Double Decker biscuit. 'Hurray!'

She caught it. 'Hurray! And with regard to his

559

father?'

'Oh, for fucksake, you. Gie me a break. The man drowned. How and why . . . well, I've apprised L Division, that's where the incident occurred. Beyond that . . . it's got nothing to do with me.'

'Fair enough. And, that last pile?'

Instantly, the mood altered.

'This is the case relating to the attack on Maria Harris.'

A dark wash dampened the air. The whiteboards, the pinboards, all the wallpaper of the incident room came into sharp relief. On one wall was Cassie's matted hair that hid her eyes, her hand reaching up in the same open grasp as the bodies in the printworks, those four tangled remains which faced Cassie in their sculpted pose. Each so close to escape, so far from life, the same life that bimbled on regardless, in the streets and homes and offices and pubs, in the lanes where people pished and drank and walked their dogs and that handsome boy lay dying. Him there, in a square of his own, the one she held and sang to.

You're a police officer, Anna. This is what you do. You speak for the dead, and the desperate living.

'Is the case solid?' asked Anna, focusing on her biscuit.

'There is nae case.'

'What?'

'Och, there's semen alright, but it isny Chaddha's. And it disny match anyone on file.'

'*Fuck.*'

'Plus, it wisny inside her either.'

'Sorry Tom, I don't understand.'

'Maria Harris wisny raped. Indecently assaulted, aye, I mean there's tears and scratches round

560

her . . . down below, but your man, whoever he is . . . well, it looks like he bottled it.'

'Eh?'

'I mean, he never followed through. That wisny urine in her hair, doll, it was spunk.'

That sounded worse, it shouldn't sound worse it was *good* news surely? That Maria had been battered senseless, not raped. If you had a sliding scale of fates you would not wish, where would this one sit, would you count yourself lucky? Would you walk glad in your garden at night and thank your good fortune and feel safe?

'It's still down to Chaddha though,' she said, defiant.

'Of course it is, doll. But we'll never be able to prove it.'

There was sand under Anna's nails, still there from yesterday. She used her thumbnail to pick it out.

'How is Maria? Has anyone seen her?'

'Wee Claire Rodgers has been out a couple of times, but I think they really just want left alone.'

'Yeah.'

The sand was damp in the heat of her fingers, forming a neat yellow ball. She flicked it into air. 'I saw Fraser had another four-week line in. Think I should go out?'

'I wouldny. Claire was pretty upset last time she came back. Fraser wouldny even let her in. But she seen Maria at the window. Said she'd shaved all that lovely hair off. Claire was greeting when she telt me. Said the lassie looked like something out of Belsen.'

Not hungry. Anna slid the biscuit along the desk, watched it spin in the fluorescent light, until

561

it came to rest by some bits and pieces of bagged evidence, the mistaken, irrelevant stuff that had not been carted off to the SCDEA. Mostly junk, rubber gloves, tinfoil, a pair of kitchen scales. A kiddies' ink pad and flower-shaped stamps. A signet ring of tired gold. Anna stretched over, lifted the ring in its clear plastic bag. The label recorded where it had been seized, whose property it was.

Manju Jaffar. Deceased.

What about Manju? Manju who stayed at home.

'This got a place to go yet?' she asked.

'Aye, I was gonny ask you about that. Should we give it to thon nurse at The Meadows. Patty?'

'Padma, you mean. I take it you're not going anywhere with this? You still don't think Manju's death was murder?'

'Not on paper, no. Attributable to Cassie dying, with the shock and that—aye, maybe. But if you're asking me if somebody went in there and shoved her, then we've found nothing to back that up.'

A plain, unremarkable ring. Anna held it in her palm, the plastic separating the metal from her skin, so she could see it, but couldn't touch.

Just like Manju in a busy street and her baby at the window. She felt a welling in her throat, a warm-cold instant of understanding.

'Well, in that case,' she said quietly, 'I think the ring should go to Carol Jenkins. You should get someone to take it there.'

'Yeah?'

'Yes. She was Manju's next of kin after all. And look,' Anna held the bag out, even though he wouldn't be able to see it from here, 'the initials match.'

'Oh, aye.' Cruikshanks was building a tower of Kit Kats.

CJ. For Carol Jenkins. Or for Christopher Jenkins, her dad.

'Could you no do it for me?'

'Sorry Tom, but there's other stuff I've still to do. I—'

Cruikshanks's mobile began blaring 'Walking on Sunshine'.

'Oop. Scuse I. Fishing calls.' He answered. 'Hello, Tom Cruikshanks, Great White Shark here. Oh *hello*, pal. How you doing?'

He beamed, gave Anna the thumbs up. She took it as a signal to leave. As she jumped down, though, Cruikshanks waggled his fingers, motioning her to stay.

'You're taking the bloody piss, mate. No kidding? Mmhm. Mmhm.'

Some juicy gen Cruikshanks was desperate to share. Anna was in no great hurry, really. She didn't have to meet Rob till three. And the other thing on her to-do list . . . Well. If she faffed about long enough, her courage might not have to desert her after all; it's just that she would run out of time. Dithering here was as good as anywhere, so long as you didn't stare too hard at the walls. If you did, they started to stare back, like you'd roused them, woken all the sleeping faces that had ever hung there. Hundreds and hundreds of eloquent pleas.

'Aye, naw, that's brand new.' Cruikshanks was grimacing at her, making wind-up signs. 'Be great to see you back, boss, really great. Cheery now. Cheerio. Well,' he clicked the oyster-shaped cover. It was quite an effeminate phone for a man; Anna suspected it was his daughter's cast-off. 'Fuck a duck. Wait till you hear this. That was Donny Sangster on the phone, our erstwhile Deputy Dawg. He's coming back next week.'

'Good for him.'

'Naw, that's no it. He's coming back because JC's going.'

'She's going?' A rapid dash of joy. At last, something that was properly fair and equitable. On the way home, Anna would buy champagne. Well, Prosecco maybe, and a big chunk of smelly cheese.

'Yus! Where?'

Cruikshanks sat heavily on to a computer chair. 'Up the road to Pitt Street. She's just been made ACC Community Policing.'

His face was flipping like one of his fish: grey and slightly gawping. 'Sangster thinks they rushed it through before the Joint Board elected their new convenor. I don't bloody believe it.'

First Anna's head shaking, then her shoulders. Laughter, seeping up unbidden, possibly hysteria, but it felt good to get it out.

'I do. Oh, Jesus . . . I do. Hamilton gets her just deserts. A bloody promotion!' She clapped Cruikshanks on the back. 'And I get an old man I can flirt with—that's not you, I mean. Glory be, thank God for that.'

*   *   *

Laura and Rob were cooking at Anna's house tonight—red snapper and wilted rocket. That's if Alice let Rob into the kitchen. Supine belly offered in adoration if he was in the lounge, Alice would crouch, ears down, fur livid if he attempted to

564

move elsewhere. And they'd yet to introduce the whole concept of 'dog'. But it didn't matter; it was another 'challenge', not a problem. See, she knew all those management courses were packed full of tasty usefulness. She felt light-headed. Hamilton's departure was absurd and obscene, but it gave her some respite to decide what she wanted to do next. Subsumed by the weight, the glory of her new office, Hamilton might choose to simply leave Anna alone. She had pushed Anna to the wire, seen her cut. It was for Anna to decide if she would bleed or scab.

'Actually, I will have some water. Thanks.'

She should have been on her way to meet Rob now. But, instead, she was standing in a tenement flat in Govanhill. *Things to do, number two.* The flat belonged to Constable Stuart Wright, and he was offering her a drink. All very civilised, considering.

Even after she'd knocked, Anna hadn't expected to be let in the actual door; thought she'd be conducting this whole exchange on the landing outside. At least Stuart's wife wasn't home—Stuart had never been one for confrontation. No, Stuart had been quiet. And thoughtful. And different.

Right up until she was climbing the stairs, she was positive she wasn't coming in, was very definite on that. A quick rap on the door, a scrawled-on parcel stuffed through the letter box; that was going to be it. So how had she found herself here?

'Cheers. Ta.'

Anna cleared her throat, had been going to say something else, about how lovely the room was. And it was, with its soft cream sofas and walls of pale yellow and green. Wooden blinds slicing

565

shadows and light, Stuart Wright before her with his quizzical face.

'Is that okay? Can I get you anything else? A biscuit or something?'

'No, thank you. I just wanted to see how you were.'

'I'm alright.'

'Good. Good. Any plans for coming back to work?'

'No. Ma'am, why are you asking me this? You don't even work in the East any more.'

'I know, I know.' She took a breath in. 'Stuart, I've spoken to your divisional commander, and there's likely to be an acting sergeant's position coming up at Baird Street. With your service and experience, he thinks you'd be an ideal choice . . . if you did feel able to come back. I know it doesn't guarantee promotion, but—'

'I don't need your charity, ma'am.'

Anna walked to the window. The tenement was high; he had a cracking view across the south side. There was Hampden football stadium, where U2 were playing in a couple of months. She would be on duty then, on a Red Day, in charge of the whole security operation, and loving every minute of it. Might even jook backstage and get Bono to sign her tits. *Joke.* Though he could always sign her bra. It was cotton; that would be ethically sound. Northwards, heading into town, was Govanhill, with its sari shops and second-hand shops, then on to where the Central Mosque hunched by the Clyde. New apartments were being erected all along the river's empty banks, *executive* flats, sealing off the river views from those who couldn't afford them. All beyond and beyond, in a glorious panorama, stretched Anna's city, as far as the eye could see. Green grids to north and south.

In the foreground down below, three kids played in the street, weaving sticks in some intricate pattern. The smallest lugged out a plank, which they seemed to be using as a prop. Anna wasn't sure if it was a den or a barrier or some apparatus to be jumped over. Whatever it was, the structure would not stay upright, and then the two who had not brought the plank began to swing it at the younger one, striking him on the backside, before he limped off in high dudgeon.

'Ever since I joined the police,' she said, still watching the street outside, 'I've heard older cops say: "The job's fucked." And I always put it down to seen-it-all cynicism, or the reluctance of the old dog to accept the new. But it's not.'

She came back to where Stuart stood. He was staring at his feet; Anna was an embarrassment. 'It's to do with a system that destroys you from the inside out. What other job shows you all the shite of the world, makes you deal with it all, and sets you apart; gives you all this power, all this responsibility, so you think you're really someone? Then it doesn't even let you take charge of your own world.'

It was true. The system told you, from day one, to act on your own initiative, then it shafted you when you did. It punished the slow and the courteous, rewarded the fast, the furious and the fickle. Hamilton's promotion was a perfect illustration—and maybe Anna's was too. The system sent you where it chose, changed your shifts, your days off, your annual leave. It planned your career, made you wait on the whim of those in

567

power, forcing you to become embittered or obsequious.

No longer. Anna no longer cared.

Stuart tried to interrupt. She raised her palm. 'No, let me finish. I'm on a roll here. You start off all bright-eyed and eager to please, desperate to make your mark. Then you watch and wonder as others get on, or get listened to at least. And *you* don't. I mean, the days of the Masons are over, but there's always another elite, another *gang*. Who you play golf with, who you're shagging, who you know and what they can do. And don't get me wrong, Stuart, I've taken advantage of that, more than once. But then the game stops working for you, or the rules change, and no bugger tells you. However it happens, the music stops at some point, and you're left without a chair.'

That's where Anna was. Watching the game, but not understanding it any more. People like Hamilton and Johnny and Claire, apparently they were the future of policing. Slick operators all, and not one you'd trust to watch your back. So what of Anna? If she didn't fight to retrieve a chair of her own, she'd end up hanging on the sidelines, marking time until her pension, and all that enthusiasm, that clarity of right and wrong and trust and truth would become a thin gruel of resentment.

She didn't want to feel that way about the job. It hurt, really hurt inside.

'That's what I did to you, Stuart. And I'm sorry.'

She took the box from her pocket, opened it. 'I was so wrapped up in my own career, I didn't take the time to find out about yours. Here.'

Anna lifted out a blue and white striped ribbon,

supporting what looked like a giant ten-pence piece. She was proud of the sentiment, but she didn't want the Queen's heid dangling on her breast, thank you very much. When it was her turn—*if* she was still here—she'd ask for one with a Saltire, or a thistle like on your hat. And be told to accept what she'd been given, or take a running jump.

She offered Stuart his long-service medal. 'Please. Take it. You've earned it, with every one of your twenty-two years. Because, see at the end of the day, the job's *not* fucked. Everything else might be. But the actual job—all that guarding and watching and patrolling. That's not.'

His hair was greying at the sides, Anna noticed. Standing there, the medal swinging from her fingers, watching him watching his feet. Was he going to make her beg?

'You sure it's not?' Stuart's head came up, his eyes sharp. 'You sure?'

'Nah,' said Anna. 'But it sounds good.'

He laughed. He *was* different. She'd never really known him at all.

'Here.'

Stuart took the medal, held it up to the window. To the stripes of light that painted both their faces.

'Thank you. Ma'am.'

Outside, the kids had finished their den. Only the youngest was still there, rearranging the entrance. Anna checked her Audi for scrapes—the plank had been swung suspiciously near, but it was fine.

'You wanting your car washed, missus?'

'Not today, no. But thanks.'

The boy stuck his tongue out, Anna laughed.

She drove through Govanhill, up through Mount Florida and the long climb of hill towards Castlemilk and countryside. Got there just after three. She hurried inside the gate, over to the same low spot, with the view of the valley and the river below. A day of holding baggage to the light, and now this one last thing to be unpacked. *Last Call*. There used to be a programme on the telly called that, or maybe it was *Late Call* and Anna was getting mixed up with the comedy spoof of the same thing. In either eventuality, a minister-of-the-week would sit in a high-backed leather chair and dourly bid the viewers goodnight, with a pithy snippet of sermon guaranteed to keep your conscience wrestling in your dreams.

It would be fitting, actually, if there was a cleric here, seeing as it was a cemetery, but there was not. Just the long dark streak of Rob and the russet coil of Laura. Waiting, and smiling. For her.

'Hiya beautiful.'

Rob's mouth glanced hers. She nodded, swayed a little on her heels. Last Call. Once Anna had done this, she could go home. Shut the door on this and work. On poor Fraser and his ruined life she could not fix.

Laura was too close to the edge, her clever, curious nose bothering her.

'Careful, you.' Anna's arm went out, guiding the child back from the rim.

'But I want to *see*.'

It was only a little hole, a couple of feet cut square from the soil, but deep. And wide enough to catch a heel.

'Anna, she can wait in the car, it's fine.'

'No.' As she said it, Anna saw the triumph zip

from Laura to her dad. 'Laura, look. I don't want you hurting yourself. How about if we both kneel down, eh? If you fall in there you could break your ankle.'

Laura knelt, Anna beside her. Head low, dizziness rising. She pressed the flat of her hand on to the earth, steadying herself on solid ground. Thick springs of grass through her fingers. Weeds too, she didn't want weeds here. She twisted, then ripped them up by the roots. Shook the grit away, looking at what fell to earth. Traces of her were threaded through that mud, even after . . . she worked it out in her head . . . thirty-four years. The space they'd dug was a discreet one, no evidence of her dad's coffin beneath.

She'd helped exhume a body ten years ago, some suspect buried before the advent of DNA. Then his past, and science and the long, digging arms of the law, had chased him to ground. It was a family plot, and the suspect's mum had died after him, so they'd to prise her out first. Only the coffin rotting that Anna could see. Quick out and away. But the man, the man had been different. Splintered, spongy wood that caved to dust and bleach-white bone. Chunks of matted hair, which came off in your hands. They tried to lift him in a oner, then the head broke off, rolled away, and one of the cops picked it up, held it like a bowling ball, through eye sockets and the nose. *Calm down, pal. There's no need to lose the heid.* And they'd laughed and laughed till the tears came.

'Excuse me, hen.'

The gravedigger squatted beside her, began lowering the wee casket into the space. It banged against one side, righted itself on the other, then

571

sat quietly, its dull brass looking up at her. Her mother's names, dates, titles: *Loving mother & beloved wife.* Anna had erased the mention of Teddy in their lives. If he was that bothered, he could get in touch. Put a complaint in writing.

'I'll leave yous a minute, folks.'

She could hear Rob's voice say *thanks*. A deep, far-off man's voice.

Lying with her mum, waiting in the grey light for her dad to come home. *Fee-fi-fo-fum*, he'd shout up the stairs, and they'd giggle. They liked to share the bed, she had forgotten that; cold feet touching warm legs, her head on her mother's gown. You'd see the car headlamps lighting up the curtains, knowing he'd bring them their breakfast: tea for Mum, toast and milk for her.

All the dusty sadness of thirty-four years. You let it go.

Her back was stiff, her bum had corners. Anna pulled herself to her feet, kissed her fingers to the headstone. 'Bye Dad. Bye Mum. Love you.'

Over by the far wall, the man climbed up into a mechanical digger, back to finish what he'd started at another lair. A mound of fresh soil shrouded the gap he was working on. Bare earth, bare bones, emerald trees. Birds flared overhead as he started up the engine, crows cawing and wheeling on unseen currents. Metal tang of mud and blood ties.

'Do we just leave it?' she said to Rob.

'Yes. He'll come back and fill it in once we've gone.'

Anna was aware of a small hand taking hold of hers. Over the weeks, it had begun to feel familiar, this mini-hug. A shell, easing round hers until the pieces fitted, sometimes sweaty, sometimes sticky,

572

but always a solid little weight.

'Did you say a prayer?' said Laura.

'Mmhm.'

Laura checked to see where her dad was, but he had wandered off to speak to the gravedigger. 'You know . . . you know when we were on Space Mountain, and it was all scary in the dark? I think it feels like that. But it'll be okay.'

'Oh, pet.' Anna bent to hug the child, kissing at the crown of her head. A furious redness, smelling of apple shampoo, of the chips they'd had for lunch, of earth.

'Okay, my two gorgeous girls?' Rob linked his arm with Anna's. 'Let's go.'

On the way out of the cemetery, Anna noticed a new arrangement. A big hunk of polished granite, with a granite bench half circling the stone, and paviors marking out where bedding plants might go. Almost like a garden. The stone was smooth on the surface, edges still raw. She wanted to read what it said, on the grey engraved with gold. There were words below a carving of a single hand cradling a baby:

**DONATED BY SANDS
IN MEMORY OF CHILDREN
WHO DIED BEFORE OR AT BIRTH.**

Don't put your hand near the fire, Annie-kins.

But you do, don't you? Fascinated by the flame, aware that it will hurt, and wanting to feel it, to prove that you can, that it will not sear flesh from bone. All over the earth, people firewalk. They shut their eyes and clench their jaw and expose clean feet to scorching coals. All the world is tiny clusters. Just cells and mucus and swimming black eyes. You can hear them at night, beating in an echo chamber.

'Alright?' Rob's lips, vibrating on her ear.

'I'm alright. You alright?'

'I'm alright.' Rob nudged Laura. 'You alright, Gingernut?'

'*Da-ad.*'

EPILOGUE

Dawn, and the tang of salt water is rising with the sun. Light kisses low grey buildings, the depots and the warehouses. The guard peels off some notes, then seals the envelope with tape. Fortunately, the men who said they will take this package across the sea are not bright men. They have no learning, unlike him. He has told them that the Mirror Man will check, and if it does not reach its true destination, he will kill them. They have heard enough of the Mirror Man to believe this, but not sufficient to know that he is locked behind bars. They are blinded anyway, by the notes the guard hands them now. They see only the colour of money, not its substance, nor its true worth. They don't realise it is only paper.

The men move off, the guard remains at the quayside. He has made it all the way to Rosyth. He has retrieved the money he lodged in the service station vent—because fortune shines on the gracious. He tries to laugh at this, inside. Feels only the pinprick hollow of his heart. He has addressed the envelope to his son. He can do no more.

An ominous vapour swallows the light, and the sea turns platinum, capricious. There is blood still, dried in a dragonskin on his clothes. There is a smell of fish that he cannot seem to escape and a hole in the sky where the sun was. The sea shines like a carpet, like a magic carpet stretching far. He steps from the jetty, on to it.

A simple step, with his hands clutched hard round the rocks that weigh his pockets down. They are hard and rough. They are his salvation.

The fall is sudden. Is quiet. As the cold shock of brine bites his open wounds, the guard sees the cinema in his town, sees the blackness and the curtain which falls in satin ruches like water, this is water. Great runnels of salt and spume are pouring over, he is plummeting in a swollen liftshaft, the current dragging everything with him. He begins to thrash. Instinct, a force more potent than he, tells him to hold his breath and he fights it fights it fights it and the visions of what he has done swim darkly with him, in curls of copper and grey. Down and down, the images remain, they do not fall behind even as his eyes and mouth are filling. Flashing and refracting in unending mirrors.

And he hears her whispering, hears it roll out like the sea. The monsters live among us.